A Fatal Distraction

A Fatal Distraction

Samyukta Bhowmick

JUGGERNAUT BOOKS
C-I-128, First Floor, Sangam Vihar, Near Holi Chowk,
New Delhi 110080, India

First published by Juggernaut Books 2024

10 9 8 7 6 5 4 3 2 1

P-ISBN: 978-93-5345-466-1
E-ISBN: 978-93-5345-222-3

Typeset in Adobe Caslon Pro by
R. Ajith Kumar, Noida

Printed at Replika Press Pvt. Ltd, India

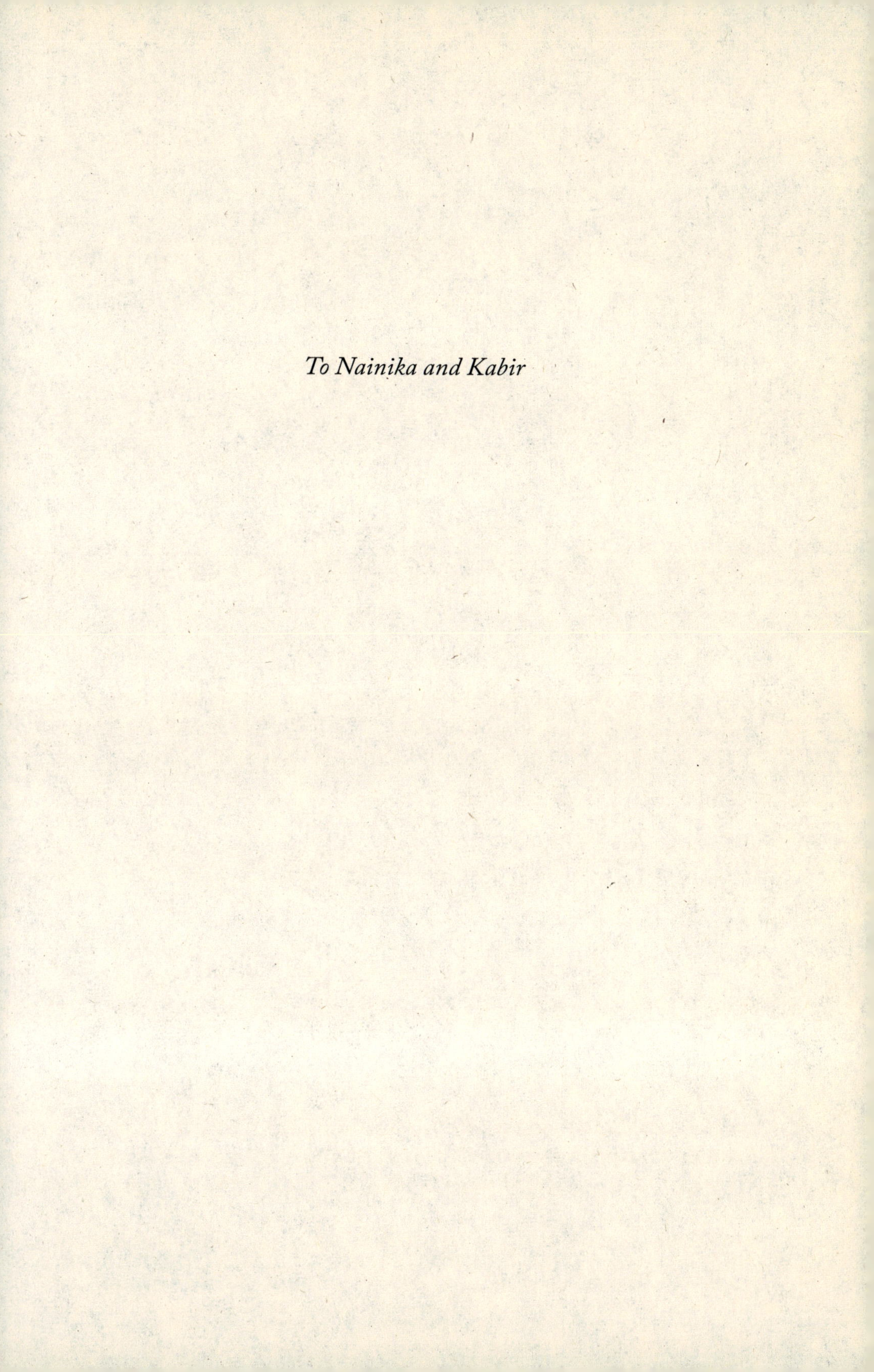

To Nainika and Kabir

Contents

Prologue

A little way down the road from Kajal Puri's rambling farmhouse in Chhattarpur, her neighbours Mr and Mrs Ahuja were on their morning constitutional. They took a morning walk every day and had done so with only a few exceptions throughout their twenty-two years of marriage. Yesterday had been one such exception, when their lane had been clogged up with police cars, press and rubbernecking bystanders.

'I always thought that Kajal would bring trouble to this colony,' said Mrs Ahuja.

Mr Ahuja grunted. He agreed, but he was focusing on his breathing, which his doctor had told him must be in sync with his walking. Deep inhales and deep exhales. Suddenly, he stopped. Were those clothes he could see discarded in the bushes?

Still breathing noisily, Mr Ahuja pointed his wife towards the bushes with his phone. He watched as she strode towards the offending garments, watched as she froze. And then froze himself as his wife began to shriek in terror.

The Tangling

1

A Small Work Problem

i

Dhritiman Bhattacharya—DB to his friends—was worried, but not unduly so. With the happy oblivion of a man unaware that he would be murdered that night, he was preoccupied with what he considered a small work problem.

DB was the managing editor of a disappearing breed, a Delhi tabloid. The *Delhi Daily* was an afternoon paper that had once been handed out by the dozen at busy intersections to bored commuters. Now, with all the entertainment said commuters could possibly want fitting into pocket-sized phones, circulation had dipped dismally.

While other tabloids had disappeared altogether, the *Delhi Daily* clung on. This was partly due to the fact that it was the pet project of the family that owned it, the influential Kapoors who owned a power company, two supermarket chains, a handful of snack brands, a music label, TV channels, and magazines in addition to their little newspaper. And it was partly due to DB.

He had been the managing editor ever since the *Delhi Daily* was founded and through a mix of amiability, pliability and instinct for self-preservation had managed to avoid most of the political squabbles that make life difficult for editors in India.

The paper had been conceived as a bit of fluff; a city go-to, with a mix of local news, particularly lurid crimes, gossip and reviews. But gradually, being of a serious bent of mind, DB had reinvented it as something more substantive. Now, reports about local political corruption rubbed shoulders with earnest features about Delhi's crumbling infrastructure and public goods.

The Kapoor family's scion, Abhishek Kapoor, had viewed these changes with an indulgent air, in the beginning dropping one or two hints to DB about the nature of tabloid journalism.

'Leave the serious stories to TV!' had been one of his refrains, and DB would only smile politely. (And, as an old-school journalist, if he had been baffled by this statement, he was too professional to show it.)

And soon, the strategy started to pay off, with stories about admissions scams, money laundering, bankrupt builders and high-living liquor barons going viral, after which Abhishek had mostly left DB alone to run things as he wanted.

Even so, DB could never quite shake the nagging doubt that someone from the Kapoor family would suddenly be called upon to replace him. And the main candidate in his mind had always been Anika, Abhishek's daughter, who was a columnist at the newspaper.

There were only two features that had remained consistent with the *Delhi Daily*'s previous avatar. One was the two pages of word games, which DB secretly enjoyed in his rare moments of leisure. And the second was Anika's column.

As he sat in his office, a grey building on one of the busy roads near Connaught Place, DB considered Anika. In his mind, she had deliberately set out from the start to be as controversial as she could. Her column, 'Naming Names', was ostensibly about cutting through the noise with hard-hitting truths and exposing those in power, using information gleaned from her insider status. And it had been popular for a while—until it became clear that Anika's inclination was to use her few inches of print real estate less for hard-hitting truths, and more to settle personal grudges and spread gossip. The enemies she made, and the constant threat of legal action that trailed her, had made her an increasingly less likely successor to DB in the eyes of her father. And today, DB was going to stub out any lingering ambitions Anika might have of occupying his chair once and for all.

DB was essentially a decent man, and not given to vendettas. So he didn't view his upcoming meeting with any sort of pleasure or relish, as one might when about to vanquish a long-standing rival. He also didn't view it with any dread—it was simply a workplace problem that he was finally going to solve to the satisfaction (he hoped) of all parties.

But he knew that Anika could be . . . unpredictable. And so, he was a little worried.

A cough distracted him from his ruminations. He looked up and saw his colleague Mridula Majumdar, who had stumped in without waiting for permission. She sat down on one of the rickety office chairs facing his desk and said, without preamble, 'Well, DB, I hope you know what you're doing.'

DB's office was a neat and orderly space, frugal but with signs everywhere of his devotion to the *Delhi Daily*. A few framed front pages hung on the walls, masking the peeling paint and the water damage, and copies of the paper, some dating back years, were stacked in piles on cabinets and shelves. His desk was a wide affair, strewn with drafts of articles yet to be published. He liked to print them out and edit them in the old-fashioned way, with a red pen, which he bought by the dozen and kept in his drawer.

'What do you mean?' asked DB, tentatively. He reached for a pen and started clicking it. 'You mean . . . how she'll take it?'

'My darling DB, even you can't be this oblivious. This meeting with Anika. You know she's going to go off.'

'I don't know that, and neither do you,' said DB. 'Anika can be very reasonable.'

Mridula snorted. It was a sound that came very naturally to her. She had a range of snorts through which she managed to convey complex, nuanced messages. (This one conveyed disbelief, a generous portion of an eye roll and just a soupçon of pity.)

DB flinched and briefly wondered if he should perhaps be more worried. While he was an excellent editor and could trim the fat and get to the guts of any story with a butcher's muscular efficiency, he was less certain when it came to the more conventional rules of social etiquette, and rarely knew how to read the room. Like that time when he mentioned casually to his sister-in-law that, in his opinion, her husband was likely embezzling with a free hand from his employer. ('I thought she would feel better knowing!' he had said later to his wife, after the inevitable showdown. And in his defence, although she did not feel better knowing *in that instant*, she did in the long run—in the very long run, when the divorce had finally gone through.)

'Anika has quite a successful career as a writer now,' he reasoned, as much for his own benefit as Mridula's. 'She barely shows up for work anymore. She just turns in her stuff via email. And, well, I *did* run it by her father.'

'A fact that may make her more angry, not less,' said Mridula.

'Do you know, I'm not sure,' said DB, in a thoughtful tone, and then added hurriedly, in response to Mridula's eyebrow lift (also very eloquent), 'Well, I just wonder if she may be in on this plan? Her father agreed with . . . alacrity, if I can put it that way. It made me wonder if it isn't a sort of family scheme.'

'A family scheme?'

'Well, I went to him with my idea, you know—of expanding. I think we need an expanded city desk. I think we need boots on the ground. I think we need . . . well, I don't have to tell you,' said DB.

'Yes, yes, I'm with you on all that. So, you went to him—and you expected that he would shoot down the idea, didn't you?'

'I did. And he didn't. He just made the point that if we expanded in one place, we'd have to cut in another. It all came so organically, that I wonder if he was trying to make it seem like my idea, but it was actually his idea in the first place.'

'Really?' said Mridula. 'It sounds most unlikely. And—I mean this in the kindest way—you know you're not exactly best at reading that kind of subtext.'

'Is there a kind way to mean that?' asked DB, coldly. 'Look, it's all conjecture, I agree. But based on certain things he said . . . for instance, he definitely hinted that we were paying some high salaries that weren't pulling their weight. And if you really boil that comment down, who are the high salaries here?'

'Not me,' said Mridula with a short bark of a laugh.

'And I had to assume he didn't mean me. Firstly, I'm hardly raking it in. And, secondly, if he meant me, he wouldn't have made the remark *to* me, you see?'

'Yes, yes, he didn't mean you, innocent. But his own daughter?'

'She does make up rather a large percentage of our compensation costs.'

'Hmm. If you're right, it's quite fascinating. These industrialist families are all so ruthless.' Mridula sounded quite impressed.

'Well, that's the point, isn't it,' said DB. 'It's not the way you or I would treat a child of our own, but with these people, who knows? We've all heard of worse. And . . . er, he's not wrong. In the early days, she used to pull publicity at least, but she doesn't anymore. And some of her recent columns have been . . . well, they've been downright personal. I've been wondering about the risks of litigation. That so-called "anonymous" piece she wrote about the plastics tycoon and his mistress? We all know who that was about. I expect a show-cause notice any day. It really distracts from, well, from our actual work.'

His tone had become fretful. 'You know, I really didn't think she would cut up rough. Maybe subconsciously, I thought that if it was coming from him, from the family, that maybe she wants to leave, and this is a roundabout way of getting there.'

'*Very* roundabout,' said Mridula, grimly. 'But I don't think so, you know. This column is important to her. She uses it like a weapon.'

DB shifted uncomfortably. 'You're right. Oh dear, I hope she won't be unpleasant.'

This time, Mridula had to laugh outright. 'My dear man. I think if there's one thing I can say with certainty, it's that she will be unpleasant. I have no idea if you're right about her father—if so, that will make her even more angry, because I assure you, she has no idea of leaving. This column is important to her. It underscores everything else—the books, Instagram, her whole social media profile. Oh yes, I think she will be unpleasant.'

'She's never behaved that way with me.'

'Well, the rest of the office has seen that side of her more than any other. It may be your introduction to a whole other part of Anika's personality.'

'Oh, dear,' said DB again. 'Well, I'm glad you're facing the music with me.'

Mridula nodded grimly. She also wasn't the type to partake in gossip, and she also felt no pleasure in the upcoming conversation. But unlike DB, she was under no delusions about Anika's inevitable reaction. He would need the cavalry.

'Of course,' she said. 'I wouldn't let you face the fire alone.'

ii

Anika Kapoor was an attractive woman in her early forties. She was very slim and always wore clothes that looked simple but were actually unfathomably expensive. They hung just so, and she moved in them with a rather arrogant grace. She had long hair that fell almost down to her waist, the one jarring note in her otherwise modern silhouette. She thought the hair made her distinctive. And, somehow, in a country full of women with long, straight hair, it did.

She had taken her time today coming into the office. She had pushed this upcoming meeting out of her mind—it was a skill she had subconsciously acquired over the years, the ability to distract herself with various sundries while something unpleasant lay ahead. Sometimes in her procrastination, she found that by the time she got around to it, the unpleasant thing had just gone away. And so, she picked her clothes with care, and ate her breakfast, such as it was, slowly. She stopped for more coffee.

But then she was finally on her way. She could put it off no longer. She sank back in the passenger seat of her car and stared out the window, caught a faint glimpse of her own face reflected in the glass, and instantly felt a stab of disquiet. Dark thoughts rose quickly to the surface, as though they had been waiting for just such an opportunity, right below the surface of her mind, to manifest themselves.

She stared at her reflection. *Who was she?* Anika Kapoor, columnist, bestselling writer and all-around successful Delhi Socialite. She looked as immaculate as ever, not a wrinkle on her skin or a crinkle in her clothes. But—she gripped her armrest—these days, she felt more and more unravelled.

From a young age, Anika had been taught to believe in positive aphorisms—where there's a will, there's a way, she learned. With faith, one can move mountains. Believe in yourself and never give up. As she grew older, she continued to parrot these sayings as doors opened up before her (as they tend to do for the unusually wealthy). If she'd been asked, she would have said with a good deal of indignation that her success came through determination and hard work. She had never had to question this.

Any obstacle she'd had to deal with was swept away. There were, in fact, only one or two—one was the editorial leadership of the *Delhi Daily*, which she had no sooner realised she would not get than convinced herself that she never really wanted; and there was one romantic entanglement that, even now, she could not make sense of. But that was it.

The rest of her life had been, essentially, strewn with roses. She had written a number of moderately successful books. She was touted as a social media 'influencer' by people for whom this was a thing. She had a long-running column in the city's favourite afternoon paper. The fact that her family owned the paper seemed beside the point.

A lifetime of privilege had sheltered her from life's uncertainties—until now.

This meeting with DB, she considered, may well be the final straw. DB did not often call her into his office, and she knew that this meeting meant an end. An end of something. Her grip on her armrest became tighter. She thought back to a conversation she had had with her father not more than a week before.

'Beta,' he had said. As though she were a child of eight. 'When are you going to take this seriously? When are you going to take your life seriously?'

She had looked at him scornfully. He represented a bygone era, an era where power lay in tangible assets, things (or people) that you could point to and say that you owned. He didn't understand that power today meant something completely different—the power of social media, the power of influence, of intangibles. These were out of his grasp.

She had said as much to him, and his face had changed colour.

In the ensuing argument, she felt she had given as much as she got. They had both left in a furious rage, hers a futile one, but his, she thought, may have been more fruitful.

When the car finally turned into her office, a burst of sunshine caused her already faint reflection to disappear completely, and she felt a moment's panic. *Where was she?* She remained impassive, but her knuckles whitened as she further tightened her grip on the armrest.

She shook herself. *Pull yourself together. You'll survive this—like everything else.*

As she marched into the office and had her usual effect of making people jump and scurry out of her way, she felt a little better. And as she came upon a pretty young woman who was trying desperately to avoid her eye, she stopped.

'Ah, Devika. Have you reworked that story yet?'

'Anika,' said Devika, trying to sound determined. 'I . . . I've only just got in.'

'I sent you an email about this last night, Devika,' said Anika. 'Do try and remember that we're a newspaper—so we should try and get things out quickly, no? Don't you think?'

'Yes,' said Devika, looking down.

'We can't go on like this. We really can't, Devika. I don't want to make an example out of you, but I'm afraid we may have to. If the story's not on my desk by this afternoon, I'm reassigning it. And if I have to reassign it, I'm not sure what the point is of keeping you on staff. The last draft you submitted was just hopeless, I'm afraid. Hopeless! Now, take this as a learning experience and maybe next time you'll have a story that we can actually print? It involves going out, Devika. Talking to sources. Corroborating sources. Working for your living. I know your generation likes their comforts, but this isn't the way . . .'

As Anika went on, Devika's lower lip started to tremble.

iii

Fifteen minutes later, Devika had fled to meet her boyfriend Ishaan in a secluded conference room.

'I could kill her,' sobbed Devika, 'I really could.'

Ishaan looked worried. Not because he felt Devika would commit homicide, but because . . . well, partly because his girlfriend was crying on his shoulder, and he felt bad for her, and also partly because he felt anyone was likely to walk into the room at any moment, demand to know what was going on and jump to the most embarrassing conclusions. How would he tell his mother he had been fired because they thought he had been making out in the office?

'I know,' he said, 'I know.' He tried to pat her head and simultaneously take half a step away without her noticing.

Eventually, her sobs subsided, and she looked up at him. He stopped stealing looks at the door and assumed an expression of utmost sympathy.

'You're so sweet,' she said, and moved away a little. 'I don't know what came over me.'

'It's Anika,' he said, 'I understand. She has this effect on everyone.'

'I just . . . I sometimes think she targets me, you know?'

'I know,' Ishaan nodded. 'But she doesn't. Believe me. She's the same with everyone.'

'You should read this email,' said Devika, her voice quavering again. 'There are so many people copied on it. And she called me out, so condescendingly.' She pulled out her phone, and Ishaan was torn between his all-consuming curiosity about the email and his equally potent desire to end this little tête-à-tête before his pain of a boss wandered in and caught them. He wavered, and then curiosity won. He leaned over to look.

'*I think it is a poor idea for Devika to make suggestions for the inputs to . . . blah blah blah*,' read Devika, ' . . . *without first understanding the system more generally. I think it is a great idea for Devika to understand the system better, as I think she will then contribute to it more effectively, and I value her thoughts. Hence my offer to explain to her* . . . ugh! She just goes on and on!'

'Oh, wow. That is rude,' said Ishaan, his boss forgotten for the moment.

'It's beyond rude!' said Devika. She gave a frustrated little scream. 'Ugh! She just makes me so mad! And it's relentless, every single day. And what's more, it's getting worse. Everyone can see it. My boss, my friends. I don't know if my work is worse than anyone else's, but right now it feels like I'm being singled out. I don't even want to come into work anymore in the mornings.'

'That's what she's like,' said Ishaan, sympathetically. He pulled her to him. His boss would just have to lump it. 'She picks and picks and picks away until she finally gets to you. It's . . . it's a kind of sadism.'

'But why *me*?'

'Who knows? Maybe it's because you're so pretty . . .'

Devika gave a watery giggle, and at this, Ishaan threw caution to the winds and leaned in quickly. After all, you only live once.

iv

'DB,' said Anika, walking into DB's office. 'You have to do something about our features team. They're just not pulling their weight.'

Why don't people say hello anymore, thought DB peevishly. But he didn't want to sound churlish, given the nature of their upcoming discussion, so he merely said, 'What have they done this time, Anika?' in what he hoped was a discouraging tone. This was a constant refrain of Anika's. She seemed to think that she should be the de facto leader of this team without actually ever being in the office or deigning to take on any daily management tasks.

'That story about the plight of gig workers. It's a little immature, no? It reads like an undergraduate essay for a writing seminar. And borderline Marxist too. You seem to be running some sort of Bengali communist cabal!'

'It's hardly immature to write about workers' rights,' said Mridula mildly. 'The way things are going, most of our readers will eventually become gig workers at a certain point.'

'Oh, are you here, Mridula?' said Anika, raising an eyebrow. There was a short, awkward pause. Finally, she continued, 'They're all a bunch of kids. And they seem to be getting younger and younger. I just had to talk some sense into a so-called journalist who looked like she was about twelve years old! And their ringleader, that Monami. She might think she's French or something, with a name like that, but the *Delhi Daily* isn't her private Jacobin Club.'

'Let's not get personal here,' said DB, bristling. The gig worker story had been his idea, and Monami, as far as he knew, was a very respectable Bengali name. 'After all—'

'But it could be harmful to the *brand*, DB,' said Anika, barrelling on, 'if these kids assume they can do what they like! Let's face it, that Monami is practically a kid herself. They need some overseeing, DB. We have to think about the optics here.'

'Never mind all that now,' said DB, after trying and failing to come up with a more diplomatic response. 'Anika, we've called you in here for a different reason entirely.'

'Oh?' said Anika. DB wasn't sure why she sounded surprised. He had mentioned very definitely in his meeting note that he had a specific matter to discuss, and anyway, she couldn't possibly think she had been called in to debate the failings of the features team. More mind games of the rich and famous, he assumed.

'Er, yes.' He braced himself. This was it. *Best foot forward.*

2

Marks of Worry

Kajal

The feeling of unreality that had been following Kajal Puri around for weeks now gathered around her. It folded itself into her skin, burrowing into the light hairs on her arms, which stood on end.

She looked around her garden. She was the one stationary figure in a blur of activity. In a corner, men were building a makeshift bar. Two or three cleaners and gardeners darted about like tall geckos in the grass, bustling, clearing, moving furniture.

The pre-monsoon clouds gathered and seemed to watch with her. She sat on a long cane lawn chair, sitting bolt upright despite its curve, and smoked. There was nothing for her to do now, anyway, but wait.

Once or twice, she looked down at the book in her hand, new from the publisher but already looking wilted through repeated fingering and page turning. She had left her usual marks of worry on the text: little fluorescent Post-Its to mark where she would be reading; passages of interest (she thought) on pages with corners folded down; quotes she might be called upon to refer to, highlighted and underlined.

The name on the front—her own!—the rather lurid-looking cover made up to remind one of those Forties thrillers, a heavily made up and scantily dressed woman running from some offscreen terror. Was it all really happening? At this point, she couldn't be sure. She took a long drag of her cigarette.

Keep it together, Kajal told herself, and, despite the muggy mid-afternoon air, gave a small shiver. It had been a long journey to get to this point. She couldn't lose her nerve now, or allow herself to be distracted by silly anxieties. *It'll be all right. It's been planned to the last detail.*

Her feeling of unreality stretched, and settled in comfortably.

Samar

At the other end of Delhi, in a dilapidated office building in a leafy neighbourhood, Samar Chishti was also waiting.

Despite the general air of having seen better days, his was a nice office. Unlike the *Delhi Daily* building, which had a touch of the Soviet, barren and overlit, Samar's room mouldered gently, overrun with houseplants. Outside was green too. Just behind his desk, there was a large window that looked out onto a banana tree. Or rather, the banana tree looked in, its leaves pressed against the glass like a good-natured but persistent neighbour. And Samar himself was of a piece with his surroundings, rumpled, weedy, but undeniably attractive. With his tired, kindly eyes and utilitarian, khaki shirts with too many pockets, he looked like a lost naturalist, one who had started out full of energy, hunting for butterflies, but then given up and decided to nap under a tree instead. It was a cosy office, popular with his colleagues, as was Samar, and it was a rare moment that found him there alone.

This, though, was one of those moments. His mind was focused on the ordeal ahead of him, and his face drooped until it was a picture of almost comic misery.

A young head popped around the corner. 'Samar, Dhritiman's here. Shall I tell him you're on the way?'

'Yes, yes. Coming,' said Samar, showing no signs of movement.

'You look as though a close and very dear relative has just passed on,' said the young head, cheerfully.

Samar sighed. His misery was such that he chose to confide in this young man, whose name he could not for the moment recall.

'It's Anika. I have a feeling I'll run into her.'

'Ah, yes, Anika,' said the young head, immediately dropping his jaunty air and adopting the serious expression everyone adopted when Anika's name was mentioned. 'Hmm.'

'Yes,' agreed Samar. 'I couldn't skip it, could I?'

'You are doing the conversation with the author,' pointed out the head, not unreasonably.

'Couldn't someone else?'

'The launch is in . . .' here the head produced an arm and checked a watch on its wrist, ' . . . two hours.'

'What about Dhritiman? Surely DB could do it.'

The head remained tactfully silent. DB, while beloved, was not an engaging public speaker given his tendency to ramble and his happy assumption that what was fascinating to him would be fascinating to one and all, however obscure the topic. As a speaker, DB was an explorer with a broken compass and each sentence he began was terra incognita.

Samar sighed. 'No, I suppose not,' he said, and finally made a move to unwind himself from his chair. It would have to be faced, he supposed.

It'll be quick, he told himself. *Quick and painless*.

Jemin

Jemin Sequeira, fashion designer extraordinaire, moustachioed, soft-bellied and cheerful, sailed down the garden path. He spotted Kajal, sitting on a lawn chair with the air of an uncoiled spring, and trotted across.

'Darling!' he said. 'Here I am. I've come early to help!'

He sat down rather carefully next to her. The chair was a traditional wooden one in the old Bengali style, and looked robust enough, but one never knew with Kajal's furniture. Like her home, which stood imposingly before them, it looked very grand, but tended to be well worn, creaky, leaky and cobwebby in places. And like her home and her furniture, Kajal too was an elegant ruin, her long face extravagantly lined in middle age, her linen shirts loose and carelessly buttoned, her silver hair tousled. She could, Jemin thought, be quite fabulous. If she would submit to a makeover, from head to toe.

Kajal, unaware of Jemin's scrutiny, gestured towards a young woman who'd just stalked out of the house, and was now barking orders at the workmen.

'Does it look like Vasudha over there needs any help?' she said. They watched Vasudha for some moments in silence. The young woman was wearing jeans and a t-shirt, and had her glossy long hair pulled back into a severe ponytail. Glasses were propped up on her head, and she would sometimes pull them down to her face and peer through them severely at some unfortunate person.

'It's a good look though, we must admit,' said Jemin at last. 'All she's missing is one of those clipboards and clicky pens.'

'She has a clicky pen,' said Kajal, with a straight face. 'She clicks it while berating the help.'

'Well, at least she's doing the thing thoroughly. That's rare in this unfeeling age. You must admit, she gives one a sense of . . . a sense of . . .'

'Mortal dread?'

'I was going to say reassurance. Of complete competence, you know. Like one of those devastatingly efficient secretaries that used to do shorthand all over the place in the 1920s. Ah, Vasu!' he added, as she spotted them and walked briskly over. 'I don't mean to criticise you, darling, and, as I was just saying to Cash here, I love that you're really, you know, committing to the thing, but . . . well, this is a very casual look, no?'

'I'm going to change later, Jem,' said Vasudha, blinking at him seriously. 'Jemin, where are all the models? They should have been here hours ago. They're going to be dressed as the victims, you know.'

'Yes, we all read your several emails about the matter, Vasudha,' said Kajal, rather testily. 'And I think I also mentioned to you that it all seemed a bit gimmicky to me.'

'Now, now,' said Jemin, as Vasudha looked stricken. 'We've had this all out on WhatsApp, let's not get into it again. I think, you know, Cash, it's a rather cute idea. It might make for some good photo-ops.'

'If we get any press,' said Kajal.

'We'll definitely get press, Ms Puri,' said Vasudha. 'Several journos have RSVPed. And even some models, thanks to Jem here.'

'It was a mistake to have it here,' said Kajal, as though she hadn't heard. 'It's too far from everything. And . . . well, look at my garden.'

'We'll clean up after ourselves, Ms Puri,' said Vasudha, some coldness finally creeping into her tone. 'Now Jem, whenever you have a second, I did want to discuss the booth.'

'Yes . . . er, yes. Just give me a moment, and I'll be with you.'

Vasudha trotted off, and he turned to Kajal.

'Now. What's eating you?'

'Nothing's eating me. What's eating *you*?'

'Nothing's eating me. I'm totally fine. I'm . . . I'm positively thrilling at the very idea of this moment. Being here, launching your book, rubbing your colleagues' faces in it . . .'

'What do you mean? Whose faces?'

'No one's, no one's,' said Jemin hastily. 'I'm sure they'll all be delighted. You mustn't be nervous.'

'I'm not nervous at all,' said Kajal. 'I'm just wondering . . . I don't know, it all seems too much.'

'Is there such a thing as too much?' said Jemin. 'Nowadays, we should take what we can get. And you're getting a full-on, all-singing, all-dancing, honest-to-goodness book launch. How many authors can even say that nowadays? Only politicians and movie stars, you know. Your colleagues will be green.'

Kajal looked at him, an eyebrow raised. 'My colleagues again. You're talking about someone very specific, aren't you?'

'Maybe I am,' said Jemin, with a grin. 'Anika will be hopping. I'm wondering if she even shows.'

'Oh, she'll show. It'll look too churlish if she doesn't. The whole *Delhi Daily* crowd is coming. And isn't her husband essentially paying for the whole thing?'

'Hey now,' said Jemin, rubbing his nose in mock indignation. 'I am the official corporate sponsor of this here book launch.'

'Sorry,' grinned Kajal.

'Oh, I'm only joking. Of course, he is paying for it. I would be lying in some gutter somewhere if it weren't for Shekhar. And actually, now that I come to consider it closely, there's an almost double deliciousness, a kind of chocolate-covered coating around the already very chocolatey cookie, in the fact that he is actually paying for his wife's arch-rival's book launch!'

'Oh, please! I'd hardly call her an arch-rival.'

'A nemesis?'

'We've butted heads once or twice, that's all,' said Kajal. 'And anyway, out of the two of us, she's the bestselling writer.'

Jemin snorted in a way Mridula would have approved of. 'Bestseller, I don't think. You know it doesn't take much here, right? What is it, a few thousand books sold or something? Anyway, there are some surprises in store for our friend Anika tonight.'

'What do you mean? What surprises?' said Kajal, sharply.

'Oh, nothing, nothing. Nothing for you to worry about, anyway. Your launch will go just swimmingly, trust me. And trust Vasu over there.'

Kajal looked at him suspiciously. 'Are you planning anything, Jem? I wish you'd tell me.'

'*Moi?* Not at all. Just looking forward to my reunion. With Anika, you know. It's been so long since I saw her.'

Kajal frowned. Her relationship with Anika had always been patchy. They had happened to join the paper around the same time, over fifteen years ago now, Kajal as a lowly staff writer and Anika, of course, as the heir apparent. Kajal had tried to be friendly then but was quite crudely rebuffed. And now, after years of professional bickering—as Kajal rose up the ranks to become a senior editor—theirs was a relationship that could never quite be mended.

'I don't think I knew that you knew her?' she said.

'Oh, we go way back,' said Jemin. 'We used to be quite close, you know. Once.'

Something in his tone made Kajal look at him more closely. 'That's not why you wanted to sponsor my book launch, is it?'

Kajal had been trying for weeks to understand why she was feeling a sort of . . . pulling along, as though she was caught up in an unstoppable tide. Was this the reason?

'No, of course not! The idea! You know why I'm sponsoring this . . .'

'No, I don't think I do, really.' There had been so many weeks of planning to get to this point, and now Kajal felt as though she'd lost track of why they were even here. 'Why did you?'

'Well, let's see. *Someone* suggested it. I think it was Samar? And it's a very good idea, you know. Just business wise and all that.'

'Business wise?'

Jemin laughed. 'You know I have no head for these things. Someone suggested it to me, and I thought, throw a party for Kajal? Yes, please! And here we are! Don't overthink it!'

'Okay . . . because she's not one to mess with. She can be really ugly.'

'Anika? Don't I know it,' said Jem, with more feeling than usual. And then he abruptly changed the subject. 'Don't give it a thought, darling! Focus on what you're going to say! Have you been through the questions with Samar? Not that he's going to be like that dreadful man on Hard Talk. Softball questions only, he promised. Now, if you'll excuse me, I must go and consult with dear Vasu on the placement of this booth. Aren't you just thrilled to have a booth, as well as a bar, as well as victims, in your garden, *Ms Puri*?'

Continuing to grin, and completely ignoring her look of exasperation, Jemin jogged off towards a semi-constructed booth, which seemed to consist of a wobbly wooden picnic table, which was now being wreathed in tissue paper.

'No, no, no, no, Vasu!' he exclaimed, sounding aghast. 'We'll have to do better than that. What about . . .'

While half his mind grappled with the situation at hand, with the other half he contemplated the evening ahead, acutely aware of feeling a wicked, almost reckless glee. Would there be fireworks ahead? He very much thought there would.

3

A Cartoon Anvil

The *Delhi Daily*

There was a very pleasurable buzz in the reception area of the *Delhi Daily*. A group of young people had gathered, voices raised, laughter bursting out every few seconds. They were looking forward to the evening with a characteristic, fun-loving wholesomeness. Not that the idea of a book launch held much promise in and of itself. But now, after a tedious week—varying from dull to miserable and punctuated by stretches of doomscrolling on social media or (for the old school) playing minesweeper at their desks—they felt enlivened by the prospect of that mystic event, one that is so rarely seen in the wild nowadays, a no-strings-attached, non-wedding-related open bar.

Among them were the aggrieved features team, for whom the week had been particularly tough.

'Anika's not even our boss,' they had complained bitterly to their actual boss, Monami Chatterjee. They felt comfortable with Monami, a relatively young newcomer, who looked like them, all low-rise baggy denim and fresh-faced enthusiasm. She had done a degree in journalism in New York and then returned to Delhi as quickly as she could. Her father joked that he was surprised she hadn't met herself on the way back.

'What can I say? You're preaching to the choir,' Monami had said, looking sympathetic. She had felt relatively confident about the gig workers story, secure in the knowledge that it had been approved by DB, who was a red-hot communist. But, like Devika, she had had to deal with the fusillade of Anika's scornful emails, which copied all of the editors, throughout the week. While the most caustic remarks had been directed at Devika, a fair amount were aimed at Monami too, and—lest they feel left out, no doubt—the rest of the features team.

Now they were preparing to shake the dust of the office from their feet, at least for the weekend.

'Have fun, guys,' said Monami. 'Enjoy yourself. You deserve it.'

'Why aren't you coming?' demanded a younger team member, Sapna. 'You deserve it too.'

'I would have, I am so annoyed to be missing it, believe me,' said Monami, feelingly. She had promised her mother she would be home for a family dinner. Her mother had insisted on it with a weird intensity, causing Monami to suspect that it was to be another "suitable boy" family event. Her mother considered herself adept at handling these introductions with subtlety and tact, which usually meant many family members aggregating in one place until finally someone was produced from behind someone else with the air of a conjuring trick. The only solace was that this unfortunate person would normally be looking even more disconsolate than Monami did—solace, that is, only until she realised it was actually rather offensive. The least these men could do was be devastated by her lack of interest.

'Just ditch your thing, and come with us,' said Tina. Tina was on the news desk, a woman in her early thirties with short hair that nicely framed her frank, expressive face.

Monami sighed. 'The last time I did that, you wouldn't believe the fuss. It's easier to just go. I'll text on the group in case I'm done early, okay? And I'll meet you . . . but not in Chhattarpur.'

'Is it Chhattarpur? That's going to take hours. I didn't know old Cashew Nut lived in bloody Chhattarpur.'

'I've called an Uber and he says he'll be here in three minutes,' said Ishaan, peering into his phone.

'I like the way Ishaan thinks the app is the driver speaking to him personally,' sniggered someone else.

'If that car is here in three minutes, I will personally hand you six months' salary.'

'Oh, you're right . . . I think he just cancelled on me. Welp, trying again.'

'What do they call it when you keep doing the same thing but expect a different outcome? Let's see . . . it's on the tip of my tongue . . .'

'Oh, leave him alone,' said Devika. The entire group burst into that very distinctive 'oooohhhh' sound that only young people know how to make collectively when they're trying to be suggestive. 'Defending your boyfriend, is it!' 'You guys are adorable!'

'I can't believe you're being this lame and ditching,' said Tina in a low voice to Monami. 'I'll be stuck with this bunch of kindergartners the entire night.'

'Isn't Samar going to be there?'

'Yes, but he'll have his own friends. He gets very strange when he's around his own age group.'

Monami bit back a response that this was understandable since Samar was twenty years older than Tina. She had stopped questioning her friend's dating habits a long time ago—and she was hardly in a position to, anyway, given that she was about to go home to be introduced to a prospective suitor by her mother.

'Not coming, Monami?' It was Shamik, a short man with a soft, oleaginous voice from whom everyone liked to steer clear. 'That's a shame. What about you, Tina?'

'Yes, I'm coming,' said Tina, unconsciously taking a step away from him.

'How nice. Can I drive you?'

Tina looked most alarmed at this prospect. 'Oh! Er . . .'

'Please let me,' Shamik continued, still speaking very softly, almost in a whisper. 'I'll get hopelessly lost if someone doesn't come with me.'

'Oh, well, er . . .'

Luckily, at this moment, Ishaan interrupted them. 'Come on, guys. Are we going?'

'Shamik was just saying he was driving,' said Monami, smoothly. 'You guys should ride with him. If you don't mind of course, Shamik?'

'Of course not, of course not,' said Shamik, trying to look genial and succeeding in only looking more nervous. 'Er, it's not too many of you, is it? I tend not to do well with too many loud noises in the car.'

'Oh, we'll be quiet,' lied Ishaan. 'You don't mind some music though, right?'

Taking him firmly by the shoulders, he steered him towards the group standing near the door who broke into a small cheer when they learned they could now hitch a ride for free. Shamik threw an agonised glance back at Tina, but she merely called back, 'If your car's too full, no worries, Shamik, I'll just call a cab.'

'Poor guy. We should be nicer to him,' said Monami, ruefully. 'It's too bad!'

'Nope,' said Tina. 'This is one time where I'm judging the book by the cover. He looks like a serial killer, as far as I'm concerned, and he sounds like one too. Not taking any chances with that!' Tina turned to the others. 'Right. I'm going to buy some cigarettes and get a cab. Anyone who doesn't fit into Shamik's car can come with me!'

She opened the main doors and the sounds of Delhi traffic immediately rushed through, filling the air with the angry beeping of horns, the staccato revving of autorickshaws, the grunt and screech of buses.

Devika hung back a little.

'Er, Monami. I just wanted to say thanks for all your support earlier,' she said. 'With Anika, you know. I really appreciate your response to her email.'

'No worries,' said Monami. 'That's kind of my job.' Monami had not been a manager for very long and she felt her responsibilities keenly. 'Don't mind her so much. I know she's intimidating, but it's just noise. She can't exactly do anything to us. If you think about it, DB didn't ask us to change a single thing about the story. She's probably more frustrated than anything else.'

'I guess so,' said Devika. 'I don't know why she has to be so unpleasant.'

'Sexual frustration?' suggested Ishaan, who had come back to see what had happened to Devika.

'Why is that your answer to everything?' laughed Devika. 'And anyway, I doubt she's lacking in that department. She's married to that dish, Shekhar Malhotra.'

'Those dishes are usually all talk and no trousers, believe me.'

Monami started to laugh, too. 'Where do you get these pearls!'

'And anyway, I doubt that,' said Devika. 'Not this guy. I had to interview him when he acquired the House of Jems. Such a sweetheart!' She sighed, before adding, 'And just oozing sex appeal.'

'Hey now,' said Ishaan, putting his arm around her. 'Incidentally, I can also acquire your house of gems. If you know what I mean.'

'Ishaan!' said both Devika and Monami together, Devika with horror and Monami with a belly laugh.

Ishaan laughed too, and Devika batted his arm. 'Not in front of my boss!' she hissed.

Monami sighed, suddenly feeling old. The two of them would go off, have fun at this party, make out in a corner if they could find one without any elders bearing down on them, and generally just Be Young. Meanwhile, here she was, tottering into senility, spending the evening with her parents, and still no long-term dating prospects. It was the struggle, she felt, of her life.

'I'm hardly the *boss*,' she said, knowing as she said it that the protestation was both futile and wholly untrue. Anyway, it didn't matter because they were hardly paying attention, Ishaan tugging on Devika's sleeve and trying to steer her out. Her expression had turned from horror to indulgent laughter. Monami could see that she had already started to forget about all the trials of work. 'I'll see you on Monday.'

'Bye!'

'Please behave yourselves in public, you never know in this current political climate . . . ' said Monami, feeling, as she heard herself, the acceleration of her descent into old age.

'Okay, auntie,' said Ishaan, with a grin, confirming Monami's fears. 'Have a good weekend.'

Ishaan's arm draped casually around her shoulders, Devika giggled as they sauntered out. Their spirits were high, as only young spirits can be, particularly when they have no idea that a cartoon anvil is about to fall on their heads. Ishaan was wondering if they could in fact risk making out in the back of an Uber in this conservative climate. Devika was also wondering if Ishaan would risk it, and her mood lightened. Somewhere, a worry still tugged about Anika, but she decided to let it go, just for this evening. Anika would keep until Monday.

Vasudha

Vasudha contemplated her handiwork with a grim satisfaction. She had set out to decorate the garden for a book party—no, a *murder mystery* party—and that's what she had done. She had murder props, decorations that suggested crime, and soon she would also have servers dressed as murder victims. She had done, she considered, the thing thoroughly and well. With everything else going on, she could at least feel proud of that.

She would have been surprised and saddened to view the scene through Kajal's eyes. To Kajal, the accessories looked garish, like they were part of the set for a children's play—a dubious chalk corpse outlined on the grass; handcuffs hanging, precarious and plasticky, from the trees; and murder weapons that seemed to be lifted straight from a giant game of Cluedo.

But to be fair to Vasudha, she was hardly in her element. She was an ambitious girl, having grown up in the shiny environs of a Gurgaon high-rise. When she had graduated college, it was with one aim and that too a singularly unimaginative one: to find a job at the nearest multinational, she didn't much care which one, as long as it would get her well on the way to an IIM or a US business school, that in turn would get her well on her way to earning a crore a year by the time she was thirty.

So what was she doing here, throwing elaborate parties for struggling designers and first-time novelists, in overgrown gardens deep in the suburbs of Delhi? Where had her life gone off the rails? At this point, she barely knew herself. She sighed and closed her eyes for a second. *One thing at a time.*

'Right. Models. Over here. Asha, you take this dagger-through-the-head hat. Suleiman, maybe you can do the noose?'

Suleiman took the noose, grinning.

'So, we just have to wear these with our outfits? Nothing else?' he asked.

'Nope, nothing else,' said Vasudha. 'Just look murdered.'

Shekhar

Being the husband of Anika Kapoor was not an easy task, even for Shekhar Malhotra, with his *filmi* good looks and very flat stomach, the two weapons that had allowed him to overcome most of life's obstacles.

In the beginning, when they had got married, it had been so

simple—almost miraculously so, he had felt. That was the magic of the wealthy and powerful, their ability to simplify everything. Nothing fazed them, and the usual troubles that plagued the rest of the city—problems with parking, power cuts, water bills, flooding—never seemed to intrude into their lives.

He had once been so far outside that rarefied world that the term outsider almost didn't apply. Irrelevant would have been more accurate. He often thought that Delhi society was like a vast galaxy, containing multitudes of solar systems, some major and some minor, and each with their own sun, and each with their own orbiting pathways that would never intertwine with, say, the solar system down the road. If Anika and her family had been the sun in her solar system (or one of the major planets, anyway), Shekhar had not even been an orbiting rock or a fleeting asteroid in the farthest reaches of black space in that solar system. No, he had been in another galaxy altogether—far, far away. And far, far more dull. Since as long as he could remember, it had been his ambition to escape this dusty outpost. And almost by magic, he had done it.

And now? He frowned as he contemplated the evening before him. Soon he would have to make his way through their sprawling Jor Bagh apartment, knock on the door of his wife's room which was situated strategically at the other end, and begin the elaborate charade of going out as a couple. *Here goes nothing*, he thought.

4

It's a Nice Crowd

6.30 p.m.

Samar and DB came up the path. DB looked about him delightedly, like a child at a circus. Samar looked about him warily, like an adult at a circus.

When they saw Vasudha's setup, DB gave a cry and seemed to stop just short of clapping his hands.

'Look!' he said. 'Murder victims!'

The models Vasudha had hired now hung around like wraiths about the garden, arrayed in drooping black, with various signs of their demise spotted about their person. One wore a noose, loosely knotted like a French scarf. Another had a dagger rather jauntily sticking out of their back.

Samar sighed. 'This is what you get when you let an intern set up a book launch, it seems,' he said, sadly. 'You don't have to sound so thrilled.'

'Well, I am thrilled!' DB was an avid mystery reader, and determined to be excited about this book. The fact that he had an advance copy and had fallen asleep trying to read it the night before did not deter him in the slightest. 'Where's our gracious hostess, I wonder?'

'Is that her, stomping towards us?'

'Hey. Samar. DB,' said the aforementioned gracious hostess, trying to smile sunnily but actually grimacing at them both in a pained way. 'Thanks for coming.' Her day had been filled with dark omens, and to have actual wraiths floating about her garden now seemed like the final straw. She was feeling the strain.

'You know I wouldn't miss it for the world!' cried DB.

'And you know I *couldn't* miss it for the world,' said Samar gloomily.

'Maybe we should just call it off?' said Kajal.

'I wish.'

'Now you two!' said DB, turning off his genial air and glaring at them both.

'One of you has written this book. The other has published it. This is a joyous day!' he thundered. 'What's wrong with you both?'

There was a brief silence at this outburst. Samar and Kajal seemed unsure how to proceed, and looked at each other.

Finally, Kajal said in a sulky voice, 'I wasn't seriously suggesting calling it off.'

'What's bothering you?' asked DB. 'I thought you'd be excited about . . . er, about all this.'

They all looked at the garden. It was finally ready. In addition to all the murder props and wandering ghouls, fairy lights dotted the space, and plastic lotuses with diyas in them had been put into the little fountain that gurgled and spurted in one corner. The overall effect suggested a lawn party that had been tragically interrupted by a crime wave, and closely followed by the onset of the zombie apocalypse.

In the middle of it all, a little podium had been set up, surrounded by chairs arranged in neat rows, and next to it a demure stall with Kajal's book prominently on sale.

'Oh, I am. I am excited. It's just . . . I don't even know what it is. Ignore me.'

'It's probably just nerves,' said DB kindly.

'It's not nerves. Why does everyone keep saying that? I am never nervous! I just . . . I don't know. I have a feeling. And actually, I am very good at predicting these things. Something about my birth chart. It's . . . it can be uncanny.'

'Well, what's your birth chart saying about tonight?' Samar asked, half-amused and half-exasperated. It had been a difficult road to publishing this book; Kajal was a first-time writer and every edit, every editorial suggestion, had first been recoiled at in horror, and then hotly contested for days. It had strained their friendship almost to breaking point. The least she could do was be somewhat pleased on publication day, when their mutual labour finally tottered forth into the world.

'I just have a feeling,' said Kajal again, reluctantly, as though the words were being physically pulled from her. 'Something's not right.'

'Is it the corporate sponsorship?' said Samar.

'If you can call Jem that,' said Kajal.

'Maybe you feel like you're selling out,' continued Samar, helpfully.

'I don't, actually, but thanks,' said Kajal, glaring at him.

'Oh, everyone's going corporate nowadays,' said DB. They had wandered up to the bar, and now leaned against it. 'That's nothing to worry about. Paid content. Advertorials.' He shuddered gently.

'Speak of the devil,' Samar said, as Jemin joined them. 'We were just decrying all you corporates and how we sell our souls to you.'

'Gin, please,' Jemin said to the bartender, who had appeared like a genie. 'Splash of tonic. What are you talking about? Me, corporate? I'm the creative talent. If anything, I've been corporatised myself. Or do I mean incorporated?'

A trickle of guests had begun to arrive. Some reporters and photographers quickly busied themselves talking to and taking photos of the murder victims, who grinned incongruously. Vasudha had reappeared, also dressed in black, the glasses gone and the hair let down.

'And remember, don't start the food until the conversation's done,' she could be heard hissing at a sullen-looking waitress.

'The clicky pen's gone but its aura remains,' murmured Kajal. 'I'm so longing for the day that girl will quietly exit my life. Today, one hopes.'

'She's done a good job, you know,' Jemin said, seriously. 'You guys will moan about corporates, but look around. Would you have pulled this off otherwise? She's even got a couple of models on the RSVP list.'

'Do models come to book launches in Chhattarpur?' asked Samar doubtfully.

'And more importantly, do they read?' asked Kajal.

'Oh, Cashew Nut, you naïve little fish. They don't have to read. Models mean photos, and models mean page three, and all the gossip blogs and Instagram reels. All that lovely media exposure that money can't buy.'

'Helpful,' interjected Samar. 'Since there's no marketing budget, you know.'

'Enter House of Jems, and enter Vasudha, and all this free PR. You're welcome.'

'It's a nice crowd, you must admit, Kajal,' said DB, looking around him with the air of a benevolent parent.

The garden was filling up with people; women in saris talking into mobile phones; girls and boys in hipster t-shirts; some drifting barwards as though drawn by invisible strings, and some sitting down determinedly in chairs close to the stage. Through it, familiar faces filtered: Delhi's regular book launch crowd, well-known writers, bloggers, journalists. Kajal started feeling a little otherworldly: could all of these people be here for *her*?

A few tried to wander up to Kajal and Samar but were summarily blocked by Vasudha, who bustled up to them with a sad-looking young woman trailing behind her: 'Kajal, Samar, shall we begin? Ayushi here will be live tweeting your conversation. If you could look at her sometimes, that would be great, so she can take some photos for social media . . . Oh, and Ayushi, remember the Instagram stories too, ya?'

Ayushi nodded with an air of one who would be elsewhere.

Samar looked at Kajal, smiled, and offered his arm: 'Shall we?'

7.00 p.m.

There was a smattering of applause as Kajal and Samar stepped out in front of the audience and sat down in the two armchairs placed for them, facing each other at a self-conscious angle. Samar started by making a short and humorous speech in which he described Kajal's novel as 'a romp' and a throwback to a time when murders were 'charming, and old-world'. 'No severed fingers and Scandinavian-style torturers here, folks,' he said, to indulgent smiles. 'You keep expecting Miss Marple to show up to solve the whole thing.'

Kajal kept her smile frozen in place, but privately wondered if all this was strictly complimentary. She would have to have a word with him later.

'So, Kajal, tell us about this book.'

She glared at him, and he looked taken aback. But then, fighting the temptation to retort sarcastically that he had already told everyone about the book (and it was *not* a romp), she launched into her prepared speech.

'Well, Samar, thank you for that, er, kind introduction. This novel has been several years in the writing . . . '

The conversation continued comfortably, as these conversations tend to do. Kajal settled in, and started to relax. Her sense of unreality faded into the background.

Standing a little way behind the seated audience, Jemin was looking around expectantly. The book launch to him was a mere appetiser, and he was waiting for his entrée.

'Hello,' said a voice next to him. He looked around to see a familiar face, but one he could not, for the moment, place.

'Hello,' he said, cautiously. She was a pretty girl with a pixie haircut, a look, he thought, so cloyingly cute it could only be an effort to disguise insanity.

'It's Tina,' said the girl, clearly trying not to look affronted that he didn't remember her. 'We met at Samar's place a few weeks ago?'

'Ah yes, of course. Sorry.' Samar's new squeeze. He didn't know where he picked them up from. Jemin assumed it was a midlife crisis on Samar's side, but he had no idea what the girls got out of it. He looked at Tina curiously. She was gazing at the stage like a little terrier with her ears perked up.

'So, congrats,' said Tina, after they had listened to the conversation between Kajal and Samar for a few minutes in silence. 'What a great turnout. At a book launch, in Chhattarpur. I don't know how you did it.'

'Thanks. I'd love to take credit, but I don't think I can. I didn't do anything.'

'Of course you did. It's the House of Jems, you know. We wouldn't get this kind of a crowd for old Cashew Nut otherwise, beloved as she is.'

Jemin considered this idea. He hadn't really thought about it, but now that he thought about it—why *were* all these people here? As Tina said, it definitely wasn't Kajal, she was completely unknown in this world, and not the kind of woman who would make many waves in it either, with no political or industry connections, no great personal wealth, and no ambition to acquire either. He had said to Samar and DB earlier that it was Vasu's hard work, but the girl would have to be a miracle worker. Was it then, in fact, him? And his baby, the House of Jems, once so bright-eyed and full of potential, and now so . . . well, he still had some brick-and-mortar stores left, so there was that. Shekhar said they were doing well, and online was more profitable. But online just didn't have the glamour and the romance, did it? He sighed.

As though she had read his mind, Tina said, 'House of Jems is going in a different direction now, isn't it? Is that what made you guys sponsor this? Just curious. I've never heard of a fashion brand tying up with a publisher before.'

'You're not writing about this, are you?' said Jemin, in some alarm. 'For the *Delhi Daily*? Someone did give me a list of talking points, but I don't remember any of them. Something about brand synergies.'

Tina laughed. 'No, I'm not writing about this, I'm just curious. I mean, it's worked out very well for old Cashew Nut, she would never be able to afford it herself. And you know publishing houses, they never spend a penny on stuff like this, let alone have open bars. Not for first-time novelists who aren't Members of Parliament or international cricketers. But what's in it for you?'

'Marketing came up with it. One of those marketing strategies, you know,' said Jemin, saying the words tentatively, as one might do when talking about a rare species of marine life. 'But Shekhar okayed it instantly. And when you think about it, it's actually a very good idea. There's a lot of overlap in our clientele. Reading books in English is so niche, you know. Look at most of our writers, let alone our readers, and our publishers. They're all from well-to-do families. They're the only ones who would go into something so frivolous, where you're unlikely to actually make any money. I mean, it's not a hard-and-fast rule, of course, but it's pretty consistent. And they shop at our stores. If not the high end, the, you know, the prêt line.'

'That's interesting. I never thought of that,' said Tina. 'I guess you're right, in a sense. And Shekhar would know, of course,' she added. 'I'm sure his wife is quite the high-end shopper.'

'Well, she doesn't shop at the House of Jems,' said Jemin grimly. 'You know her?'

'I do. I work with her. As in, she's a colleague at the *Delhi Daily*. Are you . . . not friends?'

Jemin gave a short laugh. 'No. No, I can't say that we are.'

'Ah, good.'

He looked over at her. 'You are also not a fan, I perceive.'

'Good guess,' said Tina. 'No, not a fan. She's beyond obnoxious at work. Swans around as though . . .'

'As though she owns the place?'

'Yes. And yes, before you say it, I know she literally does, or her family anyway, but you know. That doesn't mean she has to be a total douche about it all the time.'

'She doesn't seem to have any other settings,' said Jemin, sympathetically. 'I suppose the whole Samar thing doesn't help, either. With you, I mean.'

'What Samar thing?'

Jemin turned to her to check if she was joking. Nope, those pixie eyes were fixed on him with a kind of unsettling intensity that he recognised all too well. All signs of the terrier had vanished. She still looked like a pixie, but a pixie like Tinker Bell who was to his mind one of the most violent and destructive characters in all of English literature.

'Did they . . . date?' she asked sharply.

Jemin considered this. Could their relationship be described as dating? He sighed.

'Look, I'm sorry. I don't know why I always put my foot in my mouth. I thought you knew, but you know, one should never assume. You don't know how many times I've asked women who aren't pregnant when they're due. I'm just that type of person. Just forget it, please?'

'No, no. Thanks for telling me, really, I appreciate it. I . . . don't know why he wouldn't have mentioned it, that's all. I mean it does feel like a bit of a betrayal, but . . . oh well . . .'

Her voice got lower and angrier. Jemin felt helpless.

'I'm sure he was going to tell you,' he said weakly.

'How long did they date?'

That word again. Samar and Anika's relationship was many things, but it wasn't casual.

'Er, well, I'm not really sure how long their relationship lasted.'

This was true anyway. Because he wasn't fully sure that it had ever ended.

'Before she was married?'

'Er, no,' he said, feeling worse and worse. Why were the young, despite their modern haircuts and jaded airs, so terribly naïve? 'No, in fact. I mean, I don't know, of course. But I don't think so.'

'No? What, you mean she was having an affair with him while she was *married*?'

'Er, I feel like this is now a conversation you should have with Samar,' said Jemin. 'Or . . . or maybe forget it altogether. You know?'

'Poor guy, I wonder if he even knows,' said Tina, not listening.

'Who?'

'Her husband?' said Tina. She tried to keep her voice offhand, but it was clear she was outraged.

Jemin sighed. The young were endlessly surprising to him. They were more conservative than most senior citizens he knew.

'Oh, I wouldn't worry about Shekhar if I were you.'

'Of course you wouldn't. Okay. Well, I feel like I need to process this. Thanks again.'

'Look, again, I'm so sorry—' started Jemin. But she'd already gone. He looked after her guiltily. He knew he'd be hearing from Samar about this . . . but really, it was Samar's own fault for getting involved with a woman with a haircut like that. It was just asking for trouble.

Jemin had been so engrossed in this conversation that he almost missed what he was looking for: Shekhar and Anika had finally arrived. They were clearly Making an Entrance, and there was a flutter around them as they looked around, said hello to some people, stopped for air kisses with others, smiled beatifically, and glanced at the interaction in front of them on stage, all while somehow looking supremely uninterested. She was in her usual black, in a shapeless tunic, loose pants that fell just above the ankle in a neat line, and a bright silk stole around her shoulders. Was it one of his own, he wondered, an eyebrow mentally raised. An interesting choice if so. Her husband was dressed as though he was about to head to a golf game, in a pastel polo shirt and light slacks.

He caught sight of Jemin and waved.

Jemin waved back. *Will you walk into my parlour*, he thought.

5

Armed with Sharp Objects

8.00 p.m.

The reading was over, the canapes were out, the bar was open. The corpses milled around and posed for pictures. Cigarette smoke floated up into the air and the usual little knots of people formed.

'Darling!'

'Haven't seen you in so long. How was Italy?'

'Oh, the usual, you know. So hot nowadays, one just longs for some *nimboo pani* but it's all limoncello and Aperol spritzes and whatnot.'

'I know exactly what you mean. We didn't even bother with Italy this year. We really went off the beaten path . . . to Croatia, you know. And it was charming, just charming. All those little cobblestone roads.'

'Oh, did you? I think Anika and Shekhar went to Croatia too. You didn't bump into them? Zagreb and King's Landing all over their Instagram.'

'Those two? Darling,' here the speaker, a thin woman with high cheekbones, wearing a light-as-air kurta and culottes, leaned in. 'We weren't on their flight, but Ambika was. You know my sister-in-law? She said that Anika was on her flight, but Shekhar wasn't. They didn't travel together.' She raised her eyebrows meaningfully.

'Didn't travel together? But they were both there?' said the other woman, leaning in as well, and enjoying herself thoroughly.

'They were both there, but they didn't go together, and I don't think they stayed together. Just took a couple of photographs together for social media. In my opinion, anyway.'

'Oho,' said the other woman, clicking her tongue. 'What have things come to? Taking a holiday just for social media?'

'They probably both had holidays. Just not with *each other*.'

They exchanged meaningful glances. The second woman finally said, with a sigh, 'So it's that way, is it? I suppose only to be expected.'

'Yes, one is liberal of course, but it's true that if the backgrounds don't match, it's really doomed from the start. Say what you will, but there's something to be said about arranged marriages.'

'But so sad, isn't it. They were such an It Couple. Back in the day.'

'Yes, back in the day.' They looked at each other meaningfully again, before jointly breaking into laughter.

8.10 p.m.

'It's so interesting that the House of Jems is sponsoring this,' said a bearded man in glasses to his companion, another bearded man in glasses. 'I thought they were, you know, down and out.'

'I did, too!' said the second bearded man. 'They're closing shops all over the place.'

'Trust Jem to run the business into the ground even after it was acquired by the great Kapoor coffers.'

They watched Jem, who was drinking at the bar and roaring with laughter at something. The first bearded man shook his head sadly.

'He had so much potential. He could have been the next . . . I don't know, the next Sabyasachi, or something.'

'I've heard that Shekhar's moving on to his next thing,' said the second bearded man. 'Deepika Something.'

'Oh, I think I've heard of her,' said the first bearded man. 'But I thought I heard that the Kapoors were pulling out of Shekhar's holding company?'

'Oh, is it? I didn't hear that,' said the second man, practically bristling with interest. 'Because of House of Jems?'

'Well, partly, but maybe also because of the marriage, you know. Anika and Shekhar. It's a bit, shall we say, rocky?'

The two men were quite close to Anika and Shekhar at this point, and they watched them for a minute in silence. The couple was in a group, the husband talking animatedly, the wife laughing softly at something he said. They certainly didn't look, at that moment, as though they were having marital problems.

'One never knows, does one?'

The second man agreed that one never did.

8.15 p.m.

Kajal was feeling a curious mix of exhilaration and anticlimax. Her book was launched, it was out in the world! Soon she would be sitting at a little table, signing copies for people. Soon she would see it in shops, in airports, on people's shelves. What had she thought would go wrong? It hadn't happened. Nothing had gone wrong.

Samar had handed her a large gin and tonic which she sipped tentatively. Her spirits lifted and she looked around her. Some well-wishers had come up and were engaged in earnest conversation, to which she now tried to listen.

'I just think that genre fiction is making such a comeback, you know?' said a girl. 'People are less snobby about it.'

'Oh, I so agree. Thank goodness. I hated that whole thing, like, if it's written by a man, it's literary, and if it's written by a woman, it's chick lit.'

Both women, neither of whom she recognised, stopped and turned to her expectantly. Kajal felt a momentary panic. Had she written chick lit without realising it? 'Er, well, my book is much more in the thriller category,' she hazarded.

'Oh, I wouldn't say that!' said the first woman kindly, confusing Kajal utterly. She looked around for escape.

'Anyway, these things just take time,' said the second woman. 'Look at Sherlock Holmes. I'm sure Conan Doyle was regarded as a thriller writer in the nineteenth century. But he's on most college literature syllabuses now.'

'No, he's not,' said Kajal.

'Darling!' said a welcome voice fruitily behind her. 'Congratulations! Launched!'

'Thanks to you, Jem,' said Kajal, clinking glasses with him. 'All thanks to you.'

'No, no,' said Jemin, looking pleased. 'It's all you! I just helped assist at the birth, you know. Er, Samar, can I borrow you for a second? I may have to warn you about something.'

'What have you done now?'

Kajal lost track of the conversation as her colleagues from the *Delhi Daily* suddenly encircled her.

'Kajal! Congrats!' 'Just bought the book!' 'Amazing party!' The young team crowded around her, clapped her on the back, gave her hugs.

She allowed herself to relax a little in the warmth of this open praise. Normally, she thought of the features team as kids, but their unironic energy was now a welcome change from her intangible fears.

Jemin had pulled Samar away, and out of the corner of her eye, Kajal saw them engaged in an energetic chat. Samar was doing a lot of dramatic head-clutching, and she deduced she was probably missing something good. She started, cautiously, to relax.

8.30 p.m.

'I really can't believe you, Jem. You're an incredible ass,' said Samar, half-crossly and half-distractedly. He took a large gulp of his whisky. 'I was working up to telling her about all that. Now she's going to make the most incredible fuss.'

'Sorry, sorry. What can I say? In my defence, it's hard to keep up with all your stories. You must admit. It's not easy.'

'Well, well, the two masterminds!' said a cheery voice behind them.

They both jumped as Shekhar walked up, his wife Anika a little behind him. His handsome bonhomie presented an almost ludicrous contrast to the rest of the group. Anika had a quiet pent-up look, like she was waiting for the tiniest signal to let loose a storm. Samar looked apprehensive, and Jemin's cheeriness was now replaced by a guarded expression.

'Congratulations on a successful launch! And . . . maybe a successful long-term relationship?'

Shekhar raised his glass and they were all forced to clink.

'Er, thanks Shekhar,' faltered Samar. 'This was a really good idea in the end.'

'Oh, this is just the beginning!' said Shekhar. 'But it's promising, very promising. I really think we've hit on an innovative format with this idea. Books and clothes! It's so Indian, isn't it? I can't think of another country this would work in.'

'If it works, it's more a commentary on the extreme elitism of writing and publishing in English in India than anything,' said Samar, feeling as though he was babbling and trying desperately to avoid Anika's eye. 'I mean, I hope it works, obviously. But, er, it's a sad reflection on our society if it does.'

Jemin stifled a guffaw at Shekhar's expression. He looked like a proud parent who has trotted out their firstborn to recite some extensive epic poem by heart, only to have the guests start throwing tomatoes and jeering her off the living room carpet.

Finally, after wavering for a few seconds, Shekhar forced a laugh.

'You publishers,' he said, as one's elderly uncle might say 'you scallywags'. 'Always over-intellectualising everything.'

'Hardly an accusation Samar here is accustomed to hearing,' said Anika, softly, speaking for the first time. Her tone was simultaneously honeyed and barbed, and it made Samar flinch.

Shekhar sighed. 'Anika. Be nice.'

'Sorry, darling. But it wasn't an accusation—just the truth. Especially with all this . . .' She waved her wine glass around at the party still in full swing. 'What's actually going on here? A mid-market, schlocky little book—and all this? And what's the tie-up, anyway? Oh, I know you've explained it to me, but I can't say I really get it. Is the murderer a designer? Was the murder done with one of Jemin's off-the-rack scarves? Cashew Nut over there is hardly my idea of a fashion brand ambassador.' Anika laughed. It was a laugh armed with sharp objects, a laugh that fought dirty with switchblades and razors.

'I did explain it to you,' Shekhar said, with a bit of an edge to his own voice. 'We're trying to appeal to a very specific set of young women. Young professionals. They're overwhelmingly readers of genre fiction—thrillers, romance—and they like to dress well. But they want more than Fabindia, and don't want to spend a fortune. It's one of those perfectly overlapping Venn Diagrams.'

'The book is called *Murder by Design*, too,' said Jemin, a little condescendingly. 'It's set in the fashion industry, you know?'

'Kajal's covered the fashion industry for years, too,' put in Samar, wondering if they weren't piling on a bit. 'She may not be a fashion brand ambassador, but she's something of an industry insider.'

'That's all rubbish,' said Anika, shortly. 'I don't know what's going on. But it's very *odd*.'

'Is it?' said Samar. This was going off on a different tangent than he had expected. And while it wasn't exactly a pleasant conversation, he preferred it to talking about what he had feared they were going to talk about—Anika's own books. Unfortunately, that seemed to be exactly the direction in which Jemin seemed to want to take the conversation.

'I expect,' said Jemin, smiling like a krait might when sizing up a lizard, 'Anika doesn't like all the fuss over Kajal. Do you, Niks? Especially when your last book launch was held at—where was it now, Café Turtle?' he laughed. 'And not the Khan Market one, either.'

This seemed to hit home. Anika snapped around to look at him, and her eyes sizzled.

'You always were such a malicious bitch.'

Delighted to have gotten a reaction out of her, Jemin threw back his head and laughed. Samar was conscious of heads turning to look at them. He'd been dreading meeting Anika, dreading this conversation, and now it was taking place, it seemed to him, under a spotlight, with megaphones and lots of foam fingers pointing at them with signs saying 'Listen here!'.

Kajal's conversation with her *Delhi Daily* colleagues had trickled to a stop, and they were now openly staring at Anika and Jemin. Kajal looked over at them too, her face now as dark and brooding as the starless sky above them. A little further away, Ayushi had perked up and was pointing a discreet phone camera at at the scene. She wondered briefly if she could work this apparently drunken spat between two society queens into the Instagram stories without anyone noticing.

'Oh, don't be like that, my dear!' continued Jemin. Unlike Samar, he was blind to the attention he was attracting. He was focused on Anika and his voice, though he tried to keep his tone as jocular as ever, rose in pitch until it became shrill and brittle with anger, maybe even madness. 'And *I* hear there's not even a *mid* market for your next book. But never mind! You can always publish it yourself. What did you once say to me? The universe always pays its debts. Wasn't that it?'

Anika and Jemin now seemed to be on a stage of their own. She slowly took a packet of cigarettes out of a little beaded clutch and took her time taking one out and lighting it. 'Are you enjoying yourself, Jem?'

'I am, rather,' he replied. 'I'm at a party. What's not to enjoy?'

'Well, enjoy it while it lasts. I meant what I said: the universe pays its debts. One way or another, they get paid. Luckily, I've never owed anyone anything. Can you say the same?' Here she blew some smoke rather dramatically in Jem's direction.

'Anika . . . ' Shekhar's voice sounded like it was coming from the middle distance and they both ignored it.

'Oh, I think some debts go beyond money,' said Jemin, his tone low but still bright with menace. 'And yes, I think I've paid my debts. My debt to you, certainly. Don't you think I have? Don't you think I've given you things that go beyond money?'

The party had started to murmur again around them, as people turned back to their own conversations. A few metres away, Kajal continued to stare at Jemin and Anika, even though she could no longer make out what was being said.

Anika finally gave a short laugh. 'Beyond money? Typical of you. But it doesn't count, you know. Not towards the universe. Samar, you'll be hearing from me.' She turned to look at him, and he flinched. 'We have a contract. Don't think you can weasel out of it, just because I haven't made you look good. Grow up. Both of you.'

With that, she threw her smouldering cigarette onto the lawn and stamped it out rather viciously with her heel. Then she turned and walked away, her heels stabbing into the grass.

'I'm so sorry. She does like her dramatic exits.' Giving them an apologetic shrug, Shekhar followed his wife over the lawn.

6

Our Cue to Leave

9.30 p.m.

The party, rather than winding down, seemed to be picking up, much to Kajal's alarm.

She had signed books, made pestilential small talk and plastered a most unnatural-looking smile on her face until her cheeks had started to hurt. Then she stopped, and resumed her usual expression, which was halfway between a scowl and an eyeroll. It seemed to make people less interested in approaching her, and the line of autograph-seekers soon dwindled.

But as she looked around, her garden was fuller than ever, and who were all these people, anyway? Who had invited them? They had wandered into the house, and some, she noticed furiously, were even on her first-floor balcony! The nerve!

Leaving her little table, she tramped back over to the bar, where she met DB's wife, Meena. A woman in her early sixties, amiably dishevelled despite her silk sari, Meena was in a buzzy, happy state. She did so enjoy these book launches.

'Here's the celebrated writer!' Meena gurgled. 'Many congratulations, Cash!'

'G&T,' said Kajal shortly to the bartender. 'Thanks. Enjoying yourself?'

'Immensely,' said Meena. 'I haven't been to a party like this in years.'

'Neither have I. And I certainly haven't thrown one like this in years.'

'The place looks marvellous,' said Meena. 'You should really entertain more. Maybe now you will, now that you're a bona fide writer?'

Meena was always hoping to be invited to literary salons. She had held high hopes of hosting some with DB, but he had strict ideas about early bedtimes.

'Who are all these people? Where's that blasted Vasudha?' said Kajal, ignoring Meena. 'Hey, Samar!'

Samar, who had been slumped against the bar, sipping forlornly at a whisky, looked up. 'Yes?'

'Can we start wrapping this up?' said Kajal. 'Where's your minion? I'm ready for bed. Why are all those people in my house?'

'I thought you'd be upset about that,' said Meena blurrily, looking up at the balcony. 'There's someone, er, ashing into your champa tree.'

Kajal made a strangled noise. 'This is Vasudha's doing.'

'She's not my minion,' said Samar.

'Is that Anika?' said Meena, still peering up at the balcony. 'So unlike her. You should tell her, you know. She shouldn't be ashing into a tree.'

'Is it?!' said Kajal, looking up too. 'She certainly shouldn't be inside my house, for one thing. The nerve of that woman. Trash-talking my novel at my book launch, and then casually sauntering into my home.'

'Well, darling. I think I'm ready to go,' said DB, wandering up with a benevolent expression on his face.

'Of course. Let's.' Meena gave him a distracted smile and wandered off towards the house, still looking up at the balcony. As she approached, she heard Anika call down to a waitress: 'Excuse me, can you get me a drink, please? Just a Coke or Sprite or something.'

The waitress stopped short. 'Madam?' she said, in a sort of disbelieving tone, as though it would shortly be revealed that Anika was merely joking. But Anika merely said, 'Coke or Sprite,' again, and the waitress nodded in a dispirited way and trudged off towards the bar.

'Anika!' called Meena, brightly. But the other woman had turned back to her phone and seemed to be saying something furiously to the person at the other end. Meena stood blinking up for a few minutes and then trotted a little unsteadily towards the house.

9.45 p.m.

Tina and her friends were making their afterparty plans.

'Well, this was more fun than I thought,' said someone, in a self-satisfied tone, as though they had personally organised the party themselves. 'Where to next? What's near Chhattarpur?'

'I'm going home,' said Sapna, which remark was met with a chorus of boos. 'Well, I am! I feel completely sloshed.'

'Where are Ishaan and Devika?'

'Probably inside, making out somewhere.'

'Ew,' said Tina. 'Cashew Nut would be horrified.'

'So, where to next? Are we near Gurgaon?'

Various complicated discussions were entered into on the advantages of drinking in Gurgaon versus Delhi. Finally, it was decided that, since most of them lived there, they would head back into Delhi.

'Are you guys saying bye to Kajal and DB?' asked Tina, darkly. 'You go on, I'll wait.' She had been in a funk the entire night after Jemin's revelation and had avoided Samar. Annoyingly, he hadn't seemed to notice.

Tina's friends joined the group of Delhi Daily staffers at the bar, which now included Vasudha as well, looking flushed and excited.

'Going already?' DB asked them as they wandered up.

'Already?!' said Kajal. 'It's almost ten. I thought everyone would be gone hours ago.'

The group burst into laughter.

'That's our cue to leave, anyway,' said someone. 'Says our gracious hostess!'

'No, no,' said Kajal, unconvincingly. 'But DB here is usually in bed by ten.'

'I've been enjoying myself,' said DB with a slightly shamefaced smile. 'You threw a great party!'

'It was hardly me. The kudos all lie with Vasu here,' she said, glaring at her. Vasudha smiled.

'Oh, it was a joint effort. But we sold at least twenty copies and our social media's doing wonderfully too! Let's toast—to a successful launch! Does everyone have a drink?'

No one did except Samar and Kajal, who had been half-heartedly sipping her gin and wishing it was a soothing pre-bedtime jasmine tea.

'I think this calls for some bubbly,' said Vasudha, giddily. 'I think there was a bottle.' She disappeared behind the bar, and soon her head popped up, brandishing a bottle. 'Found it! Now, who can do the honours? Samar? I'll get some glasses.' Her head disappeared again. Her energy, thought Kajal, seemed manic, nervous, as if the launch were about to start instead of it already being hailed as an unqualified success.

Samar gave a comical shrug, and started to struggle with the bottle. Soon, the usual pop was heard, and the group gave a small cheer.

'Glasses!' announced Vasudha, reappearing like a pantomime fairy, with a tray of champagne flutes. There were at least ten, and she started pouring quickly. Soon everyone had a glass and they all raised them dutifully.

Vasudha called out: 'So . . . we toast. To Kajal! To the first in a long line of books!'

Everyone made the usual conventional noises. 'Hear, hear.' Tina's friends joined in, 'To you, Kajal!' 'Cheers!'

'Thanks,' said Kajal, trying to look more relaxed and less like she wanted everyone to go away.

They all drank.

'And now, we really must be going,' said DB. 'I have to find that wife of mine and drag her away.'

He moved towards the house, and Kajal and Samar followed him. 'Now, DB . . . you will carry a review, right? Who will you give it to?'

'Of course, of course,' said DB, coughing a little. 'We'll give it to the regular reviewer, er—I don't think it's been assigned yet.'

'Just don't give it to Anika,' said Samar, feelingly.

'Oh, no. As a matter of fact, she, er . . . she won't be with us for much longer.'

Samar and Kajal both stopped what they were doing, glasses held aloft, mouths slowly rounding into Os. 'What?' they both said, comically in unison.

'Yes, we've, well, we've had to tell her that we're discontinuing her column, and her editorial position with us. Very awkward and all that,' said DB. 'She's very expensive. And her readership numbers had just gone way down, and with all the controversy she kept creating—not always good, you know.'

Here, he had another coughing fit and had to stop.

'Have some more sparkling,' said Samar vaguely.

'Yes . . . I think, I think I'll just sit down.'

Samar and Kajal kept walking, leaving DB by a bench. Kajal was still digesting this news. In her world, people like Anika, with her connections, did not just have their columns dropped.

'*Well,*' she said, after she had stopped goggling. 'That is . . . certainly going to upset the apple cart.'

'I . . . almost feel a little bad for her,' said Samar softly.

Kajal shot him a look. 'Really? After her behaviour tonight? Don't,' she said. 'She's used that column of hers as a hatchet for long enough. I'm glad they've finally come to their senses. Strange that the family didn't intervene, though . . .'

'The family? I don't think—'

Suddenly, they heard a flurry of shouts. Near them, people huddled over a figure lying prone in the grass.

'I knew this would happen,' said Kajal. 'Someone can't handle their booze. This is why one shouldn't have open bars. Not on my lawn, anyway.'

'Most likely,' said Samar, but he went to have a look anyway.

As he pushed his way through a growing crowd, he found a tight circle of people at the centre. And in the middle of this circle lay the prone figure of Dhritiman Bhattacharya.

Samar was on his knees immediately, and cradled the man to a seated position.

'DB? Dhritiman?'

DB didn't answer but continued to make a dreadful choking noise, grasping now at his throat.

Time slowed as Samar seemed to see things happen through a wall of jelly. Someone screamed. Someone suggested getting an ambulance. Someone called for ice.

But it was no use. In less than five minutes, Dhritiman Bhattacharya was dead.

7

Earthworms after Rain

i

It is a sad fact, but one that must faithfully be recorded, that after a murder of a sensational nature, private detectives pop up like earthworms after rain.

It was true after the death of Dhritiman Bhattacharya.

Online, the hashtag #WhoKilledDB? was trending at the very top, closely followed by #WhoIsDB? A handful of true crime podcasters were promising to follow every turn of an investigation that had yet to begin. Already, the reporters and editors at the *Delhi Daily* were forced to switch off their phones as their colleagues in the rest of the media tried desperately to track them down for quotes.

A handful of staff braved the reporters camped outside the suddenly inconveniently located *Delhi Daily* building on Bahadur Shah Zafar Marg, Delhi's Fleet Street where journalists could be found taking cigarette breaks at all hours. The book launch had taken place on a Friday night. By Saturday afternoon, the office, which would have usually been half empty, was simultaneously abuzz and muted. People gathered in shocked circles. Some sobbed, others merely looked dazed and found themselves asking the same questions repeatedly, 'But how . . . ?' and 'Why . . . ?'

Mridula Majumdar had sat still, toadlike, in her office, all morning half-listening to the muffled voices of her colleagues outside. Contrary to appearances, she was deep in thought.

DB had been a colleague for many years and her first reaction had been a blank incredulity that such a thing could happen. She had felt numbed by it, and was shortly overcome by a wave of grief, a feeling she was unused to, not being by nature a particularly emotional or even social creature.

Long years had taught her this. And far from seeing it as a personal failing, she wondered what need there was for anyone to be a social creature, especially in this day and age. When we were all relying on each other for food and shelter and entertainment, maybe. If I were a hunter, and you were a gatherer, and we lived in some remote corner of the Amazonian rainforest—possibly. But today? When you could do your job, all your shopping, order in from restaurants, and watch movies, all without ever having to encounter, let alone speak to, another person? Then why? Why all this pointless chit-chat?

The simpler truth was, of course, that Mridula just didn't like people. And hadn't from the tender age of three, when she knew nought of hunters, nor gatherers.

At work her blunt manner, her blunter haircut and her inability to sustain small talk meant people gave her as wide a berth, albeit for different reasons, as they did Anika. But Mridula had also earned a grudging respect. Her memory and attention to detail were legend and *Delhi Daily* writers who worked with her had learned to be careful and rigorous—she had once pulled a guest column at the last minute because the columnist in question, a very respectable Delhi ad man and general mover and shaker, had plagiarised himself. By all means be wrong, she had told him, but don't be boring and repeat yourself, especially when it wasn't all that original the first time around. He had kicked, he had screamed, he had invoked his close friendship with the owners, but she had stared him down, reducing him to weak blustering with her unblinking gaze.

And DB always backed her. A personality like Mridula's did not need (luckily, because they usually did not have) many friends. But DB had been one of the few colleagues who had come close to crossing that line. If she had been asked whether she had any friends, she would have first cast about wildly, and then offered up maybe three names, among which his would have featured.

So today, she grappled with her grief. Held the despair at bay.

And then she found she couldn't; she needed to understand first. And she just didn't understand. She had questions about DB's death, and not philosophical questions like her colleagues, whose voices continued to trickle through to her in sobs and gasps. She, very literally, didn't understand.

Collecting herself, she picked up the phone to dial Kajal. It was so difficult to know what to do under these circumstances. Mridula didn't want to come off as inquisitive. Because, frankly, she wasn't. But she did need to understand.

ii

Monami Chatterjee had also sought solitude that morning. She was sitting alone in an empty conference room, on a cracked leather office chair, considering her options. An unwitting bystander would have been impressed, certain that the young woman's otherwise flawless brow was furrowed because she was considering profound questions and thinking beautiful thoughts. She had that kind of face.

In actuality, Monami did not think many thoughts that could honestly be called profound, or beautiful. Few things moved her deeply. Good food was one; the ability to get a Wi-Fi connection in unexpected places was another. However, today our imaginary bystander would have been partially correct as she was in fact grappling with deep questions. Like Mridula, she didn't understand. But where Mridula felt the pull of truth, she felt the pull of that mythical character, the amateur detective. All those years raiding her parents' shelves, seeking out Poirot, Marple, Lord Peter Wimsey and, going back, Holmes and Dupin, and now a real-life, cold-blooded murderer was out there to be caught.

Like most of her colleagues, the news of DB's death had first shocked her into a dumb stupefaction. But she and DB had not worked together very much at all. And after the initial bewilderment had worn off, the whole situation was suggestive of certain possibilities. They gnawed at her like a little knot of puppies with a chew toy.

She was interrupted in her musings by a ping on her laptop, announcing that a meeting had started online. She had sent a note to her team this morning that they would of course be cancelling their usual Saturday morning team meeting, but whoever wanted to talk, just talk, could join. She watched as people started to join the online meeting. Clearly, everyone wanted to talk.

Taking a second to check her camera and straighten her hair, she joined the meeting too, trying to arrange her features into an expression that showed sympathy, solemnity and strength all at once. This leadership gig was a doozy.

Her team comprised the writers Devika, Sapna, and a serious, spectacled girl called Nandini; Ishaan, who was considered a de facto member; and the youngest was a newcomer named Karthik, who, like Monami, had not been at the launch. They were all in the online meeting, peering into their webcams in various stages of haggardness.

'Hi, guys,' Monami began. 'Thanks so much for logging on this morning. It can't have been easy. How are you all?'

There was a moment of silence, and then Sapna spoke up, hesitantly, 'It's been . . . hard. We've been on the phone all morning with legal, with news, with marketing.'

'They've told us to get lawyers!' burst out Nandini. 'My parents are so worried. We don't have a lawyer.'

'The company will figure out a lawyer for you, I'm sure, Nan. Don't worry about that. The most important thing is . . . how are you all doing? Mental health-wise, I mean.'

'Well, let's see, our names and our photographs are all over the news,' said Devika. Her eyes were red-rimmed and puffy, and she looked as though she had been crying all night. 'Our names! They're listing them . . . over and over.'

'I know,' said Monami, sympathetically. All morning, since the news came in, she had been torn between wishing she had been there, and being devoutly thankful that she hadn't.

'It's . . . it's immoral!' said Nandini. 'Why should we be dragged into it, just because we were there? We had nothing to do with it.'

'It's the twenty-four-hour news cycle,' said Monami, soothingly. 'I'm sure they'll drop all of you once the police make an arrest.'

'Who . . . who will they arrest?' asked Ishaan in a voice that sounded very unlike his usual tone. Monami noted that like Devika, he also was looking almost physically ill.

'The way the news is reporting it,' said Monami, carefully, 'it feels like they'll arrest the bartender. Gaurav something.'

There was another silence at this.

'But . . . but why would he do this?' said Karthik timidly.

'That's the million-dollar question, Karthik,' said Monami. 'And also one that, unfortunately, the Delhi Police is unlikely to ask.'

'We've thought about this,' said Nandini. 'We've got, er, a bit of a WhatsApp group going with others who were there.'

'And?'

'It definitely couldn't have been the bartender. He was on a break or something when the whole thing happened. In fact, the person who was pouring the drinks was the publishing intern, Vasudha. She literally poured the drinks herself.'

'What exactly happened? Can you talk about it?' Monami had been itching to get to this question.

'We were saying goodbye . . . ' started Sapna.

'Who's we? And what time was this?'

'Around . . . I don't know, around ten o'clock, I think? It went on much longer than we were expecting. You know, for a book launch. We were deciding where to go next, and someone suggested saying goodbye to DB and Kajal. So we all went to where they were . . .'

'Who's we?' asked Monami again. 'And who's they?'

'There was a whole bunch of us. Let's see, me and Nan. A few people I don't even know, I think from the desk?' ('You can get their names from the news,' put in Nandini, sourly.) 'You know how people just tend to materialise when a cork pops. And "they" were DB, Kajal, that publishing guy Samar.'

'Wow . . . so that's, what, ten people? More? What about you, Ishaan? Devika?'

'We weren't at the bar,' said Ishaan sharply, still a bit ashen-faced. 'Anyway, get on with it, Sapna, I couldn't really follow the WhatsApp messages after a point.'

'Okay, so Vasudha suggested a toast. It was definitely her idea, no one else wanted to do it. You could see that Kajal was just dying for the party to be done so she could go to bed. But Vasudha insisted, she took out a bottle and a bunch of glasses and just started dishing them out. We all drank. And then we started to, you know, disperse. DB wandered off with Samar and Kajal, I think. And then it happened, almost immediately. No one could believe it at first, we all thought it was a heart attack or something. Someone called a doctor. And . . . I guess he wouldn't sign the death certificate. We thought it was best to just . . . take off. So we left.'

'Rather lucky, that,' said Monami. 'You didn't bump into the police?'

'No. But we're all sure to get our summons now,' said Ishaan, gloomily.

'There were quite a few people from the *Delhi Daily* there. The news is having a field day,' said Monami.

'It's immoral!' burst out Nandini again. 'They're saying that anyone could have done it. But literally no one apart from Vasudha could have.'

'But what on earth could her motive have been? A girl who's got her whole career in front of her, I'm guessing a completely normal background, no red flags anywhere that we know of—it doesn't make any sense,' said Monami almost dreamily.

There was a short silence.

'Maybe it was a heart attack after all?' suggested the youngest, Karthik. 'Doctors always get this sort of thing wrong. And people nowadays are dropping dead of heart attacks constantly . . . this guy I know from the gym— '

'They had to have been pretty sure to make it public like this,' said Monami, waving away the guy from the gym. This was no time for pointless side discussions. 'No, I think he must have been poisoned. I wonder if . . .'

She trailed off and her team looked at her expectantly. She hesitated, unsure if she should be making wild statements in her new avatar as a team lead, but then resolutely plunged in, 'Could it have been someone else there? Not, what did you say her name was, Vasudha, but maybe someone just standing around near him? In all the bustle he or she may not have been seen slipping something into DB's drink.'

The team considered this, and then Devika said, tremulously, 'Who?'

'Yes, who? No one had it in for DB. He was—he was just this sweet old man,' said Nandini, sounding perilously close to a sniffle.

Monami frowned. This was the nub, because she had no idea.

iii

Kajal had been impossible to reach, but Mridula got through in the end.

'What is it, Mridula?' she had said. As though there hadn't been a murder at her house the previous evening, as though a close colleague hadn't died.

'What is it?' Mridula had repeated.

'Yes, what is it? You've never called me before. I know you're not calling to offer your condolences. So, what is it?'

Mridula paused. This is where social skills would have been an asset. 'I *am* calling to offer condolences, actually,' she had said, with an impressive amount of indignation given that this was a blatant untruth. 'DB was my colleague too.'

'Yes. I know,' said Kajal, heavily. 'I'm sorry. He was . . . I still can't believe he's dead.' She had started sobbing and Mridula had felt completely out of her depth. For anyone else, this would have been a point of connection, of shared grief. But somehow, for Mridula, it wasn't. She wasn't sure why. The most she could do was to hear Kajal out.

And once Kajal got going, she found she had a lot to say. And it was strangely comforting to speak to someone who she knew would not pass along the conversation.

The morning after DB's death had passed in a fog. And there was no space to process it. Already, the news vans had gathered around her home, and young journalists peered through her gates. The police were in and out.

'The *police*. At first, I thought it was a heart attack, and that was bad enough. But now . . .'

'Yes. It seems it was . . . foul play,' said Mridula, sensing a way into what she wanted to talk about.

Kajal made a guttural sound, halfway between a groan and a sob.

'*Foul play!* It sounds so dramatic, and who could have wanted to do that to DB? I'd understand if it were someone else, but DB?'

'I know,' said Mridula. 'The news is saying . . . that the police have arrested the bartender.'

'The *bartender?*' said Kajal incredulously. 'I hadn't heard that; I can't face the news. But what does the bartender have to do with it? He wasn't even there.'

'I think it's shorthand for "we have no suspects",' said Mridula, drily. 'They're just pitching on the most convenient person. But it's nonsense, and it's not going to end there. They'll be working behind the scenes.'

Again, a groan. And then, Kajal fell silent.

'I think,' said Mridula, 'We have to do something.'

'Do? What can we do?' Kajal's voice sounded different now. What was it? Stress? Fear? Or something else?

'Well, we can investigate,' said Mridula, bluntly. 'Find out what really happened. There are so many rumours floating around on social media. The police will never get to the bottom of it.'

'Rumours? What rumours?'

'Never mind all that now,' said Mridula tactfully. She didn't want to waste any time on the chief rumour of the moment—that Kajal must have done it because she had motive, a supposedly torrid office romance (based on one picture someone had unearthed of her and DB sitting close to each other, a bottle of beer at their feet, at an office party nearly ten years ago) that must have soured, and opportunity, the fact that it had happened at her home. 'It's all nonsense. But we have to act. DB is dead. No one understands how, or why. Many of our editors and young journalists were at your party. Questions are bound to be asked. We have to be prepared.'

Another sob echoed down the phone.

'I can't . . . with all this.'

Mridula felt a touch of impatience.

'You must. The *Delhi Daily*'s in the eye of the storm. We have to take a position.'

'Marketing is putting out a press release . . .'

'Not that kind of position. I mean something deeper. Find out what really happened.'

'What does the rest of the office think? What's everyone else saying?'

This is just what Mridula didn't know. Sounds of conversation had filtered through her door, and for the first time, she had wished she could just wade in and join the chatter. But she knew if she did, said chatter would immediately cease. It would be as if the resident Tyrannosaurus rex had wandered down to the watering hole to shoot the breeze with the triceratopses and other lesser dinosaurs that she would normally interact with only for snacking purposes.

'They're all rudderless without DB,' Mridula said. 'No one's thinking straight. But we need to get out in front of this. Why, half the features team was there, and all their names are being bandied about as though they're suspects. It's the most sensational thing to happen in Indian journalism for years.'

'Well, call Monami in. Features is all her. I don't know what you expect me to do about it. I'm already knee-deep.'

'I'm not expecting you to do anything. But yes, Monami. That's an idea . . .' Monami Chatterjee had possibilities. She was more malleable, in Mridula's eyes, than the rest of the senior team, who she unkindly (but maybe not inaccurately) thought of as a frankly doddering group of old men.

'Right,' she continued, sounding more brisk now that a plan of action had occurred to her. 'Look, we may be by to talk to you shortly. It'll be important to . . . you know, look around. Talk to your staff. Talk to you.'

'Come here? It's a media circus. Don't come here,' said Kajal.

Mridula raised her eyebrows. Pointlessly, since the other woman couldn't see it, but she hoped it came through in her tone.

'But we have to—it's a news story. It's *the* news story! The other media is there, but not us? We're the only ones who may have the inside track on this one, unlike . . . all of the rest of the time.'

'Fine. Okay. I guess we have to get a *Delhi Daily* team on it. Shall I tell the others?'

'Oh, yes please—thanks,' said Mridula, relieved. Now she could bypass the triceratopses and get on with it.

8

Mortal Enemies

i

The team meeting was continuing.

'I spoke to Tina this morning,' said Devika, hesitantly.

'Did you?' Monami hadn't been able to reach her herself. She'd left her one missed call and one voice message, and then hadn't liked to do more. 'And where was she during all of this?'

'She didn't come with us, she had some sort of falling out with Samar.'

'Oh? What about?'

'I'm not sure. Something about Anika, I think. Anyway . . .'

'Anika!' This was something else Monami had been hoping would crop up. 'She's been very silent. I would have expected her to be on the news already, milking it to the last drop.'

As soon as the news had broken, she had felt a kind of astonishment that DB had been the victim and not Anika, who half of Delhi must have been gunning for. And then when the facts had become undeniable, she had felt a keen suspicion that Anika, if not the victim, had nonetheless been involved in some way. Who else at that party even had a motive to get DB out of the way? It had been an open secret that Anika thought she should have his job. And who else would have the brazenness, the audacity? Only Anika, from one of the richest families in India.

'She had had a massive showdown with Samar and Jemin earlier . . .' started Sapna.

'A massive showdown? About what?'

Various painstaking explanations were entered into, and the entire scene acted out. If the whole thing hadn't ended in tragedy, they would have had a good laugh over it. It would have probably been the single item on their team meeting agenda that morning.

'And Kajal heard it all?'

'Oh, yes. She looked *furious*. She was finally starting to relax and then she just sort of . . . turned to stone again. She didn't say anything, but you could tell she was pissed off.'

'And where was DB during all of this?'

'I don't know. Wandering around. Socialising. He was actually having a whale of a time,' said Sapna, sadly.

'Hmm. And what did Anika do after this . . . massive showdown?'

'I don't really know. I didn't see her.'

'I saw her husband take off,' said Ishaan. 'He left quite early. But she wasn't with him.'

'I think I saw her on the balcony when we were toasting,' said Nandini. 'She was talking into her phone. Sounded like she was having quite an argument with whoever was on the other end.'

'Oh,' said Monami, disappointed. 'She wasn't part of the group that was toasting?'

Everyone shook their heads, decisively.

'Oh, well.' It wasn't important that she be there, Monami thought to herself. She could have just paid the bartender. Or the intern. She tried to follow this train of thought, and then realised that her team was looking at her expectantly. 'Well, look. I'd like to work on this as a story.'

There immediately rose a chorus of protests.

Devika said, 'Mona, we can't.'

Ishaan said, 'I agree. We absolutely can't.'

'Hang on, hang on. I know none of you can. But I think I should. I don't think we'll have a choice, really,' said Monami. 'It's a story, and it's a story that's pretty much focused on the *Delhi Daily*. We'll have to follow it up in some way.'

'I guess the news desk will do that . . . ' started Devika.

Monami snorted. 'That bunch? They'll just go to the press conferences and report what the police tell them. We have to dig deeper. I'll have to clear it with . . . well, with someone at some point. But we can't lose any time on this.'

Finally, Devika said slowly, 'Talk to Tina. I spoke to her this morning, and she was . . . I don't know, she just sounded off. Oh, I know we're all off right now, but she sounded really weird. She said . . . she said that she had seen the whole thing, that she was watching it all. And she said it was like watching a play.'

'That's not weird,' said Ishaan. 'She was probably high. There were quite a few joints going around. Er, reportedly.'

'Maybe,' said Devika. 'But she sounded so odd about it. She said that as she was watching, she felt that something was going to happen. That it would end in some sort of dramatic way. And it did.'

There was a short silence. Monami looked thoughtful.

'Cashew Nut felt it too,' said Sapna, suddenly. 'She was saying it all night.'

'What?'

'Just that something was going to go wrong.'

'You see? This is the kind of thing that the news desk is just not going to think about or ask about. We have to use, I don't know, some imagination and all that. We owe it to DB, guys.'

As though on cue, a highly theatrical cough sounded by the door. Monami turned her head sharply to see Mridula Majumdar peeking around the door like a belligerent owl in one of the more unpleasant children's fairy stories. Mridula was known unofficially as the office Boo Radley, and the sight of her never failed to unsettle.

'Oh, er, yes Mridula?' said Monami, uncertainly.

Mridula didn't say anything for what seemed like an interminable age, and then finally grunted: 'Can we talk?'

ii

That Saturday morning, Samar lay in bed. He lived alone in a roomy apartment on Amrita Shergill Marg, a stone's throw from Khan Market, and his usual weekend breakfast routine was to stroll down to one of the coffee shops there and buy some coffee and a *pain au chocolat*. He would often bump into friends and make a morning of it.

Today, of course, all that was out of the question.

For one thing, he felt that he couldn't move, that if so much as a fingertip left the sanctity of his bed, the universe would start to collapse. He stared up at the ceiling, the peeling paint, the cracks and the lone spider's web that had been growing since the start of the summer and that he hadn't bothered to ask the cleaning lady to sweep away because he liked watching it grow.

He wished he could snap his fingers and a bottle of beer would magically appear. Or a joint. Come to think of it, he did have a joint somewhere, or a few Ambien. Could he sneak out of bed for the worthy purpose of finding them?

He found he couldn't. His limbs wouldn't move. Instead, his mind raced.

Mostly, he felt resentful that he couldn't think of DB. What a friend he had been, for many years. But now he could only think about DB's purple face, that dreadful choking sound. And in the periphery, the low but present dread.

Unlike the *Delhi Daily* team, he had stuck by Kajal that night until the police arrived. And although they hadn't accused him of anything, and he certainly hadn't said more than he needed to, he had had his fair share of attention.

I suppose, morally speaking, he thought, I am responsible. It was my book launch, in a manner of speaking. I took him there. I literally drove him to his death. I may as well have handed the glass to him. Put it right in his hand. The drink of death. Samar shook his head. *This way madness lies.*

He had been told in so many words that his movements would be carefully watched and that he should not try to leave Delhi.

He started to giggle. It seemed funny, when he couldn't even leave his bed.

The whole evening now took on an air of fantasy, of extreme surrealism. Cashew Nut's book launch. The wandering corpses. The weird exchange between Jemin and Anika. All that stuff about the universe. Everything had been weird, even before DB's death. Kajal constantly saying that something was wrong, that something would happen.

This thought stopped his internal monologue short. How could she have known that?

He shook his head again. At times like this, he thought of reaching out to only one person. But that was just the person he couldn't call. Or could he? If there had ever been extraordinary circumstances, these were those. He felt a sudden rush of energy—he had to speak to her. Nothing else made sense, but they could weave together their own stories and make their own meaning. They always had. He reached for his phone.

iii

Kajal considered the phone in her hand.

Phones. She had never really thought about it, but they had somehow changed from something one *had* to something one *was*. And not just in the old-fashioned sense of being made distinctive by a personalised phone case or wallpaper. They were an extension of your physical self, in many cases nowadays only functioning when being held, or looked at, by their owners.

The only difference was, of course, that phones were easier to replace or mend than, say, an arm or a leg.

With this sudden thought of missing limbs, Kajal shuddered. Why were bodies so complicated? We never think of them when we're alive. We pump them with bad food, cigarette smoke, alcohol. And if they hurt anywhere, we consider them a nuisance. But one thing goes the wrong way . . . a little drink, a little poison . . . and that's that. Our bodies turn against us.

Like, to come full circle, our phones. They were a veritable treasure trove of information about us, from whom we contact, to what we say to them, to what we watch or play in our spare time. Each phone had been imprinted with the personality of its owner, so that we were only entirely understood by our phones. And those who had access to them.

As if on cue, the phone in her hand started to ring. She stared at it, vibrating urgently, as though it were an alien. Presently the ringing stopped. She put it back in her pocket with a shudder.

9

Skeletons Always Lurk

i

Safely in her office, which when compared to Samar's florid space, or DB's cosy one, closely resembled a Spartan soldier's barracks, Mridula cleared her throat. Monami, who was still thinking of Boo Radley, looked nervous.

'So, I, er, happened to overhear your conversation back there,' began Mridula. 'About this whole business of DB.'

'Oh, yes?'

Years abroad had inculcated in Monami the habit of calling everyone, including older people, by their first name, but the Delhi-convent-educated girl in her still felt the old urge sometimes, particularly in situations like this, to call people 'sir' and 'ma'am'. She bit back the 'ma'am' now.

'Yes. I agree with you. I think we should investigate.'

'You do?'

'Yes, I do. I agree with you entirely—there's more to the story, and the police won't figure it out. They won't even scratch the surface. I don't have a lot of faith in the news channels, either. You know what they're like. Create a Hindi film plot out of the whole thing. Then sell it so that in the end, even the police are calling them for tips.'

'Wow. Okay, great. You agree? Wow.'

Monami hadn't meant to say 'wow' twice. But she could see where this was going, and her mind was already trying to work out whether she could back out of the room in some sort of socially acceptable way.

Mridula was also experiencing extreme discomfort. Like Kajal, she too thought of the 'young' as one objectionable monolith. But whereas Kajal regarded them with an indulgent suspicion, Mridula found them merely tiresome. This whole interaction was already exhausting her.

'There have been too many cases in the recent past,' Mridula went on. 'So many murderers going scot-free . . . but it's not corruption I'm thinking of. It's sheer incompetence. Remember the Talwars?'

Monami nodded at the mention of the famous murder case. On the most circumstantial evidence, and amid a showy media trial, the Talwars had been arrested for the murder of their child, only to be released years later on the determination of a mistrial.

'The police, as you know,' continued Mridula, 'have already picked their main suspect. The bartender.'

'He doesn't seem to have a motive, though,' said Monami, feeling unreasonably as though she was being childish by insisting on this point.

This feeling was corroborated by Mridula saying airily, 'The police couldn't care less about any of that. They just need someone to charge. What we need is an investigation.'

Monami sighed. 'I was going to investigate with my team,' she said, sadly.

'Oh, no. You have to be completely impartial.'

'Of course, we would be,' said Monami, a little offended.

'I'm afraid your team can no longer be impartial,' said Mridula. 'Why, they're all implicated up to the hilt on the news! It's nonsense, of course,' she added hurriedly. 'But if they're part of the investigation, they can't be impartial. It's an obvious conflict of interest. Our own internal standards wouldn't even allow it.'

Concealing her surprise that there was such a thing as the newspaper's internal standards, as she certainly hadn't heard of any in all her time there, Monami nodded.

'I suppose so. But it's absurd to think one of them might be involved.'

'I agree it's unlikely. But we can't rule anything out. One thing is clear—it's most likely to have been one of the people who was drinking with DB at the time. And that's a relatively small group, and it includes your team and several others at this paper. And who knows what kinds of motives there may have been? Skeletons always lurk in cupboards in newspaper offices. Petty jealousies, rivalries, resentment over some perceived slight . . . these things build up.'

Skeletons always lurk . . . Despite herself, Monami felt a small thrill.

Of course, Mridula quashed any semblance of adventure immediately by continuing, in a deeply prosaic tone: 'Right. I think we'll have two lines of enquiry here. The first is—who? We'll have to interview as many people as we can who were at that party. Who was around, but also who wasn't, who spoke to whom, what was said. The whole kit and caboodle. And the second is motive. That will be harder, I think. That will take some digging.'

'Speaking of motive, we should start with the senior staff,' said Monami, trying to keep her voice determinedly casual. 'Just to keep it democratic, you know.'

Mridula looked at her shrewdly, and grinned. 'Got any theories?'

'Who, me?' said Monami.

'No need to do the whole *who, me* act,' said Mridula, with a cackle. 'I know there's no love lost between you and Anika. I know she makes herself quite pestilential when it comes to features. And I also know that she sticks out a mile here. Where is she, for one thing. I would have expected her to be sticking her nameplate over DB's office by now. But what you may not know is . . . she may have had another motive.'

'Who? Anika?' Monami's ears perked up, almost visibly.

'Yes,' said Mridula. She wasn't used to passing news around. But if they were investigating, Monami would have to know, she supposed. 'DB had to make her position redundant. Just yesterday, as a matter of fact.'

'What?' Much like Kajal and Samar had earlier, Monami goggled. She reeled. She would have clutched her head if she had thought of it.

'Anika . . . was getting fired?'

'Got. Made redundant, not fired. I thought these things would be all over the grapevine. This office doesn't seem to have one. Yes, she was told that her column wouldn't continue, and, unfortunately, we couldn't keep her on the payroll.'

'She must have . . . she must have been wild about it.'

'She actually handled it very professionally.'

Mridula thought back to their meeting the day before—had it only been the day before?—with DB. The unpleasantness that she had foretold hadn't come to pass, and she had been impressed with Anika's grace under pressure. She'd come close though; particularly when DB had mentioned that they had got upper management's—essentially her own family's—approval, there had been a moment where Mridula had thought she detected a wavering in Anika's eye, a warning sign before losing her temper, and lapsing into the usual furious reaction. However, her eyes had merely flickered and other than a deepening of the iciness, and a definite drop in her manner from formally polite to borderline unpleasant, she had held control. Mridula had almost admired her for it.

She now wondered, swayed by the gleam in Monami's eye, whether this was indeed a motive for murder, and the desire for it had been birthed right there, in front of their eyes.

'I . . . I don't even think I can process this.' Monami stood up and started to pace up and down the room. Her leather sandals made an unpleasant swishing sound on the floor that immediately set Mridula's teeth on edge. This is why she couldn't work with people. 'It's almost too perfect. Are we supposed to believe that it's a coincidence that DB gets murdered on the same day that he fires her?'

'Please sit down,' said Mridula with a sigh. 'You're treating this like a joke. If Anika is involved, and that is a very big if, it's not going to be at all easy to prove it. You know the country we live in. You know who her family are. In fact, we should hope she was *not* involved, because if she was, she's almost certain to get away with it.'

Monami stopped her pacing with a dismayed look.

'You think so?'

'Let's be serious. We need to be very systematic about this. First of all, we don't even know if she had the opportunity. She was at the party, yes, but could she have gotten the poison into DB's drink?'

'She could have paid off the bartender,' said Monami. 'And maybe the police are actually correct for once in our nation's history.'

'Also,' continued Mridula, ignoring this, 'If detective fiction has taught me anything, it's that cold-blooded murders aren't usually committed out of spite alone. It's usually for reasons that are much more practical.'

'Maybe she thought if she killed him, the firing would be *off*?'

'Can you please stop calling it a firing? She wasn't fired. She was made redundant.'

'That sounds worse, just so you know, but okay.'

'Just being accurate,' snapped Mridula. 'And it's hardly likely that she would believe that, since not only was I present at the interview, but her own family is also aware. It wouldn't just go away. Anika's not a childish person, and for someone in her position, this would be a most unlikely step to take. Think of what she has to lose. Her social standing. Which is basically all she has, so . . . everything.'

'She probably thought she'd get away with it,' said Monami. 'You know people like her never believe they'll ever be held accountable for anything.'

'Well, we'll definitely have to talk to her.'

'Did you say her own family was aware? I thought they would have kicked up a fuss.'

Mridula nodded. 'Yes. But they didn't.' She thought back to DB's comment that it had been their idea in the first place. Had Anika had this impression, too? 'That part is curious.'

'Sounds like there's a story there,' said Monami, hopefully. *Skeletons always lurk.*

'But is it connected to DB's death? That's the question,' said Mridula.

'The way things are now,' said Monami, 'I can't think of a single person at this office, or anywhere in Delhi, that would have had a motive to put DB out of the way. Except for Anika. There's no one.'

'Well, that's why we have an investigation. We can't act on instinct. I agree with you on the surface, but we just don't have any data right now. We're reporters, right? Let's find out the facts and report them. Now, we'll need a plan, and let's set up a weekly meeting to discuss details. Or more if necessary. I'll put it in your Outlook.'

Monami sighed. There was no romance in the world.

ii

Early the next morning, a little way down the road from Kajal Puri's residence, Mr and Mrs Ahuja were on their morning constitutional. They took a morning walk every day and had done so with only a few exceptions throughout their twenty-two years of marriage. One exception had been yesterday, when their lane was clogged up with police cars, press and rubbernecking bystanders. They had muttered to each other about it, but finally decided that it would not be worth the hassle of picking their way through the crowd for their usual exercise and had taken a turn around their terrace garden instead.

Today, they were determined. While two police cars remained like sentinels outside the Puri gate, the lane was more or less clear. As they walked, the last of the straggling press cars drove by, showering bougainvillaea petals on them as they passed.

'I always thought that Kajal would bring trouble to this colony,' said Mrs Ahuja for about the twelfth time since the day before.

Mr Ahuja grunted. He agreed, but he was focusing on his breathing, which his doctor had told him must be in sync with his walking. Deep inhales and deep exhales.

'Whatever the media says, I'm sure she had something to do with it,' continued Mrs Ahuja, still retreading familiar ground. 'People don't just get randomly poisoned at other people's houses without the owners knowing about it. Please!'

This last came with a majestic snort.

In this Mrs Ahuja was not being perhaps wholly just to Kajal, who had been an exemplary neighbour for over two decades, as had her parents before her. Their garden was full of flowering trees that bent attractively over the wall of their property and into the street beyond. They were faultlessly polite. And they never held parties, except for maybe the odd, dignified Diwali do. However, as far as Mrs Ahuja was concerned, once was more than enough, especially when that party produced a corpse and brought news vans and pushy reporters to their picture-perfect neighbourhood.

Mr Ahuja grunted again, although now with more purpose.

'Clothes—hpph—in—hpph—bush—hpph,' he said, between decisive exhales. He pointed with his phone, which he clutched with the same firmness that his forefathers had once held their walking sticks.

Mrs Ahuja looked over. She was keenly against any littering on their street and was the terror of the neighbourhood WhatsApp group in this regard.

Sure enough, there was what seemed like a pile of black clothes in the long grass on the side of the road just ahead of them. She marched over, already bristling. They looked like good clothes, too, silk perhaps, with the way the sun glistened off the fabric.

As she drew closer, she stiffened. Something was wrong; this was no pile of mere clothes. Was . . . was there a body within?

She clasped a hand over her mouth, but her screams still carried down the street, shattering its air of sleepy privilege.

For there, in the long grass behind one of the flower beds planted so recently under her own watchful eye by the RWA, lying almost as though she had just passed out after the party, was a lifeless body that the police would later promptly identify to be that of Ms Anika Kapoor.

10

Venomous as Snakes

i

'Two! Two murders!' said Deputy Commissioner of Police Akshay Kumar, bitterly. Thanks to his name, he was a man who understood that life is funny, but not ha-ha funny. 'And what have you fools done? You didn't even discover the second body! You imbeciles!'

The man to whom these words were addressed somehow looked both shamefaced and mutinous. Inspector Dave had not had a good day, but he persevered.

'My men tell me they looked everywhere,' he began, to disastrous effect.

'Your men are BIGGER IMBECILES THAN YOU!' roared the DCP, his face growing a delicate shade of plum. The men behind Inspector Dave fidgeted. 'Do you know how this makes us look? Do you want another national incident on our hands? The press is already likening this to the Aarushi Talwar case and demanding a special probe. All because of you and your travelling circus of a team!'

This time, Inspector Dave prudently chose to remain silent.

'Now . . . just give me a summary of what you did and leave your report on my desk. And then get out of my sight! We'll have to deal with you later, after we clean up your mess!'

Resisting the temptation to clear his throat dramatically, Inspector Dave began his account. They had arrived at the scene of the crime at 11.27 p.m., approximately thirty minutes after the call had come in. Once there, they had discovered one corpse, that of Mr Dhritiman Bhattacharya, aged sixty-two. Mr 'DB' as he was known, was the founder and editor of a paper called the *Delhi Daily*, a daily newspaper which covered a mix of news and . . .

'Yes, yes, yes, yes, yes,' barked the DCP. 'That wretched tabloid. I know it. Stick to the facts.'

The facts were that there was a dead body, and it appeared that the cause of death was due to some kind of poisoning. There were six people left on the premises, as the fifty or sixty guests and staff had all disappeared hastily when they heard the police were en route.

'Who were these people? And whose place? Private?'

'Yes, belongs to a Kajal Puri. It was her book being launched. She is also working at *Delhi Daily*; this Mr DB was a colleague. Additionally, there was a Mr Samar Chishti, who works at the Sea Lion publishing company, a Mr Jemin Sequeira, a Ms Jyoti, the housekeeper, Karim, the driver and Poonam, the cook. Mrs DB was also there, but she was in no state to be questioned.'

'Hm. And what had been happening? A book party?' said the DCP.

'Yes. This Kajal wrote a book it seems, on some designer murder or something. Ms Kapoor and her husband were guests also.'

'Where is he? Have we tracked him?

'He's in Hong Kong, we've called him back. He left the party early, it seems, to catch his flight.'

'Hm. Anyway, go on with your most unenlightening report.'

'We questioned everyone,' said Inspector Dave, sullenly. 'It was clear what had happened. There was poison in his drink. The party had been going on just as usual—drinks, snacks and all. And then suddenly, in the middle, this old man drops down dead.'

'Old? How old did you say he was?'

'Sixty-two, sir,' said Inspector Dave, mopping his brow, having suddenly recalled attending festivities for DCP Kumar's sixtieth birthday the year before. There was an icy silence.

'Er, as I was saying,' said Inspector Dave, continuing valiantly. 'Suddenly, this . . . er . . . this man falls down dead.'

'Analysis? Autopsy?'

'Yes, sir. The drink was unfortunately not recovered, there had been so much chaos, you know. Guests, and then medical persons.'

'Wonderful,' said the DCP. 'Autopsy?'

'Results haven't come yet, sir. It seemed to have been such a clear-cut case,' Inspector Dave said sorrowfully.

'And you suspected the bartender? What was his name?'

'Gaurav, sir, Gaurav Rana. But we didn't arrest him, sir, the media reported that wrongly. We just brought him in for questioning.'

'And what did you find?'

'He had been taking a break when Mr DB started to choke. He accused one person who he claimed had been behind the whole thing, and she herself had poured the last set of drinks. A Vasudha Chaturvedi.'

'Who was she? A waitress?'

'She was an intern at this publishing company, this Sea Lion. She planned the whole event, it seems.'

'Age?'

'Twenty-four.'

DCP Kumar sighed. 'Motive?'

Inspector Dave hesitated. 'There wasn't a clear motive. We thought . . . we thought she must have, you know . . .' he finished by tapping his forehead significantly.

'Or maybe,' piped up an overenthusiastic constable at the back, 'we thought it might have been a sort of filmi stunt that went wrong.'

The DCP looked up. Usually, the junior members of the team were content to melt into the wall, like the ivy-green wallpaper. 'Who are you?'

Inspector Dave turned and glared at the unfortunate interloper. 'Police Constable Khurana, sir. Newly joined.'

'Come forward, Constable Khurana. Explain yourself.'

Constable Khurana came forward, looking both nervous and thrilled. 'Well sir, well, it was a very strange scene, sir. All sorts of stunts were happening. There were handcuffs, daggers everywhere . . .' He took a quick look at his superior who gave a curt nod and then looked abstractedly through the window behind the DCP's head as though he had washed his hands of the whole affair.

'Inspector!' said the DCP. 'Please explain this.'

'It's as I said, sir. It was a book party. The book was about a murder. So they had lots of props, lots of stunts. Tape with "crime scene" on it. There was even a chalk outline of a body in one corner. It was damn confusing, that much I can frankly say,' said the Inspector. 'When we first got there, we didn't know who to look for, or what had happened. The whole thing was just like a setup. So, we thought that maybe this also was a stunt, and it just went wrong. I was very suspicious of Mr Chishti also. He seemed to be in charge of the whole thing. I thought between them they had cooked up some publicity stunt for their book. I would have arrested them, if I could.'

'And what a great day that would have been for our civil freedoms,' said the DCP. 'And now . . . Anika Kapoor,' he said. 'I wonder how she fits in.'

'She was there at the party, sir, with her husband, Mr Shekhar Malhotra. Very well-established business family,' said Inspector Dave, feeling that he was now on firmer ground.

'Cause of death?'

'She was strangled,' said the Inspector, with relish. 'Strangled by the scarf she was wearing.'

'So, someone had to have a good deal of strength,' said the DCP, thoughtfully. 'Rules out any women, possibly. Her husband?'

'He had left the party early, as I said.'

'Hmm. And her body is found . . . two days later. Outside the house?'

'Yes. Just down the road.'

'Curious. Very curious. And there are no CCTVs on that road?'

The Inspector had just been treated to a twenty-minute lecture on this subject by Mrs Ahuja. 'No sir. But they will be installed shortly, according to the residents' association.'

'After the horse has already bolted,' said the DCP. 'What was her time of death?'

'Prima facie, the medical examiner said that she'd been dead for over forty-eight hours.'

'And there were no . . . no other marks on the body? After lying in the grass for two days?'

Inspector Dave raised his eyebrows. 'No. But this one will be an easier one to investigate, there will be plenty of motives . . .'

'Unfortunately, you won't be the one investigating it,' said the DCP, curtly. 'This is a Special Crimes investigation now. I'll take one of your men though, for continuity. How about you, Constable Khurana? Up for it? Now, the rest of you, file out. You'll be hearing from me soon enough.'

The men filed out, uncertainty writ on their faces. On one hand, they had been let off much more lightly than they had expected. On the other hand, it was galling to think of that young pimple Khurana getting in on a high-profile case like this.

Their leader fumed inwardly too. Special Crimes! Always taking over when the going got good. And this one had just got very, very good. He thought back to that night. Long though it had been, it had been a peek into a world that he did not enter much—a world that inspired equal amounts of envy and disgust. That farmhouse, the imported liquor, the absurd snacks. It was always amusing to come across that class of people in an atmosphere of crisis, when they and their perfect place in the world were thrown off axis. It took a lot to shatter their eternal calm, but this murder had done it. He thought back to all the nervous faces, the tears, the blank looks. He was still certain that he was right—there was obviously a mad man or woman at work, someone who thought that a murder would be the perfect publicity for a book about murder. A girl with her way to make, perhaps, or a cool-as-cucumber editor. And in that world, isn't anything possible? he asked himself. You don't even have to be insane—that lot just think that the world is theirs to take, theirs to change, theirs to do with as they like. And isn't it?

With that, Inspector Dave shook the rarefied dust of Kajal Puri's farmhouse from his feet, and stomped back to the grit of everyday Delhi, to the streets and people he knew and understood.

ii

Meena had not been able to cry since the death of DB. Not even when she saw his lifeless body for the first time. She had become frozen, and now, even three days later, she felt the same way. Her extended family, aunts, uncles, cousins, sisters-in-law, had gathered around her in solidarity but now they too started to fall back. 'It's the shock,' they had said to each other when they first saw her white, gaunt face. 'It's delayed reaction.' But soon even they couldn't explain away her tearlessness.

Her children had flown in from Texas and California, and their wails had filled the house. They hugged her, cried, shook in her arms. But still she could not. She asked them practically what they wanted to eat and spent hours cooking their meals. Through it all her mind seemed to stay blank. Then they too withdrew, quietly making funeral arrangements, all the drudgery and everyday duties that surround a death and somehow drag it down from the unknowable to the mundane but make it all the more terrible in so doing.

Now, finally, she was alone. And the news of Anika's death had come. Meena's mind was slowly unwinding itself, and she seemed to see before her a series of images. Somehow, Anika's death had not surprised her. Why? She seemed to have anticipated it.

She had gone back to the house, she remembered, to talk to her. There was something about her up there, on the balcony, something she thought she must correct. Anika's behaviour had always been bad, Meena had always known it. Like her late husband, she was not an envious woman, wasn't malicious, didn't gossip. When she met Anika at staff parties, she had felt only a pleased curiosity, knowing of her famous family, and a frank appreciation of her glamour, her beautiful clothes. Once, she had felt pity, when she had overheard a fight between her and her husband in a parking lot. But only once.

There had been something about her that night though, a strangeness she couldn't place . . .

Her mind seemed to slowly thaw and whirr back into action, but as it did, the gush of remorse and guilt that hit her was worse than the blankness that had been there before. She had left her husband, left him, right before he died. And for what? To do what? She had to physically put up her hands to her head to block the feeling out. She would never forgive herself. It was something that could not be forgiven. With her hands squeezing her head, she felt her thoughts become walled in again, and the emptiness creep back. This . . . this vacuum . . . was better, at least. She walked slowly into the kitchen, each step an effort, and looked around for something to do.

iii

Shekhar Malhotra, his legs stretched out in his business class seat, looked out of the window at the early evening sky. He was thinking. The call from Delhi had come in while he was in a meeting, and he had had to step out. His colleagues and clients had all been very decent: shocked and insistent that he take a flight back that very afternoon. After that, it had been a blur. This was the first breath he had been able to draw since taking DCP Kumar's call, he realised. That this was a Special Crimes case had come as a surprise. Though he supposed that it was inevitable.

The setting sun filled the aeroplane cabin with streaks of straw-yellow light. Shekhar sipped on his scotch and closed his eyes. His head fell back on his headrest.

Anika, gone. It was hard to comprehend. Was she really gone? Maybe he would get back to Delhi to find that it was all an illusion, she would be at home as usual, wearing her now-customary grimace.

It hadn't always been like this. She had been a different person when they got married, so many years ago now, adventurous, impulsive. They couldn't keep their hands off each other. Unconventional? No, maybe not that. Her family ties were too strong. Even her most 'rebellious' years had seemed to be out of a playbook—The Wild Years before One Settled Down.

The only thing that wasn't in the playbook was their marriage. It had surprised everyone, including him. It was true that they had fascinated each other from the start, like calling to like. They were almost the same person, with the same ruthless attitude to life, the same self-regard. They had had a fling, a heady, sex-fuelled fling. But marriage? Even now, years later, thinking about it, he could relive his shock, the physical thrill he had felt.

Everyone had attributed it to his looks, of course. He was hardly a catch without them. No one knew anything about him, he seemed to have emerged fully formed, tall, chiselled out of marble like some Greek sculpture, and so carefully, studiedly spoken. He's estranged from his family, Anika told her sceptical, disapproving parents. His father was in the army, so they never stayed in one place for very long. The lies had brought Shekhar and Anika closer together, had given their marriage a private, illicit charge.

He remembered the conversation he'd had with her father just before the wedding. The much-venerated Abhishek Kapoor, pompous, overbearing, someone who signed his emails, even personal ones, with a line of his degrees under his name. Both her parents had viewed him as little more than a gold digger.

'Well, Shekhar,' he had said, and managed to make even this opening sound sneering (or was that the meticulously maintained and ever-growing chip on Shekhar's shoulder speaking?), 'You've pulled it off.'

By this point, Shekhar had known not to rise to this bait. He had even enjoyed the taunting up to a point . . . because he knew it was little more than a powerless vent. He had, in fact, pulled it off.

'Pulled it off, sir?' he had said, knowing that this faux-innocent tone would merely infuriate her father further.

'Yes, pulled it off. Oh, well done, well done. I really didn't think you would. But don't think,' he said, coming so close that had Shekhar leaned forward a quarter of an inch, he could have touched the other man's forehead with his nose, 'that you will see a penny of her money. You divorce her, you leave her . . . you get nothing.'

'Oh Abhi, darling,' Anika's mother, Leela, had said, her words laced with contempt. 'Leave the poor boy alone. He won't leave Anika. They're two love birds. Aren't you?'

Sly and sarcastic, Leela was an even more dangerous proposition than Abhishek. For decades she had fought to preserve her marriage and thus her place at the top of Delhi's social hierarchy. With little in the way of brains or talent, Leela developed a scathing tongue and an expression of unstinting disdain, as if perpetually stepping around a drunk who had passed out on the pavement. Shekhar never knew what Leela was thinking and had sometimes caught her looking at him with a kind of malevolent intensity that alarmed him.

The only ally he had had back then in Anika's family was her sister, Anita.

Anita was only two years older than Anika but was already considered the dependable old maid of the family. She was serious, hiding her undeniable good looks behind a mask of no-nonsense professionalism. She headed a few of the family businesses, and, most of the time, she made it plain that she had very little time for her more frivolous younger sister.

Shekhar had expected her to be as distant and suspicious as the parents, but she was surprisingly welcoming, telling him that she was happy her sister was settling down with him.

'I didn't really expect her to get married so quickly,' she had said. 'I thought we'd be hearing about her affairs for years.'

'You still might,' said Shekhar, and she laughed, a disarmingly pretty, tinkly laugh.

'Somehow I don't think so,' she said, and she blushed a little, which surprised and delighted him.

Anita would have to help manage the parents now, he thought. Who knows what kind of a state they'd be in, and people like that—rich, arrogant, used to having their way—in situations out of their control can lash out, become as venomous as snakes. His thoughts turned again to Anika. Was she really gone? The idea, particularly in this suspended, honey-light-filled state, seemed absurd. He struggled to think, even as he felt his sluggish and exhausted mind give in to sleep.

iv

A different kind of grief had permeated the Kapoor household than the Bhattacharya household. Here it found expression in truckloads of white flowers covering every surface, a room that was constantly filled with relatives, family friends, and, unfortunately, those who simply wanted an excuse to see the famed Kapoor residence in Vasant Vihar. A prayer meeting was always underway, and the chanting of priests and pealing of bells filled the house, it seemed to Mrs Kapoor, from morning until night.

Unlike Meena, Mrs Kapoor could not stop her tears. She wept, she wailed, for once with no thought to her hair and makeup. She could not handle the puja room and stayed upstairs in her private suite, visited only by her husband and her daughter.

Today, she and her husband were alone. At some point she expected that she would run out of tears, but for now there seemed to be an endless supply. Her husband was white-faced, wan.

'We know he did it,' sobbed Mrs Kapoor. '*We know*. It couldn't have been anyone else.'

'He couldn't have, baba,' said Mr Kapoor. 'He wasn't there. That's what we know. The only thing we know.'

He sounded tired, hopeless.

Mrs Kapoor jumped up and grabbed at her husband's clothes. With her hair loose and her face devoid of her usual heavy makeup, she looked crazed. He felt a little afraid of her in that moment. He had always known that rage flowed through his wife like lava, rage that could, and on occasion had, scorched all before her. Both his daughters had inherited that capacity for anger. Leela was feared by all the women in their extended family, and most of the men. But Abhishek, around whom she tried to maintain an icy composure, had never seen his wife so unhinged.

'Abhi,' she screeched. 'He did it! He killed my baby. And he's going to get away with it!'

'Leela, Leela,' said her husband. 'Calm down. He did not kill her. He couldn't have. Look, I'll call Anita. She'll know what to do. But you must calm down. There are so many people downstairs.'

But Leela Kapoor could not be calmed. For once in her life, she didn't care who was downstairs, who heard her, what people would say. Her world had broken and she needed to lash out.

11

As Murderers Tend to Do

i

Monami and Mridula sat in a coffee shop near their office. Mridula was sipping from a drink towering with whipped cream and drizzled chocolate. Monami couldn't take her eyes off it.

'So, where are we?'

'Nowhere.'

Monami was feeling glum. The discovery of Anika's body had thrown their office—and it seemed the nation—into disarray. From a random, rather theatrical death, which of course shocked everyone but about which everyone also felt a certain amount of excited curiosity, they had gone to what some were calling 'The Great Journalist Purge of 2024'. And their paper was the target! Panic ensued. Who would be next? Some reporters refused to show up to work, others wrote long, overwrought social media posts and letters to the government. Monami had no fears for her personal safety, but was aggrieved at losing her primary suspect.

'Let's review the situation,' said Mridula. She took a very loud slurp of her drink and then fished out a dog-eared notebook from an ancient leather handbag. A pen was stuck in the spiral. She pulled it out, clicked it open in a way that Vasudha would have approved of and poised it over an open page. If this were the olden days, mused Monami, she would have licked the nib.

'The position has obviously changed drastically since the last time we spoke.'

'Our main suspect, herself topped,' agreed Monami, sipping on her own coffee, an americano in which she had determinedly added no sugar but now was rather wanting some as she confronted Mridula's tower of froth. 'It's so like Anika to ruin things, even in death.'

'Don't be flippant. She wasn't our main suspect, for one thing. She was also a human being, for another.'

'I know. Sorry.'

'Now, I'm assuming we don't buy all this purge nonsense . . .' Mridula paused here and glared at Monami as though she had brought the theory forward into the world.

'No, no. Just silly,' Monami said hastily. She had spent a little bit of time pleasurably contemplating the idea that a depraved lunatic was on the loose, picking off *Delhi Daily* journalists one by one. She had to admit it sounded unlikely, even to a fertile imagination like her own. 'But now hear me out. I'm sticking with my Anika theory. While I agree it's an unexpected roadblock that she's dead, if anything, this could also just clinch that she was guilty.'

Mridula sighed and laid down her pen. 'Okay. Let's hear it.'

'Okay. So . . . why else would anyone kill her? She obviously had an accomplice. In the death of DB, I mean. She waited for them after the party, to meet her in the road. And then, they got into a violent quarrel, you know, as murderers tend to do, and her accomplice strangled her.'

'Is this the Twitter theory?'

'It's a Monami Original,' said Monami with dignity. 'Twitter's very set on that fashion designer guy.'

'Jemin Sequeira? So they've moved on from Kajal? That's interesting.'

'Oh, the Kajal camp still has takers. You know, she and Anika weren't exactly the best of friends either. But that theory's absurd. Cashew Nut!' Monami paused to chuckle, and then went on earnestly, 'But yes, the main theory of the day is that it was Jemin Sequeira, with his scarf. They had had words just before, you know. The social media person from Sea Lion took a video, and it's all over Instagram. They start off very loudly, with Anika talking about Kajal's book being schlocky and mid-market and a whole host of other things. Just being her usual obnoxious self. And then she and Jemin get into it, and it gets quieter and harder to make out. But based on that video alone, those are the two frontrunners.'

'Hmmm.'

'But that completely ignores the DB angle. Once you look at both, Anika is the only real alternative. There's literally no one else who has both a motive for killing DB, as well as a potential reason to be killed herself.'

'Well, if you're asking about motives to kill Anika, surely there were any number,' said Mridula, frowning. 'Lots of people didn't like her, she rubbed many, many people the wrong way. With her attitude, with her column.'

'True. But is it likely that Anika happens to be murdered on a completely unrelated motive, on the same night that DB is killed?' Monami almost added, *think, woman, think*, but prudently refrained.

'Of course, of course. But we can't allow ourselves to be blinkered. There are other possibilities.'

'Such as . . .?'

Mridula didn't answer immediately; instead, she concentrated on scooping out all the chocolate liquid from the bottom of her tall glass. Finally she said, 'The way I see it, there are two options. Option One, the two crimes are related. As you say, she's somehow implicated in DB's murder. Either by being responsible for it, or she could be implicated in another way that doesn't seem to have occurred to you.'

'How?'

'She could have seen something.'

'You mean, about who killed DB? That's an idea . . .' said Monami. She tried to piece it together: 'So, she saw who slipped whatever-it-was into DB's glass . . .'

'From the balcony, she would have had a good vantage point, too.'

'And then she tried to . . . what, confront them after? That would be silly. And she wasn't really silly.'

'She was arrogant, though,' Mridula said, waving her straw to make the point and leaving little chocolate drops on the table. Monami wiped them up meticulously with little paper napkins. 'As I believe you yourself have pointed out. She wouldn't dream of the possibility that she would be killed herself.'

'That's true,' said Monami. The thought of Anika as an eyewitness, bravely striking out to challenge a murderer, unsettled her.

'And Option Two, the two crimes are completely unrelated. No—' said Mridula, as Monami's voice immediately rose in protest. 'It's pointless to speculate.'

'Okay, but how could they be *completely* unrelated?'

'What do we know about Anika's murder? She was found strangled, a little way from Kajal's house. The prevailing theory is that she left the party with everyone else, met someone . . .' ('The accomplice,' put in Monami.) ' . . . in the street, they argued, she was killed. There's no more yet—no witnesses, no other theories. So, it could be completely unrelated, why not? Someone could have taken advantage of the chaos.'

Monami shook her head. 'Having just witnessed a death, be inspired to kill someone? It's too far-fetched.'

'It is, but then this whole thing is far-fetched, isn't it? Listen. Imagine that you are one of the, let's face it, many, many people that Anika had targeted in some way, in her personal life, with her column. You've been carrying that around with you for *years*. You've thought about killing her before. But you can't, you can never get her alone, or you can never work it so that it wouldn't be traced back to you. Maybe you don't even think about it that seriously to begin with. But the thought grows and grows. It's many years later now, and you've been living with it constantly in your mind. And then suddenly, one day, this happens—maybe you've been drinking. Everyone's upset by the death of a beloved colleague. Many people are in tears. *No one is noticing what's going on around them*. No one. Maybe you see Anika, similarly dazed, and you think, this is it. This is my shot. And you take it.'

There was a brief silence. Mridula broke it by adding, practically, 'Or, it could be Option One. She could be the culprit. Or she could have seen something. There's really no way to know for sure.'

Monami was still distracted by the picture Mridula had painted. 'What kind of person would do that, though? Carry the idea of murder around with them . . . for years?'

'That's what we have to find out, isn't it?'

And thus began their first investigation together.

The Untangling

12

No Stranger to Murder

i

'THE MURDERS THAT HAVE GRIPPED THE NATION' flashed the banner on the television screen.

'Ever since the gruesome double deaths occurred, the crimes have gripped the minds of the people,' said a reporter standing outside Kajal Puri's house. A guard glowered at her from nearby. She ignored him.

'We are here, outside the scene of the crime in the outskirts of Delhi, trying to find a glimmer of truth. The personalities involved are no less than a leading newspaper editor, and a prominent socialite, Anika Kapoor. The venue? A book launch party, which was being held right here. One poisoning, and then almost three days later, thanks to police ineptitude, the discovery of the strangling. Scenes that have shaken even Delhi, no stranger to murder, to its core.

'Under these circumstances, there is enormous pressure on the police. Calls are mounting for arrests to be made. However, the days go by, and the whole thing remains more enshrouded than ever in mystery.'

'Have the police reported any fresh developments, Akanksha?' asked a disembodied voice from the studio.

The channel had been running the video clip from the launch on a loop, and the entire recorded interaction between Jemin, Samar, Shekhar and Anika took up a corner of the screen throughout the day.

'It's been very difficult to get any information from DCP Akshay Kumar, who's now in charge of the case. He's rebuffed several attempts at interviews,' said the reporter, with an air of personal grievance. 'But speculation has been rife. It has been particularly directed at four people: Ms Kajal Puri, the journalist and writer in whose home the murders occurred; the designer Mr Jemin Sequeira, of course a well-known name on the Delhi party circuit, founder of the House of Jems and whose scarf the victim was literally strangled with; a Ms Vasudha Chaturvedi; and Mr Samar Chishti, the editorial director of the publishing company Sea Lion.'

'Names we will all become very familiar with over the coming days and weeks, no doubt,' said the studio anchor smugly. 'Anika Kapoor was of course part of the influential Kapoor family, whose holdings include a controlling share in India Now Media. Viewers will have seen her sister, Anita Kapoor, on our channel just last night on Ashwin's programme.' The picture gave way to some snippets from that interview.

'This has really brought to light the shocking police procedures in this country,' said a small but fierce-looking woman with her hair pulled back in a neat bun. Looking closely, one could see that she bore a faint resemblance to Anika, but where Anika was distinctive, with her hair and haughty chin, her sister chose to cultivate a bland, if polished, anonymity.

'My sister's death happened in the most public way possible,' Anita was saying on the clip. 'The ensuing scrutiny of our family has been incredibly painful, only exacerbating our grief. But we will bear the scrutiny and the intrusions in order to keep up the pressure for as long as it takes to ensure that justice is done. What are the police doing? They didn't even discover my sister's body until days later!' Here the fierce tirade stopped momentarily as the speaker's voice broke a little. She stopped, took a breath and continued calmly. 'How much valuable evidence was lost, how much disintegrated over those hours? We want answers. This will not be one of those cases that the system drags out for years. It seems fairly clear that there are really only a few persons that are indicated . . .'

'Hard-hitting words there by Ms Anita Kapoor,' said the anchor, as the producers cut back to the studio. 'She seems to make reference to a very specific set of suspects. Presumably these are the names you were just mentioning?'

'Yes,' said Akanksha. 'And thanks to social media, rumours are already rife. Our viewers have already seen the fight that appeared to take place between Mr Jemin Sequeira and Ms Kapoor just moments before her death.'

'So, he's Suspect Number One?' said the studio, with perhaps more jauntiness than a double murder being covered on national television warranted.

'It's not clear. Mr Samar Chishti, a prominent person on the Delhi literary scene, may also have had a motive. It appears they had been . . . er . . . romantically involved. We . . . well, we obviously can't point any fingers, but both these men are clearly implicated,' said Akanksha, contradicting herself superbly.

'Thank you, Akanksha. Anything else?'

'As I said earlier, there's also the author of the book that was being launched, who it can be said lured both victims to her home. This home. Ms Kapoor was heard making some disparaging remarks about the book Kajal Puri had written and was launching. And she has not left this house, according to the neighbours, in days. Is it the shock? Or a guilty conscience?'

Akanksha stopped, looking pleased by this dramatic finish.

'Right. Er, good questions, Akanksha. Hopefully we'll have some developments soon. It also seems like a very pointed attack on the *Delhi Daily*, our media colleagues?'

'Absolutely,' said Akanksha, putting on a serious face. 'The *Delhi Daily* is one of the last newspapers of a certain . . . type here in Delhi. They've made a lot of enemies over the years with their stings and their society gossip. It could be someone with a major grudge against the paper, looking to take the editors out one by one.'

'What a state of affairs!' said the anchor with gusto. 'Is the media no longer safe in the nation's capital? We'll tackle that question tomorrow night, with members from the ruling party and the opposition in our primetime debate.'

ii

Abhishek and Leela Kapoor sat on a sofa and waited for their daughter. Abhishek had finally put his foot down and insisted that everyone get out of their house. '*Just get out!*' he had shouted. And they did, family, friends and staff alike, in a confused rush, some holding puja paraphernalia as it still burned. Now, a heavy mix of tuberose and incense hanging in the air was the only sign that they had ever been there. The house was empty, and every little noise reverberated across the marble floors and high-ceilinged halls. Leela thought she could even hear echoes of noises that had stopped days ago. The puja bells, for instance—they rang in her ears incessantly, even in the depths of the night when she could not sleep.

She and her husband now sat very still on a sofa in one of their drawing rooms. Abhishek stole a glance at his wife. After three days, she was now finally quiet. But the silence—of her, of the house itself—which he had thought himself desperate for, now unnerved him. For years, he had been a blur of movement from his morning yoga routine to his tennis and after-dinner drinks at the club. Now he didn't know what to do with this eerie emptiness, these vacant hours.

It was like he was paralysed, like someone had picked him up and put him in a jar of formaldehyde.

Now they stirred as their daughter, the sharp-faced woman they had been unseeingly watching on TV walked in. She, too, looked tired and shaken.

'Anita.'

'Anita.'

It was painful for Anita Kapoor to see her parents in anguish like this. They pawed at her arms pitifully and brought her to the couch to sit with them. She put a hand on each of them, her father's knee bony and vulnerable, her mother's hand cold and parched. They had never been an emotionally forthcoming family, and now they communicated through gestures more than words.

'How was the interview?' asked her father, finally.

Anita shrugged. 'I said what I had to say.'

'That police inspector . . .' said her mother, and tailed off.

'We're working closely with him, Mumma. Don't worry. We'll get whoever did this.'

'Don't worry? Get whoever did this?' her mother was suddenly shouting, and they all jumped at the outburst. 'Don't talk like one of your American TV shows. We all know who did this! We *know*.'

Anita sighed. 'We don't know. You're being . . .' She hesitated, not wanting to say the word *crazy*. It hung, unspoken, in the air. 'It wasn't him.'

'Yes, don't . . . don't be ridiculous, Leela,' said her father. 'You know that's not true. He was on a plane for god's sake.'

Anita looked at her father, a once powerful man who now seemed old, frail. He seemed to wilt further in the light of her stare.

'We want an investigation,' he said, and she could tell he was trying to sound like his old self. 'We want our own private investigation.'

'You want me to hire a private investigator?' Anita sounded tired.

'We want our papers on this.'

'Our papers *are* on this.'

'We're watching the news!' her mother screamed again. 'They're talking about all sorts of nonsense! And they're not moving quickly enough! We know *he did it*!'

'He didn't do it!' snapped Anita, suddenly at breaking point. 'He didn't do it! What is your evidence, apart from your crude snobbery?'

There was silence. Anita was breathing deeply.

'I don't think you're thinking straight,' she said again, in a voice that was almost frighteningly calm. 'If you insist on going down this route, you'll only bring an unwanted spotlight on this family's problems—and there are many of those—and the press will relish the chance to swoop in like vultures. Is that what you want?'

Her parents remained silent, wrapped in their grief and hopeless rage.

'I understand your pain,' continued Anita, 'I . . . I feel it myself. But this mindless prejudice of yours will only make a mess of the investigation. We cannot let that happen. I will not let that happen.'

Without waiting for a response, she stood and walked out of the room, slamming the door behind her. Abhishek and Leela looked at each other.

Leela repeated, in a shaky whisper, 'We have to do something.'

'We won't stop until Anika's murderer is found,' said Abhishek, reaching for his wife's hand. 'But you must rest. You must have a clear mind. I can't have you breaking down now, we've got to stay strong.'

iii

Mridula and Monami drove up to Kajal's home, which loomed before them. The imposing colonial façade, once a bright sunflower yellow, after decades of monsoons and neglect, was now a kind of runny off-white. Nonetheless, its bones were fine and behind rolling iron gates its grandeur remained evident.

Today, there was a clutch of press vans in front of this gate. Akanksha could be seen speaking earnestly into her mobile phone, with a harassed-looking cameraperson next to her.

It took quite a lot of determined beeping and shouting before the crowd parted and let the little car through. Mridula negotiated her tomato-red Wagon R (an uncharacteristically flamboyant choice) up the short driveway. In front of them was the garden, mulchy, messy but still impressive in its expanse. The brown leaves in the grass didn't crunch underfoot so much as softly squish into the earth.

They were met at the door by a woman wearing a bright salwar kameez whom they recognised as Kajal's long-time housekeeper.

'Hello, Jyoti, is it?' said Mridula, in Hindi.

'Yes,' said Jyoti. 'You're here to see madam?'

'Yes. She's expecting us,' said Mridula, and added as the housekeeper looked sceptical, 'We're from the newspaper, remember?'

Jyoti drew aside. 'She's upstairs.'

They followed her through the wide hall and up the stairs. The inside of the house continued the outside theme of faded grandeur, a once imperious manse on its last legs. The floor was a scratched green marble, the stairs were wide and flat, the stone worn smooth. It was the kind of house that made one nostalgic for one's grandmother.

Upstairs, there was a wide landing, a long passage and doors to what seemed like half a dozen bedrooms. A roomy balcony, which wrapped around the outside of the house, let in a leafy sunlight that washed gently through the entire space.

They found Kajal sitting in a long planter's chair on this balcony. She jumped in a slightly theatrical way when they came up behind her.

'Mridula,' she said.

'You know Monami, of course,' said Mridula.

'Er, yes,' said Kajal, nodding vaguely. 'So, here you both are.'

'Yes. Can we go through it? All of it.' Mridula had never been one for long greetings or preambles.

Kajal shrugged. 'What do you want to know?'

They sat in wicker chairs at a round coffee table. Monami approved of the balcony, broad with a grey terrazzo floor and thick balustrade. A number of flowering plants had been placed carefully in painted pots, roses, champa, hyacinth and pink and yellow oleander. Birds called from the trees in the overgrown garden below; as Monami watched, an emerald-green bee-eater flew by. She could see how Kajal might be protective of this refuge, and not allow too many people in.

'Tell us about the launch. From the beginning,' said Mridula, unmoved by the idyllic scenery.

'The beginning? I don't even know when that was,' said Kajal. 'The whole thing was an act of madness. We should have just done a signing at Oxford Bookstore. That was the original plan, you know. Instead, this . . . absurdly over-the-top . . .'

'So, why did you do it?' Mridula said.

Kajal almost sprang out of her chair. 'What do you mean?'

Mridula and Monami both stared at her.

Then Mridula said, 'I mean, why did you have the launch then, instead of the signing?'

Kajal slowly sat down again.

'Oh. Sorry. I'm all on edge. We got the sponsorship—with the House of Jems . . .'

'Who came up with that idea?' Mridula had taken out her dog-eared notebook again and was busily writing in it. 'Samar?'

'I'm not sure. Someone from marketing, Jem said. Maybe Vasudha? She was an intern at Sea Lion, but she had originally worked for Jems, so it was very natural for her to make the connection.'

'Vasudha had worked for Jems?'

'Yes, I think so. In marketing, I thought. But it seems she wanted to get into publishing, so he found her the job at Sea Lion.'

'Jemin did? I see,' said Mridula, still writing in her book. Then she looked up, but Kajal was looking out over her garden, to the vans and journalists beyond the gate. She seemed to be on the verge of saying more and wondering how to frame it. Mridula gestured to Monami that they should stay silent.

Finally, Kajal frowned and said, 'I wondered if it *was* Vasudha's idea, you know. It seemed like . . . I don't know, I wondered if it had originally come from Jemin himself.'

'What made you think so?'

Kajal paused. She was recalling how uneasy she had felt in the days and even weeks leading up to the launch. Of course, after the unreality of the murders, this feeling had come back with the force of a cyclone, and permeated her entire being to the point that she found she couldn't complete simple tasks, or even thoughts, without harking back to it all. Why had she felt uneasy? She still didn't know.

'Nothing definite,' she told Mridula. 'But the entire time, I had a sensation of being . . . pulled along in a certain direction, if I can put it that way. I can't even put my finger on why or how. But you think that all along, you've made a series of random decisions, if you know what I mean? We got the sponsorship, so we did the launch. We needed a big space, someone suggested we do it here, so we did it here. And then suddenly, you find that you've ended up in a certain situation, and you can't help but wonder if it's been . . . very *specific*. Do you know what I mean?'

'Vaguely,' said Mridula, tapping her pen on the coffee table. 'But is it just a feeling? Can you point to anything that you're basing this on?'

Kajal shook her head. 'It wasn't even a concrete feeling until the day of the launch. I was uneasy that morning. My own book was being published, and I somehow couldn't even enjoy it. And I didn't know why. I was sitting down there in the garden, listening to Vasudha throwing her weight around, and Jemin came in. And it suddenly struck me that Jemin was the only person who really seemed happy with the idea. He was . . . he was positively *glowing*.' She frowned.

'Maybe he thought it was a good business opportunity?' hazarded Monami.

'Do you know Jemin?' asked Kajal. Monami shook her head. 'Then you don't know why that suggestion is, I'm sorry to be blunt, absurd. A good business opportunity? That's the last thing that would excite him, honestly.' She hesitated again. 'Look, I don't want you to go away and start suspecting him without any proof. I've gotten to know him during this whole process, and I don't honestly believe he would hurt a fly.'

'Yes, yes,' said Mridula. 'Disclaimer noted. Go on. Was there anything else?'

'Well, he may have been planning something involving Anika,' said Kajal, miserably. She explained the conversation they had had that afternoon. 'It sounded like she was his whole focus. Now, again, I don't want you to think . . .' she trailed off.

'That's very interesting,' said Monami, and she and Mridula looked at each other.

'And then they had their whole showdown. Have you heard about that?'

Monami nodded. Kajal was clearly not a TV news watcher. But Mridula shook her head and said, 'Tell us.'

'It happened right after the reading. I was a little distance away, so I may not have been totally accurate in my hearing,' said Kajal. 'The person to ask is Samar, he was with them. But essentially, Anika was questioning, loudly, the reason for the book launch. She said the book was schlocky, badly written. So why the sponsorship, why the glitzy party?'

'And you heard this?' said Mridula, thoughtfully.

'Oh, she wasn't even trying to keep her voice down,' said Kajal, and though Anika was now dead, she couldn't keep the bitterness out of her voice. 'You know what she could be like. She was beyond insolent. And she kept harping on the point—*why*? Why? The others kept giving her reasons, the market, I don't know, synergies and whatnot, and she kept saying that it was nonsense and that there was something else going on.

'And then Jemin started rubbing it in that she was just jealous because her books haven't been doing well,' said Kajal. 'And I think that shot really hit home, because of everything she's been going through recently. I suppose you knew,' she said with a sudden change of tone, to Mridula, 'that she was being let go? You never said.'

'What should I have done, put out a news alert?' said Mridula. 'Go on with what happened.'

'Now that I know *that*, I guess it all makes sense. Anyway, when Jemin made that comment, it may have been the straw that broke the camel's back. She got very quiet and muttered something to him, and he muttered something back and Samar and Shekhar just stood there looking uncomfortable and awkward.'

'You didn't hear it at all?'

Kajal shook her head. 'But it somehow drained the glee from him,' she said. 'From Jemin, I mean. He just looked incensed. And when I thought about it later, I don't think I saw him after that. He wasn't at the bar when we were doing the toast, when DB died. He didn't actually resurface until later, when we were calling the police. Isn't that odd?'

13

A Bit Forrader

i

After a brief silence, Mridula said, 'But you don't suspect him of killing her?'

Kajal jumped up and stood near the balustrade. 'I . . . I just can't imagine him doing a thing like that. The idea's absurd. *Strangling* her? No.'

'When was the last time you saw Anika?' asked Monami.

There was a pause before Kajal answered this question. She looked away again, out over the balcony, past the press vans, past the rooftops of the other farmhouses, the green surrounding them.

Finally, she said, 'She was up on my balcony. While we were toasting. That was the last time I saw her alive.'

Mridula said, 'What time was that, roughly?'

'Probably around ten or ten-thirty? I wasn't really checking. It seemed ages. I didn't think the party would go on so long. I thought it must have been midnight when we were toasting, but of course it wasn't.' Kajal sighed. 'If everyone had just gone home after the reading, nothing would have happened.'

'But everyone stayed.'

'Everyone stayed. It was more like a party in the end. My book was . . . it was almost secondary.' Again, the same note of bitterness had crept into Kajal's tone.

Mridula raised her eyebrows, but she only said, 'Tell us about the toast.'

'It was all Vasudha's idea. She suggested it and opened a bottle—a new bottle. I was not pleased with her, let me tell you. I was annoyed with her already, for throwing this big party in my house, and then she suggests opening a bottle at midnight. I mean, I thought it was midnight, you know.'

Mridula nodded.

'Why were you annoyed with her for throwing a party?' asked Monami, tentatively. 'It was all for your book, wasn't it?'

'It was not,' said Kajal. 'She had done her best, because she's nothing if not competent, and at the end of the day, it was a good *party*. But was it a good book launch? It was all so juvenile. She had lots of props out—you know, a chalk outline of a corpse, various murder instruments hanging from trees, a toy revolver and all that. And she made the servers, who were part-time models I think, working for Jem, wear these ridiculous costumes—one was wearing a noose around their neck, another one had a dagger sticking out of their back. That kind of thing. Very childish.'

Monami privately thought it sounded like a lot of fun, but out loud she said, 'It definitely doesn't sound like any book launch I've been to.'

'Well, exactly.'

Mridula was still busily writing away in her notebook. 'And the toast. She opened the bottle herself?'

'No, Samar opened it, as a matter of fact. There was a big pop. Vasudha poured.'

'And everyone drank from it?'

'Well, some people already had a drink, I suppose. Me, for instance. And Samar, for another.'

'So neither of you drank the wine from the bottle?' said Mridula.

'No,' said Kajal, looking at her sharply. 'We didn't.'

'Interesting. We'll need a list of names of who else was in this crowd. Can you put something like that together?'

Kajal nodded. 'I'm not a hundred per cent sure, but I've been thinking about it, and I think I could.'

'Okay, that would be helpful,' said Mridula. 'Now, Kajal, this is important, so if you need to think about it, take a few minutes. What exactly happened—how did DB get that drink in his hand? Did someone hand it to him? Did he pick the glass up himself?'

'I've thought about this moment over and over again,' said Kajal, turning around and walking back towards them. The sun was behind her, and they squinted to look at her face. 'It's not very clear. Vasudha poured the drinks, and they were all sitting on a tray. She handed out a few, and I think a few people just picked theirs up. I wasn't really paying attention, to be honest.'

'Who made the toast?'

'Vasudha. She said, "Here's to Kajal, and many more books to come," or something very conventional like that.'

'So, everyone was looking at Vasudha?'

Kajal stared at her. 'Y-yes. Are you suggesting that someone would have had enough time to slip something into DB's drink then? She spoke for about five seconds.'

'I'm just trying to think of the possibilities,' Mridula said. 'There seems to have been a very small window. That's the one that strikes me as the most likely, no?'

'I . . . suppose so. But they would have been seen!'

'Do you remember how everyone was standing? Who was DB standing next to?'

Kajal closed her eyes.

'I think Samar,' said Kajal, slowly. 'But you can't really think—'

'Where was Vasudha?'

'She was still behind the bar.'

'What happened next?'

'DB wanted to go home. He went off looking for Meena, his wife, you know. Samar and I went with him. I asked him who was going to review the book, and Samar jokingly asked him not to give it to Anika. And then he dropped the bombshell on us—that Anika was leaving the *Delhi Daily*! Samar and I did some goggling over it.'

Monami nodded, understandingly.

'And then . . . then . . . it happened. He started coughing . . . it only took three or four minutes.'

Her voice broke, and they all fell silent.

'Poor old DB,' she said, after a minute or two. She had teared up.

'Yes,' said Mridula. 'But he did love detective stories! Maybe a part of him is enjoying this. The entire country's trying to solve this mystery. Well, the media and some people on the internet anyway.' She sighed and dabbed at an eye with some crumpled tissue paper she'd foraged from her old satchel. It was the first near-human reaction Monami had seen from her up until this point.

Kajal gave a watery chuckle. 'That's true. But oh, just thinking of him kills me. He was so happy with the book launch, he loved all the murder victims, and the chalk outline and all the rest of it. He was the only one who did, unironically. And he loved my book too. Schlocky and poorly written as it is.'

There was a moment of pensive quiet. Then Mridula said, 'Can we see where the body was found? Anika's, I mean.'

ii

They looked down at the trampled grass behind the rather bedraggled flower bed in the street. Kajal had refused to battle through the press to accompany them, and so the housekeeper Jyoti had brought them instead. She stood watchfully a little distance behind.

'So the theory is that she leaves the party and meets the murderer here. They get into a fight. And down she goes. If this were a detective story,' said Monami, wistfully, 'there would be clues just lying around. We'd find one or two each.'

It certainly didn't seem like there was much to see now. There was a tangled row of tea roses by the road, and the body had been found behind these, under a large jamun tree. The grass had grown quite high, obscuring most of the soil around it.

Monami stepped gingerly into the long grass—she was essentially a city girl and understood it to be a basic truth that long grass existed only to hide snakes—and poked at it with a stick she'd picked up.

'I can't see anything now. The grass is all trampled.'

'The police were everywhere,' said Jyoti, with pursed lips. 'They stayed for hours. And they were aggressive, especially the second time. They seemed to think that we had murdered her ourselves!'

'Of course,' said Mridula. 'They would say that. Always looking for the easiest people to blame, the police.' She had slipped easily into casual Hindi. 'You can't trust them.'

Jyoti nodded eagerly. 'As though we would do this! They must be idiots!'

'They are, unfortunately. Mona, two inches to your right—what is that glinting there?'

Monami looked in the direction pointed to, and swooped down with a delighted exclamation, all thoughts of snakes forgotten.

She brought up the object and showed it to Mridula.

'It's a phone.'

The phone lay in the palm of her hand, the screen cracked, and the case covered in the reddish soil of the flowerbed. Jyoti drew her breath in sharply.

'Is that . . . is that hers?'

Even with the cracked screen it was clear the phone was new—sleek and flat; it took up almost Monami's entire palm.

'It's the latest iPhone, I think. Could be hers.' She felt a rising excitement. 'I wish we had one of those Ziploc bag things that detectives are always using.'

To her delight, Mridula now drew out exactly such a bag from the recesses of her capacious satchel, and gave it to her with the ghost of a grin. Mridula seemed quite pleased, both with the find and with herself.

'Before you bag it—I think that's the term—let's see if it switches on.'

Gingerly, using the end of her dupatta to cover her fingerprints, Monami pressed down on the power button on the side of the phone. Nothing happened.

'Let's go in and see if it'll charge,' she said, looking around furtively at the knot of press and the two police cars further down the road. They were all still trying to get a picture of Kajal who, emboldened by her visitors, had come out of her house to yell obscenities at the photographers. Mridula, knowing that no one was watching, slipped the phone into her handbag.

Monami was a little shocked. 'Don't we need to hand that to the police?'

'We do, and we will,' said Mridula. 'But once we do, we'll never see it again. So, we might as well figure out whose it is first. It's their own fault for not spotting it in the first place, isn't it? Come on!'

iii

Everyone held their breath as Mridula clicked the phone into a charger.

Nothing. Not even a flicker.

There seemed to be a collective group sigh.

'That's a shame,' said Mridula, trying not to sound grumpy but failing. A first clue coming to nothing is dispiriting to anyone. 'Anyway, I'm sure the police will be able to make something of it.'

'Will they?' asked Kajal.

'They should,' said Monami, thinking back to various CSI episodes she had seen. 'Not sure how good their technology is, but it should be easy enough to get into a phone these days. Particularly if she had been backing up to the cloud.'

'The cloud?' From Kajal's expression, it was clear that to her the cloud was the purveyor of shade or rain and nothing else.

'It's very technical but from what I understand they can . . . I don't know, reimage it or something, and pretty much recover all the data. Anyway, we should get going and hand this in, I suppose.'

'Yes,' agreed Mridula, whose brow was still furrowed. 'I have to say . . .'

'What?' asked Kajal, who still seemed to be digesting the 'cloud'.

'It's a bit surprising that the police didn't find it, isn't it? Even for them. I mean, we found it pretty easily.'

'I didn't see it,' Monami pointed out.

'I'm sure you would have if you'd kept looking,' Mridula said, kindly.

'It could have been more hidden when they were here,' suggested Kajal. 'There are plenty of animals that wander down that road, you know. Dogs, cats. The occasional cow. They could have moved it more into view.'

'That's the other thing that's been bothering me about all this,' said Mridula.

They all waited patiently. Jyoti came in with some tea things on a tray.

'It was one of the first things I thought when I heard about her body being found. That it wouldn't just lie in the street for almost two days. The police may not have found it, but the dogs and cats definitely would have. Not to mention the cows, rats, jackals and mongooses. The kites and eagles. You get the idea.'

'Well,' said Monami impatiently. 'What are you saying? What does that mean?'

'I think the body was moved. And whoever moved it, must have dropped the phone. The police should be able to tell us when . . .'

There was a devastating crash behind them and all three wheeled around. Jyoti's tea tray had smashed to the floor.

'Oh no! I'm so sorry!' wailed Jyoti. 'Your beautiful tea set!'

'No, no, it's fine. You're not hurt?' said Kajal, rather perfunctorily. It was clear she was not pleased. They all helped Jyoti clear away the pieces and she disappeared to get a mop for the tea and milk.

'We're all on edge,' said Kajal. 'Jyoti's feeling it as much as anyone. She's not used to seeing this kind of thing happen in this house.'

'She's been with you for a while, has she?' said Monami, thoughtfully.

'Almost since I was a child. And her mother before her, too. I don't know what I'd do without Jyoti.'

She said this last as Jyoti walked in and hugged her affectionately. The housekeeper, already tremulous after the crash, now seemed completely overwhelmed and cried openly on her employer's shoulder.

'I think you'd better go,' said Kajal to Mridula and Monami. 'We'll have to pick this up later.' Her voice was gruff.

Mridula looked a little surprised, but she nodded at Monami, and they moved towards the door. As they walked out, Monami looked back to see her patting Jyoti on the shoulder as they both bent down to mop away the milky pool on the floor.

iv

'Well, now we're a bit forrader, as they say, aren't we?' said Mridula as she turned her engine on. It sputtered and died almost immediately.

'Who says that?' asked Monami. Her mind was whirling with half-formed theories and vague impressions.

'People,' said Mridula, vaguely, trying the engine again. This time it took, with an encouraging chugga-chugga-chugga. They drove slowly out of the gates, with the press peering into their windows curiously as they had before. 'What have we learned?'

'Kajal and Jyoti are involved in some way,' said Monami, promptly. 'I didn't think Kajal could have been involved at all. Old Cashew Nut! It's incredible. But after that scene . . .'

'Yes,' said Mridula. 'They're definitely holding something back. But why? I can believe they did something silly, like find Anika's phone in the house and throw it away in a panic. Your revelation about the cloud must have come as the most awful shock! But I can't believe they would have anything to do with actual murder. So, why not just tell us?'

'Yes, if it was as innocent as that,' said Monami, 'wouldn't they have just come clean, not shoved us out like that? They may have not wanted to say anything to the police, but to us?'

'I'm not sure,' said Mridula. 'She may be trying to protect Jyoti. We'd have to get the police involved. Much safer just to deny all knowledge.'

Monami chewed on this. 'Maybe. And you're right, it must be something innocuous that they're hiding—they wouldn't have had anything to do with DB's death, and I can't see them having anything to do with Anika's either. That would be ludicrous.'

'Oh, I'm definitely not ruling anything out,' said Mridula. 'I think it's unlikely, but we just don't have the data right now.'

'What? Not Cashew Nut,' said Monami, laughing. 'Are you seriously considering her as a culprit? She wouldn't have had the strength to strangle anyone, for one thing.'

'We have to consider everyone, Monami,' said Mridula. 'Everyone. Maybe I don't consider her seriously, but you heard her when she was talking about Anika, about what she said about her book. And I've known them both for years; believe me, there's no love lost there. Imagine how you feel, how your colleague Devika feels, and then imagine that going on for a *decade*. That's where Anika and Kajal were. And if anything, I'm understating it.'

Mridula paused for a second, and then continued, 'I'm not sure I bought everything she was saying, either. Her feelings about the book launch, for instance. Now, again, I know Kajal, we've worked together for many years. And she is quite laid back about most things. But her first book? She's dreamt of nothing else for years. She would have been all over that launch. And she was also *very* careful to draw our attention to Jemin. The fight, the fact that he wasn't at the toast. No,' Mridula shook her head. 'I don't rule her out for a second.'

They drove on for a while in silence. The ride from Chhattarpur to central Delhi was not a quick one, especially with the daytime traffic jams and road works. But it seemed to pass quickly for them both, lost as they were in their own thoughts and theories.

'We'll have to get into that phone,' said Mridula, finally breaking the silence as they turned into a wide, tree-lined avenue. 'It might give us some clues about the time of death, and also tell us who she was talking to up there on the balcony. But in the meantime, how do you feel about squeezing in another interview tonight? We're quite near Amrita Shergill Marg. We could pop in on Samar.'

14

This Weird Magnetism

i

'This channel's investigation into the shocking double homicide that has rocked the nation continues,' barked a bespectacled newsreader. 'Today, we have a representative from the Delhi Police, a spokesperson from the ruling party, a spokesperson from the opposition, a lawyer and a feminist, and a friend of one of the victims, Anika Kapoor, who can tell us how the family and friends of the deceased are coping with their loss.'

With an abrupt change of volume, the newsreader continued in a voice that one assumed was supposed to sound sympathetic but was merely sotto voce barking. He turned to the young woman next to him, who blinked in the studio light.

'Let's start with you, Ms Prachi Mehra. You knew the deceased. You have in front of you a panel of people who are able to shape the action around this. What would you like to say, and what would you like to see happen next?'

'Thank you, Pranav,' said Prachi, a little breathlessly. 'Well, first of all, I must say that the inaction has been shocking. To commit a crime so brazenly, in broad daylight—'

'The crime took place at night,' said Pranav, frowning.

'In broad daylight *as it were*, Pranav; it's a figure of speech, you know,' Prachi said in a superior tone. 'But absolutely in the public eye, and there have been no arrests yet! My poor friend's body wasn't even discovered by the police in their first investigation, and I think we should have some answers about why. Anika was an absolute pillar of society, and this treatment is disgraceful. Her columns had, over the years, called out various instances of injustice and corruption. There were numerous people at that party that night who had their daggers out for her. Er, I mean . . .' said Prachi, tailing off.

'Right. Care to name any names?'

'Oh, I'm not sure I could name them,' said Prachi. 'But let's just say that there were multiple people there, starting with professional rivals, targets of her columns, and even personal relationships that had gone off the rails, that the police could be pursuing.'

'Mr Samar Chishti is a name that has been mentioned in this regard,' said Pranav, encouragingly.

'Well, it's absolutely not for me to say, but yes, he absolutely *should be* looked at as a Person of Interest,' said Prachi, bafflingly. 'Not only did they have a personal relationship, but he was also her editor. Her editor, you know. And she'd sent him a manuscript—her memoirs. His publishing company had a long history with her writing, and, suddenly, he refuses to publish her work? Has anyone found this manuscript? Is anyone even looking for it? The contents could be very telling . . .'

ii

Samar let Mridula and Monami into his apartment wearing track pants, an old, stained t-shirt and a harassed look.

'Come in, come in, come in, come in,' he said, running a hand through his hair, which already stood on end. 'Tea? Coffee? Only instant, I'm afraid. I've run out of beans, in more ways than one.'

'Where's the help?' asked Mridula, looking around. 'You're alone?'

Samar winced. 'We thought he'd better go and stay with my mother for a bit.'

'And . . . how are you managing?'

'How does it look?'

Monami had never been inside this apartment, and it looked all right to her—despite the dust bunnies in corners, and the many cup rings on various surfaces. Books were crammed into shelves and piled on tables and chairs. A Bakelite phone stood in a corner, on a Chinese chest of drawers. All the furniture looked like it had been transported straight from the early twentieth century. She found it soothing.

'Rough,' said Mridula. 'You should get someone to do the jharu-pochha, at least.'

'There are times, Mridula, when one does not think of jharu-pochha,' said Samar with dignity.

'Well, one should, Samar. You'll get bugs soon.'

'You didn't stop by to lecture me about housekeeping, I suppose?'

'No. No, we didn't.'

Mridula sat down rather gingerly on a long leather settee. Monami took a comfortable-looking armchair, and then wondered guiltily if she were taking Samar's usual spot. He had disappeared down a corridor and could be heard clattering glasses and bottles.

He reemerged, rather sheepishly, with a bottle of whisky and three glasses.

'I'm just going to assume you don't want tea or bloody instant coffee.'

Mridula shrugged and started clinking ice into her glass. Monami raised her eyebrows but dutifully followed. It was good whisky, too.

'So, Samar,' said Mridula, after everyone had been handed their drink.

'Hang on, what shall we drink to? Murder? Yes, let's drink to murder!'

No one moved.

'Tough crowd.'

'Don't get maudlin, that's my advice,' said Mridula, drily. 'Why don't we drink to truth? Finding the truth.'

Samar laughed softly. 'I'll drink to that, but it seems a bit of a wasted toast.' They clinked glasses, and he continued: 'I don't think anyone will ever get to the bottom of this. The thing's like something a mystery writer would have dreamed up. And you think the police are going to solve it?'

'I definitely don't think that. Hence, you know,' Mridula pointed to herself and Monami.

'Ah yes, the amateur sleuths! Well, why not,' said Samar, taking a long glug.

'Let's try to get to the bottom of this before you get to the bottom of that,' said Mridula, looking rather pleased with her pun. 'Your glass, I mean.'

'Don't explain your jokes, Mri. They're bad enough.'

'We want to ask you some questions, get your side of the story.'

'My side of the story! Everyone wants that. What will you give me for it?'

'Come on now, Samar. Be serious. This isn't a joke.'

'I know it isn't, my darling Mri. It is certainly not a joke, a fact that is borne in on me every time I have a visit from our charming police force, which is quite often.'

'Well, we better get going then, before they come and arrest you,' said Mridula.

'Ha. Ha.'

Monami felt like telling him that she didn't think Mridula was joking, but she didn't want to further dampen his mood. Despite the forced jollity, she could see he was feeling the strain. His eyes darted around the room as they talked, and his fingers drummed restlessly against the arm of his rattan chair.

'So, let's start with the party. What can you tell us about it?'

'The party. The party. That's that Peter Sellers movie, isn't it? So apt. It does feel like we're in a farce sometimes.'

Mridula and Monami waited.

'What can I tell you? Well, what would you like to know?'

'Let's go all the way back. How did it come about? Whose idea was it?'

Samar sighed. 'The ironic thing is, I knew it was getting too big. These large book launches are always more trouble than they're worth. Small book launches, that's the way to go. Or perhaps go digital. Make the writer go on Instagram Live. That's what marketing keeps telling me, anyway.'

'We'll make a note of that,' said Mridula, suppressing an eyeroll. 'So, clearly, this wasn't your idea.'

'It was not. You know me, I would never have thought of this in a million years. We would have had our usual little coffee shop launch, or done it on Zoom or something, and that would have been that. Mind you, it also wasn't a bad idea. It was a nice way to break through all these . . . austerity measures we're usually up against. Vasudha had just come to us from Jem and Shekhar, and naturally she put two and two together. Jemin agreed, and there we were. An absolutely first-rate launch: large crowd, open bar, the works. Most importantly, someone else project-managing the whole thing. All very nice.'

'So, the sponsorship was Vasudha's idea? It's been suggested to us that it came from Jemin,' said Mridula.

'*Jemin?*' Samar laughed. 'He's a lovely chap, but sponsorships and all of that would be totally beyond him. No, no. Definitely not his idea. I thought it was Vasudha's idea, personally. She put two and two together, as I said.'

'Lucky Kajal,' said Mridula.

'Yes, it would have done really well for her,' agreed Samar. 'If not for all the . . . all the murder and mayhem, you know.'

'It was a good launch, then? Many books sold?'

'I can't remember now, but yes, I think so. We were celebrating at the end. That's what Vasudha said, here's to a successful launch, or something like that.'

Monami glanced at Mridula, understanding that she was picking up on Kajal's statement that it had been a good party, but not necessarily a good launch. But what was she getting at? That had just been Kajal being grumpy. Still, she couldn't help but admire the older woman's attention to every lead, however small and seemingly inconsequential.

Mridula was still following up on the Kajal question.

'But she doesn't seem to have been too enthusiastic? Kajal, I mean.'

'No, she wasn't,' said Samar. 'DB and I found her that day looking . . . well, less than enthused, as you say.'

'Any idea why?'

Samar shook his head. 'We were both surprised. We thought she would have been glad about her book being launched. But . . . well, she was quite grouchy. She said she just had a feeling. Prophetic, as it turns out, no? She says there's something in her birth chart, and frankly I'm starting to believe it.'

'Okay. Hmm. Tell us what happened with DB.'

'There's nothing to tell. We were all standing around, doing a toast, waiting to get out of Kajal's hair. We'd almost pulled it off, and there was that air of *it's finally done*. Probably coming mostly from Vasu if anything, she'd been working so hard on this. And then . . . this happens. It was quite surreal.'

'You opened the bottle?'

'I did,' said Samar, looking hard at Mridula. 'Your sources are correct.'

'So, it was definitely a new bottle. Can you confirm that?'

'Yes, and even if it wasn't, everybody had a drink from the same bottle. Vasu poured them all out in front of us. Whatever it was, it wasn't in the bottle.'

'Everybody? You included?' asked Mridula, almost casually.

'No, I actually didn't drink from that bottle at all. I already had my whisky.'

He raised his glass at them both and took another glug.

'I see. Do you remember who else was in this crowd? Who was DB standing next to?'

'He was standing next to Suspect Number One, yours truly, on one side. And one of the kids from his paper on the other—I don't know who it was.'

'Short? Tall? Glasses? Boy? Girl?'

'I really couldn't tell you. I think it was a boy with glasses.'

That could have been any of them, really.

'We'll need a list of names from you. Do you think you can remember exactly who was part of this group?'

Samar sighed. 'Honestly, no I don't think so. I could try, but there were so many people that it was just a blur. People seemed to be coming out of the woodwork. You know how it is at these things, especially when someone opens a bottle. People just pop up. There was me, Kajal, DB, Vasu. And then a bunch of kids, I suppose from the *Delhi Daily*, who seemed to know Kajal and DB.'

'No one else from Sea Lion? What about Jemin?' asked Mridula, and Monami could tell she was still trying to keep her tone casual.

'I don't think Jemin was there. But I can't actually remember,' said Samar, frowning. 'No one else from Sea Lion.'

'Okay. And what did you think had happened at the time?'

'Like everyone else, I thought he'd had a stroke, or a heart attack. I was absolutely flummoxed when the doctor started asking questions.'

'What exactly happened after? Did you see Anika?'

'No, not at all,' said Samar, shortly. 'We'd had some words earlier, which I'm sure you've heard about. And seen. I can't switch on the news, every time I turn it on, they're playing that damn clip.' He paused and sighed deeply. 'And then I think we avoided each other. I was at the bar mostly.'

'What was your relationship like with Anika?'

Samar made an indeterminate movement. 'Me and Anika? We . . . we go back a little way.'

Mridula and Monami merely looked enquiring. He looked back at them, it seemed to Monami, for a long while. The silence ticked like a metronome, the tension rising to its strict rhythm. She thought that he was trying to come to a decision, just like Kajal had in their interview. To tell, or not to tell? He startled her by answering this question out loud.

'Well, I may as well tell you two rather than our friendly police force. The truth is that Anika and I . . . well, we were involved.'

'Involved?' said Mridula. 'How do you mean?'

'I suppose you must have an idea. We, well, we had a really long relationship, if you want me to be totally blunt about it.' He looked off at a wall behind them. 'You can't possibly imagine how strange it feels to be telling you two about this. No offence.'

'I can imagine it must be odd,' said Mridula, and her voice had become surprisingly gentle. 'I'm sorry, Samar. You must be suffering a good deal more than you can let on.'

Samar buried his head in his hands, and they were afraid for a moment that he would start to cry. When he raised his face again, he looked pale, and his voice sounded ragged, but he held himself together. 'First, DB. My friend. Then Anika. It's crazy. It's . . . it doesn't seem real. Her, dead. I can't wrap my head around it.' He took another large gulp of his drink and slumped in his chair, the parts of his handsome face displaced, like in a Cubist portrait. All sign of the devil-may-care man who had let them into his flat had now dissipated, the bravado replaced by shock and undisguised sorrow.

Mridula and Monami glanced at each other again. For the first time in a long time, Monami felt keenly the strangeness of the journalist's role as observer—she was present at a scene she ought not to be present at, an interloper in someone's private grief. But this was her job, to try and tease out these stories, to get to the truth.

Samar was continuing, 'I can't explain to you how we were. We'd been together since school. On again, off again. For many years.'

Mridula said, her voice still very soft, 'What happened?'

'We had a relationship when we were at school,' said Samar. 'We were children. Babies. Neither of us possibly dreamt that it could mean anything, much less . . . what it became. After school, she broke up with me. I expected it. We were from different worlds. I had no ambition. And all she had grown up with was power and money and the pursuit of more power and more money. But . . . we couldn't somehow quit each other. We went to different countries. For years, we worked with oceans between us. But we kept coming back. And the strangest thing is that I could slowly feel her becoming a different person. Especially after her marriage. She became the sort of person we used to laugh about when we were younger, losing her temper at the drop of a hat, saying unforgivable things to people, treating her colleagues like trash. But all her prickliness, her sourness, her impatience . . . all of that just seemed to fall away like snakeskin when we were together.'

His voice seemed to come from far away, the words part of a personal reverie rather than addressed to his interviewers. 'She was essential to me, like air. And I was the same for her. It wasn't really sexual. Or it was more than that. And it wasn't really love.' He gave a short laugh at this thought. 'It was just us. We held this weird magnetism for each other that we couldn't explain; we just knew it was there, we felt it.'

Inevitably, it was Mridula who punctured Samar's dreamy soliloquy with the cold pinprick of reality: 'And her husband?'

Samar's voice went flat. 'Yes, her husband. I don't think he knew. But I was never sure, really. You've heard the rumours about them—

they drifted apart. They may even have had an open marriage, I'm not sure. I . . . I have to say I was a little surprised when she got married to Shekhar. Not out of jealousy, you understand. We were beyond that. But he seemed to appear out of nowhere. Not that I know him much better now. But, back then, it was strange to see them together—as if Anika was using Shekhar to attack her parents. Attack their values, their obsession with their social standing.' Samar paused. 'But to answer your question, I don't know if he knew. It sometimes seemed like he was off doing his own stuff, if you know what I mean. But we never talked about that. Actually, we never really *talked*. It's not like we were constantly texting each other or anything like that. I had other relationships.' ('Tina,' thought Monami. 'Poor Tina.') 'She had her marriage. What we had together was a private refuge, like an attic or a treehouse, somewhere you go to get away from everybody else.'

'When was the last time you spoke with her?'

'It was during that party. That whole very theatrical "showdown". With the whole world watching. Oh, god,' Samar leapt up from the sofa and started to pace up and down. 'I can't bear to think about it. But at the same time, it's all I can think about. Her face, her strange anger. The dramatic way she walked away from us, her heels drilling holes in the grass. Yes, dramatic, that's the word.'

'It was all . . . an act, you think?'

'No . . . no . . . not in the way you're thinking. I'd been dreading this meeting because it was true that she had sent us a manuscript, and it was true that Sea Lion wasn't publishing it. It wasn't my decision. I thought she would feel that I had betrayed her.'

'By not publishing it?'

'Yes.' Samar looked miserable. 'But I couldn't. It was out of my hands.'

'And that's what your last conversation was about? Her manuscript?'

'No. It was more the kind of subtext of the conversation though,' Samar sighed. 'You've seen the clip. Shekhar came up to us, all hearty and *congratulations on the launch*! Poor chap. And Niks—Anika—immediately started to lay into everything. Why the over-the-top party, why the sponsorship for a first-time writer, what was the reason and so on and so on. And loudly and rudely too, with Kajal in earshot. It felt like the entire party just stopped and looked at us.'

'What did you make of those questions? About the book launch and all that? Was that just her usual . . . spitefulness? Sorry,' Mridula added, a little lamely, at the end. They were all so used to talking about Anika just as they liked, without worrying about anyone actually having a personal connection with her being present, anyone who might take offence.

'Oh, don't worry about it. I know what everyone thought about her. To be honest, I thought she was just creating a diversion. It was always so awkward when we met in front of her husband. Luckily, it happened rarely. Usually, we would just say the first thing that popped into either of our heads. Unfortunately, this time what popped into her head wasn't, well, it wasn't the most diplomatic, with Kajal right there. She wasn't actually angry. Well, not until she and Jemin got into it, anyway.'

'Ah, yes. Tell us about that?'

'Now *that* was dramatic,' said Samar. 'I don't know the details . . . I don't!' he said, defensively, as Mridula grunted in disbelief. 'As I told you, we didn't really talk. We all went back decades. School, you know. Jemin knew us when we first got together. But I was out of the country when they had their . . . beef. I never heard the details; they were both very cagey about it. Something about money, I think. I didn't really pry, either. You know how awkward conversations about money can get.'

'What was the conversation about, exactly? Money?' asked Mridula. She sounded a little frustrated, and Monami understood why. It was like casting about for a light switch in the pitch dark.

'Basically, Jemin said something about her being jealous about this launch, and she accused him of enjoying his own bitchiness. She said something like, *enjoy yourself while you can, because the universe always pays its debts*, and then he scoffed and said, *some things go beyond money*, or somesuch. She didn't like that, and they sort of glowered at each other for a while. Honestly, I thought they were both being a little dramatic. They're both like that, you know. It was what first brought them together. Anyway, I assumed it was something to do with a loan she'd given him.'

'Ah, there was a loan?' Mridula sounded relieved to have got somewhere concrete at last.

'Yes, I think so,' said Samar. 'But I would ask Jemin. Or Shekhar. I think he was involved in some way.'

'Her husband?' Mridula sounded surprised.

'Yes. Again, no one has really told me the story, but from various hints and reactions people have had, I think Shekhar had something to do with their falling out. The one thing I know for sure is that they fell out very shortly after Niks and Shekhar got together. Almost in the same week, or the same month, or something like that. You should ask Jem. I'm sure he would tell you.'

'Oh, we will,' said Mridula. 'We'll go see him next. But there's something I'm not understanding here. Their deep dislike for each other, Jemin and Anika, I mean, but the House of Jems was actually bankrolled by her husband?'

'Yes. He probably saved Jemin's business, as a matter of fact. The pandemic's been so hard for everyone.'

'He didn't know the history, or his wife didn't object?'

Samar just shook his head. 'I can't tell you about any of that. You'll have to ask him. Or Jem. My guess is that he knew, he couldn't have *not* known. She's hardly quiet when it comes to her grudges.'

Monami wondered when he would stop talking about her in the present tense.

15

An Act of Vengeance

i

'Now, about this manuscript . . . ?'

'The manuscript!' Samar laughed, hollowly. Monami had never heard anyone do a hollow laugh before, but she recognised it instantly as such. People were always laughing hollowly in books. 'I see the news has picked up on that. I don't know how thrilled the family is going to be with Ms Prachi Mehra.'

'Ah, the family were involved? They didn't want it published?'

'Well,' said Samar, hesitating. 'I don't know for a *fact*.'

Mridula sighed again. More groping for light switches. 'What was the manuscript about? Was it a memoir?'

'Yes. But a very quickly put together one.'

'Was it any good?'

'It sort of depends on what you mean by *good*. Literary merit? Not really. It was quickly put together, as I said. She just wanted to get something out.'

'What was actually in it?' asked Mridula. 'Family? Friends? You?'

'Yes, sort of all of the above. She had put everything that she could put into it.'

They waited. This time, neither of them pressed him, and just waited. Finally, Samar sighed.

'I have to say, you two are getting more out of me than our police force. Maybe it's the whisky,' he said, and, as though resigned to it, poured all of them some more, waving away their protestations, and took another large gulp. 'About six months ago, she came to see me. Something had happened, and she was furious.'

Samar paused again. He was wondering how to describe this meeting. How it had taken him back to their early days, when they did actually talk, when they knew everything there was to know about each other. It felt somehow strange, but also completely natural, for her to have come to him in the same way, more than twenty-five years on, as though not a single moment of time had passed.

'What was she furious about?' Mridula nudged him.

Samar shook his head. 'She didn't tell me exactly what, but I'd seen her like that many times before. It was her family. She's always been a bit at odds with her family. Always felt as though she didn't quite fit in . . .'

This had also been a theme back then; it had always been a theme. She had always felt like an outsider, whether or not it had started as an affected adolescent stance (he could never be sure), ultimately, it had become her reality. 'But this time, she said, was different. She said she had to do something about it. And her response was to write a book. She tried to frame it as something else, but I knew what it was—it was a sort of juvenile shaking of the fist. They'll be sorry, that sort of thing. I tried to talk her out of it. It felt childish. But she didn't want to hear it. She was determined.'

Samar hadn't been able to put it into words that whatever had happened, whatever she was angry about, this act of hers would drive the final wedge through her relationship with her family. She would never be able to repair it. But she was beyond reason. 'She . . . she didn't listen, and she was also angry with me for not instantly supporting her. What could I say? I said that I would read it when she was done, but I couldn't promise anything.'

He tailed off again. He had played and replayed that scene with Anika so many times in his head, to understand if he could have done anything differently, and if he had, would anything have turned out differently.

A moment or two later, he gave himself a little shake, like a dog trying to throw off spots of water. 'So, she wrote this book, like . . . like lightning,' he continued. She put everything that she could possibly put in it, every barb, everything that might possibly wound. Her early years, her parents, her sister. It's not that she was revealing secrets, but she had painted a portrait of a dysfunctional family, each member consumed by their own demons. There was not much love to go around, not much affection or warmth, just an overwhelming sense of responsibility to protect their wealth and their position. You can see why a family like the Kapoors, so beholden to an image of themselves, an image they maintain at all costs, would hate for such a book to come out in public, a book written by one of their own, no less.'

It had been a difficult book to read, knowing that she had been holding all of this toxic rage inside for years. It had explained so much.

He stood up suddenly, feeling the vertigo of the last few days. Mridula and Monami watched him.

'It was . . . it was a bombshell,' he said, simply. 'It was more than that. It was a personal cry for help. It was a public denunciation. It was . . . rather frightening.'

'Can you give us any details?'

'Well . . . she was careful in one sense,' said Samar. 'There was nothing that could be called libel, or anything like that. No shady business practices. No, it was more . . . more insidious than that. It was more humiliating than defamatory. There was a chapter about her sister in childhood that was just . . . well, it was just mean.'

'But true?'

'I have no way of knowing, but my guess is yes. Stories about her wetting the bed, missteps with boys, cruel childish acts, something that happened at the beach once. They were the sorts of things that could be said about anyone, but when you're running a business empire you don't want to appear so vulnerable, so small, so human.'

'The sister, you mean?'

'Yes, Anita. She's pretty much the next in line, it's common knowledge that she'll be the next CEO.'

'And Sea Lion passed on publishing this book? It sounds like something that would sell quite well.'

Samar nodded, and sat back down. 'Of course. Literary merit aside, as I said. And that could have been fixed. But yes, everyone loves gossip. Any publishing house would have wanted to take it. A publishing house in another country that is.'

'You mean . . . ?'

'Her family stepped in. She came to us first because of me, but what she overlooked was that her father and our CEO are bum chums, stalwarts of the old boy network, playing doubles on the grass courts of the Delhi Gym before a stiff scotch at the bar. This part, obviously, is off the record, you understand?' he glared at them both suddenly. 'I don't have a shred of evidence or anything. This is just what I think. They must have got together and decided that this sort of thing would be bad for the nation or something, you know how these captains of industry are. And decided to pulp it before it was even published.'

'Sounds very likely to me.' Mridula seemed to hesitate before asking, 'Were you in it?'

'Yes, I was. And I didn't care, before you ask. Did I love it? No. Would it have been very awkward for me had it been published? Possibly. But I wouldn't go out of my way to not publish it.'

'Would she have found another publisher?'

Samar nodded. 'I should have thought so. If she was smart, and she was, she would have found someone to take the risk or she could have self-published. There would have been a market for it for sure.'

Mridula and Monami looked at each other. Monami was sure the same thought flashed through their head at the same time. *Motive?*

'Can we read it?'

'If you can get to my CEO, sure. He's the only one who has a copy. And her family, obviously.'

'Hard copy only? No email?'

'She sent it to me printed,' said Samar. 'She used to send all her copy to us that way—she liked the heft of it, she said, when it was all bound up. And my preferred way of reading is offscreen, so it worked for me. I only had the one copy. And since my CEO asked for it . . .' he shrugged. 'I don't have it anymore.'

'So, to summarise,' said Mridula, and her tone was grave, 'Anika came to you six months ago, and said that she was writing a book. A book that didn't make her family look good. Six months later, the same family relieves her from her position at the *Delhi Daily* . . .'

'And in such a clever way too,' Samar interrupted her. 'Making DB do the dirty work. Sneaky. I wonder who thought of *that*.' His voice took on a new undertone, one that Monami had not heard yet. It was many, many layers down, buried under the vagueness and the easy manner, but it was in there somewhere—an admiration for ruthlessness.

Mridula seemed to be struck by Samar's statement. She paused for a few moments, and her owlish face looked even more sombre, more calculating than usual, as she looked at Samar.

'I've been thinking and thinking about this,' Samar continued, snapping Mridula out of her thoughts. 'Can you imagine? On a day like this. Her family's essentially won. She's lost her job; she can't publish her book. She's down and out. And then . . . then she dies! In such a violent way. It honestly has been driving me nuts to the point where I've started believing all of Kajal's guff about birth charts. That must be it, right? It was written in her stars. This was a run of bad luck, her own personal *kaliyug*.'

He seemed to sink further into his chair, and his voice got lower, 'And even more than that. I don't think there was a single person at that party who was a genuine friend of hers. Isn't that something? She went to the book launch of a colleague, someone who should have been a friend. But she wasn't a friend. Oh, and it wasn't just Kajal. Niks lived her whole life in Delhi, and she didn't have any friends here. She had a social circle, of course; when she threw parties, half of Delhi would show up. But everyone was kind of wary of her. If you think about it, I was probably the most genuine, the most feeling relationship she had. I was probably the closest to her of everyone there, and even I had been dreading running into her. Dreading it, because I thought she would make a scene about her book, about Sea Lion not publishing it.' His voice finally lowered to the point where they had to strain to hear him.

'Samar,' said Mridula softly. 'Who do *you* think did it? You're right, you probably were the closest to her out of everyone. So, who do you think did it?'

Samar, still seemingly in a daze, stared at her as though she had asked him something so outlandish, so grotesque, that his brain needed time to process her audacity. But surely, Monami thought, he must have considered it, the most obvious question of all.

'I . . . I don't know who killed her. I simply don't know,' he said, as if it were the first time such a question had occurred to him.

Mridula and Monami looked at each other, and rose to go. 'Well, this has been most enlightening, Samar, thank you,' said Mridula. 'You've certainly given us a lot to chew on.'

They made their way slowly to the door, Samar following them. 'It was helpful to me too, to finally be able to talk freely about me and Anika,' he said. 'Thanks for that. Of course, I assume you'll keep it to yourselves? It's all off the record, and all that.'

'Yes, we'll keep it to ourselves, Samar. For now. But it may have to come out eventually. Depending on where our investigations take us.'

Samar looked annoyed by this, but only shrugged.

'Oh, and by the way, Samar, there may be some reason to believe now that Anika was killed much earlier,' said Mridula, casually, as he opened the heavy wooden front door. 'And maybe inside Kajal's house, with her body being moved later. What do you think of that theory?'

Samar started. 'She . . . she was on the balcony when DB died,' he said. 'We all saw her.'

'You think it could have happened that way?'

He took a moment to think about it. Finally, he shook his head. 'I don't really see how, unless Kajal herself is implicated, and that is nonsense. There's no way. When DB died, she was a ball of energy, rushing in and out of the house with cushions, with ice, and whatnot. She wouldn't have had time. And then after that everyone left.'

'You stayed with her, didn't you?'

Samar nodded. 'I did. And Jemin too. But if you're suggesting—'

'We're not suggesting anything. Just getting everyone's story straight. Bye, Samar. Thanks for everything you've told us.'

ii

Back in the car, Mridula and Monami looked at each other.

'It could be just an act,' said Monami, before the older woman could say anything. 'But it wasn't. He's shattered. He couldn't have done it.'

Mridula said nothing. She started her car up and they puttered away.

'Can I give you a ride to a metro station?' she said, finally. 'Or home?'

'Thanks, no. Just drop me anywhere, I'll take an auto.'

'I'll drive you home,' said the older woman firmly. 'It's been a long day.'

'Oh, you don't have to . . . ' said Monami, surprised by Mridula's offer.

'That's fine. Where do you live? CR Park, right?'

Monami found that she didn't have the strength to argue, and just nodded. They drove in silence to her busy little neighbourhood. This late at night, the traffic had subsided, and it was a peaceful ride home under yellow street lights.

Once parked outside her house, Mridula turned to her. 'Becoming too real?' she said.

Monami looked at her. It was as though Mridula had read her mind. It was uncanny, and not wholly pleasant. The thought gave her a little creepy feeling down her spine.

'Yes. I don't know how you knew, but that was just what I was thinking. That interview was hard. I've always seen Anika as little more than, well, little more than a cartoon villain, if you know what I mean. There wasn't a third dimension to her. She was Wile E. Coyote.' She didn't know if this reference would mean anything to Mridula, but the older woman nodded, and she continued. 'To see Samar like that . . . he loved her . . . was mourning her . . . and . . . and . . .'

'And?'

'And her family. I hadn't seen anything through her eyes at all. Of course, if her family really was behind pushing her out of the paper . . .'

'No. That was a failing on my part. I should have listened to DB,' said Mridula. 'He suspected it. I didn't believe him.'

Monami shot a look at her. Mridula's face was grim, her mouth set in a very straight line. And although she was perfectly still, Monami thought there was a new energy about her. A menacing crackle seemed to emanate from her, like from an electrified fence with barbed wire running along the top, the kind that's used to guard a bleak prison house, made of slate-grey bricks, surrounded by Siberian tundra. Monami moved a little further away from Mridula, shrinking against the window.

'Don't blame yourself.'

'I don't. Go on with what you were saying. You no longer see Anika as a cartoon villain? It's taken you long enough.'

Monami would have preferred more of a sympathetic response to what she felt was a searing and compassionate insight. She frowned. 'I know, I know.'

'You need to start thinking of the victim as the victim, as a human being. She had been hurt badly, by her own family. Now, I know you have your pet theory. And I'm not suggesting you tear it up or anything like that. Could Anika be the culprit? She could be lashing out, like a wounded animal. I still think it's unlikely, but I don't think we've ruled it out. But . . .' Mridula stared at the little green patch that passed for a park in front of Monami's street, 'a few things about that interview were interesting, no?'

The electricity from the fence seemed to dissipate a little, and the barbed wire seemed less sharp. Mridula turned back to look at Monami, and she felt less of a need to melt into the upholstery.

'Definitely they were. Er, like what, would you say?'

'What could have happened six months ago?'

'You think it could have a bearing on her murder?' asked Monami.

'We don't know. But it's strange, isn't it? What reason could her family have to push her out of the newspaper? That's why I didn't believe DB. It's such a peculiar thing to do.'

'Maybe she was embarrassing them?' suggested Monami. 'She was trying to be an influencer, you know, so she kept trying to keep a high profile and annoying people with her insults and indiscretions. Maybe her family felt she was a nuisance? And after all, what did they really do? They didn't make a public hue and cry about it. Just quietly went through DB. If she didn't kick up a fuss, no one would even know. They might assume she'd left the paper of her own accord. In fact, I think that's what people *would* assume.'

Mridula looked at her thoughtfully. 'Do you know, that's very insightful of you,' she said.

'There's no need to sound so surprised.'

'You're absolutely right. They didn't make a hue and cry. But *she* was going to.'

'The manuscript?'

'Yes. The manuscript.'

'You really think that could be a motive for murder? But who? Are you saying . . . are you suggesting it was Samar? No! I can't believe it of him.'

Mridula looked at her, and a small smile came over her face. 'Because of his sad story? He does look so fetching when he's rueful. I would have thought you would have been outraged on behalf of your friend Tina.'

Monami turned red, and again wondered at Mridula's perspicacity. Did nothing get past this woman? 'That's . . . that's not really serious,' she said.

Mridula laughed, though to the recoiling Monami it sounded like the aggressive honk of some great matriarch of a goose. 'Either way,' Mridula said, composing herself, 'we can't just take his word at face value. Detective work 101, you see. He might be desperate to stop the book from being published. We don't know what's in it; maybe he's been portrayed really poorly. In fact, we only have his word for their entire relationship. It may have been sexual, nothing more. And he may have gotten tired of it. He was there, on the spot. He was careful not to drink from the bottle that poisoned DB. And he stayed behind with Kajal, while everyone else left, to wait for the police.'

By the end of this speech, Monami felt dizzy with tiredness. It had been a long, emotional day, and she couldn't take one more second of it.

She got out of the car abruptly. 'Thanks for the ride.'

'No problem. Onward and upward!' said Mridula. Monami narrowed her eyes. Mridula obviously wasn't tired, and, however murky the journey, she was obviously still enjoying herself.

16

The Sort of Thing That Makes Your Soul Slowly Leave Your Body

Jemin Sequeira's studio in Qutb was often showcased in magazines like *Architectural Digest India*, with surrounding copy full of words like 'riotous' and 'exuberant'. He had decried the global taste for minimalism with every fibre of his being. 'Less is not more,' he was fond of saying to anyone who would listen. 'More is more! It just seems so obvious.'

There was barely a clear surface in his studio. Every inch of the walls was papered in a bright green silk that matched the treetops outside his French windows. The floor was tiled in a black and white marble checkerboard pattern, and everywhere there were piles of fabrics, on his leather Chesterfield sofa, on the floor, strewn across his wide Jaipur-carved desk. He himself sat at this desk today, looking like he was trapped behind it.

'Thanks so much for coming,' he said, a little warily. 'Samar called ahead. He thinks you can help . . . shed some light?'

Mridula and Monami sat down on the wide, squashy chairs in front of him.

'Nimboo pani? Water? Tea? Something stronger?'

Since it was 11 a.m., Mridula said, firmly, 'Nimboo pani would be great, thanks. Mixed; water, not soda.'

'Same,' nodded Monami.

'Sure.' Without any warning, he gave a deafening bellow: 'Charu! *Teen* nimboo pani, mixed!' and got an answering echo before resuming, 'Now then.'

'Right.' Mridula took out her notebook, on cue. 'Just a few questions. I assume you've already spoken to the police?'

'You assume correctly. They've been hounding me day and night. There's really no other word.'

'Can you tell us what happened? In your own words.'

'Where should we start?' Jemin already sounded tired, and this was just the first question.

'Why don't we start at the beginning,' said Mridula. 'You sponsored this launch?'

'Yes, and it's seeming like a dumber decision the more I think about it,' said Jemin, bitterly. 'I don't really question Shekhar on these things.'

'Ah, it was Shekhar's idea?'

'It came to me through Vasu, but yes, I believe it was Shekhar's idea, originally. Something about demographics, or synergies, or buying power. Very MBA. Vasu wouldn't have come up with it herself. She's a dear girl. But she's essentially a doer. She has no imagination. She would never have thought this up on her own. She wouldn't even have *thought* to think it up, if you know what I mean. It's our education system. It encourages one to colour within the lines, not draw new ones.'

'Right,' said Mridula, glancing at Monami. Monami thought she knew what the look meant—*are you keeping score? Kajal thinks it's Jemin's idea, Samar thinks it's Vasudha's idea, Jemin thinks it's Shekhar's idea*. 'And just to be clear—Shekhar owns the label?'

'Yes, his holding company owns it,' said Jemin. 'They bought us out a few months ago. Honestly, it's been a godsend. He handles the business side: the invoicing and the accounts payable, and accounts receivable, and supply chains and all that, all the sort of thing that makes your soul slowly leave your body, and I handle the creative. It's like a match made in heaven.'

'And . . . business is booming?' Mridula sounded like one of those uncles that corner young people at dinner parties and ask how the job hunt is going.

'Oh, yes. Booming is the word,' said Jemin, but still vaguely.

'We heard some stores had to be closed,' said Monami.

'Oh, did you?' Jemin seemed to lose some of his blurred focus and looked at her sharply. 'But that's all part of the strategy, you know. Ask Shekhar, he'll tell you. Something about focusing our ground, or, I don't know, consolidating our advantage. It's all business-school speak, but it sounds wonderful.'

'And it's all still rolling in?'

'Why are you asking about my business?' asked Jemin, abruptly. 'This is a bit off topic, isn't it?'

'Just getting some background,' said Mridula. 'So, your relationship with Shekhar is good, is it?'

'With Shekhar?' Jemin sounded surprised. 'Yes, of course. He's quite a nice guy, you know. A total nerd, of course. But I don't hold it against him.'

At this point, a young woman came in with three glasses on a tray. They stopped talking as she put the glasses down carefully on coasters in front of each of them. Monami sipped her drink, glad of the coolness. There was a storm coming, and the inside of Jemin's office, with its wide-open windows, was just as muggy and oppressive as, if not more than, the day outside.

'Thank you,' said Mridula to the young woman, and she nodded. Then to Jemin: 'So your relationship with Shekhar is good. But I understand you didn't get along very well with his wife?'

'No, that's true. I can't say I did.'

'Any particular reason?'

Jemin stood up slowly and walked to the window. 'You both knew Anika, of course, and so you know that one doesn't exactly need a reason. But, in my case, it was quite prosaic, I'm afraid. I owed her rather a lot of money.'

This bald statement, simply made, surprised both Monami and Mridula. Mridula's eyebrows rose. 'So that was it, was it?'

'Yes. You wouldn't know it, but we were rather good friends once. She, Samar and me. Of course, the two of them went off in a different direction sometimes, but we were all . . . friends. She gave me rather a large loan with which I started my first venture, maybe you've heard of it? It was called Fashion Pops!' said Jemin. His voice took on a dreamy tone. 'It was such a fun idea. Pop-up fashion shows, you know. The models were desperate to take part. Most of the time they're so jobless, when the season's not on I mean. So, we would work with these designers to have micro shows in different places. We went everywhere! This being Delhi, we did shows at cocktail parties for millionaires, and we did toddler birthday parties too. You wouldn't think it, but pop-ups at toddler parties became quite the rage. Some of those mothers . . . ' he trailed off.

Monami, who had a sister with two children and plenty of small cousins, nodded understandingly. She could definitely see this catching on.

'What happened?' she asked.

'Well, it didn't work out,' said Jemin, bluntly. 'It was just sort of a fun idea, and, on some level, I suppose I thought it would help me launch my own brand. It didn't. I don't have an earthly head for business, you know. There were no . . . what does Shekhar call them? Revenue streams. Those mothers drive hard bargains.'

'And Anika helped you launch this business?' said Monami. She was surprised; Anika didn't seem like the sort of person who would throw her money around.

'Yup. She didn't have a head for business either,' said Jemin, cheerfully. 'Besides, as I said, we were friends. And it didn't take much—it's not like we needed office space. But yes, I did need a rather large . . . er, capital injection . . . in the beginning, to sweeten the deal for the designers I worked with.'

'Did she introduce you to Shekhar?' asked Monami.

Jemin threw back his head and laughed at this. 'No, no! *She* introduce *me* to Shekhar? Not at all. No, not at all. Shekhar found me all by himself.'

'And how did she react to the fact that he bought you out?' Mridula said, frowning a little in the face of this mirth.

'Do you know, I'm not sure. I imagine she did everything she could to talk him out of it. But he was quite insistent. He'd done all this research, you know, something about the market and, I don't know, points of entry and all that. I guess he thought we'd be a steal. And frankly, we were.' He grinned at them both. 'And thanks to him, we've just been exploding. Unlike me and Anika, he does have an earthly head for business. And easy on the eyes, too.'

'Once your business started doing better, you didn't want to pay her back?' asked Mridula.

'Oh, I'm sure I would have, at some point,' said Jemin. 'But no, I didn't. I suppose I became . . . pig-headed about it. She was so . . . so offensive every time we met, that it put my back up. And please, it's not like she needed the money.'

'We hear that you locked horns over a debt earlier in the party,' said Mridula. 'What was that about?'

'Oh, did Samar mention that?' The hint of strain on Jemin's face, which had ebbed and flowed with their conversation, now grew more pronounced. 'You know how Anika could be. Always with the drama. I think partly she was super annoyed at Kajal getting this major book launch—she spent quite some time getting digs in, knowing Kajal was listening. And . . . I don't know if Samar mentioned . . .' he hesitated.

'If you're talking about the, er, nature of their relationship, yes, he was most forthcoming about that,' said Mridula.

'Oh?' Jemin looked surprised. 'Well, then, you know. She always did up the drama whenever her husband and Samar were talking to each other. I think she must have felt awkward in those circumstances. Understandably. And so, I suppose she'd just say the first thing that came into her head.'

There was a little pause at this, and finally, Mridula said, 'Okay. So overall, you were happy with this book launch? It went well for you? The sponsorship and so on?'

Jemin shrugged. 'Well, as I said, I don't really question Shekhar on these things, and I assumed it came from him. And . . . well, I have to admit, I was intrigued. Anika's colleague. Someone she would, in the usual scheme of things, be quite contemptuous about. Her husband actually sponsoring the launch so that it becomes one of those big parties. It was all so deliciously *ironic*, you know. I think that was why I didn't hold Vasu back when she came to me with some of the most preposterous ideas. It wasn't wholly conscious, I assure you. But at some level, there was certainly a part of me that felt a bit of schadenfreude that Kajal was publishing this book with a big-brand publisher that had just rejected Anika.'

'You knew about Anika's book?' said Mridula.

'Yes, Samar and I are quite close. I suppose he shouldn't have, but he told me. Anyway, it's not like publishers and writers have a doctor-patient confidentiality clause,' he added defensively.

'What did he tell you, exactly?'

Jemin looked at them again with that sharp look that was at odds with his usual chumminess. 'What do you mean? He told me she'd submitted a book to him, and that his higher-ups were passing on it. She would be furious. He was just a bit uncertain and maybe nervous about how to break it to her, or rather how to break it to her so that she actually took no for a no and didn't keep after him about it, which is what I gather she was doing.'

'He didn't tell you what the book was about?'

'A memoir, I gathered.'

'Nothing more?'

'No, nothing.'

'You didn't read it, for instance?'

'Read it? How on earth would I?' Jemin sounded genuinely surprised. 'And even if I could, why would I want to? I assume the book was deathly dull, so to speak, which was why the publisher was passing.'

'They were her memoirs; you weren't curious as to whether you were in them?'

'Not particularly. I knew Anika, she was far too careful to put anything too real in them. She would never risk it. And anyway, nowadays, any publicity is good publicity.'

'Jemin, do you have any idea who would have wanted to get DB and Anika out of the way?'

Jemin stood up again and walked to the window. Monami watched him and wondered why all their interviewees were doing this, turning their faces away, walking around, making their expressions hard to read. Kajal had done the same, and even Samar had paced. Was their restlessness a product of stress? Or guilt?

'I do have a theory,' he said finally. 'Firstly, there doesn't seem to be any rhyme or reason to both murders. Anika by herself—yes, I guess, maybe. Any number of disgruntled colleagues or acquaintances at that party. But Anika and DB both? No.'

'And so?' prompted Monami.

'I think one of them was a mistake. DB, to be specific.'

'DB . . . was a mistake?' asked Monami. 'How?'

'Well, firstly no one had a motive to kill him. That sweet old man? I didn't really know him, but there seems to have been no reason to get him out of the way. And secondly, think about the way it happened, through a toast. It would have been very easy to get the glasses mixed up. I thought maybe someone else was being targeted.'

'Interesting,' said Mridula. 'Who?'

'Who what?'

'Who did you think was being targeted?'

'Oh. That I don't know,' said Jemin. 'The only person at that launch that anyone could have wanted to kill was Anika. Maybe she was the target, and something went wrong?'

'That's quite a theory,' said Mridula. 'She was nowhere near the fatal toast.'

Jemin shrugged. 'It's not perfect, but it's the only theory that makes any sense to me. But try telling our police force that.'

'And who do you think was behind it? Do you have a theory about that?'

'I do, actually. It's just a theory, but again, it's the only one that makes any sense to me.'

'We're listening.'

'I don't have a shadow of proof,' said Jemin. 'You understand? This is just a theory.'

'We understand. Go on.'

'I think it was Vasudha,' said Jemin. This was the first time anyone had actually plumped out a name, and both Mridula and Monami were taken aback. Sensing their astonishment, Jemin continued, a little defensively, 'I think it could only have been her. She poured the drinks. She had it in for Anika.'

'Did she?'

'Well, she has quite a pash for Shekhar, you know. Poor kid. Just moons around him constantly. He doesn't mean to, of course, but he really encourages that sort of thing, just being so good-looking and then not having an earthly idea of the effect he's having on women. And men. Both,' he added, with a wry laugh.

'I see,' said Mridula, cautiously. 'I think I see.'

'I think she wanted to get Anika out of the way,' continued Jemin, 'maybe subconsciously she'd been planning it all along.'

'So, you think she's insane?' said Monami.

'That's a bit harsh,' said Jemin, looking at her.

'If you think she mixed poison in someone's drink, ended up killing someone else by mistake, and then killing her initial target anyway, you must think she's crazy,' said Monami. 'It's what the news is suggesting, too,' she added. 'One of their theories, anyway. Not quite the detail that you have, but that she's crazy.'

'Well, if the shoe fits,' said Jemin, shrugging again.

Monami thought that this was a strange and somewhat heartless reaction from someone who must have worked with Vasudha for many months.

'You think she could have strangled Anika with a scarf? One of your scarves, in fact? Why do you think Anika was wearing it, by the way? If she was not exactly your biggest fan?'

Jemin reddened at this, and his expression broke into something approaching anger. 'That's the one thing that makes me more convinced than ever, actually. I've been thinking and thinking about this, and I'm more convinced than ever that what she wore was *not* one of my scarves. It was similar, very similar, but it wasn't one of mine. Firstly, I can tell, and secondly, she would never wear a House of Jems scarf. And so it follows that it must have been planted by someone who wanted to distract suspicion away from themselves—and onto me.'

'And you think that's Vasudha?' asked Monami.

'Look, I'm not making out a legal case against her. I don't want to throw around too many wild accusations. But if I think of who at that party hated Anika, and who would have known what sort of scarf to source, well, she sticks out a mile.'

'Where were you,' said Mridula, 'when the toast was happening?'

Monami wasn't sure if it was because he was caught off guard by this sudden change in topic, but for whatever reason, Jemin looked taken aback at this question.

'I went off for a little bit to smoke a joint to calm down, if you must know,' he said. 'I hung out with the waiters and the models. The models were my crew, I know some of those kids really well. It was calming after all the BS.'

'You didn't see Anika at all? Even after DB . . . ?'

'Honestly, at that point I wasn't really noticing anything. Everything had gone out of my head. It was just the most shocking thing I've ever witnessed. I have to say Kajal handled it brilliantly—unlike me. I just . . . I became rooted to the spot. But Kajal sprang into action, called for water, splashed his face, called for a doctor, was literally running up and down until he arrived.'

'Everyone else?'

Jemin shook his head. 'I think we all just hung around, kind of shell-shocked. Vasu fell to pieces. The models were also totally out of it. I told them all to go home.'

'When did you leave yourself?'

'Me? Er, well, I stuck around for a little while, rallying around Kajal, you know. But when it seemed like she was okay, and the police would have to be called, I left.'

'So, you have no idea who might have done it? You didn't see anyone in the road as you were leaving?'

'No one at all.'

As she had done with Samar, Mridula waited until the end of the interview to say, casually, 'By the way, we have some reason to believe that Anika may have been killed earlier than previously thought, and her body was moved. What do you think of that theory?'

'What do you mean? When do you think she was killed?' said Jemin, frowning.

'We think her body may have been moved to the street, and she was actually killed at Kajal's home, before everyone went home.'

Like Samar, Jemin took a minute to chew on this theory. His eyes went slowly back and forth between Mridula and Monami. He looked confused, and maybe a little scared. 'I don't see how that can be,' he said, finally. 'Who would have moved her?'

'That doesn't gel with your Vasudha theory?' said Mridula, watching him closely.

'How could it? She wouldn't have been able to move the body. No, I'm fairly sure she was murdered right out there, in the street.'

'Okay, well thanks for your time, Jemin.'

17

A Vision

i

Monami left Jemin's office again feeling the strain from the night before. She was thinking deeply as she broke into a jog to catch up with Mridula, who seemed to be moving at the pace of a drill sergeant. And in so doing, she almost collided with a young man.

'Oh, sorry,' she said. And then she looked at the man she had bumped into and felt a reflexive need to smooth her hair and straighten her clothes. For he was a vision, this young man, dark and lean, with large eyes and a rather scruffy beard, the kind of man who looked like he might have been a poet living in early twentieth-century Paris. 'Oh. Hi.'

'Oh, hi,' responded this vision, grinning.

'Hi,' said Monami again, with a corresponding grin. Why couldn't a man like *this* pop out from behind a relative's back during one of those 'family meetings' her mother was always planning, she asked herself.

'Visiting Jemin?' said the Vision. 'A nice change from his usual visitors these days.'

'Oh?' said Monami. 'Why is that?' If this man was reflective of the usual standard, she felt she and Mridula would be more of a downgrade than a step up.

'The police, you know.'

'Ah, yes. Of course.' Beside her, she felt Mridula reappear, a sinister presence at her elbow.

'But you're obviously not police,' said the Vision. 'You're far too attractive.'

'Ha ha!' said Monami, and felt her mind slowly go blank. She had always been terrible at flirting. The only circumstances under which she could flirt were (i) if she were given hours to prepare, and (ii) if the man in question wasn't disconcertingly handsome. Then, in a controlled environment and if she remembered her lines, she was okay. But when unusually attractive men were sprung upon her without warning, all hope was lost. On some level, she knew she should say something cool and flirty back. But what?

'Ha ha!' she said again, and heard the words come out surlier than she had intended. The Vision looked surprised. Monami looked desperately at Mridula for help.

Mridula had been watching all this with an air of great interest, as Jane Goodall might watch her chimpanzees.

'You are very attractive too.'

Monami froze. Had she really heard these words come out of Mridula's mouth? For a few seconds she closed her eyes. Finally, she had found something even worse than her usual inability to flirt: Mridula flirting on her behalf.

'Oh. Er, thank you,' said the Vision, sounding alarmed.

'Are you a model?'

'I am.'

'Were you one of the models at Kajal Puri's book launch?'

Monami felt almost weak with relief that this was the direction in which Mridula's remarks had gone. She opened her eyes again.

Unfortunately, the smile had disappeared from the Vision's face, and he looked nervous. He darted a glance at the closed door to Jemin's office.

'I was. You . . . you're not journalists, are you?'

'We *are* journalists,' said Mridula, in a voice that conveyed a schoolteacher's indulgent pride at a favourite pupil's clever guess. 'That's absolutely right.'

'I'm sorry, I can't talk to the press,' said the Vision. He threw Monami a look of regret, and said 'sorry' again.

Mridula said, 'We totally understand, but we were hoping you might help to clear Jemin. It's better to talk to us than the police.'

'The police?'

'Yes. They'll want to corroborate his alibi, and he says that when everything was happening at the party, with DB, you know, that he was hanging out with his models and servers. That's you, no?'

'Er . . . yes.'

'Super. Well, make sure you make it clear when you speak to them. You know, they get muddled very easily.' Mridula smiled a grisly smile at the Vision and prepared to move away. Monami could see that he was rattled.

'He was with us. He was with us the whole time,' he said. 'I don't think the police suspect him, do they?'

'Oh, they do,' said Mridula, seriously. 'It's a dead heat between him and Samar. Samar Chishti, the publisher, you know.'

The Vision looked grave, but made no move to walk away from them and Mridula pressed her advantage.

'So, can you corroborate that Jemin was with you the entire time? He didn't disappear for a few minutes at any point?'

The Vision hesitated again and then said, 'No, after the argument he had with Anika, he was with us the whole time. We had a stash of beer that we, er, kept restocking from the bar. And the bar had separate servers. Once we were done sort of making our presence felt, we thought we could relax.'

'You were there just for the atmosphere?' said Mridula, frowning.

'Well, we were wearing House of Jems clothes, as well. But all black to blend in with the serving staff, for some reason. And that Vasudha had the really—I mean *really*—corny idea to dress us up as murder victims.' The Vision seemed to have recovered some of his aplomb, and rolled his eyes at Monami. 'She really put everyone's backs up.'

'I can imagine,' said Monami.

'I had to wear a noose! How can you show off clothes wearing something like that around your neck? Jemin should have stopped her. Of course, he had his plans, but he should have stopped her. I've been around for ten years, and I've never seen anything like that. It was quite pitiful.'

'Ten years? You must know Jemin quite well, then,' said Monami.

'Yes, I do,' he said.

'What do you mean . . .' began Mridula, when, suddenly, the door to Jemin's office flew open. He stood framed in the doorway, and seemed to stiffen at the sight of them. His eyebrows arched, he walked towards them in what Monami felt was a threatening way.

'Suleiman,' he said, in an artificially loud voice. 'I thought I heard your dulcet tones. What are you saying to the sleuths?'

'Oh, nothing, nothing,' said the Vision hastily. 'They were asking me a few questions, about That Night.'

A look passed between them and Jemin, his eyebrows still raised, said to Mridula, 'I wish you'd have asked before talking to my staff. Did you get what you wanted?'

Mridula raised her eyebrows in turn. 'I think so. My apologies for not checking with you, but we literally bumped into . . . I'm sorry, did we catch your name?'

'Suleiman,' he answered.

'We literally bumped into Suleiman. Or rather, my colleague here did.'

There was a pregnant pause, during which Monami felt the prospect of getting Suleiman's number, or at least giving him hers and hoping for the best, fade rather rapidly into the distance. Oh, well, she thought. We'd have had nothing to talk about.

ii

'Well?' said Mridula to Monami, once they were in her car.

Monami was still recovering from her close brush with Suleiman, and had to think about this.

'He's definitely hiding something,' she said at last.

'Jemin?'

'Yes. The beef between him and Anika is somewhat cleared up, but it doesn't all seem perfectly clear yet, does it?'

'These are definitely deep waters,' agreed Mridula as she navigated delicately around the Qutb Crescent. 'The relationship with the husband isn't totally clear yet either.'

'Yes. He doesn't seem to let his wife's grudges stand in the way of a business deal.'

'A business deal,' said Mridula meditatively, 'that only happened a few months ago.'

'You think that's what Anika was upset about?'

'It's a possibility, no? What did you think of his mistake theory?'

'Not much,' said Monami, 'unless we're suggesting that we're dealing with a sociopath. If it was a mistake, I don't think the murderer would have just hopped on to Anika next. Unless it was Anika herself, of course, who killed DB. As I keep saying.'

'Yes, you do.'

'Why, what did you think of it?'

'I thought it was a possibility very early on.'

'Did you?' said Monami, sceptically. 'You never said. Was that Option One or Option Two?'

'Yes,' said Mridula, answering the first question and ignoring the second. 'DB's death as it stands makes very little sense. No one seems to have had a reason to kill him.'

'What did you think of Jemin trotting out his theory of it being Vasudha? I thought it was rather mean of him.'

Mridula nodded. 'It was. But mean or not, it's a theory. We don't have enough evidence there, but I thought his theory about Vasudha and Shekhar *was* interesting.'

'Her crush on him, you mean?'

Mridula nodded. They fell into silence as a thunderstorm broke out suddenly, and lashed rain against their windscreen. Monami considered the character of the murderer—was it someone filled with such all-encompassing hate that he or she just killed without compunction? And when the first attempt didn't work, tried again? But then it would have to be a sociopath, someone with literally no regard for human life. Monami shivered a little at this idea, and at the little droplets of rain that came through the window beside the driver's seat which would not close all the way. She looked over at Mridula and tried to read her mind, but Mridula was focused on the road in front of her, her usual frown furrowing her brow.

'That model also let slip a few interesting things, didn't he?' murmured Mridula. 'I would have liked some more time with him. What a pity you didn't get his number.'

Monami turned sharply to look at the woman sitting beside her, searching for signs of leg-pulling, but Mridula's expression was inscrutable.

'Well, I would have, if you hadn't interrupted me.'

'Of course you would have,' said Mridula, and now Monami was sure she detected a bit of a smirk.

18

Sidebars

i

Mridula let Monami go on to the office and proceeded to a small market in Vasant Kunj, not far from Mehrauli. As she entered a café, a compact man with neat silver hair and tidy features rose and made his way towards her.

'Mrs Majumdar?' he said, curtly.

'Ms,' corrected Mridula, as they sat down and looked carefully across at each other. 'And you must be DCP Akshay Kumar.'

The man inclined his head. 'I understand you have some evidence for me?'

Mridula hesitated for a beat before bringing out her bag with the broken iPhone in it. The Deputy Commissioner beckoned to a man, also in civilian clothes, sitting at a table close by, and he jumped up and ran over to them. 'Please take this, Khurana, belonged to the murder victim Mrs Kapoor. We'll need all the data on it, fingerprints, everything.'

The man nodded and whisked the bag away, taking out his own phone and dialling busily as he did so.

The DCP then turned to Mridula, but before he could speak, she jumped in. 'I'm surprised you asked me to meet you here?'

'Are you, madam? Why? It's quite close to our police headquarters. And I thought it would be more convenient for you.'

'You didn't want to meet me at your office,' said Mridula. It was a statement, not a question.

The DCP looked at her for a moment and then spread his hands out. 'Maybe I didn't. Maybe I wanted to keep this . . . unofficial.'

'Why?'

'How did you find this phone, madam?' asked the DCP. 'I find it very interesting and . . . curious that you did so.'

Mridula's eyebrows flickered, but she dutifully told the story of how she and Monami had gone to visit Kajal, asked to see the scene of the crime, and found the phone just lying there, glinting in the grass.

'Just lying in the grass?' he asked.

'Just lying in the grass.'

There was a brief silence. Finally, DCP Kumar continued, 'May I ask what you made of that fact? How did you think the phone got there?'

'I think we were supposed to think that it had fallen off Anika's body or that perhaps she dropped it. And . . .'

'And the police missed it?'

Mridula repeated the action the DCP had made moments ago and spread out her hands in a gesture of acquiescence. 'As I say . . . I think that's what we were supposed to think.'

'Ah. And is that what you did think?' pressed the DCP.

'I think that, for one thing, the phone didn't fall out in the street, because the body didn't fall there in the street.'

'Ah. And why do you think so?'

Mridula was suddenly tired of this game, and she snapped. 'I'm not sure why you're asking me these questions, if you're trying to evaluate me in some way, but must we sit here and waste time? I thought so because it's obvious. A body could not be left in the street for two days and be undisturbed. This is India. It would have been discovered almost immediately, if not by humans, by any amount of wildlife. After two days, it would be more likely to have been discovered as a pile of bones, picked clean by kites.'

'I agree. Yet you would be surprised by how few people have come to this conclusion,' said DCP Kumar with a touch of unexpected irony. 'The only conclusion the news media is drawing, for instance, is that the police overlooked the body. And if they get wind of this phone, the conclusion they will draw is that we overlooked the phone, too. When I can tell you myself that my men and I, personally, went through every inch of that lane, and there was not a chance that the phone could have been undiscovered. Let alone a body.'

'The body was moved,' said Mridula, slowly.

DCP Kumar nodded. 'The body was moved. And the phone was dropped . . . accidentally? Or on purpose?'

'You have a theory, I suppose,' said Mridula, feeling thankful that she hadn't asked Monami to accompany her to this little sidebar chat. The interview seemed to be taking an ominous turn.

'I *do* have a theory, madam,' said the DCP, making the word madam sound like an accusation, almost as if he had said 'murderer'. 'My theory involves your friend and colleague, Kajal Puri.'

'You think Kajal moved the body?'

'I think *only* Ms Puri or one of her household staff could possibly have done so, yes.'

Mridula merely waited. The DCP seemed annoyed by her lack of reaction.

'I think they moved the body,' he continued. 'And overlooked the phone in the process. When they found the phone, possibly in the same place that they found the body, they panicked. And they called a close friend, a trusted colleague, someone who wasn't as implicated as they were, perhaps, and asked them how to get rid of it. This friend, or colleague, understood that this was an important piece of evidence, and, to her credit, advised them to hand it in to the police. However, *not* to her credit, she may also have advised them to indulge in a little piece of . . . shall we say . . . theatre? Maybe she thought that the police would simply swallow the rather implausible story they told.'

Mridula sighed. Men, and particularly men in positions of power, were so tiresome.

'Why don't you just come out and say what you would like to say, Deputy Commissioner?' she said. 'Are you accusing me of something?'

'I am not accusing you of anything, madam,' said the DCP, leaning forward. 'And that is because I have no evidence to do so. And it is also because you have turned in what I consider to be a very valuable piece of evidence. But the fact is that some concealment has taken place here, some tampering with timelines and locations. We are watching all of your colleagues very closely, madam.'

'Including those of us who are not under investigation,' said Mridula, scornfully. 'I understand you perfectly.'

'You don't understand anything,' said the DCP, finally losing his temper. 'But I would like to impress upon you, madam, that we are not a bungling band of fools as the media would like to make us out to be. We see more, and we do more, than you could possibly know. So, either you have tampered with evidence and if that's the case, we *will* find out, or you are simply involving yourself in a case that frankly you have no business being involved in. Either way, you are not doing us any favours. So maybe in your own interest, you can get out of our way and let us do our jobs?'

'For my own interest?' said Mridula. 'Are you threatening me?'

At this, the DCP seemed to lose some of his anger and laughed.

'Threatening you? No, no. We don't threaten little old ladies. I'm just informing you of some facts. If you obstruct our investigation, you'll get yourself and your newspaper into hot water. And when the stakes are this high, it'll be *very* hot. That's all. Have a nice day, and stay dry, madam.'

With this, the DCP pushed his chair back and marched out of the café. Mridula watched him, hoping the swinging doors would hit him in his backside on the way out, but there she had no luck.

'Stay dry,' she muttered to herself. 'Now was that a reference to the rain, or the hot water that we're supposedly going to get into?'

She too got up, and Monami would have perhaps been gratified to note that her brows were now furrowed, and the sense of enjoyment she had got from last night's interviews had been dispelled.

ii

When the DCP got back to his office, still huffing and puffing with indignation that Mridula had the gall to interfere with police business, he found a distinguished guest waiting for him.

'Mr Kapoor,' he said. 'It's an honour.'

Abhishek Kapoor rose from the somewhat shiny leatherite armchair they had placed him in and extended a firm hand. The two men sized each other up; the DCP had been expecting this interview since the start of the case but had expected that it would take place with a little more fanfare than this. An unexpected visit, no personal assistants or lawyers or man Fridays in attendance? No message of warning from the Commissioner? This was not his usual experience of Delhi's business elite. And so he felt his guard go up as he sat down behind his desk. Khurana had also entered the room and was standing quietly by the door, looking muted but undeniably thrilled to be in the same room as these two men.

'DCP, I've come to ask about your progress on the case.'

'Ah. I thought you had a direct line to the Commissioner, sir,' said the DCP.

'I do, of course I do,' said Abhishek. 'But I wanted to hear it directly from you. One gets such conflicting reports.'

'Of course. Well, we have made some progress, I'm happy to tell you. In fact, I've just come from an interview where we have secured quite a key piece of evidence. Your daughter's phone.'

'Anika's phone? It's been found?' Abhishek's tone was curiously flat, as though he could understand on some level that this was a good thing, but it wasn't quite registering.

'Yes, it was found just outside Kajal Puri's residence yesterday.'

'Interesting. And has it told you anything yet?'

'We've just sent it off for analysis. Khurana?'

That young man jumped a little at his name and nodded tremulously.

'Er, yes sir . . . sirs. I've just handed it in and we should be hearing more shortly.'

Abhishek nodded with the same air of dispassion. 'Good. Good. That should tell us . . . well, it should tell us something. Her text messages, who she was calling, her emails . . .'

DCP Akshay Kumar looked at him curiously. His guard was now a little lower; he understood that this man had not come to rake him over the coals or accuse him of not doing his job.

'Is there something in particular you wanted to know, sir?'

'I want to know if you have any particular suspicions yet?' said Abhishek. 'The news, social media, everyone seems to be going in different directions.'

'We have some leads,' said the DCP cautiously. 'It's a very tricky case.'

Abhishek Kapoor merely nodded and waited for him to continue.

'In most cases,' continued the DCP, 'we can track motive, and opportunity. In this case, it's curious—there are motives, many, er, personal and professional, shall we say. But the opportunity is more limited. There are only a handful of people who could have got to your daughter when she died. And, tied together with the death of Mr Bhattacharya—yes, it's tricky.'

'I understand. When you say a handful of people, can you elaborate? I imagine it's the same names we hear about in the news?'

'That's so,' said the DCP, nodding. 'We have our eye on Ms Kajal Puri, for one. The video evidence is quite damning that your daughter and she had a falling out that evening. We've had multiple witnesses corroborate that Ms Puri was quite furious after overhearing your daughter disparage her book. And I find this discovery of the phone rather, shall we say, fortuitous.' The DCP frowned, thinking back to his highly unsatisfactory conversation with Mridula. That woman had nettled him. 'Equally, your daughter had quite a . . . er . . . long-standing relationship with Mr Chishti.'

'Samar?'

'Yes. He was also on the spot, as it were, and he may have had a motive. This manuscript . . .'

Abhishek waved that away. 'That manuscript is no motive for murder. For one thing, I don't believe she would have ever published it. My daughter may have talked a tough game, but she was nothing if not loyal to her family. And it's certainly not a motive for Samar. He barely featured in it.'

The DCP digested this in silence. 'It would be helpful if we could see the manuscript,' he said tentatively.

'I don't see why,' said Abhishek, 'I can try to get it for you. But really, Deputy Commissioner, I don't think that has any bearing on the case. It's just the media with their usual penchant for theatrics.'

The DCP thought this was somewhat ironic, given that at least one or two of these media channels were owned by Abhishek Kapoor himself.

But he prudently made no comment. 'And finally, we have Mr Sequeira. He was also on the spot, and there was also no love lost between him and your daughter. Between us, we think that he is the most likely suspect under these circumstances. His personality . . . he seems the type to lose his head and commit a crime without thinking. He owed your daughter money. They also, according to this viral video, had quite an altercation.'

Abhishek sighed. If his wife had been here, she would have been jumping into the fray, asking if they had done this or that, if they had interviewed this person or uncovered that clue, in fact what on earth were the police doing? Was this what we paid our taxes for? And so on. But Abhishek found, even if his thoughts had played along similar lines, that he just didn't have the energy.

Instead, he asked, in a tired voice, 'Who is this child, Vasudha? How did she get involved?'

The DCP shrugged. 'It's unfortunate. She worked for Mr Sequeira as an intern at the House of Jems. We don't have many leads on the Dhritiman Bhattacharya angle, but it seems clear that she was in the best position to administer that poison.'

Abhishek shook his head. 'It just doesn't make sense.'

Constable Khurana, behind him, gave an almost imperceptible start. For this is what he had been saying all along. It just didn't make sense—he had risked his personal relationship with the DCP many times by saying this, tentatively at first and then more boldly as the case was formed, particularly against Jemin. And here was the victim's father, saying the same thing! He felt most vindicated.

DCP Akshay Kumar, who was a perceptive man, caught this start and tried to control his irritation. It wouldn't do to give it away in front of the victim's father, but Constable Khurana had used the same phrase, verbatim, to him so many times that he was starting to develop a sort of Pavlovian response to it. Instant eyeroll and a tendency to groan. He bit both back now.

'I understand,' he started, 'that it must be very difficult to think about these things in conjunction with your daughter's death. My suggestion would be, sir, that you leave us to create a case. We will bring it to you as soon as we can, and when we do, it will be complete. We'll leave no stone unturned, I assure you.'

'Thank you,' said Abhishek, heavily. 'I appreciate that. And can I ask . . . has anything else come to light? Or is it just these three or four people you're focusing on?'

'Oh, we're casting our net wide, I assure you. Those are the three or four names the media is focusing on and it's true that when we look at opportunity, on the surface, they are the most clearly indicated. However, we have to look for motive as well, and we're looking far and wide. Your daughter's professional enmities in particular. Not just through her column—there were a number of legal cases in the works against her, you must be aware—but also her colleagues. And there are one or two names who may link the two together. Your daughter and Mr Bhattacharya.'

At this, Abhishek seemed to lose some of his enervation.

'Her colleagues? That's interesting.' His eyes seemed to focus on a point in the middle distance for a whole minute, until finally he seemed to come to a decision. 'Well, thank you, DCP, for your time. It's much appreciated.'

He stood up, nodded and walked out, his shoulders thrown back as though he had suddenly rediscovered his authority. DCP Kumar, a little worried, watched him leave.

19

They Don't Share Your Beautiful Nature

i

Sunder Nursery was in magnificent form. The recent rain made the grass and the trees shimmer, and the air itself seemed to come alive. There was a restless, coiled-spring feel about everything. And as usual, the peacocks cried mournfully in the background.

On any other day, Monami would have had her phone camera out, trying to frame photos against the grey sky, the foliage, the champas in bloom and the stately Mughal reflecting pools dotted with bright pink lotuses.

But, today, she wanted to talk murder. She and Mridula found an empty bench (the café had flooded and was being industriously pumped), dusted it thoroughly for bugs and got going.

'Okay, let's recap,' said Mridula. 'What's our position?'

'Right,' said Monami. 'We've interviewed three people so far. Kajal, Samar and Jemin. And those three interviews have clarified approximately nothing and led to around a zillion follow-up questions.'

'Be serious,' said Mridula, with a frown. 'I thought some of them were most enlightening.'

'I have started with some notes, if that helps.'

'Ah, notes. I thought I'd never hear the words. Go on, then.'

Monami gazed down at her phone screen, which looked like this:

Conversations had: Kajal, Samar, Jemin.

Points of interest:

Kajal:

- Claims didn't want a launch at all—was unhappy about it
- Thought the launch was Jemin's idea
- Said Jemin had disappeared during the toast and was planning something beyond the launch (maybe around Anika?)
- She and housekeeper Jyoti are definitely not coming clean about the phone (or body??) (who was Anika talking to?)

Samar

- Says launch was Vasudha's idea
- Was standing next to DB during the toast and didn't drink from the bottle
- Had a long relationship with Anika. Could have had a (very, *very* thin) motive to suppress the manuscript

Jemin

- Says launch was Shekhar's idea
- Owed Anika money—could be a motive there. Probably lying about financial status—his business is folding
- Was he in Anika's manuscript? He says he hasn't read it
- Anika was strangled with a House of Jems scarf (fake?)
- Disappeared during toast
- Thinks Vasudha did it
- Wasn't happy about us talking to Suleiman—why??

Question: Was DB the intended victim of Murder A? If not, who?

'Very . . . interesting,' said Mridula. 'You know notes are supposed to be objective? It's pretty clear you suspect Jemin.'

'Discounting Anika herself, he is *obviously* the forerunner here,' said Monami. 'He hated Anika; he had a number of motives there. He seemed to be planning something according to Kajal, and Anika was actually strangled with a House of Jems scarf or a knock-off which . . . I mean, it may be nothing, but it may also point to the murderer making a point. Which Jemin would, if he were guilty.'

'What's the point he would be making? *Police, arrest me, I did it?*' said Mridula. 'He'd be drawing attention to himself quite a bit. And what about a motive for DB?'

Monami shrugged. 'You did have an Option Two: the crimes aren't connected. Maybe DB was a mistake, and Jemin used it as an opportunity to get even with Anika.'

'Lots of speculation,' said Mridula. 'Do you mind if I add a few more questions?'

And to Monami's anguish, she reached over casually for her phone and started to type into it with one ponderous finger:

Question: Why is no one owning up to the launch idea?
Question: Why was Kajal in a terrible mood on the day of her launch?
Why was Jemin in such a good one?
Question: Why did Shekhar buy House of Jems?
Question: Where was Anika after the DB incident?
Question: When and where was she killed?
Question: Why did her family want her out of the family newspaper?

'Some of those questions aren't really questions,' said Monami, reading over her shoulder. 'Kajal and Jemin's moods, for instance?'

'It's just a point of interest,' said Mridula. 'Would you be in a good mood before planning a murder?'

'I would if I were insane,' said Monami, darkly.

'You think Jemin is insane?'

'I think this is an insane set of circumstances, and if I look around for who is most likely to be insane, well, it's him. And what about Shekhar buying House of Jems? Why is that a question?'

'It's another point of interest,' said Mridula, mildly. 'I find it interesting that Anika and Jemin were on such terrible terms, but her husband goes out and buys his company? A company that, despite what Jemin Sequeira says, doesn't seem to be doing terribly well. There's something there that we're not seeing.'

'The family business?'

'Another interesting thing. It's such an unusual step. Why?'

'It is interesting, but does it matter? I don't think it can have any bearing on who killed her. Also, it seems a little beyond the scope of the investigation, if you know what I mean. No, I think Jemin's the forerunner in Anika's murder. And as for DB, I'm sorry, but Anika's still the forerunner there. And now, I do have a theory about that intern.'

'Vasudha?'

'Yes. I think she was the accomplice. Kajal said she was out of her element. Even Jemin suspected her. Could it be that Vasudha wasn't implicated in Anika's death, but was actually Anika's accomplice? She could have put something in DB's drink while Anika was making herself very showily visible elsewhere? And then, maybe Jemin was right, she could have got it wrong in some way. I think someone said that she was inconsolable after DB's death. Maybe it didn't go the way she had planned.'

'So, you think that Anika paid her to put something in DB's drink?'

'I think it's a possibility, yes.'

'Doesn't say much for the girl. As you say, all fingers point to her. Why would she implicate herself in such a public way?'

'Maybe she needed money?'

'Doesn't seem like it. From my research . . .'

'Research?' interrupted Monami.

'Yes. I typed her name into Google.'

'What, with one finger? That must have taken a while.'

'Anyway,' said Mridula, taking the high road, 'she's from a very well-to-do family. Grew up in Laburnum—you know, that fancy complex in Gurgaon. Her father is one of those well-paid executives, it seems.'

'That might make her more mercenary than anything. A need to keep up that lifestyle.'

'Slightly on the character assassination side,' said Mridula. 'But I concede it's a theory. You've said something else interesting there . . . no, it's gone. But it'll come back. Just the smallest glimmer.'

'It does explain everything. Anika and Vasudha are responsible for DB's death,' said Monami, not to be side-tracked by glimmers. 'Meanwhile, Anika's death is explained with your own theory—the fact that someone else swooped in and took advantage of the chaos. Everyone was distracted. Maybe Anika stood outside and waited for Vasudha to come out so that they could, I don't know, debrief, or she could pay her, or something. Then, someone else, let's call them X, comes out and intercepts her. They exchange words—she's her usual Anika self, so it all goes downhill quite quickly. X strangles her. There,' finished Monami. 'Done and done.'

A family with two children wandered by, the mother throwing Mridula and the gesticulating Monami a curious glance. Monami wondered if any of their conversation had reached her, and what she might have made of it. She didn't seem unduly alarmed, though, and gently shepherded her children down the path until their whoops faded away.

'And X is Jemin?' said Mridula.

'X could be Jemin. I think so far, he's the likeliest.'

'You don't have a very long list of points next to Samar,' said Mridula. 'He passed your inspection? But if you think about the kind of relationship he had with Anika, he would be just as likely, if not more so, than Jemin.'

'I don't see Samar doing this,' said Monami.

'Yes, he has quite a way with him,' said Mridula. 'It makes all women very sympathetic to him, for some reason. But if you think about it, he's simply bursting with motives. The relationship. The book.'

'The book is the only thing that makes me question him,' said Monami, meditatively. 'We only have his word for it that there was nothing suspicious in it, and that he didn't care if it got published. He even said it could have been mildly embarrassing to him. Maybe he's understating it, and it would have been *wildly* embarrassing.'

'Yes. If you think about it, at this point, it could really be any of them. Kajal was no fan of Anika, who insulted her book. She runs upstairs after DB's death, runs into Anika, and acts instantly. Afterwards, she's horrified at what she's done—but still. *She kills her.*

'Samar. He and Anika went way back. There are deep waters there, deeper than you or I could possibly know. He essentially told us as much. He has his reasons—he doesn't want to publish her memoirs, she's becoming a nuisance, he's fallen out of love with her—take your pick. But again, the result is the same. He takes advantage of the chaos. *He kills her.*

'And now. Jemin. As you said, the likeliest of the lot. They have history. He needs money. Anika's putting pressure on him to pay up. He runs into her when the others are toasting, or outside. They have words, round two of the battle they'd already begun on the lawn. And this time it's too much. He loses control. *He kills her.*'

Mridula paused to take a breath and stole a look to see how her audience was taking it. Monami should have been wide-eyed, but she merely nodded phlegmatically. She was starting to get the hang of this gig.

'I agree. I still think Old Cashew Nut is the least likely, and I can't see Samar doing it either. But I agree we can't rule them out yet.'

'And that's not even the end of the suspect list.'

'It's not?'

'No. That list doesn't count those who may have had a motive for DB too.'

'What do you mean? That's only Anika, isn't it? Who else had a motive to kill DB?'

'Can't you think of anyone? We're missing some names from the office, don't you think?'

'Who?' asked Monami, bluntly. 'You don't mean—'

'I mean Ishaan, Devika and Tina specifically. They were all there. They all seem to have conveniently disappeared when DB was killed. Where were they?'

Monami snorted. 'Wherever they were, they couldn't have had anything to do with it.'

'All three of them had motives for getting DB out of the way, too,' said Mridula calmly.

'What?' Mridula was gratified to note that Monami looked wide-eyed now. 'What do you mean?'

'Well, let's say Devika and Ishaan were plotting to kill Anika,' said Mridula, raising her voice to drown out Monami's immediate reaction of incredulity. '*DB could have corroborated their motive for killing her*. Being their boss, he knew, more than anyone, how much Devika hated her. All the details, all the little slights and her emails to him full of bitter complaints about her. Of course, she didn't know he bcc-ed me on all emails, so I know too. But still. She couldn't have known that. She could have thought that the extent of it would have died with DB.'

Monami fell silent.

'And Tina? Her name hasn't come up yet, but she's probably the only one who *actually* had a motive for DB.'

'Tina?' Monami stared at her.

ii

Unaware that their names were being dragged through the mud in this cavalier fashion, the features team of the *Delhi Daily* were eating cold samosas in the office cafeteria.

'No one seems to be getting anywhere,' said Ishaan.

'Everyone's just scared,' said Devika. 'I'm scared. The most plausible explanation is still that it's someone who's just crazed. It could be someone in this very office.'

They all looked at each other. Tina said, with a ghost of a smile: 'It's such a shame it can't be Mridula. She fits the bill so well.'

'I know, and if you think about it, isn't it suspicious that she wasn't there? It's almost as though she was giving herself an alibi.'

'But if she was, she did,' observed Ishaan gloomily.

'Still. She's the likeliest person.'

'It's usually the least likely person,' said Karthik.

'Then it would be you, Karthik,' said Devika. Karthik looked taken aback.

That was when Shamik walked in, and this banter abruptly ceased as the same thought seemed to occur to all of them at once.

'How about Shamik?' said Devika, under her breath. 'He's another likely suspect, no? How much do we really know about him?'

'Aw, you girls are always laying into him,' said Ishaan, but he sounded uncertain. 'I agree he's . . . well, he can be weird, but he's harmless. He may have bored them to death, but I can't see him doing anything more violent than that.'

'I don't know. I always said he looked like a serial killer,' murmured Tina. 'He'd probably have a motive for Anika, too. She was always so rude to him.'

'Isn't that jumping to conclusions?' said Ishaan. 'I mean, I agree we don't know much about him, but that's because we don't really hang out with him.'

'He's definitely odd, which is probably why we don't hang out with him.'

'Not the same thing as assuming he's a murderer.'

'Also,' said Devika, 'if hating Anika is a motive, then we all had one. I mean, I know it's horrible to be killed like that, but really, she was the worst.'

'Oh no, he's coming this way!' hissed Tina. 'Quick, pretend to be discussing the case!'

'We *are* discussing the case,' said Ishaan.

Shamik was one of those unfortunate people who wanted to be social but was always finding himself on the periphery of social groups. This was partly due to his age, as he was a good ten years or so older than most of the young features team, and partly due to his earnestness, a trait that the group tolerated in their youngest member, Karthik, but saw as faintly distasteful in someone who in their eyes was practically an Uncle. However, they tolerated him; as Ishaan had said, they generally thought he was harmless, and also, he had a soft spot for Tina, which, together with Tina's clear annoyance about this fact, was an endless source of amusement to the entire office.

He now wandered up to them with a studied nonchalance.

'Talking about the case?'

'Isn't everyone?' said Tina shortly.

'I, too, am thinking about the case. Mind if I join you?'

Everyone made neutral noises and shuffled their feet as Shamik slipped into an empty chair at their table.

'I was upstairs on the balcony,' said Shamik, abruptly. 'I . . . I watched DB as he died.'

Everyone had been showing signs of restlessness, but fell quiet at this. Even Tina thawed a little.

'Oh?' she said.

'Yes. It . . . it was quite a strange and unique vantage point. I could see the whole garden. In fact, I stopped watching him, and I started watching everyone else,' said Shamik. 'I watched you, for instance, Tina.'

'Me?' Tina froze again. 'Why did you watch me?'

'I was watching everyone,' said Shamik. 'I watched Anika clomping around on the balcony. She was making a lot of noise, and sort of whisper-shouting into her phone. But when . . . when it happened, my attention was attracted to the garden. And I watched . . . I watched everyone's faces. And I noticed you. You were watching too.'

'Me?'

'Yes,' said Shamik, almost dreamily, unaware of the rising hostility with which Tina was looking at him. 'You had such an interesting look on your face. It was as though you were expecting something to happen. And, when it *did* happen, you seemed rooted to the spot. You weren't upset, you didn't start forward, you just stayed there, staring.'

'Shut up, Shamik,' said Tina. 'You're talking nonsense. Even for you.'

Shamik looked as though he had been abruptly brought back to earth.

'Oh. Oh, I'm sorry. I don't mean anything was *wrong*. In fact, if you'd been more upset, it would have seemed so disingenuous. I . . . I admired your restraint. You know, with the history you and your father had with DB . . .'

'What history?' said Devika, looking between Shamik and Tina. There was a tense silence, which Shamik seemed to finally grow aware of.

'Oh . . . oh, I thought everyone was aware. We're all friends here . . .' Shamik grew more and more flustered. 'I . . . forgive me. I didn't mean to say the wrong thing.'

'It's probably best you don't say any more,' said Tina in a low voice. She stood up. 'Also, we're *not* friends.'

She turned away with such force that her chair fell over with a clatter. Without bothering to pick it up, she marched out of the cafeteria, leaving her friends and Shamik staring after her.

'Oh dear,' said Shamik, sounding genuinely dismayed. 'I'm always saying the wrong thing.'

iii

'Tina?' repeated Monami. 'What motive would she have had?'

'Yes, I think, actually, if anyone at that party would have had a motive for killing DB, it would have been Tina.'

Monami gaped at her. 'Why?'

'She never told you? About her parents?'

Monami shook her head.

'Her father was a very senior journalist in Delhi, many years ago. You've heard of Mukesh Shah, no?'

'Vaguely,' said Monami, wrinkling her eyes. 'Who was he?'

'Well, he was Tina's father. That is what's pertinent here. He was arrested for extortion—back in 2015 or 2016, I think. Tried to blackmail a politician into paying him to not publish damaging news. It was DB who broke the story that led to his arrest.'

Monami was silent. This was all news to her. And she considered Tina a close friend.

'The fact is that while her father was undoubtedly guilty, the sting itself was borderline. Many people at the time said that it was illegal—journalists wearing wires, pretending to be something else to trap someone into doing or saying something. It's not quite kosher.'

'I had no idea.'

'Well, I think DB felt guilty about it on some level. He reached out to the family afterwards, and offered Tina a job at the *Delhi Daily*. I think only a handful of us knew about it. She's changed her name and everything, hasn't she?'

'Yes,' said Monami, slowly. 'She's definitely not a . . . what did you say? Shah?'

'And she does stand out in one way—from the very beginning. She wasn't part of the toasting group, she says she watched it from a distance, and that it looked like a play. I thought that was very interesting, back then. And, of course, she had a motive for Anika, too.'

'Anika?'

'Yes. Because of her family, Anika was one of the few people who knew about Tina's history. And bad enough as that might have been, it must have been further complicated by the . . . well, the Samar angle. Did she know about his relationship with Anika?'

'Even if she did. To go from that to strangling her! She's not . . . I mean, she's not a psychopath. And anyway . . . ' Monami paused, struggling to put her thoughts into words. 'You yourself said that murders aren't committed out of hate alone. Remember? It has to be something more immediate, more urgent.'

'I agree,' said Mridula, using her dupatta to wipe off the droplets of sweat on her forehead, and pointing it at Monami's phone. 'I agree. But there's a whole *Delhi Daily* angle that we can't afford to ignore. They need to be on your list.'

Monami continued to shake her head. 'No,' she said. 'I can see Anika paying someone. I can see Anika paying this Gurgaon chick. But Tina? No, it doesn't make any sense.'

'You're assuming it had to have been Vasudha putting the poison in DB's drink. Remember there was a whole *Delhi Daily* crowd there. She could have persuaded anyone to do it on her behalf. Remember that Samar said that on the other side of DB was a boy with glasses. That could have been any of them, even one of the girls in dim light could have looked like a boy with glasses. And maybe she didn't tell them what her real plan was. Maybe she said it was just a prank, that it was *bhang* or something.'

Monami was reduced to silence. This was worryingly plausible.

Many of the *Delhi Daily* crowd who had been there that night might have been amused by the idea of a prank, only to be scared into silence when things got out of hand.

'I find it interesting that Devika and Ishaan were absent from the toast, too,' Mridula went on. 'All three of them—Tina, Devika, Ishaan. What is stopping us from suspecting all three of them from being X?'

Reluctantly, Monami added the three names to her list.

Tina. Devika. Ishaan.

'Right. That's the office. We're still missing one name. Maybe the most important one of all.'

'Vasudha?'

Mridula nodded. 'She's either the culprit, or she's a victim. We have to find out which. And . . .'

Monami waited patiently. Surely there couldn't be more people to add to the list. It was long enough.

'All our theories about X. All these suspects,' said Mridula, finally. 'None of them answer any of the questions.'

She pointed at the questions she had just added to Monami's one:

Question: Was DB the intended victim of Murder A? If not, who?
Question: Why is no one owning up to the launch idea?
Question: Why was Kajal in a terrible mood on the day of her launch? Why was Jemin in such a good one?
Question: Why did Shekhar buy House of Jems?
Question: Where was Anika after the DB incident?
Question: When and where was she killed?
Question: Why did her family want her out of the family newspaper?

'Are the questions important?' said Monami, exasperated.

'Remember why we started down this path. We wanted to use our imaginations. That's what the police won't do. And I can't help thinking that there's a whole dimension we're still missing. We need to dig much more deeply into Anika's background. By all accounts, she was going through a difficult time. Her family asked her to leave a long-standing job. She writes a book, which she can't get published. Her husband buys a company from someone she has an ongoing feud with. I think Samar was right that she was at the end of whatever rope she had. What frame of mind was she in at the party?'

'The kind to commit murder?' said Monami, hopefully.

Mridula shook her head. 'After all that, you think she would have set her sights on murdering DB? I rather think not,' said Mridula. 'She may have been in a murderous mood in general. But why would *he* have been her target?'

'The face of the family action to oust her?' suggested Monami.

Mridula shook her head again. 'She would have known that he was working on her family's orders. And that explains why she handled herself so well at our meeting, by the way. I doubt she would have taken such immediate revenge on DB. From the way she used her column to settle scores, Anika knew better than most that revenge is a dish best served cold.'

'So, what do you think, then?

'I don't know. All we know about her at the party is that she was her usual arrogant self. Going after Kajal's book. Going after Jemin. But was she just going through the motions? Playing a starring role in the film "Being Anika"? We have to find out what was on her mind. I think we have to go visit her family.'

'Would they see us?' said Monami, doubtfully.

'The father would,' said Mridula.

'How can you be so sure?'

'Because he just emailed me to ask for a meeting,' said Mridula, smugly.

20

Tunnel Vision

As they made their way back to their office, the rain came down again, and as so often happens in the Delhi monsoon, the water started to rise in the roads and underpasses and traffic drew to a crawl. Mridula drove carefully, leaning forward, glasses on her nose, peering with a particularly peeved expression at the car in front of her as they inched along.

Monami was glad of the silence, as she felt apprehensive about the meeting ahead. The powerful Abhishek Kapoor, whose face had glowered at her from many magazine covers. What would he be like?

They had to park a little way away from the office and run to the entrance. By the time they got to Mridula's office, they were bedraggled, and Mridula looked even grumpier. The young man who sat at the front desk chased after them.

'Er, ma'am, Kapoor sir has come, and he's in your office!'

'Yes, yes, we know.'

'He's been sitting there for a while.'

'Okay, thanks.'

'Shall I ask the boy to bring some coffee?'

'That Nescafé stuff? If there's nothing else, then yes. And maybe some of those butter biscuits.'

'Okay.' Still looking alarmed, the receptionist raced off. A visit from Abhishek Kapoor was not an everyday occurrence.

They entered the office, and Mr Kapoor got up from a chair. He was, to Monami's surprise, smaller than she had pictured. She had expected that he would tower over them, but here he was, maybe half a head taller, no more. And the recent tragedy (she assumed) had made him look somehow shrunken and frail. His cheeks had caved in and the bags under his eyes could have held a week's worth of groceries.

'Mr Kapoor,' said Mridula, briskly. 'So sorry to keep you waiting. The rain.'

'Yes,' said Abhishek. 'No problem.'

Normally, he was a stickler for punctuality, and he surprised even himself with this response. But he had honestly not noticed the time ticking by, lost as he was in his thoughts about how to approach this conversation. His wife and his daughter seemed to be sitting on each shoulder, shouting opposing instructions at each other over his head.

'Thank you, first of all, for suggesting this meeting,' said Mridula, taking charge. Monami was impressed at her tone, so efficient, so purposeful, so different from her usual demeanour at work meetings, which fell more into the general begrudging and resignation area. 'We were very happy to get your email. We've been hoping to get a chance to connect and talk about what happened to Anika, and to DB. I think you could shed a lot of light on the matter.'

This seemed to genuinely surprise Abhishek.

'Me?' he said. 'I'm just as much in the dark as anyone. More so, in fact. This whole thing has come as a bombshell. My wife . . .' he trailed off, and then fell silent.

Mridula shot Monami a look, and Monami knew what she meant—again, with this peek into Anika's family mourning her. In death, Anika was coming to life for Monami.

'I can understand, this must be very difficult,' said Mridula, using the same tone now that she had with Samar. 'But you can tell us things about Anika. Things that may prove essential.'

'My daughter wanted me to bring my lawyer,' said Abhishek, as though he hadn't heard. 'But I decided not to.'

'Oh?' said Mridula, going with it. 'Your lawyer? Why?'

'You ask why? This is an emotional matter for the family. It's imperative that we have control over what . . . what is said about us. About our daughter.'

'I see,' said Mridula, and fell silent. Clearly this man had something he wanted to say, some reason he was here. It was maybe not the reason she had thought.

'But I didn't want to bring my lawyer,' said the old man again. 'I wanted to talk to you privately. This is a very sensitive issue. You see?'

'I think I see,' said Mridula.

'I hear from the other editors that you are investigating this matter.'

'Yes, that's right. And Monami here.' Mridula nodded at Monami, but Abhishek continued to look only at her, as though Monami wasn't there. Normally she would be outraged at this Indian-uncle behaviour, but she decided to give him a pass. The man was clearly suffering.

'May I ask if you've come to any conclusions?'

'Of course you may. Unfortunately, we have not,' said Mridula. 'We've found out a few things, and I have been sharing them with the police. You may know that we found Anika's phone outside Kajal's house, and I handed it over to DCP Akshay Kumar.' Monami couldn't suppress the slight smirk that always arose at the mention of this name. She quickly looked away as she felt Mridula's glare on her. 'He was . . . well, he was less than gracious about it, I must say. Seemed to think we were getting in the way.'

'Yes. Yes, the police can be difficult,' said Abhishek. 'But I've just come from a meeting with the Deputy Commissioner. He's not a bad man. I encourage you to work with him.'

'Of course. We have no reason not to work with the police.' Mridula suppressed a grin, thinking back to her recent interview with the DCP, and imagining his reaction if she offered up her services as a colleague.

'They are pursuing one angle quite diligently. Do you know about that?'

Mridula hesitated. 'It's difficult to say, since we don't have an inside track with them. We're getting all our news from, well, the news. If I had to guess, I would say Mr Jemin Sequeira.'

'You're right,' said Abhishek. 'Why did you think Mr Sequeira?'

'Because he's the most convenient,' said Mridula.

'Ah. Nothing else? No evidence has led you that way so far?'

'My colleague and I have just been discussing the case,' said Mridula, rather impressively. 'And we've been making out quite a good case against quite a few people. There's really nothing to single anyone out—yet.'

'Quite a few people.' Abhishek sighed, and looked at the floor. Monami felt desperately sorry for him. She knew what he was thinking: what they had all, at some point or another, thought about this case. 'The DCP said the same. Personal enmities, professional enmities. Legal cases against her. So many enemies for her to have had. So many people who might have wanted to kill her! It's incredible.'

Mridula tactfully remained silent, and watched Abhishek as he followed his train of thought.

'And we, her parents, not aware. I'm . . . this has been so hard for us. I hope you understand.'

'I do,' said Mridula, patiently. 'Can I ask . . . what do you think about the police's angle? Do you agree with it?'

Abhishek took his time before answering.

'The fashion designer,' he said, finally, 'and my daughter had a complicated relationship. They were good friends once. We've had Jemin over to the house countless times when they were in school. Samar Chishti too. Another name that has been brought up in this regard. It's inconceivable to me that one of them could be responsible for this.' He shook his head.

'So, you don't agree with it?'

Surprisingly, Abhishek shook his head again. 'Ah, now I don't say that, I don't quite say that. That was many years ago. Who knows what might have changed since then? Adults always have more complicated relationships than children. Something could have turned in them, turned them against each other.'

Mridula and Monami waited. Monami couldn't really understand what he was getting at. So he didn't think it was Jemin. Did he think it was Samar?

'The police theory,' continued Abhishek, 'as far as I can make out, is that while poor DB was dying, Jemin Sequeira sought out my daughter, and killed her. Then he solicited the help of some of Kajal Puri's staff and, together, they concealed the body. When the coast was clear, they laid her in the street.' His voice took on the monotone of a newsreader.

'And . . . and you want us to disprove this?' asked Mridula.

'I want you to continue your investigation,' said Abhishek simply. 'I want you to talk to everyone you can think of. And I want you to report back to me.'

'I see. You want us to report directly back to you. What if we find out something we think you may not like to know?'

Abhishek gave a humourless chuckle. 'What can I possibly not like to know now? No, I want to know everything.'

'May I ask . . . why? If you don't want us to disprove the police theory, then . . . why?'

'The police,' said Abhishek, 'have what we call tunnel vision. No? They would like to tie up a case nicely and neatly with a bow. They find a likely explanation. They pursue it, to the exclusion of all else. That is not what I want. No, what I want is the truth. You understand?'

'I . . . think so. You think it may be as they say, but you're not convinced. Is that right?'

'Yes, exactly. I want to understand all the possibilities. I want to understand what could have happened, what we can rule out, what must have happened. And I may have disproportionate faith in our country's media,' Abhishek's voice took on a tone that Monami felt must have been his more natural way of speaking, as the phrases fell easily now from his lips, 'but I think that we are the ones to do that. Not the police, who frankly can be inept, with all due respect to them. No, it must be us. The media. That's what makes our nation, our democracy, great.'

Monami could see why he was a titan of industry. If she were younger or less jaded, she might have wanted to applaud.

However, as usual Mridula seemed unmoved. 'Well, we have no arguments with that at all. That is essentially why we have wanted to pursue this case, too. To find out the truth. For both Anika and DB, who was a beloved colleague at the *Delhi Daily*. But for us to do that, Mr Kapoor, we need some information from you. Can you answer some questions for us?'

At this, the wind seemed to go out of Abhishek's sails, whether it was the implication that he had overlooked the death of DB so far in their meeting, the further implication that DB had been a beloved colleague while Anika had not, or the prospect of questions, Monami could not be sure.

Either way, he faltered out: 'Questions? For me?'

'Yes. I think it would very much help to establish Anika's frame of mind on the day she died. That very morning, for instance, my colleague DB and I had to undertake the rather unpleasant task of breaking the news to her that she would no longer hold her long-term editorial position at this newspaper. My colleague DB's opinion was that this decision came ultimately from her family, only to be handed down by him. I wanted to ask you, is that true?'

Abhishek did not respond. He didn't look alarmed or indignant, he just looked at her, as though waiting to see what she would say next. And Mridula pressed on: 'This book, now, also. We understand that this book, which was not going to be published by Sea Lion, but which she may have published elsewhere, painted your family in a negative light, and could have been a source of much unpleasantness, if not cause an actual downturn in your business fortunes. Now, my question to you is, did you ask DB to relieve her of her position at the paper as a result of this book? Or was it the other way around? What was your relationship really like with your daughter?'

It was at this moment, when Abhishek's face seemed to turn to wax, that the receptionist opened the door, poked his head inside and said heartily, 'Coffee? I have biscuits!' When no one responded, he carefully opened the door, trying to balance a tray of cookies in his other hand, and ushered two office boys in. They shuffled in, eyes down, and placed three saucers and three cups in front of Abhishek, Mridula and Monami. Then one of them brought in an oversized flask and started, slowly, carefully, to pour coffee into each cup. Monami thought she saw his lips move in silent prayer. When this fraught exercise was completed without incident, the receptionist, with a grand final flourish, placed the biscuits on a small table, and then, finally becoming conscious of the lack of response and the glassy-eyed look of the VIP guest, backed uncertainly away.

'Er, enjoy,' he said, and shut the door carefully behind him.

This little interlude seemed to have given Abhishek the space that he needed to answer Mridula's questions. As the door closed behind the trio, he said, with a sharper tone than Monami had heard from him yet, 'May I ask why you want to know all these things? These are private, internal affairs. Family affairs.'

'We think they have a bearing on the crime,' said Mridula.

'How can they?' asked Abhishek. 'How can these things have any bearing on the crime?'

'It would explain Anika's frame of mind. It would explain her actions.'

'Her actions did not get her killed,' said Abhishek, frowning. 'Maybe it was a mistake to come here.'

'Excuse me,' said Mridula. 'You have just asked us to investigate, to do what the police will not. We have done exactly that, and we are now doing what you've also asked us to do—laying those findings in front of you. Our investigations have led us to these questions, and we believe that this is how we will find out what *did* happen, not what may have happened. This is the downside of having a free and open media.' Mridula gave a dry chuckle. 'They will always find out some uncomfortable truths. We still have something of a functioning media in this country, as you so eloquently said just now. And this is what we bring to you, warts and all.'

Although Mridula's words and delivery weren't as grand as Abhishek's, Monami felt a warm flush of pride wash over her at them. She marvelled again at Mridula's hidden talents. Where was all this depth of thought, of feeling, usually? She kept them buried away under that brusque manner, and the array of snorts. A philosopher in a rhino's skin.

Even Abhishek seemed to be swayed by her words. He continued to look at her thoughtfully for a while, and then gave a dry chuckle of his own.

'Well, well. Maybe you're right. I knew there was a reason I came to you, to this paper. The *Delhi Daily*. DB's paper,' he said, musingly. 'He reinvented it, you know. It used to be mostly about gossip, page three. He changed it to be more . . . well, more of the paper you describe. Uncovering truths. The pursuit of justice. Yes, there's a reason I didn't go to my TV channels. I came here. And maybe you're right.'

They waited for him to say more, but he seemed to have gone underwater, to have sunk back into his own thoughts again.

'I can only tell you,' he finally said, haltingly, 'that it's not what it seems. Things are not how they appear. Now that I've heard your side of it, I can see that we must have come off as most heartless, to you and your colleague, DB.'

He paused here and sighed so heavily that Monami felt like reaching out to him to pat his knee.

'I can only tell you,' he said again, 'that I wasn't pushing her out. Oh, no. It was the other way around.'

'The other way around?' asked Mridula, tentatively. She also seemed to understand that Abhishek Kapoor was in the grip of some powerful emotion, and she didn't want to upset this precarious balance.

Abhishek put a large hand up to his forehead and kept it there.

'Yes. I *was* trying to push her—but I was pushing her to come closer to the family business. I felt that she was wasting her life with her connection with this paper. In the beginning, I thought she may have wanted to lead it someday. But, over the years, it slowly became clear that that wouldn't happen. Her columns, the controversies . . . they didn't drum up publicity for the paper, and they didn't help our business. If anything, the opposite. I had fallings out with friends, I had business relationships break over it. I never confronted her though, I thought she would come around to seeing it my way.'

'But she didn't see it your way,' Mridula said softly.

'She didn't see it my way,' agreed Anika's father. 'She thought I was old-fashioned. And she could be incredibly stubborn. As I'm sure you both know.' He directed a rueful smile at them both.

'But what she couldn't see is that her talents didn't lie in writing. She had wanted to be some sort of cultural influence, but she wasn't. Her books, I was told, always got publicity but sales were modest. I don't deny that she had some notoriety, though it seemed to do more harm than good. But if she had been trained, guided, she would have been a . . . a force to be reckoned with in business. She was quite ruthless. And at the same time, she was loyal to her family, to her principles. Whatever you say, I am sure that she would never have published that manuscript. If anything, it may have been a last hurrah on her part, something to get out of her system, before she finally came back into the fold.'

The old man seemed to grow even older by the end of this speech. He looked at them both and gave another sad smile.

'You probably think that this is just wishful thinking from an old man full of regrets. But it's true. And so I can tell you with utmost certainty that her state of mind, as you put it, on that last day, wasn't as dire as you may think. She understood from the meeting with DB and yourself that it was a message from me. But it wasn't the message you may have thought it to be. She knew, from a conversation we had had last week, that I was waiting to welcome her back into the family business. She just had to say the word.'

'I see,' said Mridula, still cautiously.

'If you don't believe me, go speak to Shekhar. And speak to my daughter, Anita.'

'That would be very helpful, thank you. And thank you for everything you've shared today. It's more helpful than you know.'

Abhishek looked at her. 'I'm not sure I should have. But I'm more emotional nowadays than I have ever been.' He sighed again. 'It's probably a good thing I didn't bring my lawyer.'

21

Detritus from Another Planet

Shekhar and Anika's palatial apartment wasn't far, and about twenty minutes later they were pulling up to a sleek gate. Amid Jor Bagh's wide avenues full of enormous shady trees, Mridula's Maruti Wagon R seemed smaller, ricketier, the once jaunty red paint even more faded.

They were ushered in by a smart-looking housekeeper, who didn't ask any questions. And now—here they were. The late afternoon sun seemed to have a different quality than it had in Sunder Nursery. There, it had been more golden, more alive. Here, it slanted rather coyly and self-consciously through the louvres of wooden shutters. One of the shutters, slightly ajar, revealed a blaze of pink bougainvillaea. Inside, though, the room was shorn of colour—everything was white, beige and sepia-toned. Even the light as it filtered in, faltered and turned pale.

Monami considered the space, as she had considered the others. She and Mridula were alone, and, usually, when left alone in fancy apartments, she was an inveterate wanderer and looker. She would examine expensive-looking knick-knacks, handle them gingerly like rare detritus from another planet. But here, she somehow didn't like to, and contented herself with just a few furtive glances.

It was a beautiful apartment, decorated sparely in a somewhat traditional fashion: a Mughal miniature here, a 'modern' bronze sculpture there. But it didn't seem lived in. The books on the shelves, for instance, were piled horizontally, one on top of another and colour-coordinated, suggesting a kind of affected artistic sensibility, but also that they were never pulled out and read. The sofas were simply stiff with cushions. One felt obliged to sit, as Monami and Mridula did, on the edge with back upright, leaning forward awkwardly to sip the tea that had been placed on the rather distant coffee table.

She tried to imagine Anika and Shekhar living here, the cocktail parties they would host, the low hum of polite conversation. She could imagine it easily, high heels on the carpet, smokers on the balcony, the quiet laughter and cigarette smoke carrying out into the manicured parks beyond.

What she couldn't imagine, though, was them sitting alone together, perhaps sharing some tea on the sofa or talking about their day. It wasn't that kind of room.

They had been waiting for about ten minutes when the door opened, and Shekhar came in. Monami stood up. Mridula didn't, whether on purpose or because her low perch made this physically impossible, the world would never know.

'Hi. Thanks so much for seeing us,' Monami said, as the one standing member of their partnership. They shook hands. Up close, Shekhar was very handsome, as Devika and Jemin had said, still broad of shoulder and trim of waist. One thing their investigation was certainly doing was opening her up to a side of Delhi that had apparently been hidden from her all this time. The Delhi of Handsome Men, just wandering around as though they lived here.

'Thank you for coming,' Shekhar said, gravely. He was dressed casually, in a cotton kurta and white pyjamas. There was no outward sign of mourning, apart from a faint tiredness, and a tendency for his gaze, which Monami could imagine was usually quite direct, to wander off. He ran his hand through his hair. 'I hope it wasn't too out of your way.'

'Oh, no,' said Monami, and could feel Mridula give her a stern look. She sat back down and tried to sound less earnest. 'We were just in the office. At ITO, you know.'

'Ah, yes. Without traffic, that's quite a short ride.'

'Yes, there wasn't any, now that the rain has stopped.' Feeling herself start to ramble, Monami clammed up.

Shekhar nodded absently and sat down opposite them. He leaned forward a little. His looks were smoother, more deliberately styled than Suleiman's appealing boho scruffiness, and the whole effect was not really Monami's type. ('The suited-and-booted type,' as her father would put it, 'Not for our Monami! If he looks like he's got a steady income, forget about it.' He would then laugh uproariously, but her mother somehow would not.) But in this intimate space, with the light slowly fading, he certainly created an effect, like one of those upright Bollywood heroes with good hair who pine but will not act unless the match is thoroughly approved by all the ancestors on both sides of the family. Nerdy but wholesome, and with a certain sex appeal, as Devika had said, all the same.

'Are you working with the police?'

'Not technically,' said Mridula, managing to give the impression that they definitely were. 'We're conducting our own investigation at the *Delhi Daily*. It's two of our own.'

Shekhar nodded, and fell silent again, whether waiting for them to speak or thinking something through, Monami couldn't tell. But Mridula seemed in no hurry to begin either, and there was a pause which stretched over a minute until finally, Shekhar sighed, and leaned back again.

'Okay,' he said. 'I know the police are going in a specific direction. It would be interesting to hear where you're going. And if Abhishek says I can help, well then . . . just tell me how.'

'Thank you. If you don't mind, let's start with the book launch.'

This wasn't a question, but Shekhar didn't seem to notice.

'I didn't even want to go. I wish we hadn't,' he said. 'Anika loved this whole scene—book launches, parties, you know. But I said to her that we didn't have to schlep all the way to Chhattarpur. This Kajal woman was a colleague but hardly a friend. Still, Anika was determined to go. She wasn't one to miss out on parties, even kind of lame ones.'

He used Americanisms like 'schlep' and 'lame' with ease. His accent was inflected with the usual faint American twang that educated Indians these days seem to have, particularly ones that have been brought up more on Hollywood than Bollywood.

'I understand you were actually a sponsor?'

'I? Oh, I see what you mean. Jemin was a sponsor, yes. I don't really get involved in the day-to-day of these operations. And I certainly don't feel like I need to go to every marketing event.'

'Ah, I see,' said Mridula, her tone carefully neutral. 'But the sponsorship was your idea, wasn't it?'

Shekhar raised his eyebrows at this. 'My idea? Not at all.'

'Oh, when we spoke to Jemin, he said it was,' said Mridula. 'If not yours, then whose idea was it, do you know?'

'I'm not sure, now that I think about it.' He seemed surprised at the turn the conversation was taking. 'I assumed it had come from the publisher, to try and wangle some budget.'

'And you were happy to oblige?'

'I suppose I was. We're always looking for innovative marketing angles for Jems. This seemed like one. The budget wasn't exactly large, you know. Vasudha was able to pull it off on what we'd consider the equivalent of a shoestring. Although the publisher may not have thought of it that way,' added Shekhar with a small smile.

'Ah, Vasudha. It wasn't her idea, by any chance?' said Mridula.

'I really couldn't tell you,' said Shekhar, frowning slightly. 'She may have made the connection between Jems and Sea Lion. But I will say that if it was anyone's idea, it was most probably Samar's, or maybe even Jemin's. They may have thought it up between them.'

'Why do you say that?'

Shekhar shrugged. 'It wasn't really a . . . a business idea, if I can put it that way. At the end of the day, I think they just wanted a party, and this was the only way they could figure out that someone else would pay for it.'

A glance passed between Monami and Mridula. *The buck is passed, yet again.*

'I see. And you were willing to pay for it?'

'It wasn't very much, as I said,' said Shekhar. 'And frankly, House of Jems is losing so much money that this would be just a drop in the ocean. Maybe on some level I thought I should let Jemin have a last hurrah before we really got down to brass tacks, as it were.'

'Jemin is under the impression that House of Jems is doing very well,' said Mridula.

Shekhar laughed. 'No, really, he can't be. Not even Jemin would be that oblivious. Why, we've had to close stores all over the place. To be honest with you, we're quite close to just going entirely online, save some overhead.'

'Interesting. And so you were happy for the children to have one last party.'

'If you put it that way,' said Shekhar. 'What's the angle here, anyway? Why are you asking about the sponsorship? Do you think it's relevant?'

'Can you tell us in your own words what happened at the party?' said Mridula, ignoring this question.

'I didn't really stick around for very long,' said Shekhar. 'I had a flight to catch. Besides, Anika immediately got into it with Samar and Jemin, and almost immediately after, I had to leave.'

'She didn't want to leave with you?' said Mridula.

'No. I was going straight to the airport, and she said she would stick around and get a lift with someone. She had quite a few friends there—publishers, writers, you know. They all stick together. And . . .' He paused, before adding rather heavily, 'And, to be honest, she wasn't wholly pleasant to be around when she was in that mood so I, well, I kind of left her to it.'

'She didn't give you any other reason for wanting to stay behind?' said Mridula, now gazing at the ceiling.

'No. It did occur to me that maybe she wanted to get into it with Samar and Jemin again . . . which, if anything, spurred on my departure,' said Shekhar.

'What did she "get into it" with them about? Do you know?'

Shekhar sighed heavily. 'The usual thing. I suppose you've heard about those damn memoirs by now. The news channels seem to have cottoned on to them. She wanted Sea Lion to publish them, and they weren't. So, she was being fairly unpleasant to Samar. And Jemin . . . well, he was just being Jemin, which didn't help. Rubbing it in.'

'I see.'

There was another brief pause. Shekhar looked at his hands. Monami looked at Shekhar. Mridula finally took her gaze off the ceiling and looked at him too.

'I know what you're thinking,' said Shekhar. 'And, well, I don't want to go into it here, obviously. It's very personal. But we weren't in a good place, I'm afraid.'

'I'm so sorry,' said Monami.

'Thank you. It—it's very painful to talk about, as you can imagine. I . . . I just wish we'd had a better goodbye. I wish I'd at least tried to make her come home with me rather than, rather than—' here he seemed to falter a little, 'feeling relieved to go. To get on a plane. Yes, I felt relieved.' He looked at them both, miserably.

Monami wondered again at how their interviews seemed to draw the most personal feelings from people. She couldn't imagine Shekhar offering up this little titbit to DCP Akshay Kumar, for instance. And yet here he was, laying bare his soul, as it were, to the two of them. Two people he'd never met before.

'Forgive me for asking, but had you had . . . any particular fight recently? Or were there any . . . specific problems in your marriage?'

'No, no, nothing specific,' said Shekhar, raising his eyebrows slightly.

'How did she feel about you acquiring the House of Jems, for instance? I understand she was not fond of Jemin Sequeira.'

'Oh, I see,' said Shekhar. 'That was all nonsense. I made her see that. Why should I let a business opportunity go because of some childish spat? It was a perfect strategic buy at the time, and which I got more or less for a song. She didn't like it, as a matter of fact, but, well, she was sensible and saw it my way in the end.'

For Monami, the spell cracked a little and for a second, she saw another man in front of her. Someone as hard as nails, who was used to getting his way, especially when it came to his business. Once again, she wondered what life had really been like for the woman who had been so tough in the office, so abrasive and brittle.

Mridula also seemed struck by Shekhar's casual assertion of dominance. 'I see. And what about this book she was writing? Had you read it?'

'Ah, the book,' said Shekhar. He seemed now to be on more familiar ground, as though this was more the type of question he had been expecting. 'Yes. The family wasn't happy with Ms Prachi Mehra for raising that on television, let me tell you.'

'I'm sure the police would have caught wind of it anyway,' said Mridula.

'Would they? I really don't think it's that relevant either. What do you want to know about it, anyway?'

'Had you read it?'

'I had . . . glanced through, yes.'

Mridula waited for a beat and then asked, 'And what do you think of this theory that the news is peddling, that a motive for her murder could be to get this book out of circulation? To stop it from being published?'

Shekhar shook his head decidedly.

'The purest melodrama,' he said. 'First of all, it's not out of circulation. I'm sure the publisher still has it. We just have to ask Avi, er, Aviroop, you know, the Sea Lion CEO. And er, I'm really not sure it would have been published anyway, but even if it were it's certainly not a motive for murder.'

'What do you mean? Do you think she wouldn't have found another publisher?'

Shekhar hesitated, and said, a little slowly, 'I know you've just come from Abhishek. I don't know what impression he left you with, but he was fairly adamant that it wouldn't get published. And, if my experience with this family is anything to go by—what Abhishek wants, Abhishek gets.' He paused and looked at them both. 'This is confidential, you understand? It's just my personal impression. Anika was . . . well, she was ruled by her family. She would sometimes rail against their control, but at the end of the day, she toed the party line. From the snippets I read of that book, she would never have published it. It would be like publishing her diary from when she was a child. It would reflect badly on her as well as the family, and she would have known that. She, at the end of the day, she was a smart woman.' He looked down at his hands and Monami had a sudden impression of two people who, even if they were at odds with each other sometimes, were caught up in a current that they couldn't fight. He probably toed the party line too.

There was a silence as Mridula seemed to digest this.

Finally, she said, 'Could it be a motive for murder for someone who maybe wasn't aware of that? Someone else who featured in it, who wasn't family?'

'I suppose you mean Samar,' said Shekhar. He got up again, but instead of going to the window, started pacing up and down on the carpet in front of them. 'Look, I can't believe it of him. That's all I can say. I've gotten to know Samar through all this, you know, and I know all the rumours about the two of them. Do I believe them? I . . . I don't know. In any marriage, there are bound to be . . . ups and downs. And ours was no exception. There were faults on both sides. But do I think that Samar . . . *Samar* would kill her because he featured in this book in some sort of salacious way? Absolutely not. I tell you I don't believe it for a second.'

At the end of this speech, Shekhar seemed to be breathing slightly harder than before, and stared firmly at the two of them, as though daring them to contradict him.

They didn't. Instead, Mridula said, rather abruptly, 'So, what's your opinion, Mr Malhotra? Who killed your wife?'

It felt like a change of scene. Shekhar looked at her and seemed to shrink back into himself. He said, 'I . . . I can't think. I can't imagine. It all seems . . . surreal. Absurd. Do you have any theories?'

Monami looked down at her hands too. One couldn't very well say to a grieving husband that her leading theory was that his wife was a murderer, or at least an accomplice, and had therefore died a misbegotten death.

Mridula shook her head. 'It's far too early for us to have theories.'

'What a diametrically opposite way to the police approach,' said Shekhar, with the faintest trace of a smile. 'They don't think it's too early at all. Neither does the media, apparently.'

'What do you think of the media's theories?'

'The purest melodrama, as I said. People don't have enemies, not in this transactional day and age.'

Monami could think of a few people at the office who would have disagreed with him. Mridula may have been following a similar train of thought, as her next question led them to the paper.

'Were you aware that your wife was leaving the *Delhi Daily*?'

'No, was she?' Shekhar sounded genuinely surprised.

'You didn't know?' Mridula looked at him keenly.

'No! Are you sure? It seems very unlikely.'

'Had you spoken to her that day, before going to this party?'

Shekhar looked uncomfortable. 'We . . . we didn't really speak in that sense. We just spoke about logistics, I'll pick you up at seven, we'll meet there at eight, stuff like that. I guess we were beyond sharing information like this. Leaving the *Delhi Daily*, really? You're sure?'

Mridula nodded. 'I'm afraid so. I was present at the interview with DB that morning, where he let her know that unfortunately, her column would be discontinued.'

'*What?*' Shekhar goggled, as Monami had, and as Samar and Kajal had before her. 'DB discontinued her column? What right had he to do that?'

Mridula regarded him with a dispassionate air. 'The move was endorsed by her father.'

'Huh! And you're sure of this?' asked Shekhar again.

Mridula nodded. 'He didn't deny it when we saw him just now.'

Shekhar seemed to chew on this for a while.

'That might explain quite a lot about her behaviour at this party. Poor Anika,' he said. A short silence followed this statement. No one seemed to know what to say next. At least, Monami didn't, and it seemed Shekhar had also run out of fuel, and now wandered up to the window, gazing out at nothing in particular.

Mridula, as was her wont, broke the silence by listing items on her to-do list, 'Mr Kapoor asked us to keep digging. And I'm hoping you can help us with that. Can you set up two more interviews for us, please?'

Shekhar had to make a visible effort to get back to business. 'Yes, of course, if I can. Who do you want to see?'

'We'd like to meet Anika's sister. And the intern, Vasudha. She worked with you, I think?'

'You want to meet Anita?' said Shekhar, slowly. 'Can I ask why?'

Mridula shrugged. 'Just more background, you know.'

'I . . . well, I'll see what I can do, but I'm not sure that's going to be possible. Anita is going through a lot,' said Shekhar. 'She has had to take over the family business. Her father's in no state, absolutely no state, as I'm sure you saw when you met with him just now. Anita's been . . . well, she's been resilient, but I don't think she has any time to talk to the press.'

'Their own paper is hardly "the press".'

'Oh, I'm sure they're meeting regularly with one of their TV channels,' said Shekhar, vaguely. 'I'm not sure *Delhi Daily* would make that cut. No offence.'

'No offence taken,' said Mridula. 'What about Vasudha?'

'Ah, yes, Vasudha. I'm sure she'd see you,' said Shekhar, kindly. 'I'm glad you're going to see her, actually. She's been absolutely crushed by this. Do mention that you were here, and that I send her my best. She's a good kid. Let her know that I'm watching out for her.'

Monami remembered what Jemin had said about Vasudha having a crush on Shekhar, and she warmed to his kindness. 'Of course we will,' she said.

'Could you give us her address?' said Mridula.

'Sure, I'll need to call my assistant to get it.' And as he made the call, repeating Vasudha's address out loud, he walked to a side table, opened a drawer and took out a pad and pencil.

'Thank you,' he said, smiling at Monami as he handed her a piece of paper. 'For passing on my message.'

The direct look into her eyes and the flash of white teeth disarmed Monami, and, despite her usual imperviousness to clean-cut businessman types, she found herself smiling back. In her peripheral vision, she felt certain she could see Mridula rolling her eyes but she didn't care. If Mridula were impervious to the decorative charms of handsome men, so be it. Monami wasn't and had no wish to be. There were so few of them around.

22

Teetering into Insolence

i

It seemed like their time with Shekhar had come to an end, but Mridula made no move to get up from the sofa. Instead, she seemed to take her time, look around, and said, as if she were musing to herself, 'You know, it's a curious thing about this case. One or two people we've interviewed have commented on it. We never seem to get a bead on Anika herself. She didn't seem to have many friends.'

Shekhar frowned. 'I don't know what you mean. We have many friends.'

'Yes, so you mentioned. That's what struck me, that you said she had many friends at this party of Kajal's. But no one else has really said that. I'm sorry to be blunt with you. No one at the office she worked in could be considered a friend of hers. No one, really, at this party you say she was so keen to attend. But you and her father seem to agree. Her father says he didn't know she had so many enemies. You've said something similar.'

'Is "enemies" the word?' said Shekhar, still frowning.

'If one of them hated you enough to kill you, then yes, I believe it is the word,' said Mridula, rather brutally. Monami looked at her in surprise. There was a harshness in Mridula's tone that she hadn't heard her use with the others they'd interviewed. 'The sad truth is—your wife made herself unpleasant. Again, I'm sorry to be blunt, but there it is. She was not well liked. And the circumstances of her death are increasingly murky. There are no witnesses. Nobody can even pin down the time of death with any certainty. It's not an easy crime to solve. And as such, it's one that the Delhi Police are not likely to solve. They won't solve it, but they'll most certainly make an arrest. Now, the question to you, and to the rest of Anika's family, is this: Would you be okay with such an outcome? Are you just looking for an arrest, *any* arrest? Even if it's based on, to use that colourful phrase of yours, the purest melodrama? Or would you like to find the truth, find out who is actually responsible for your wife's death? I suspect that it's the latter. Is it?'

Shekhar looked nonplussed by Mridula's temerity. 'Of course,' he said, 'what else could we want?'

'I thought so. Your father-in-law said the same. Now, if you would like to find out who is actually responsible, we need to start asking some hard questions. We need to get to the truth of who your wife really was, and who may have wanted to kill her. I'm afraid you haven't been honest with us today, Mr Malhotra. You haven't helped us.'

'Excuse me?'

'You haven't been honest with us today,' said Mridula, again, although Monami could have told her that he had heard her the first time, from the increasingly black look he was giving her. 'You've told us you don't think she had any enemies; you haven't told us about her affair; you haven't actually told us anything.'

Shekhar stirred at the mention of the affair, but when he spoke, his voice was calm. 'You're teetering into insolence here, Ms Majumdar,' he said.

'Insolence?' Mridula gave a short laugh. 'Do you know what your father-in-law said to me? I asked him if he wasn't worried that I would find out something that would hurt him. And he said, what can hurt me now? I think he feels how we feel—that the time for insolence is past. All your little walls must come crumbling down, Mr Malhotra. I couldn't quite put it in those terms to your father-in-law, but that's the only way for us to get at the truth. We're not asking you these questions to report them in our paper. We're asking you to uncover the truth of what happened. Not just to your wife, but to a dear friend of ours.'

Shekhar slowly sat down again. His face was hard to read, but Monami thought he was assessing Mridula, trying to work out how seriously he should take this ungainly spinster with her bad haircut and her smug moral superiority. Still, Monami thought, Shekhar must have been impressed. Not many people would have stood up to him in this way. And it didn't feel like posturing. How could it be, in this private space? It was genuine, and her pursuit of the truth heartfelt. And that was saying quite a lot.

'I understand what you're trying to say, Ms Majumdar,' said Shekhar. 'Believe me, I do.'

He kept his gaze steady, unbothered by Mridula's own unblinking gaze—the owlish stare that Monami, like everyone else at the *Delhi Daily*, found so unsettling. But Shekhar seemed owl-resistant.

'Whatever the truth,' continued Shekhar, 'there are some things that can't be tarnished. Anika's name, her reputation, is one of those things. It's . . . it's all we have left of her. All her family has left. Do you understand?'

'Yes, of course I understand. I've worked at this paper, in this country, for many years, and I probably know better than you that there are some things that we will print, and there are some things that we will not. That's a secondary issue. To understand what we will print, we first need to understand what happened. First the story, then the spin.'

'No one is talking about spin here,' said Shekhar. 'The story is the story. I just can't imagine what you're asking about will have any bearing on this case. Apart from fuelling malicious gossip—as if anyone needs more of that now with this media circus. Anika doesn't deserve that. And neither does her family.

'I think you're taking entirely the wrong line. Anika is not responsible for her own death. Someone else is responsible. Surely you can see that?'

'Nonetheless,' said Mridula. 'To get at the truth, we must get to her character. I understand that these are hard truths. The possibility that Anika had enemies, that she may have had an affair. It's difficult to contend with—especially now. But the answer to her murder may well lie there, and we cannot ignore it. If the family wants justice, there's no other way.'

At this word *justice*, the mood in the room seemed to change. Shekhar leaned back.

'That's exactly what we want. We want justice. There must be payment for whoever did this.'

Mridula's eyebrows rose. 'I think you and I understand justice differently. I mean justice, not retribution.'

Shekhar waved this away. 'Unfortunately, it often comes to the same thing.'

'If I understand you, you think your wife was having an affair, but you don't think it had a bearing on her death?'

Monami groaned inwardly. Why this constant harping on the affair? *With the husband?*

'You think she had enemies, but you don't think that had a bearing on her death either?' Mridula continued. 'Forgive me, but that is a very naïve view.'

Fortunately, it seemed that Shekhar's mood had improved. He laughed.

'I've heard about you,' he said. 'Mridula Majumdar, what do they call you? The editor-at-large. I always wondered what that meant. But here you are, at large. And twice as natural.' He grinned. 'No wonder Abhishek asked you to keep digging. And no wonder they kept you hidden away. Are you as thoughtless as you appear? Or are you more dangerous? I rather think . . . I rather think that you're not stupid.'

'Thank you,' said Mridula. 'You're right. I'm not.'

'And I'm not naïve. I understand what you're trying to do, the psychology of the individual, and all that, but I think this case is not like that. There were a number of people at this party, and one of them obviously is more unbalanced than the rest. I think all this talk about enemies, affairs, well, it's all pot-boiler stuff. I understand that the *Delhi Daily* is a tabloid, but there are limits. And now *I'm* sorry to be blunt.' The words were firm, but Shekhar had a small smile on his face.

'I think we'll have to end this interview here,' he added, sounding almost apologetic. 'I have another appointment. This has been . . . well, it's been interesting. Thank you for coming by. I'm sorry I couldn't give you what you wanted.'

'Not at all. Thank you for your time,' said Mridula. 'This has been helpful nonetheless.'

'I'm glad to hear it. Good luck with the rest of your investigation. Let me walk you out.'

They made their way back into the lobby through the silent apartment. A muffled clanging could be heard coming from what was presumably the kitchen, but if anything, the faint noise merely accentuated the silence rather than broke it.

'Good luck,' said Shekhar again as he closed the door.

The noise echoed across the marble floors.

ii

As they walked down the stairs, Monami released a breath.

'You are not the most tactful, has anyone ever told you that?' she said to Mridula, who only grinned in reply.

'I know. That's why I asked for Vasudha's address before going into all that,' she said, holding her hand out for Shekhar's note.

Vasudha Chaturvedi
50A Nizamuddin East, third floor

'Oh, she lives quite near here. Nizamuddin East,' said Monami. Shall we go now?'

Mridula looked at her. 'Are you up for it? It's been a long day.'

It had been a long day, starting with the muggy morning at Jemin's office, and then traipsing, it seemed to Monami, all around Delhi, in the rain, the still, expectant air at Sunder Nursery, the fraught interview with Abhishek Kapoor at the office. And Shekhar, his burnished good looks and his curiously opaque manner. The twilit sky had blossomed into a pink flush, a beauty that Delhi could show only when the rain washed away the smog. There were still spots of blue, and the outline of the moon could be seen directly above them.

'There's still time before it gets dark,' said Monami. 'Let's go, I feel like we'll lose our momentum if we stop now.'

23

An Almost Perfumed Breeze

i

Nizamuddin East was a little neighbourhood that nestled in the shadow of Humayun's Tomb, a ravishing sixteenth-century mausoleum. Vasudha lived in a barsati, on top of a graceful old house that had been converted clumsily into flats. There was no lift, and they huffed up three flights of stairs, rang the bell and after what seemed like an age, heard the thwap-thwap of a pair of chappals. Then silence and another pause, as though the person behind the door was bracing themselves. Just as Mridula was about to ring the bell again, the door opened.

By this point, Monami had heard so much about Vasudha, she had a very confused picture of her in her head. By some accounts, this young woman was a conniving climber, the accomplice who had sent DB to his death. By others she was a victim, merely doing her job, and in the wrong place at the wrong time. But by all accounts, she was a competent woman, efficient, ambitious, smart, on her way up whatever ladder she wanted to climb.

So when Vasudha opened the door, in her sweats and glasses, she came as a surprise. She was a small-framed young woman with, what seemed to Monami, a childlike face. She looked at them enquiringly. 'Yes?'

'Mridula Majumdar here, and Monami Chatterjee; we're from the *Delhi Daily*. We got your contact from Shekhar Malhotra. Do you have a second to talk?'

'From Shekhar?' Vasudha said uncertainly.

'Yes, we're investigating the murders of Anika and DB on behalf of the *Delhi Daily*,' said Mridula. 'And,' she added unabashedly when Vasudha still made no move to let them in, 'on behalf of Anika's family.'

'The family?'

'Yes, Mr Kapoor has asked us to stay close to this investigation,' said Mridula,officiously. 'Do you mind if we come in and ask you a few questions? We won't be long.'

'It's just the two of you?' said Vasudha, still uncertain.

'Just us,' said Monami with artificial cheer, trying to put the girl at ease. Vasudha was obviously nervous, maybe even afraid. And Monami understood why. News anchors were throwing her name around as though her guilt was established. No doubt, like Jemin, Samar, and Kajal, she had been visited more than once by the police. But unlike the three of them, she was young and alone and vulnerable.

Vasudha had moved aside, reluctantly it seemed to Monami, to let them in, and as they came through the door on the landing, they found themselves in a large terrace space made pretty with flowering plants, potted trees and old, repainted garden furniture. The house was across the road from the crumbling wall of Humayun's Tomb, and Vasudha's terrace had a fantastic view of the white marble onion dome.

'Wow,' said Monami. 'Well, that was worth the climb. What a view!'

'Yes, isn't it?' said Vasudha, a little mechanically. 'Should we sit out here? It's so nice after the rain.'

They readily assented, as there was indeed a nice, almost perfumed breeze, one of those cool winds that are rare in Delhi's smoggy desert heat, but so enchanting when they blow.

'So, Vasudha,' started Monami, as they settled around the table. 'We're sorry to barge in on you like this. We're hoping we can help clear all this up. Do you mind if we ask some questions about that night?'

The tired look intensified on Vasudha's face. She sighed. 'Do I have a choice? Go ahead. Do you mind if I smoke?'

'Not at all,' said Monami, feeling surprised again. She wouldn't have taken this dewy young woman for a smoker.

Vasudha lit her cigarette, but after taking a perfunctory puff, it smouldered, forgotten, between her fingers. Instead, she looked off into the sky and then intently at the branches of the peepal tree that fell into her terrace from the garden next door.

Finally, Mridula spoke. 'I can imagine all this must be very hard for you. We'll be as quick as we can. Let's start with how you came to work at Sea Lion. Can you tell us? You worked with Shekhar first, didn't you?'

'Yes. I interned with him when he was making a few acquisitions. A couple of summers ago. It was . . . it was a really good learning experience.'

'And then you decided to switch tacks?'

'Yes . . . I've always been guided towards finance, business, you know, by my parents. But what I've always wanted to do was to go into writing or publishing. Shekhar was very helpful about helping me find Sea Lion and getting me a job with Samar.' Vasudha's tone was flat.

'Oh, okay. And how did you come to work on Kajal's book?'

Vasudha continued to tap her cigarette on the ashtray, even though there was no ash left to fall.

'I don't know. It was handed to me. I was an intern.'

'And how did you come up with the idea for the launch?'

This question was thrown out seemingly casually, but Monami held her breath. Would Vasudha pass the buck too?

If they wanted a reaction, none came. In the same flat tone,

Vasudha said, 'It wasn't my idea, originally. I'd have preferred to have it in central Delhi. Everything would have been easier. Not so far for things and people to travel. But then I got handed the budget. Or rather, the non-budget.'

'And you had to think—outside the box?'

Vasudha looked at Mridula then. 'Yes. I had to think outside the box. But I really can't take any credit for the idea to host it at Kajal's. We had gone to her house for something, and someone . . . I think it was Samar . . . mentioned what a beautiful space it was. And it is, you know. I mean, it's a little down at heel, but charming if you like that sort of thing. And Samar did. And she had a good-sized garden.'

'So, it was Samar's idea?'

'I think so. And Kajal was happy to host. That's why I didn't understand her attitude afterwards. When we first suggested it, she was more than fine. Excited, in fact. I think she liked the idea of showing off her old home. And then on the day, she put up this whole act of being so unhappy with the whole thing,' Vasudha's voice had now become bitter. 'Why did she pretend? I don't know. But it wasn't how she really felt.'

Mridula and Monami glanced at each other. How many ways could people see the exact same event? Every person had a different account.

'What about the partnership with the House of Jems? How did that come about?'

Vasudha shrugged again. 'Like I said, there was no budget. Jemin came to see Samar one day at the Sea Lion office . . .'

'He did? About what?'

'I don't know. But I think they discussed it. After that meeting, the plan was set. Jemin was going to sponsor the launch. Suddenly the money came in, we could have drinks, hire catering, the whole lot.'

There was another brief silence at this. Monami looked at Mridula again, but she didn't meet her glance this time, and her expression was unreadable.

'So . . . between them, you think Jemin and Samar made the plan?'

'Yes.' The answer came quickly in the same flat monotone.

'Okay. Tell us what happened on the day itself, Vasudha,' said Monami.

'It went so well,' said Vasudha. 'Everyone came, even people I thought might not. We had writers, journalists, even minor celebrities. It was, well, it was almost perfect! The food, the decorations, the . . . the models. It all fell into place. If it weren't for Kajal's strange attitude, it would have been perfect. I didn't understand her. When the whole thing was for her—her book. She acted as though we were all in her way.'

'She gave no reason for the change in attitude?'

Vasudha shook her head. 'No. Not at all. But she wouldn't have confided in me, anyway.' The same bitterness in her voice.

'Tell us about what happened with DB.'

Vasudha looked away. 'There's nothing to tell. I poured the drinks. The police think I did it. But I didn't. I have no idea why or how he died. I don't.' Her voice trembled.

'Do you have any theories about what could have happened?' asked Monami, gently.

Vasudha shook her head again. 'I can't imagine. Sometimes I think . . . I think . . .'

'Yes?'

'The theory that the news is throwing around. Oh, I know it's preposterous. But it could have been a publicity stunt that went wrong, you know? I don't want to accuse anyone, but . . . but . . .'

'But? Tell us. It won't go beyond the three of us, but it may help us to draw some conclusions.'

'Well, if Jemin and Samar were planning anything between them, this is just the sort of harebrained thing that they would do! Jemin, anyway. He would think that he was being so creative. He wouldn't have dreamed that DB would actually have died. Maybe he thought it would be a way to get reporters more interested in his store. His business is doing so badly . . . I don't know.'

'So that's your theory, is it?' said Mridula thoughtfully. 'It's interesting, but Jemin had the same theory, too.'

'He did?'

'Well, he thought it was an accident. DB's death.'

Monami thought she knew what Mridula was getting at, that it was also interesting that Jemin thought Vasudha was responsible for this accident, and here was Vasudha thinking it was Jemin.

Vasudha shrugged. 'He could be right.'

'Is there any reason you think it may have been Jemin? Apart from his penchant for overly creative schemes, I mean?'

'I . . . no,' said Vasudha. 'And look, I'm not saying I necessarily suspect him. Nothing so concrete as that. But he . . . he was the opposite of Kajal. He was . . . absolutely hopped up that evening. Seemed like he couldn't contain his excitement. And lately, he had become very involved. Kept asking me about the details. Who would be there, who I was inviting, how I would set the scene and so on. At first, I thought it was because he wanted to showcase his clothes properly. But he really wasn't interested in that at all.'

'Oh? What was he interested in?'

'The questions he was asking . . . well, they were more about the party itself, and the guests, if you know what I mean. There . . . there was something about Anika particularly. He kept asking if she'd RSVPed, if she was coming for sure. I was worried that he was, I don't know, planning some surprise. Something to do with Anika. He . . . he wasn't a big fan of hers.'

'Interesting,' said Mridula. This was the same impression Kajal had had, Monami thought.

She expected Mridula to extend this line of questioning, but Mridula had lost interest in Anika. 'What about the models? Did Jemin ask about them?'

'The models? What do you mean?'

'I don't really mean anything specific,' said Mridula. 'But tell me about how that worked—did he pick them himself? Did you?'

Vasudha no longer looked exhausted, indifferent, thought Monami. What did she look like now? Confused? Or was it fear?

'Jemin picked them,' she said, slowly, precisely. 'We have a few regulars, and everyone's kind of free right now since it's off season.'

'We met one of your regulars,' said Mridula, cheerfully. 'A very ornamental young man. Suleiman. He was interested in Monami, here.'

'Mridula!' said Monami, glaring at her. Honestly, sometimes the woman was so inappropriate. She couldn't even.

'Sorry, but he was, you know,' said Mridula, continuing down her inexplicable tangent. 'I may have poured cold water all over that flame though. I hope not.'

'Suleiman and Jemin go way back,' said Vasudha, sounding as though she welcomed the change in topic.

'Yes, he said—ten years!' said Mridula. 'Although he didn't look that old.'

'Well, models, you know,' said Vasudha, smiling. 'And I think he started young.'

'Yes, models,' said Mridula, smiling back. 'And the serving staff. Where did they come from?'

'The . . . the serving staff? From the caterer,' said Vasudha.

'Ah, the caterer. Of course. You wouldn't have a list of names? It's really imperative we talk to everyone.'

'I . . . I don't know. I could ask, but I'm not sure I should be sharing personal information,' said Vasudha. Her eyes had dropped to the stone floor and the stress seemed to have crept back into her voice.

'Never mind, I guess the police will have already made a list. We'll just get it from them,' said Mridula. 'Let's move on. Can you tell us anything about Anika's death?'

Vasudha shook her head. 'No. I didn't even see her after—after what happened with DB.'

'What did you do after the toast?'

'After DB died, you mean? I don't really remember; I . . . I was in shock. I just sort of wandered around in a daze.'

'Did you wait for the police?'

'No. Jemin suggested that I go home, so I did.'

'And you didn't see Anika at all afterwards?'

'No, I didn't.'

'When was the last time you saw her?'

'During the toast. She was on Kajal's balcony, smoking. Everybody saw her.'

'What was your relationship like with Anika?'

Vasudha's voice, which had been rising with each answer, now became defensive; she was almost shouting. 'It was fine! I barely knew her! I didn't have it in for her! I had no reason to kill her!'

There was a brief pause, and then Mridula said, 'I'm not saying you did.'

'Aren't you? Aren't you? That's what everybody else is saying. That I killed her, or him, or both. Why would I? Why would I do that?'

That was the question, thought Monami. She gestured to Mridula that she thought they should go. Aloud, Monami said, 'We're on your side, Vasudha. I know it doesn't seem that way, but we are.'

Vasudha laughed. 'I don't even know what that means.'

Monami and Mridula both stood up. Mridula said, 'I'm sorry. I didn't mean to upset you. I know it seems that everyone's against you right now, but believe me, we're just trying to find out the truth. So please think, before we go—is there nothing else that you'd like to tell us? Even if you think it's insignificant?'

'No. There isn't. I really must ask you to go, I'm so tired.'

'I understand,' said Monami, and glared at Mridula. Out of all the interviews, Mridula had handled this one the worst, thought Monami.

The rollercoaster mood, one moment playful and smiling, the other moment accusatory and poker faced. And those irrelevant questions about models and servers! What was she playing at? If she meant to put Vasudha at ease, she had utterly failed.

As they walked across the terrace to the door, Monami thought that overall, Vasudha had impressed her favourably. She still didn't know if Vasudha was responsible for either death, but she came off as an outsider, as being totally alone and, therefore more deserving of Monami's sympathy and compassion than anyone else they had spoken to so far.

And unlike the others Vasudha didn't try to hide her feelings—she had jumped at once to the right response to Monami's frankly empty words of being on her side. 'I don't even know what that means.' There was no way of knowing which side was which, at this point. There was no way of knowing anything yet.

'What are your plans now?' Monami asked, trying to soften the impact of the uncomfortable last few minutes.

'I don't know,' said Vasudha, still sounding bereft. 'All my corporate dreams have been washed away. My parents are beside themselves . . . keep asking me to come home.'

'Why don't you? It might be a good idea. Maybe best not to be so alone right now.'

Vasudha shook her head. 'I'd rather stay here. I . . . I can't go home now.'

'Well, you have Anika's family's support, which is nice,' said Monami, trying to cheer her up. 'Her husband Shekhar was just telling us to tell you to hang in there, that he's looking out for you.'

But barely had these words got out than Vasudha burst into tears, into great juddering sobs. It was like a dam had burst; she sobbed and sobbed, with her face in her hands and her shoulders shaking. Monami, horrified, patted Vasudha's back awkwardly. At least Jemin had been right about one thing—this girl really had it bad on the

Shekhar front. And now that Monami had seen him up close, she totally got why.

'I'm so sorry, I didn't mean to upset you. It's a good thing! They've got your back!' Monami looked over at Mridula for support, but the older woman was just gazing at Vasudha, regarding her outburst with a dispassionate air. We should go, Monami mouthed at Mridula, and jerked her head in the direction of the door.

'Right. Okay, well thanks again for seeing us,' said Mridula. 'Do call us, won't you? If you can think of anything else. And Vasudha? I agree with my colleague here. It's best right now that you not be alone. If you don't want to go home, I suggest you bring someone here to stay with you for a few days.'

Vasudha looked Mridula in the eye, the sobbing a distant memory.

'I prefer to be alone right now.'

'Do you? But remember that there's a killer on the loose. We shouldn't lose sight of that. *You* shouldn't lose sight of that.'

As they left, Monami looked back at Vasudha, sitting at the little table on the pretty terrace. The sun had almost set, washing the sky in a vivid mix of orange, pink and purple. The whole scene felt cinematic. All that beauty—it took Monami's breath away but also made her inexplicably sad. For years afterwards, that evening and that sky would remain etched in her mind in all its detail.

ii

'Well, that was . . . certainly something,' said Mridula when they got to the car.

'You could have been a little bit more sympathetic,' said Monami. 'That girl is suffering. What was all that guff about servers and models and whatnot? This wasn't really the time for japes, was it?'

'I suppose not,' said Mridula, somewhat meekly. 'What did you think of the whole interaction?'

'Well, Jemin was right that she's definitely got a crush on him.'

'On Anika's husband?'

'Of course,' said Monami. 'I felt sorry for her. She seemed so alone, no? I don't just mean literally.'

'I agree with you. It's unfortunate,' said Mridula.

'It was interesting,' said Monami, slowly. 'That she was the only one to really seem certain about whose idea the launch was. No? Everyone else just *thought* it was so-and-so's idea. No one really seemed certain. But she was convinced it was Jemin and Samar.'

'Yes. And she also seemed to think Kajal was faking her mood that morning.'

'Yes, I noticed that, too.'

'But she did contradict herself in one way,' said Mridula, starting up the engine.

'How?'

'You didn't notice? She said that it was her idea to go and work at Sea Lion. How did she put it? That she's always wanted to get into publishing and writing. Nonsense.'

'How do you know it was nonsense?'

'She contradicted herself minutes later,' said Mridula. 'She said that her corporate dreams were blighted, or something. What corporate dreams? If she wanted to work in publishing. Publishing! In India, where no one makes a dime!'

Monami was silent. She hadn't noticed that.

'It's interesting, isn't it?' continued Mridula in that infuriatingly conversational tone. 'You never know who to trust, who is telling the truth, and who is not. I have to say, I'm really enjoying myself. Come, it's been a long day. I'll drive you home.'

The Reckoning

21

Unknown and Unknowable Devices

i

The funeral was over. Meena was now preparing to fly to Calcutta, where the eleventh-day ceremonies would take place among white-clad friends and family in tuberose-laden halls. There would be a picture of her husband at the centre of it all, garlanded, the ordinary portrait already looking otherworldly, as though the subject's mind were elsewhere.

Meena was still trying to occupy her mind with trifling matters, to prevent becoming overwhelmed by larger ones. Her relatives had unwittingly helped, with questions about the food she would be giving up, or whether she would be wearing leather on her feet for the next few days, earnest advice given in solemn tones about what to do and what not to do, all in aid of facilitating, one assumed, DB's journey onwards. She wasn't a religious woman, but she was conscious of a devout gratitude at this moment, not for the provision of religion in answering questions about life, death, and the purpose of our existence, but rather for its capacity to fill that existence with the detritus of ritual. It occupied her days, and that was all she needed just now.

She looked at her guests, who were perched awkwardly on her living room sofa. The younger woman had a notebook open, ready to take notes; and the older woman, a friend of her husband's, who should have been here to grieve with her, had come only to ask questions.

'Well?'

'Meena,' said Mridula. Her tone was gentler today, to Monami's relief. 'We just want to ask you a few questions about DB.'

Meena's expression didn't change. She looked as though she was in a waiting room, not at a busy airport or train station, but maybe at the dentist with others ahead of her in the queue. She was not in a hurry and not bored. Just waiting.

'I really hate to bother you,' continued Mridula, a little uncomfortably. 'But we need to move quickly on this. Before the police make any unfortunate arrests.'

'The police are on the right track,' said Meena.

Mridula and Monami looked at her in surprise. They hadn't really been expecting her to say anything unless asked a direct question.

'What do you mean?' Mridula managed, finally. 'Do you know who they're about to arrest?'

'Yes.' Meena's tone hadn't changed; she didn't sound adamant, or defensive, or even particularly interested. She sounded just as affectless as before, but perhaps a touch louder. 'They know who killed him. And they're right.'

'Er, do you want to tell us who?'

Monami glanced around, nervously. In the detective stories she had read all her life, before grand pronouncements like this could be made, something would happen involving various unknown and unknowable devices but essentially resulting in the speaker coming to a quick and sticky end. At any moment, Meena, the murderer's name upon her lips, might crumple to the floor, traces of strychnine later found at the bottom of her teacup.

A strained silence settled, during which Meena stared at a spot on the wall behind them. Even Mridula started to look around her, rattled.

Finally, Meena spoke.

'I don't really know if I should,' she said. 'There's no evidence. I just know.'

'It'll help us find the evidence. We'll work backwards,' said Mridula.

Meena finally looked at her, and seemed to come in from far away, as though trying to focus an unfocused telescope.

'You've really had no indications? Who have you spoken to so far?'

'Kajal. Samar. Jemin. Vasudha . . . is it one of these names?' Monami couldn't hold it in any longer. Anywhere, a sniper might be taking aim. She resisted the urge to bark, 'Spit it out, woman!'

Rather than answer her, Meena said, 'Anika was ashing into the champa tree.'

'Anika?' said Monami, feeling a little helpless at this jump from one homicide to the next. She glanced at Mridula, who gestured at her to stop interrupting.

'Yes, she was walking up and down, talking into her phone. She was smoking a cigarette, and she was ashing into the champa tree,' said Meena, mechanically, as though reading from a script. 'It was one of Kajal's favourites, it had pink flowers. Not the usual white. Dark pink. And Anika was ashing into it. I went to speak to her, but she was busy talking into her phone, I couldn't get her attention. So, I called up to her.'

Meena was speaking very deliberately.

'I have dreams about that encounter at night,' she continued. 'Maybe her spirit is restless? Who knows. You should ask her family to carry out all the right rituals. Nowadays, people are so careless about that sort of thing. But it matters.'

'I'm sure it does,' said Monami. 'Did . . . did she say anything to you?'

'To me? No. She was talking into her phone. And then she called down to a waitress. She wanted another drink.'

'She called down from the balcony?' asked Mridula.

'Yes, she said, "Can I have another drink, please?" And then I think she asked for a Coke or a Thums Up or something.'

'What did you do then?' asked Mridula.

'I . . . I went upstairs to find Anika, as I said. And I couldn't find her.'

Meena looked at them both with an air of finality.

'You couldn't find her? Anika, you mean?'

'Yes, Anika. I looked upstairs, on the balcony. And she wasn't there.'

'Maybe she'd come back down?' suggested Monami.

'Yes, maybe. Although I didn't pass her on the stairs. All I know is I couldn't find her anywhere—I still have dreams about that, too. I don't know why. I'm looking for her through endless passages, in endless rooms. She's never there. Sometimes it seems like I've just missed her. Sometimes I find her but when I get close I realise it's not her. That waitress . . . it's always that waitress. I can't quite remember her face, of course, but she was dressed in black. And I always wake up wondering why it was so important. But in my dream, it is.'

'Does this have something to do with who you think killed your husband, Mrs Bhattacharya?' asked Monami, feeling like she was being too direct but also feeling compelled to ask the blunt question.

She hardly expected an answer, but to her surprise, one came.

'It was that Vasudha,' said Meena.

Mridula and Monami stared. They may even have been open-mouthed.

'You think,' said Mridula, quicker to recover than Monami, 'that Vasudha killed DB? Why?'

'I don't *think*, I *know*,' said Meena. 'When it all happened, I heard the outcry breaking out and I had a kind of sixth sense. That it was about Dhritiman. I was upstairs, still looking for Anika. I think . . . I think I was a little disoriented. I heard all the commotion and I just . . . I somehow knew it was about him. I couldn't move. I must have been stuck there for several minutes. Then I somehow got myself down the stairs, and I almost ran into her.'

'Into Vasudha?'

'Yes. She was running up. And her guilt—it was written all over her face.' There was a slight pause, and then, some animation finally creeping into her voice, Meena repeated, 'She looked frantic, and definitely guilty. She stared at me in horror—didn't say a word—and rushed past me, up the stairs.'

She looked at her two guests. 'At the time I didn't think anything of it, we all thought he was having a heart attack, didn't we? But I remembered it later. That look of terror. She was guilty. She knew it, and she knew that I had seen it. She creeps back into my dreams, too. Always skulking in the corners, just out of reach. But she's there. She's always there.'

The silence seemed to lengthen the very shadows in the room. Finally, Meena spoke again, heavily. 'Then, I went outside. And the nightmare began. But this I know—Vasudha killed my husband.'

'Have you told the police this?' asked Mridula.

'I tried to. But they didn't listen. Their focus is on Anika now,' said Meena. 'They barely heard me all the way through. And I know it's not—well, as I said, it's not really evidence. A look on someone's face. But it was enough for me. I *know.*'

'Maybe . . . maybe she was shocked?' suggested Mridula. 'DB had just died right in front of her eyes.'

Meena shook her head. 'I know shock. It paralyses you, roots you to the spot. No, she looked guilty. And when she caught sight of me, she looked even guiltier. She gave a start and rushed past. It wasn't shock. It was guilt.'

'Who else was on the balcony, when you went up?' asked Mridula. 'You didn't see Anika, but did you see anyone else?'

'There were lots of people there,' said Meena. 'I saw some of Dhritiman's *Delhi Daily* staff. Just kids.' She shook her head. 'They were all so shocked. One of the girls was absolutely shaking and crying. I think, subconsciously, that was part of the reason I knew something was seriously wrong, even before I went downstairs. And then . . . then I knew.'

She closed her eyes.

'Thank you, Meena,' said Mridula. 'I . . . I'm sorry I haven't been around more.'

Meena Bhattacharya opened her eyes again and said something unexpected. 'You're the only one who is helping us by trying to find out who killed him,' she said. 'This conversation has helped. It's . . . it's helped to clarify a few things in my mind.'

'Anything you'd like to share?' asked Monami, hopefully.

'I don't have proof,' said Meena, frowning. 'But mark what I say—it's that girl Vasudha. *She did it.* I wasn't so sure before—but I am now.'

ii

Anita Kapoor faced the group of businessmen sitting at the conference table in front of her. All of a sudden, she felt very tired. The men around her were almost uniformly middle-aged, all with receding hairlines and expanding waistlines. They wore oxford shirts, blazers, thick glasses. And they were all gazing at her with varying degrees of concern and sympathy, but this didn't detract from her overall feeling of being one against many. She longed for an ally, her own ally. Where was he? In a different boardroom, maybe, feeling the same thing.

She drew a deep breath and began.

'Thank you for agreeing to a mid-cycle meeting on such short notice. I'm sure you cannot have missed the current turbulence that's surrounding our family. And, fortunately or unfortunately, our family is our business. My father . . .' here she paused. As always, when she spoke at a meeting like this, she prepared by writing out a script the night before, and she remembered each word perfectly. But she knew that she must come off as hesitant. Hesitant, unsure of herself, diffident . . . all those things that men like women to be, even when, or maybe especially when, they were in a position of power.

'My father is not himself. This incident, with my sister . . . ' again the pause, the quaver in the voice. Apart from the dramatic effect, the pause also helped her to survey her audience and see how they were taking it. They were all gazing at her with the same unblinking sympathy, but she was familiar enough with this environment to know that behind the expressions, their minds were calculating. They were thinking, *was this weakness and how can I take advantage?*

'My sister is dead,' she said. 'My parents are . . . struggling. They're not themselves. My father is in no position to . . . to carry out his responsibilities. This . . . this whole thing has aged him terribly.'

Nods, and a concerned clicking of tongues. A hushed murmuring.

'At such a time, I must take an unprecedented step. It's incumbent on me to . . . to take the reins. You must understand that this is a step I take with utmost reluctance. But I have my father's understanding, and I know that this is something I must do.'

She paused again. Would there be an outburst, a shocked questioning? The seconds ticked by and there was not. She went on.

'In order to take this step, I need the approval of the board. As you know. And so, I come to you. With my hands folded.' This was a trick she hadn't learned from her father, who was always confident, and could not appear any other way. But Anita was shrewd enough to understand that a confident woman in charge scared boardrooms full of men. Certainly this boardroom. So she folded her hands and looked down at the floor. When she looked back up, she saw on each and every face, with absolutely no exceptions, the same thought strike. *Opportunity*. She took a deep breath and went on.

iii

'That was . . . creepy,' said Monami.

Mridula put a finger to her lips and started the engine. She didn't speak until they were past the little road where DB and Meena's house was, had driven out through the colony gates and left GK-II behind.

'Well,' said Monami, unable to contain herself any longer. 'What did you think?'

'It's certainly interesting,' said Mridula slowly.

'What, the look of guilt? It's hardly damning evidence.'

'That, no. But a couple of other things struck me. Three things, to be exact. What about you?'

'I guess . . . I did wonder why Vasudha was going up the stairs?'

'Yes,' said Mridula, sounding pleased. 'You noticed that? I wondered that as well. Putting myself in her shoes—if this happens, and she's totally innocent, either, like Meena says, she would be rooted to the spot, horrified. Or she would rush off somewhere to be alone. One of the downstairs rooms perhaps or a bathroom. Vasudha knew the house. Why would she suddenly charge *upstairs?* And Meena seemed to suggest that she was going upstairs quite purposefully.'

'I suppose so . . . ' said Monami, doubtfully. 'But can we take her word for it?'

'As to Vasudha being purposeful, we can't, of course, rely just on Meena's account. Vasudha may have been charging around without thinking where she was going. But, together with Meena's conviction that she's the guilty party, and the fact that Vasudha didn't mention going upstairs herself, it's an interesting thing to keep in mind. The other interesting thing is what Meena said about Anika.'

'She didn't say anything about Anika, she didn't even find her,' said Monami.

'That's the interesting thing. Where was she? One moment she was on the balcony, very visible, and the next moment she had vanished into the ether?'

'Do you think . . . that was when . . . ?'

'I don't think it would have been long enough,' said Mridula, meditatively. 'She was obviously alive, pacing . . . asking for drinks . . . ashing, and so on. when Meena was downstairs. There wouldn't have been enough time to kill her and stow the body in the couple of minutes that it took Meena to go upstairs. But . . .'

'But . . . what?'

'Some vague flicker,' said Mridula, and closed her eyes for a second, much to Monami's alarm. 'No, it's gone. There was something . . . it ties in with something you said earlier . . .'

'At least this settles one thing,' said Monami, triumphant. 'There's no way Anika could have seen who murdered DB, confronted them and got herself killed for trying to be a hero. I *knew* that was farfetched. What was the third thing you were going to say?'

'The third thing, which I don't think Meena herself realised, is about your friends, my dear.'

'My friends?'

'Yes. She said she saw someone from the *Delhi Daily* shaking and crying, and she said that was how she knew something was wrong. But she saw this while she was upstairs, as the outcry downstairs was taking place. Why would someone—one of the kids, as she put it—be shaking and crying upstairs, before they even knew what had happened downstairs?'

Monami frowned. 'Maybe she was confused, and she saw that afterwards? It really doesn't make any sense otherwise.'

'We need to be absolutely sure before we can rule anything out,' said Mridula. 'You have to speak to your friends, Monami. I suspect they know something.'

25

Tiny Signposts

i

'SENSATIONAL DEVELOPMENTS IN DOUBLE HOMICIDE' screamed the rolling ticker text under the breathless newsreader.

'We can now confirm that a husband-and-wife duo have been arrested from the farmhouse of Ms Kajal Puri in connection with the two murders that happened there earlier this week,' the newsreader shouted. 'A housekeeper and driver have now been proven beyond a doubt to have had a hand in the murder of the famous socialite Anika Kapoor and are being questioned. It's yet to be determined whether Ms Kajal Puri played a part. Akanksha? Any updates on that?'

The luckless Akanksha, now standing outside a police station in Central Delhi, framed by ancient trees, responded cautiously, sounding as though years had been added to her life in the days since she was assigned to cover this story: 'No updates yet, but Kajal Puri will no doubt be brought into the station to be questioned. Very serious charges have been laid at the door of her housekeeper and driver, and it's very unlikely that she will have been completely unaware.'

'What are the charges? Are they being charged with the murders?'

'So far, it seems not,' said Akanksha. 'The charges we have heard so far have been tampering with evidence and obstructing a police investigation. It seems that they may have . . . interfered with the body in some way.'

'Interfered? What do you mean?' the newsreader asked, the expression on his face one of outrage at the unfathomable wickedness of the world.

'We're not sure yet, but clearly this case is more complicated than it appeared at first sight,' said Akanksha, sounding more and more depressed. 'Even after these arrests, fresh questions will have to be answered—why would this couple commit this outrageous act? What was their motive? And what of the first victim, Mr Dhritiman Bhattacharya—where does he fit in?'

'Right. Stay on the story Akanksha, we'll come back to you for more details.'

'I will. This is Akanksha Goyal, with cameraperson—'

But they had cut back to the studio.

ii

The drive up to Kajal's farmhouse seemed desolate. All the press vans were gone. The grass outside the gate where they had camped was flattened and brown; cigarette butts, chips packets and miniature glass bottles were tiny signposts left of their once constant presence.

'They raced off when Jyoti and Karim were arrested,' said Kajal. 'Just fled after the police.'

'Why didn't you tell us?' demanded Mridula, sounding quite angry.

They were sitting, not on the upstairs balcony now, but in a little sitting room on the ground floor. All the windows were shuttered and there was a faint smell of damp everywhere.

Kajal groaned and reached for her teacup, as though for strength.

'I didn't know what to do. We were both terrified. But I . . . I ought to have known that the risk for me wouldn't have been as great as the risk for them. In this country . . . whenever they can arrest someone who's poorer, less able to defend themselves, they do.'

'What did you tell them?'

'I told them it had been all of us!' cried Kajal. 'I told them that I ordered them to do it. But the police didn't care. They just held up their hands and said they would be back to talk to me. And then bundled Jyoti and Karim into a police jeep.'

'Can someone please tell me what we're all talking about?' burst out Monami. 'What did you tell them to do? Why have they been arrested? Did you, did they . . .' she tailed off.

'Jyoti didn't kill Anika, if that's what you mean,' said Kajal. 'I didn't tell her to do that. But that's what it would have looked like. That's why I couldn't say anything in the beginning. You understand?' she appealed to Mridula.

'I don't, frankly,' said Mridula. 'You should have told me everything. I knew you were holding something back when we first spoke to you. That whole story and the phone being perfectly placed for us to find was too obvious. And both of you are terrible liars.'

'If you know so much about it, why don't you tell Monami, then,' snapped Kajal. 'And also tell her what you would have done differently.'

'Well, I don't know all of the details, obviously.'

'You surprise me.'

'But here's what I think, anyway. You found Anika's body somewhere. I think in your room, or somewhere else in your house. Shortly after DB was killed, and probably right after you called the police. And you knew that once the police arrived, they'd immediately suspect you. So you decided to hide her body. Wherever it was, it was somewhere good because the police obviously didn't find it . . . where did you hide it, by the way?'

'I told Jyoti to roll her up in a carpet and put it under the bed,' said

Kajal, gloomily. 'There's such a jumble down there, no one would have looked twice.'

'And then you waited for a day, smuggled the body out and put it right in the street next to your house. Brilliant.'

'Are you being sarcastic? We didn't know what else to do,' said Kajal. 'I just wanted her body out of the house. I knew it would be linked back to the party whatever we did, and I didn't want to add any fingerprints or get caught driving somewhere with the body in the boot of my car. So the next night, I went out to the press and told them I would make a statement. They all started clustering around me, and Jyoti and Karim took the roll of carpet out through the back door and put the body in the street. We thought that might be safer than doing it in the middle of the night or anything like that, when there may have been the odd person still awake and watching. Some of the press were living in tents out by the gate. Anyway, this plan worked—they could have literally strangled her there and I don't think the journalists would have noticed, they were so intent on pointing their cameras at me to capture the moment when I might incriminate myself.'

'Quite ingenious,' murmured Mridula. 'But a sad reflection on our press.'

'Yes, well. Being part of that august body myself, I had a hunch it would work. It took Jyoti and Karim five minutes and they were back. And then that ass Mrs Ahuja discovered the body the next day. And it all seemed to go according to plan—the idea being that Anika had left the party and then been killed afterwards outside my house, as opposed to inside.'

'Of course, you forgot about her phone . . .'

'Yes,' said Kajal, still dismayed by the memory of finding it later. 'It had slid off her body and was lying in a corner of my room.'

Mridula shook her head. 'You should have told me,' she said again. 'That new DCP . . .'

'Yes, he isn't so much of a numbskull as the other police, it seems.

He cottoned on quite quickly to the fact that the body couldn't have lain out there for a day and a night and it must have been moved there recently. Also, something about forensics—I guess all that C.I.D.-Crime Patrol stuff they show on TV isn't fiction, after all. Some carpet fibres were still on her, or something. And he got the time of death much more accurately than we thought he would. And once he knew all that, we were clearly indicated. He started with the driver, of course, and then got to Jyoti. We all tried to tell him what had happened, but he seemed to think I was just protecting them. Pah,' she spat.

'And what about DB?'

'He'll find a way to link them, no doubt. Anyone could have poisoned that glass, after all.'

'Please tell us everything now. Start from the beginning.'

'It all happened after DB died. I had called the ambulance, and the police, and I staggered into the house. I went into my bedroom . . . and I found her.'

'Anika?'

'Yes. It . . . she . . . was in my room. On my bed, in fact. I may have screamed, it was such a shock. Her body was so cold. Luckily everyone was in the garden, clustered around DB's body, so the house was empty. I didn't know what to do. I thought for a second that I was going completely mad. With what had happened to DB, and then immediately to be faced with another dead body. I did what I always do when I'm stuck—I called Jyoti.'

'I see.'

'I depend on her for everything. Anyway, she came, and we agreed instantly that we couldn't let her be found like this. I so regretted having called the police at that point. But they were coming. So, I went down and did a little bit more head-clutching (it didn't take much pretending, I can tell you) and kept everyone out of the house, while she and Karim found an old carpet, rolled her into it and stashed it under the bed. You know what the bottoms of beds are like . . . mine had all sorts of things under there, suitcases and boxes and whatnot. So, they just sort of moved things around and hid her there.'

'And how soon after that did the police come?'

'Quite soon, I think. By that time almost everyone had managed to leave. It was just Samar, Jemin, and me. And the staff, obviously.'

'You didn't want to confide in Samar or Jemin?'

Kajal hesitated. 'I thought about it. But I couldn't . . . you know Samar and Anika's history. It would just have complicated things even more. Honestly, I just wanted everyone out of my house so that I could sit and have a second to *think*.'

'How long did the police stay? Lucky for you they didn't find the body,' said Mridula drily.

'You know the police. They were local, and a whole circus of them arrived at once. They stayed for hours, asked endless questions, and they did look around the whole house and garden. That was a bad time for us, but Jyoti handled it so calmly. I was more of a wreck but luckily, I think they were expecting that. And in the end, they didn't find anything. They left, but half the country's press had showed up by that point. So we couldn't do anything more that night. I told Jyoti we'd have to leave it for a while. I slept in another bedroom. Of course, I didn't really sleep but I couldn't bear to be in my own bedroom for obvious reasons. And then the next day you called me, talking about social media.'

Mridula looked a little guilty. 'It wasn't only about social media.'

'The more I thought about it, the more guilty I looked. Anika had been so rude about my book, about the launch. They would say that I killed her in a rage, or that I wanted to stop her from publishing a negative review, or some rubbish. I thought they would put me in prison immediately.'

'What about the phone? Was it cracked when you found it?'

'Er, well—no.'

'I see. Did you happen to look to see who she had called last, presumably from your balcony?'

'Are you joking? First of all, I couldn't work that phone—couldn't unlock it. Second of all, the bare sight of it sent me into such a panic, I wanted to destroy it immediately. But I didn't know how to do that either, or whether these things can be traced, so I thought it was safer to leave it for someone else to find. And you two found it beautifully.'

'Jyoti wasn't so calm on that day,' said Monami, remembering the crashed tray.

'Well, at that point I think our nerves were just shot. In some ways I'm glad the truth has come out because it really was a mental strain to keep hiding it. But now they've taken away Jyoti and Karim and I'm sure they'll be back for me the moment they can put a case together.'

'They won't,' said Monami. 'I think they're still hot on another trail. And we'll figure out what happened, don't worry.'

'Will you?' said Kajal, doubtfully.

'Well, being fed the wrong information hasn't helped. But I think we will. We're quite close now,' said Mridula.

'Are we?' said Monami, unconsciously echoing Kajal's doubt. 'If DB and Anika were killed around the same time . . . well, that only makes matters murkier, in my opinion.'

'It does,' agreed Kajal. 'I've been so confused by everything. It probably made much more sense to you since you've always thought that someone may have done it later. But we saw Anika a few minutes earlier, remember? She was ashing into my champa tree. So, it literally must have happened a few moments before I found her. That's a pretty narrow window.'

'And you didn't meet anyone when you came up the stairs?' asked Monami.

'No, by that point everyone had already gone down.'

Monami wondered if Mridula was going to bring up the story that Meena had told, about seeing Vasudha going upstairs. But Mridula simply sat there, saying nothing. *Were her eyes closed?*

'So how much time would you say there was between DB dying

downstairs and you going up to your room?' Mridula said, as if she had suddenly woken up.

'It's difficult to say exactly. I've thought and thought about it. There was so much to do downstairs, I had to call the doctor, calm Meena down, all of that. It may have been about ten, maybe fifteen minutes. But not more than that.'

Mridula had closed her eyes again.

'Something is definitely . . . off,' she said, finally. 'Something we're not seeing.'

The two other women merely looked at her questioningly.

'What are we saying? That by some coincidence, two murders happened at your party at almost exactly the same time? Or that someone murdered DB and the second murderer took advantage of the chaos and killed Anika while everyone was distracted? It seems unlikely if it all happened within ten minutes.'

'It seems unlikely, but it did happen,' said Monami, wondering if she wasn't pointing out the obvious.

'It was plausible when there was more time,' said Mridula. 'This . . . doesn't feel plausible. We're missing something.'

'We're definitely missing something. We don't know who committed either murder!' said Monami.

iii

Back in the car, this time with rain pounding on the windshield, a distracted Mridula drove faster than she normally would have down the narrow Chhattarpur lane, splashing a pedestrian with mud and failing to notice him swearing loudly and shaking his fist.

'So, do we think she's telling the truth?' said Monami, who hadn't noticed the pedestrian either.

'About which part?' said Mridula, taking her eyes off the road.

'Well, all of it. She's lied once before,' said Monami. 'Imagine if she didn't find the body, but actually killed Anika in the bedroom when she found her there, alive. A crime of passion and circumstance.'

'Yes, we'll have to consider that a possibility. Personally, knowing her, I think the suggestion is ridiculous. But we'll definitely have to consider it.'

'She did lie to us before,' said Monami, deciding not to take offence at her suggestion being described as ridiculous.

'Yes, that was very unfortunate, not to mention very silly.' Mridula sounded mildly disapproving, thought Monami, as if Kajal had been caught cheating at rounders in school.

'She has a motive. One thing could have led to another . . .'

Mridula shook her head. 'Something's missing,' she said.

'Yes, you've said that before.'

'It just feels like it has to be two completely separate crimes, committed by two completely separate people, one upstairs and one downstairs,' said Mridula. 'But how can that be? It doesn't FIT!'

She shouted this last word and Monami jumped, almost hitting her head on the Wagon R's roof, seatbelt notwithstanding.

'Sorry, sorry. It's just frustrating,' Mridula thumped her steering wheel in anger. 'I feel like I'm getting old. I just thought I would be better at this whole detective thing. It feels like I can tell when things aren't right, but I can't tell what's not right about them, and I can't make them right. I can't explain them.'

'You're doing just fine,' said Monami. 'You've picked up on a whole lot of things that no one else has.'

But Mridula had relapsed into a cantankerous silence.

Eventually, she said, 'You have to go and talk to your friends. They may be able to provide the missing link. We know that Tina was downstairs when the toast was happening. Where were Devika and Ishaan? They may have been upstairs, and they may have been the kids that Meena was referring to. You have to ask them if they know anything, or if they saw anything.'

Monami, queasily, recalled the taut faces of Devika and Ishaan, who hadn't been at the toast with the others, when she had spoken to them on Teams the next morning. Could they really be somehow implicated?

'And let's revisit our two possibilities,' continued Mridula. 'Option One—the crimes are linked. DB and Anika worked at the same paper. There's some motive that links them together. And both were targeted in a carefully planned murder.'

'Right.'

'And Option Two—these are two separate crimes. DB dies, and then the second murder is purely opportunistic. Someone sees an opportunity, they seize it. In that case, we need two separate culprits.'

'From everything we've found out,' said Monami, slowly, 'it's seeming more and more like Option Two, which is surprising. I started out thinking there was no way the crimes were not linked. Which do you think it is?'

Mridula shook her head. 'I don't know. I'm almost wondering . . . if there isn't an Option Three?'

26

Haven't the Earthliest

i

Almost every newspaper office in Delhi is located near an Udupi restaurant. And, in most cases, that restaurant is named Udupi Restaurant. So it was with the *Delhi Daily* office, on a busy main road that also housed, improbably, alongside several newspaper offices and a busy passport office, an international doll museum.

Monami, Tina, Devika and Ishaan were seated around a table inside Udupi Restaurant. The tables were all made of white plastic, as were the chairs. White paper napkins wilted in stainless steel holders in the centre of each table. But anything Udupi Restaurant lacked when it came to their interior decor, they made up for in the freshness and quality of their food. Lunchtime was always packed to the rafters.

Today, the four were there during the post-lunch lull and there were only two or three stragglers in an otherwise empty room. Their waiter had a surly, put-upon expression as he brought around cups of South Indian filter coffee, and then went into the back to noisily and pointedly finish his own lunch.

'Right,' said Monami. 'This is an interview.'

'How's the investigation going?' asked Tina. 'Found anything out yet? Was it Jyoti and the driver? Has Kajal been housing the Chhattarpur Bonnie and Clyde?'

'It's weird that the police haven't made any other arrests yet,' said Devika. 'Isn't it? They were after Vasudha in the beginning and now they seem to have made a U-turn.'

'Who do they suspect now?' said Ishaan. 'Do you know?'

'Finished? No more questions, is it? I meant that *I* am going to be interviewing *you*,' said Monami. 'Not the other way round.'

'Just tell us *something*, Mona,' said Devika, sounding anxious. 'We haven't heard anything. It's been really weird.'

Monami sighed. 'Okay. First, I don't know if it was Jyoti and the driver, but it seems doubtful. It's only been a few days since the murders; they can't possibly arrest anyone yet, and besides, they don't have any evidence. Or rather they don't have any evidence that points to a single person. I would say they're spoiled for choice when it comes to suspects. Ishaan, to answer your question, I haven't the earthliest who the police suspect. We're not really working with them. And it seems to be a different person every day—Samar, Jemin, Vasudha. Now, can I ask some questions of my own?'

All three looked a little sullen, Tina shrugged and looked away.

'I'll take that as a yes. So—here's the sitch so far. It seems Anika was killed far earlier than we expected, around the same time as DB in fact. One in the garden, the other upstairs.'

Devika and Ishaan looked at each other.

'What? Something you two want to tell me?' said Monami, catching this glance.

Tina turned around and looked at them, her eyebrows rising. 'Guys?'

To everyone's horror, Devika burst into tears. 'I told you,' she said to Ishaan. 'I to-o-old you!'

'Calm down,' said Monami, as gently as she could. Mridula had been right to choose not to come to this meeting. 'Tell me what you saw. When was it—when you guys were upstairs?'

Ishaan put an arm around his girlfriend and nodded, miserably. 'We'd snuck away. There were so many rooms upstairs, we just ducked into the nearest one.'

'Kajal's room?'

Ishaan shrugged. 'I don't know. I don't think so, though. The lights were off, and it looked pretty unused. It was muggy. The . . . er, the bed was dusty.' He looked away.

'So, what did you see? Did you see who killed Anika?'

'No, no. But we . . . well, we saw her body.' Fresh muffled sobs from Devika.

'You . . . you saw the body?'

'Look, we're telling you this, and only you, okay?' said Ishaan, fiercely. 'I do not want to get mixed up with the police.'

'I mean . . . I can't guarantee that. But tell me, anyway. Please tell me. It's almost already out there.'

Ishaan sighed. 'We went upstairs . . . found a room . . . started . . . you know. And it was dark, so we were fumbling about a fair bit. We finally got to the bed . . .'

'And I bumped against something,' wailed Devika, lifting her head from Ishaan's chest like a phoenix. 'I thought it was a lumpy bolster or something . . .'

'But it was too angular to be that . . .'

'So, we switched on our phone lights . . .'

'And we saw her!' Devika burst into sobs again and even Ishaan looked a bit green.

'Was she dead?' said Monami.

'She looked dead,' said Ishaan. 'Gosh, we didn't really check. That scarf around her neck, her eyes bulging. We just assumed she was.'

'So, what did you do?'

'Are you kidding? We freaking hightailed it out of there. As fast as we could. We were just staggering around, wondering what we should do, when we heard all the commotion.'

'That's when DB died?'

'Yes. And, of course, then we didn't dare say anything to anyone about finding Anika. Everyone would have thought we'd done it.'

Monami thought back to the conversation they'd just had with Kajal. Almost the exact same words used. *So many enemies.*

She looked at her friends, hesitating. 'Guys, I'm afraid I'm going to have to take this to Mridula.'

Ishaan said 'No!' at the same time as Devika said 'You promised!'

'I didn't promise anything. But don't you see—this changes everything again. What you're saying is that *she was already dead when DB died*. That washes out the theory that it was someone just looking to take advantage of the chaos.' Monami frowned. It also seemed to wash out her own personal theory of Anika being at least partly responsible for the death of DB. But she wasn't ready to put that part away just yet. 'Who did you see when you came out of the room?'

'We didn't see anyone,' said Ishaan. 'Not before, because we weren't looking, and certainly not after.'

'Come on, you've got to think.'

Ishaan and Devika looked at each other. She rubbed her eyes a little and said, 'We really didn't notice, Mona. I mean, there were a bunch of people out there. But I think they were mostly from Sea Lion, or maybe friends of Kajal or Jemin. I think there was a waitress. We didn't really recognise anyone. I don't think anyone from the office was up there.'

'There was onc person who told us he was up there,' said Tina, suddenly. 'Remember? Shamik. You should ask him, Mona. He was not only upstairs, he was also creepily watching everyone and everything, he said.'

'Give the guy a break, Tina,' said Ishaan, quietly. 'You know he's just a weirdo. He didn't mean anything by what he said.'

'Oh, please. You guys are taking him at his word way too easily. How do you know he wasn't responsible for Anika's death? He definitely hated her—remember the shouting match when she killed his precious page one story? How do you know he's not trying to throw us off the scent? To . . . to throw the blame on *me*?'

'What do you mean?' asked Monami. 'When did he do that? Explain.'

They briefly described the scene at the cafeteria, and what Shamik had said. Monami made a mental note to tell Mridula this detail.

'We should probably talk to him,' Monami said, when they were done. 'He may have seen more than he knows up there.'

'You're missing the point, Mona,' said Tina. 'If Anika was already dead, when he was up there, he's a suspect. He has to be!'

'Maybe,' said Monami. 'Anyway, look, guys, I should go and take all this to Mridula. There's lots to discuss. But *please* just keep thinking of anything we may have missed. Now that the news is bound to come out about the earlier time of death, the police will be looking much more closely into what everyone was doing at the party, where, when, and all that.' Cue fresh sobs from Devika, which Monami ignored.

'Tina, your . . . your family's history with DB may also come out.'

Tina looked up. 'What? Why?'

'Babe, more people know about it than you think. And no one else has anything close to a motive to kill DB. He had no enemies. Everyone loved him. His finances were clear. The police are going to be desperate for anything, any sign of conflict.'

Tina was silent. This fact had not escaped her, and she had spent many sleepless nights worrying about it. But it still shook her to hear this bald statement from a friend and, more importantly, a source so close to the investigation.

She looked so stricken, that Monami leaned over and put an arm around her.

'Hey, don't worry,' she said. 'We're on your side.' The same phrase that she had used with Vasudha, but this time it meant something. The idea that Tina could be involved in this was crazy. Monami would never believe it for a minute. 'But you have to help us. Is there anything you can add? The last time we spoke you said you felt like you were watching a play. Have you thought any more about that? Why did you feel that way?'

Tina shook her head. 'I still can't put my finger on it,' she said. 'It . . . it just felt like people were being directed, if you know what I mean. Take Kajal, for instance,' she added, as everyone looked blank. 'She clearly just wanted everyone to go home. The last thing she wanted was another drink. But there she was, clinking glasses with the rest of them. It just felt like . . . I don't know, like she was being pulled by an invisible string.'

'Doesn't that bring us back to Vasudha?' said Ishaan. 'If anyone was doing the directing, it was her. She practically insisted on the toast, poured the drinks herself.'

Monami thought back to the interview with Meena. 'If it weren't for a total lack of motive, Vasudha would be my prime suspect. But . . . I don't know, guys. I met her, and . . . she is not in a good place. She's suffering. I didn't get a guilty vibe off her at all.'

'Mona, you know we love you and we think the world of you, right?' said Tina, squeezing her arm.

'Uh-oh,' said Monami. 'What's coming now?'

'Well, I mean this in the nicest way possible, but you are *too* trusting, girl. You trust everyone! You wouldn't think anyone was capable of murder. They would literally have to commit it in front of you for you to believe it.'

'What?!' said Monami, indignantly. 'I'm shocked by this libel. And hurt. Shocked and hurt. Anyway, you don't know what you're talking about. I was literally just suspecting Kajal of lying through her teeth before coming here to meet you.'

'Cashew Nut? Well, that's a start, I suppose. But you need to take it further! How do you know that Ishaan and Devika are telling the truth now, for instance? You've just swallowed everything they've said like a lamb.'

'Hey now!' said Devika. 'What do you mean?'

'How do you know they didn't kill Anika and then make up this charming story about finding her body while indulging in their sexual escapades? Gross, by the way, guys.'

'What the hell, Tina!' said Ishaan.

Monami thought again about Meena, about how she heard someone sobbing and crying on the balcony. *One of the kids.*

Tina was still talking. 'My point is, you can't just assume that Vasudha is not guilty because of a *vibe*. If you ask me, she definitely *is* guilty.'

Monami looked at Tina, searching her face for clues. 'You're right, of course. And we're not discounting her, or assuming she's not guilty. We're doing everything by the book. Mridula is taking exactly the tack you're describing, Tina. She'll not only be asking whether Ishaan and Devika are telling the truth about finding the body, she'll be asking about you, too. She may ask, for instance, how do you know that Tina's not playing a stupendous double bluff and working with Shamik as an accomplice, one upstairs and one downstairs?'

Devika, Ishaan and Tina were aghast.

Monami broke into laughter. 'I'm joking! Relax, I'm joking! No one could seriously suspect any of you.'

But the troubled expressions did not leave their faces. And, ultimately, she didn't blame them—without proof, anything was possible.

The waiter came by with their bill. Monami looked at him, in his white Udupi Restaurant uniform, and then suddenly remembered, 'Oh, speaking of questions, I do have one more about your story. Did you say you saw a waitress upstairs?'

ii

'What do you think?' said Monami. She was in Mridula's office, reporting what she'd heard. The Udupi Dialogues, as it was to be known, Shamik's testimony, the waitress—all of it.

And a completely new expression had come across Mridula's face. She was positively beaming. For Mridula, this meant a smirk now curled up one corner of her mouth, but it seemed to transform her face.

'Well, this is the first breakthrough we've had in a while. If not ever! You agree?'

'Er, yes? But which bit, particularly? The timing, right? I know Ishaan and Devika's testimony isn't the most . . . scientifically accurate, but I believed them,' said Monami. 'I wish they'd made sure she was actually dead, though. Or told someone.'

'Yes, but they behaved like the scared children they were,' said Mridula. 'Anyway, well done you! It's all very enlightening. Even something Shamik said sounded interesting . . . I must go speak with him myself,' she said and stared off into space.

'Do you think—' Monami started, but Mridula put up a hand to stop her.

'Give me a minute,' she said. 'It's all very hazy at the moment, but I think I'm having an epiphany.'

Monami stifled the urge to say, 'Well, it's about time.'

After a minute and a half, Mridula opened her eyes. The epiphany had left no trace, other than that she now looked like a smug owl instead of a dyspeptic owl. An owl that had just answered a difficult quiz question correctly.

'Well?!' demanded Monami.

'Okay. Okay. I think, I *think* I have a theory. I have to refine it, but I think this one has legs. Oh, it definitely has legs. It answers everything. Even Meena's dream and the question of the elusive waitress,' Mridula's eyes shone.

'That's . . . well, that's amazing. What is it?' said Monami, bluntly.

'Right. Well, sorry, but I do think we need a tiny bit more information. It's like the train has left the station, but it hasn't quite arrived yet.'

'You can say that again,' muttered Monami.

'I think, you know,' said Mridula, her face still lit up, 'that it's time to pay a visit to Anika's family. Shekhar hasn't set us up with an introduction, but I have no doubt Abhishek will. The famous Kapoors. Or at least Anita.'

'Oh.'

'Yes. We haven't had enough to go on before. But I think it's called for now. Definitely called for.'

'Er, what will we say to her when we go see her?'

'You leave that to me,' said Mridula, with what Monami recognised with surprise as a grin. She wasn't sure she trusted this newly giddy Mridula. It seemed most unnatural.

27

One of Those Bubbles Made of Steel Traps

i

Anita Kapoor lived in her family home in Vasant Vihar. Like Kajal's home, it stood in a quiet, leafy road, behind a sizeable garden, but there the similarities ended. Where Kajal's home could be described as woodworm chic, the Kapoor manse gleamed. Where the former had dampness creeping up the walls and smelt of mildew, the latter was all steel, marble and glass. Tropical plants and creepers had been strategically placed on balconies, and huge, discreetly lit paintings could be seen through floor-to-ceiling windows.

Monami looked through the iron gates while Mridula laboriously explained to the guard why they were there. This was different, and less welcoming, than all the other homes they'd visited. Even Anika and Shekhar's chilly Jor Bagh home now seemed cosy, with its blaze of bougainvillaea and wooden shutters. This place seemed like a fortress; it was like trying to access a building that held state secrets. The guard, automatic rifle on his shoulder, peered suspiciously at them, unwilling to let them enter even after they dropped Abhishek Kapoor's name.

How would the likes of *you*, the guard seemed to be saying with his eyes, know the likes of *him*?

Calls had to be made. And then the gates parted and the guard waved them through, still looking as though he had the gravest misgivings.

They entered a marble lobby and arrived at an elevator.

'Madam is on the third floor,' said another supercilious guard.

'I can't believe these people have a glass lift inside their house. This is nuts,' said Monami, gawping at the bronze and gold accents, the crystal chandeliers, and museum-grade art.

Mridula nodded grimly. 'Welcome to the lives of the one per cent of the one per cent.'

The doors opened and they found themselves in a vast living room. Most of the walls were essentially huge windows, and the light-filled space was dotted with low sofas, fashionably curved lamps, and soft piles of carpet. Padding towards them on one of these rugs was Anika's sister, Anita. She was dressed casually in a tracksuit and had a welcoming smile on her face, but Monami had a distinct impression of her as impermeable, untouchable, as though shielded by an invisible bubble. One of those bubbles made of steel traps, not soap and water.

'Hi,' said Anita, thrusting a hand forward. 'You're Anika's colleagues? I'm so sorry, the guard didn't catch your names.'

'I'm Mridula Majumdar.'

'Er, and I'm Monami Chatterjee.' Their names fell with a thud on the floor, and no one picked them up.

Anita continued to smile a little patronisingly.

'Do come in and sit down. I'm so glad you came. I've been feeling a little removed from all the action.' As she was talking, she led them over to a low, creamy leather sofa and indicated that they should sit.'

Mridula and Monami sat gingerly on the edge of the sofa, Monami felt a little like a stray cat who had wandered in from the outside, a cat that usually looked for trouble but here, amid all the art, leather and fiddle-leaf figs, was reduced to an uncertain silence.

'I'm glad at least someone from our own paper is working on it,' Anita said, kicking off proceedings. 'I was going to call to check, and now I don't have to. So, what have you found out? The police seem to have changed tack from blaming everything on that unfortunate intern.'

'Have you been apprised of the most recent facts?' asked Mridula, even more pompously than usual.

'You mean the arrests—this housekeeper? The driver? Yes, of course,' said Anita.

'The arrests, yes, but also the . . . implications.'

'What do you mean?'

'The timing. Previously it was thought that your sister was killed after the party, by someone out on the street. But now it seems that she was killed inside the house. *During* the party. Not long after DB's death, in fact.'

Anita stood up, sharply. 'I did know that,' she said. 'It seems to have been indicated all along, doesn't it? What does it mean?'

'It means, I think, that her death was very carefully premeditated. That's what it means. An impression has been created of the *opposite*, of the fact that this is a crime that has been carried out on the spur of the moment. But actually, I think the timing, the characters, the location, everything was very carefully considered.'

There was a short silence.

'How interesting,' said Anita, sounding a little impatient. 'And where does that lead? Basically, who do you think did it?'

Mridula asked a question back. 'What's your theory about what happened to your sister, Anita?'

Anita seemed to consider this question. She looked at the two women, and Monami got an impression of a sharp analytical mind at work. Finally, Anita said, 'I don't know how well you knew Anika?'

'We were colleagues for a number of years,' said Mridula, cautiously.

'You probably knew her as—what? Difficult? Aggressive?'

Mridula merely bowed her head.

'I think it might help if I told you something about my sister.'

'Please do. That's part of the reason why we're here. We want to know what Anika Kapoor was really like.'

'And who would know better than her sister? Well, I can tell you . . . Anika *was* difficult,' said Anita. 'She was my sister. I loved her. And I know it's conventional to say kind things, nice things, about one who has passed. Especially when they're part of your own family. But the truth is, well—she was always difficult. Always. I wouldn't say this if I didn't think it may have some bearing on her death, you understand?'

Monami felt a faint surprise at this attitude, but it was mixed with a kind of relief. Here, finally, was someone who saw Anika for who she was. Not her father or her husband's version, but one that was honest, unfiltered. Anika, as Mridula would say, warts and all. And Anita was right, who would know better than her sister?

Mridula nodded. 'Go on.'

'Even as a child. She was one of those children who couldn't bear for someone else to have something that she wanted herself. She would break toys rather than give them to other children. I remember once we went to a beach in Goa and I found this beautiful, pale pink conch shell. We had been looking for shells and we'd picked up about a dozen or so, and then I found this beauty. I was thrilled, of course, and Anika didn't say anything, but I could tell that she was jealous.'

'How old were you both?'

'It sounds so childish, doesn't it! Well, we were children. She must have been eight, and I ten. Something like that.'

'What happened?'

'When it was time to go home, I saw that it had somehow disappeared from my collection. I confronted her and she laughed, told me she had buried it back into the sand. She didn't know where, she hadn't left any markings, and there was no way to find it again on what seemed then an immense beach.'

'She buried it so that neither of you could have it?'

'Yes. I know it sounds like a small thing, but it illustrates her personality, even then. She would rather destroy a thing she wanted, make it disappear, rather than let someone else have it.'

Anita paused here, looking to see if Mridula and Monami were paying attention. Both were listening intently.

'It was like that later, too. Of course, as she grew up, she found ways to become more socially . . . let's say palatable, but underneath her nature was the same, quite ruthless.

'You can imagine, it didn't make her a lot of friends. Oh, of course she had a massive social network. Between her job, her books, and our family, she probably knew half of Delhi. But intimate friends? I'm not sure if she had even one. She had me, and she had Shekhar. And that was it.'

Mridula nodded. 'And what was your relationship like? Good?'

'Do you have a sister, Ms Majumdar?' said Anita. Mridula shook her head.

Anita then looked at Monami, who nodded. 'I do.'

'Then you know. Our relationship wasn't always good, as you put it, but we were sisters. It was . . . how shall I put it? It was us against the world. From the very beginning. I knew her, I understood her nature for what it was. I had no illusions about her, you understand? But I knew her. And she knew me. And in our family, that kind of relationship is important. You have to know who has your back. Especially as two daughters in a family full of sons, cousins, nephews, uncles—every one of whom were constantly planning some coup or other—you have to know who you can rely on. And I could rely on Anika. And she could rely on me.' Anita sighed. 'I . . . I don't want to be sentimental. That's why I told you that story. You mustn't be under any illusions about her character. But Anika, well . . . she was my sister. I feel like I've lost part of myself. That's all.'

Anita paused here, as if to compose herself. Monami was taken aback at the poignance of the older Kapoor sister's words. She had only ever seen Anita on TV or in the newspapers, and it showed how little you knew about someone from their public persona. Anita had touched her. She thought sentimentally about her own sister.

'So, when you ask me what could have happened,' continued Anita, 'who could have done it, I have to answer that I simply don't know. Because Anika made life difficult for herself, I think there were any number of people at that party who had it in for her.' Anita exhaled. 'That's the unfortunate truth.'

'Tell us about this book she was writing.'

'Ah, the book,' said Anita. 'The infamous book. What would you like to know?'

'How did you feel about it?'

'My father was convinced that she wouldn't publish it, so I . . . I didn't really feel anything, I suppose.'

'Had you read it? Reached out to her about it?'

'No, I didn't. I don't want to make excuses, but there has been so much going on. You have no idea how many hours we work. It must look like we just cut ourselves cheques for doing nothing, but I assure you that's not the case. I am busy from early in the morning until late at night. I'm at the office, and when I'm not at the office, I'm at events, or I'm working from home. There was just no time to reach out to Anika. But I . . . I can't tell you how much I regret it now.'

'Of course, I understand. And did you agree with your father's belief that she wouldn't publish it?'

'I hadn't really thought about it, to be honest. My father seemed so confident. And Aviroop Uncle is a close family friend. I thought between them, well, they must be right. That book wouldn't have been published.'

Monami had a sudden vision of the two sisters living in this hard, cold house with their overbearing, rule-bound parents, having to constantly meet some imaginary standard for how to be a Kapoor. For someone of Anita's disposition, it seemed to have b Anita had settled into the gilded cage. Anika had t

'Your father tells us he had a pretty intense ch week ago,' said Mridula. 'About her role in the famil you know about that?'

'He told you about that, did he?'

Mridula nodded.

'I wonder why. It's not like him to talk openly about o concerns.' Anita ran a restless hand through her hair. 'Th thing has changed him beyond anything I could have imagi be expected, I suppose. Yes, to answer your question, I do know that. I know that Dad wanted Anika to play a greater role in run the family business. Of course I didn't want to tell him this, but it a forlorn hope on his part. She would never have agreed.'

'You think not?'

Anita shook her head. 'Never. To Dad, you see, our business is the world. It's one of the most important in India, a fact that he's very proud of. He inherited some of it, you know, but he built a lot of it on his own. It is a legacy to be proud of. And he just didn't understand why Anika wanted no part of it. He kept thinking that it was a phase, and that she would eventually grow out of everything else she was doing, the books, the influencer stuff. He didn't realise that she had no intention of letting go of any of that. She in fact wanted to do *more* of it. She wanted to commercialise her social media profile, grow her audience, play "Anika Kapoor" for a living. He just didn't get that.'

'And so, when she lost her editorial position at the *Delhi Daily*, what do you think her reaction would have been?'

'I think she would have been furious, honestly. I wish he'd told me before taking such a drastic step, but he didn't.' Anita shook her head. Again, the gilded cage door had slammed shut, thought Monami. 'It's been most unfortunate. It's driven my father to a terrible despair, the same week that this happened, that he would . . . well, take such a step.

s just been so cut up about it.'

Monami remembered the old man seeming to grow more frail in nt of their eyes when he spoke about Anika.

'And so,' said Anita, 'I'm hoping that this police investigation will ear fruit soon. It's really not good for him to go on feeling this way. Hopefully he can get some closure. Have you got anywhere, by any chance?'

'We're making progress, I think,' said Mridula. 'We have a number of theories. Of course, we've had to rework all of our ideas in the face of this new timeline.' Without Anita having to ask, Mridula explained: 'There were any number of people at this party who had a motive, however petty, for killing your sister. But we've now found out that if she had been killed *earlier*, they would all have an alibi. They were watching DB die, and so couldn't have also been inside Kajal's house, killing Anika.'

'Who are you talking about? Someone specific?'

'Pretty much everyone,' said Mridula. 'All the names thrown around by the media, by the police. Kajal. Samar. Jemin. The unfortunate intern, as you said.'

'Oh,' said Anita. 'Well, it's good to know they've been cleared. Especially Samar, he's been a friend of ours for decades. I knew him in school, too, though I was older, of course. And of course, their relationship had changed in recent years. My mother is quite convinced that he encouraged her to write this book, to alienate herself from us. She thinks that he manipulated her.' Anita shook her head.

Monami recalled Samar's drawn face, his raw grief.

'You don't agree?' said Mridula, perhaps recalling the same thing.

'I . . . I'm not sure. It doesn't sound like the Samar I knew in school, but so much water has passed under the bridge since then. Even Jemin. They used to be so close, but he seemed to just hate her recently. I don't know what he had against her but whenever he could speak out against her or denigrate her, he would. In public, on social media. But even so, I found it so unlikely that he would . . .' she trailed off, and then said abruptly, 'So they've all been cleared?'

'Well, unfortunately, Kajal has put herself in a position where her word is not to be easily believed,' said Mridula. 'But if it can be proved that the crime took place earlier than previously thought, yes, I believe it's quite impossible for her or Samar to have committed the crime. Jemin . . . is maybe less unlikely, but he's not likely either. He was elsewhere when her body was found.'

Anita shuddered a little at the mention of the body.

'Horrible to be talking about Anika like this,' she said.

'I know, I'm sorry,' said Mridula, a little formally. 'But thank you for being honest with us today. You are the only person in your family who has been so far, you know.'

'Oh?' said Anita.

'Yes. You speak about your sister as though she's a real person, not just a . . . news headline. A reputation to upkeep.'

Anita nodded. 'We were sisters.'

'I don't think you ever said, by the way . . . had you read the book?'

Anita looked at Mridula, and there was a sudden flare of anger in her eyes. In that instant, Monami saw the resemblance between the sisters. It had been there the whole time, disguised by their differing temperaments. When Anita's mask slipped, it was startling how similar the two sisters were.

'I read some of it,' she said now, her voice not betraying any emotion. 'And, for your information, it *didn't* change my feelings towards her. I totally understand that she was lashing out. This was the only way she knew how. All the things she said in her book . . . it was just her outlet. I agree with my father; I don't think she would have published it. Once it came down to the wire, she would have pulled the plug.'

Monami and Mridula glanced at each other. Anita caught the look and said, 'I suppose you think I'm kidding myself.'

'You know your sister best, ma'am,' said Mridula, politely.

'I do. And I tell you she wouldn't have published it.'

'And you really have no theories yourself?'

'In the beginning, I thought it must be either Jemin or Samar,' said Anita, thoughtfully. 'I was so angry. I . . . I went on TV and pretty much accused them.'

'And now, your opinion has changed?'

'I'm certainly not throwing around any accusations,' said Anita, grimly. 'I have to keep my position in mind. But honestly, even thinking it through, no one else really jumps to mind. Who else could it have been? I have no idea. I suppose . . . I suppose the timeline couldn't be wrong? It does hinge mostly on Kajal, and this housekeeper. Do we trust them? Or maybe they were all in it together?'

Mridula smiled knowingly. 'The *Orient Express* trick? Maybe.'

'We need answers,' said Anita. 'What can I do to help?'

'I'll be in touch,' said Mridula. 'My next stop is the police.'

Monami started. This was news to her.

'Oh? And what will you say to them?' asked Anita. 'You don't appear to have found any answers yet?'

'There are questions,' said Mridula. 'There are some curious points about this case. Too many motives, motives that don't fit. Two murders, one with too many suspects, one with none. There's an odd cast of characters—everyone we've talked about—and there's even a waitress who inexplicably keeps making an appearance.'

'A waitress? What do you mean?' Anita snapped. 'What does a waitress have to do with it?'

'A waitress and a model.'

'What an odd little woman you are.'

Mridula merely smiled politely again. 'Ms Kapoor, thank you for seeing us.'

ii

'What . . . was . . . that?' demanded Monami, when they had finally wound their way out of the house and down the massive driveway and were back in their little car. The guard had silently watched from his guard box but had made no move towards them.

'I wanted to let her know what we'd found out.'

'About the timeline? You didn't mention Ishaan and Devika's evidence.'

'Yes, I feel it's better for her to think it rests on Kajal's word.'

'And we're really going to the police now?'

'We are.'

'Are . . . are you sure you know what you're doing?'

Mridula gave a rather lopsided grin. 'Wait and see.'

'That woman was tough as nails,' said Monami, thoughtfully. 'I think she really loved her sister, but . . . well, I'm starting to feel sorrier and sorrier for Anika.'

'Why is that?'

'Well, she gave the whole "we are sisters" speech, but when I think of me and my sister . . .' Monami hesitated, thinking Mridula might find this point childish.

'Yes, go on. You and your sister?'

'Well, I would expect her to take my side over our *parents*. I mean, that's just the basic pact. It's the two of you against the world, but the world starts with your parents.'

Mridula gave her peculiar grin again. 'That's not how families like this work.'

'I mean, why make the speech then? If you're going to stand by while your sister's slung out of a job, not support her about the book, all of it. Also, she said she didn't think it could be Samar or Jemin, but then she went back to them pretty quickly.'

There was a pause.

'So did you get what you wanted out of that interview?' asked Monami a little timidly.

'I wanted, as I said, to alert Anita to certain facts that we had uncovered. We have, and now we watch for the results.'

They stopped at a traffic light, and both glanced at their phones. Mridula opened her map app and looked for a route to the central police station.

Monami's phone had been on silent during their recent interview, and she now saw with horror that she had piles upon piles of new notifications. 'Hold on, something's happened.'

'What?'

'Oh, no, no . . .' said Monami, scrolling through the messages. She put her hand to her forehead. 'No!'

'What? What is it?'

'It's Vasudha. She's . . . she's *dead*.'

'*What?*' said Mridula. 'What? How can she be?'

'She's dead. Drug overdose.' Monami pulled up a news clip that someone had posted on Twitter.

Vasudha's little flat in Nizamuddin was surrounded by police cars, and press. They watched as a stretcher emerged from the house. A body lay on the stretcher, a body shrouded in a white cloth.

'No . . .' said Monami, almost in a whisper. 'Not another one . . .'

She thought of Vasudha, on her terrace, with the breeze blowing.

To her the investigation up until now had seemed almost academic—drawing up lists, thinking about potential motives, even the moaning about plodding work had been part of the charm. But this—this was different. The blaring sirens of the police cars and the ambulance woke her rudely from her dream. And the body . . . that young girl they had talked to just yesterday. Monami blinked back her tears. And even Mridula looked dazed. They could hear the muffled voices of reporters—'prime suspect' said one, 'overdose' said another, 'suicide' said a third.

28

Black Magic Woman

i

They drove straight to the police station at Connaught Place. The silence was only broken once, when Monami said, in a rather shaky voice. 'That poor girl. Do you . . . do you think we could have stopped it?' She thought back again to the day before. (Had it really only been the day before?) Why was that scene so imprinted on her?

After a brief silence, Mridula said, 'I wouldn't think that way. We have no idea what happened.'

'She took an overdose of sleeping tablets. This can only mean that she was guilty. Right?' Monami had been scrolling Twitter nonstop. 'Yes, the news channels have been playing it for the last hour—there's no doubt, it seems, that she was the one who poisoned DB and also killed Anika. No motive in either case except black magic woman, of course. The media just sickens me in this country.'

Mridula shook her head. 'I don't think it's that simple. It could be. But we're in deep waters. I think it's also in someone's best interest for her to look guilty, to in fact be guilty. And they've laid it all out for the police. Their case is clear.'

They passed the rest of the car ride in silence.

ii

DCP Akshay Kumar had spent the last week hot on the trail too. His actions had in many ways matched those of Mridula and Monami but multiplied by a factor of about a hundred. He had not only spoken to everyone they had spoken to, in some cases multiple times, he and his men had tracked down every single person at the party, taken statements, filled out forms, got things signed, looked sternly through their spectacles.

The case was almost clear in his own mind. He had an airtight little story all imagined out and almost ready to present with a bow tied around it to the press. And his superiors, of course. And the public. But mostly the press, which had grown more rabid by the day.

So, when he heard one of his prime suspects had committed suicide, he wasn't all that surprised. Unfortunately, that was how criminals tended to react—and especially women—when they sensed that the police were on their trail. It was a shame this particular criminal was so young, and so, let's say, camera-friendly. That wouldn't play well. But she had at least given up her accomplice, and he would be like a lamb to the slaughter. He started to—metaphorically—roll up his sleeves and plan the kill.

Suddenly, the phone on his desk rang. He picked it up.

'Yes!' he growled.

'It's Khurana, sir,' said the voice on the other side.

'Yes, Khurana? Tell me. Quickly.'

DCP Akshay Kumar's regret about his rash decision to take Khurana on board had not abated. Every time any developments would occur, you could bet Khurana would be there with an inconvenient question. But sir, this, but sir, that. Wouldn't it have been smarter to pick a less public place? Yes, Khurana, but murderers aren't always smart. But sir, wouldn't she have known that everyone would have guessed it was her only? Why poison a drink in this random way? It got on his nerves after a while.

'There are two ladies here to see you, sir.'

'Two ladies? I have a very full day, Khurana . . .' began the Deputy Commissioner.

'They're here about the Anika Kapoor case, sir. They've just been with the family, and they say they have an important update for you.'

'They're working with the family? Hmm . . . send them up.'

It was news to DCP Kumar that the family had hired private investigators. He would have to sort this out. The kudos for this case must lie with the Delhi Police, and the Delhi Police alone.

iii

They had been ushered in by a very polite guard, and Monami had been revising her mental image of the police. One grew used to Indian bureaucracy, of offices filled with bored, apathetic officials, of crowded rooms and people slouched in despair as though they had been there for days, weeks maybe, and expected to remain there until the mould grew silently between their toes and rooted them to the ground.

So, she was not expecting the shiny new central bureau building, with its spotless floors and its very able-looking personnel. She had been impressed.

This sunny optimism slowly faded as they entered DCP Akshay Kumar's office. Having so far thought of his name, and by extension him, as a vast joke, she was thrown by the irate man in front of her.

'So,' said DCP Akshay Kumar (Monami could think of him in no other way), practically hissing. 'You two. The amateur sleuths.'

Mridula seemed to think that she and the DCP were old friends and sank into a chair with what Monami could only think was an overfamiliarity which would not go over well.

It did not. DCP Kumar glared at them both.

'How are you, DCP saab?' Mridula started, conversationally. This casual tone did not seem to go over well, either.

'What do you want, Ms Majumdar?' said the Deputy Commissioner. He was usually a courteous man, but somehow this woman incensed him. He attributed it to her smugness. 'Don't you think you've interfered in this case enough?'

Mridula raised her eyebrows. 'We're here with an update. I thought we helped you the last time.'

'Helped? Amateurs have no idea the kinds of complications they cause. I thought I warned you about getting too close to this case the last time we spoke. Now, we still haven't determined exactly how the phone you apparently "found",' here he accentuated his words with speech marks scratched into the air, 'got to where you "found" it. Did your friend Ms Puri plant it there? Or did you advise her to take the course she did, and plant it yourself?'

Monami, who had never had so much as a parking ticket, started to get a shivery feeling in her spine. Should they try to make a run for it?

But Mridula didn't sound particularly worried, mostly just surprised and a little impatient at the turn the conversation was taking. 'This again. Why would we bring it to you if that were the case?' she asked, practically.

There was that smugness again! 'Maybe you couldn't unlock it, you needed us for that,' said DCP Kumar, his voice rising. 'Your friend had cracked it.'

'By the way, did you find out who Anika had been talking to on the phone just before she died?'

Monami had to admit that she admired Mridula's gumption. She would never have been able to toss out a question so offhandedly in the face of this uniformed man's wrath. His very moustache seemed to be quivering.

'As a matter of fact, we didn't,' he said. 'If you must know.'

'You mean, you couldn't find out who she was talking to, or that she wasn't talking to anyone?' asked Mridula.

DCP Akshay Kumar's bluster dissipated.

After a full minute seemed to tick by, he said, 'The latter.'

Mridula nodded. 'That's what I thought.'

DCP Akshay Kumar was silent again for a while, and then finally he laughed. 'Okay, I know you're dying to tell me. So tell me. I'll admit we were all perplexed by that little nugget. There's no way the data could have been tampered with. She was definitely not talking to anyone before her death—not on that phone, at least.'

'Ah,' said Mridula, and nodded.

'Is that what you think? That she was using another phone?'

Mridula shook her head.

'No, I don't think that. If you don't mind, I want to share with you a theory that I have been formulating. A theory that I think will answer almost everything that has been perplexing about this case. I think you're about to arrest the wrong person.'

'Who do you think I'm about to arrest?'

'Jemin Sequeira,' said Mridula promptly. 'Aren't you?'

His indulgent expression turned back into the original glare.

'How did you know that?'

Mridula shrugged. 'It's indicated. Do you have a motive?'

His glare became even more pronounced. 'Not one that I'm obliged to share with you, please forgive me for being blunt.'

'They had a falling out many years ago . . .'

'They did.'

'And do you know why?'

The DCP clicked his tongue. These amateurs. 'I can tell you this much, there was money involved. That's what we always look for—the money motive. I can tell you that is what causes around ninety per cent of all the crimes in Delhi.'

'Anika was one of Jemin's early backers,' said Mridula.

'Yes. Quite a lot of money, in fact. She bankrolled him.'

'Now it's my turn to ask you to forgive me,' said Mridula, but she didn't sound apologetic. 'Why would Jemin kill Anika on the basis of that loan? It was ancient history. She didn't need the money. She wasn't asking to be paid back. Also, during the launch, Jemin spoke about a debt that *Anika owed him*. Not the other way round. Why would he kill her?'

DCP Kumar shook his head. 'These are small details. You may be right that she didn't need the money but sadly, Ms Kapoor was one of those women for whom that didn't make a difference. She wanted to be paid back. Who said what during the party is neither here nor there. The fact is, we *know*.'

'You know?' said Mridula. 'I see. You've just found something out. Something . . . what could it be?'

'Not that it's any of your business—' began DCP Kumar.

But she interrupted him again. 'Vasudha?' she said, quietly.

The DCP summoned up all his patience. 'I suppose there's no harm in you knowing, the facts are bound to be made public shortly. Yes, Vasudha. It's a sad story, but she left a letter confessing everything. Her complicity in the scheme.'

'What scheme?'

DCP Kumar merely smiled condescendingly.

'And she accuses Jemin of murdering Anika?'

'Yes. She witnessed it.'

'*Jemin?*' burst out Monami. 'I can't believe it.'

She wasn't sure why, but this solution simply didn't work. Despite the fact that she had left their interview with Jemin wondering about him, knowing that he was holding something back. This was not the solution.

DCP Kumar merely looked at her pityingly. 'We have a confession. And an eyewitness account. She put the poison in Mr Bhattacharya's drink. Then, she ran upstairs to Ms Anika and witnessed Mr Sequeira strangling her.'

There was a brief silence.

'This confession—handwritten?' asked Mridula. 'Signed?'

Deploying that patronising smile again, DCP Kumar explained it to Mridula like he would to a child. 'The youth nowadays, they don't handwrite their notes. Everything is online.'

'She left an *online* note? An email?'

'She must have *typed* it online,' said the DCP, waving his hand around vaguely, to indicate some activity in the ether. 'But then, she printed it.'

'It was printed? But that is of course very easy to fake,' frowned Mridula.

The DCP chuckled. 'Who would fake that?'

'The real murderer.'

DCP Akshay Kumar, till now the hero in his own motion picture, wished fervently that either he, or these two women in front of him, were elsewhere. One of his team had a screensaver that showed beach shacks in Goa, with the blue sea in the distance, and a palm tree or two that looked as though their fronds were waving gently in the breeze. That's where he wanted to be. With a cold beer in hand. And that's maybe where he *would* be, once he had this case wrapped up. A national case, two murders, a public frenzy—and he had wrapped it up within a matter of days. With the help of a signed confession, but still. A signed confession he had, and he wouldn't let these two meddling women wrest it from his clutches.

'Madam . . .' he began.

'Just give me twenty minutes. That's all I ask.'

'Madam,' he said again. 'The note was signed. It was in her flat, with her body. No one else was there. It wasn't faked. We have our murderers. If you have any theories about why the phone call Ms Anika was taking somehow didn't leave a record in her phone, I would be delighted to hear them, as I must admit, it has been bothering me. Well, not me so much as Constable Khurana. But if not, well, maybe we should cut this meeting short.'

'DCP Kumar,' persisted Mridula. 'You have a very easily fakeable note from a dead girl. Yes, fakeable. Anyone could have left it in her apartment. Anyone could have administered an overdose, and then left the note there. You have a note, and a witness who accuses someone but cannot be questioned herself because she is dead. There are others out there who wanted Anika out of the way. You must allow yourself to consider some alternatives.'

'We have considered our alternatives, I assure you,' said DCP Kumar in a tone that he hoped brooked no argument. He didn't like being questioned in this impertinent way. Shades of Khurana.

'What if I were to tell you that that confession is impossible? That it couldn't have happened that way?'

'I would say you must be mistaken.'

'We have an eyewitness account—two eyewitnesses in fact—who can attest to the fact that Anika was already dead when the toast took place.'

'What? Who are these witnesses?'

'And apart from that, it's just incomplete. What about the death of DB? What was the motive to kill him?'

DCP Kumar hesitated. This was the one weak point in his case. Damn the woman!

'There was a reason . . .' he started.

'But you don't buy it,' said Mridula. 'Can you share it with us? We've been investigating too, and we can maybe help shed some light.'

After a short pause, DCP Kumar said, 'Why don't you share your investigation with me? These so-called eyewitness accounts. Which really,' he added, with a shade of reproach, 'is the way this should go, you know. We are the police, after all.' All the animosity, all the impatience had gone from his voice. Mridula hesitated for only a second before she responded to his olive branch.

'I have a theory,' she said. 'That DB *had* to die—for Anika to die. There was no other way for the crime to be carried out.'

There was another brief pause as DCP Kumar looked from one of them to the other. Finally, he sighed, and said, 'I'm going to regret this I know, but okay. Tell me.'

'Thank you. You won't regret it. Trust me.'

'That,' said DCP Kumar decisively, 'I don't.'

29

The Scapegoat

i

For the second time, Monami found herself in the colourful studio in Qutb Enclave. Through Jemin's tall windows, she could see the form of the Qutb Minar, and today by some miracle, there wasn't the usual haze of Delhi smog surrounding it, but a picturebook blue sky.

They were in the outer offices today, and she looked around curiously. There were long tables, with two or three employees at each, busily working on tablets, or on fabrics. One person was on their phone, and while they were having an energetic conversation with someone on the other end, their tone was still muted. The atmosphere was one of industry, creativity, and harmony. Monami imagined it would be a nice place to come to work every morning.

It was a shame all of it was going to be disrupted in a few minutes. She wondered what the employees would make of the scene.

She was about to find out. Mere moments later, Deputy Commissioner Akshay Kumar marched in with what looked like a squadron of officers behind him. Everyone gaped at him, and he paused a little in the doorway to savour the effect.

'Right, office is closed for the day! Please, everyone, out.'

No one moved. The gaping continued. The voice on the other end of the phone could be heard, rather loudly in the silence, saying 'Hello? Hello? Hello?'

DCP Kumar looked around again, and used his loudest, firmest official voice: 'Now, please, ladies and gentlemen! NOW!'

Jemin's office door flew open. 'What's going on? What's all the shouting about?' He stopped abruptly when he saw the cadre of officers at his door and went a little pale. 'Wh-what's all this about?'

'Ah, Mr Sequeira,' said DCP Kumar, smoothly, 'I was just encouraging your staff to take the rest of the day off so that we can discuss certain matters of a private and serious nature with you. We think you may find it more amenable, rather than having them stay here and watch.'

Jemin looked as though he was struggling to form words, but finally choked some out: 'I don't understand what this is about, but okay, guys, take the day. I'll see you again tomorrow.'

'Jem, are you sure?' said one of the employees, a young woman in a cotton sari.

'Yes, yes. Please go. I'll call you. I'm sure this is something quick.'

Confusion writ over their faces, the small team gathered their things, and slowly moved towards the door. Some threw Jemin looks of concern and sympathy and solidarity. Monami felt again that the police were making a mistake—there is no way this man is a murderer, she thought. And if he was he wouldn't have committed a murder that was so . . . calculated. Bashing someone on the head in a temper and then feeling instantly contrite, she could imagine. But cold-bloodedly seeking someone out to strangle them? She just couldn't see it.

As the team were filing out, Shekhar's shoulders filled the doorway. 'What's going on? Inspector?'

'Deputy Commissioner, sir,' said DCP Kumar, with a touch of acerbity.

'Sorry, *Deputy* Commissioner,' said Shekhar, sarcastically. 'What's going on?'

'We've received some intelligence about Mr Sequeira here that I would like to put before him.'

'Is this the way to do it?' asked Shekhar, angrily.

'We thought it would be better than taking him down to the station, yes sir.'

'Well, get on with it, then.'

'We'll just wait for a few others to join us, sir,' said the DCP. 'You've made the calls?' This was addressed to Mridula, who, sitting in a comfortable swivel chair in a corner, seemed to have appeared out of nowhere.

She nodded.

'You? Who else have you called?' demanded Shekhar.

'Just Samar, Kajal and a couple of kids from the *Delhi Daily* office. Oh, and Anita,' said Mridula serenely.

Was there a stiffening at this last name? Monami couldn't be sure. Jemin still looked confused and a little scared. Shekhar raised one eyebrow.

'Anita? Why Anita?'

'Next of kin,' said Mridula, shrugging. 'We would have got in Meena as well, DB's wife, you know, but she's in Calcutta now.'

Any response from Shekhar was lost in the clamour as Kajal and Samar entered, followed closely by Tina, Ishaan, Devika and Shamik. Kajal and Samar looked wary, even more so when they saw DCP Kumar. The others looked frightened.

'Mridula? What's all this about?'

Mridula spoke without standing up: 'It's DCP Kumar's party. Let him have a go first.'

Everyone sat down obediently on the chairs that had just been vacated by Jemin's team. Only Jemin and Shekhar stayed standing.

'So, ladies and gents. Thank you for coming. It wasn't my idea to have such a—ah—theatrical gathering. For that you can thank your friend Ms Majumdar over there,' begam DCP Kumar. 'But I do welcome the chance of having a group chat.'

'Are you going to tell us how far you've got in your investigations?' said Shekhar, sounding less impatient and less sure of himself than he had before.

'Certainly, certainly,' said DCP Kumar benevolently. 'We may even have some answers before we all leave this room. Now—to begin at the beginning. I will recap the position, that is, if you permit, madam?' He turned to Mridula with what Monami assumed was heavy irony. Mridula just did her usual shrug.

'So, on the night of September 10, the managing editor from the *Delhi Daily*, a man most of you knew well, Mr Dhritiman Bhattacharya, died suddenly at a book launch party. On first glance, it appeared that the drink he had been holding in his hand had been poisoned. This immediately posed a quandary, as the bottle had just been opened, and the drinks poured in front of a rather large group, many of whom are—in fact—here.' He paused to beam at everyone. 'We could only conclude that someone had rather deftly added the poison without being seen.'

'One of us?' asked Jemin loudly. 'I keep telling you, Inspector, it couldn't have happened that way! It's impossible. Have you even begun to investigate what else he ate and drank . . .'

'It's Deputy Commissioner, Mr Sequeira,' said DCP Kumar, no longer sounding acerbic, just disappointed. 'As it happens, we now actually have a signed confession to that murder and are no longer investigating it.'

'A signed confession? From whom?' several voices rose at once.

'Ms Vasudha Chaturvedi.'

'*Vasudha?*' 'Oh, no.' 'It can't be!' Again several voices rose, but whether there was a note of relief among all the conventional expressions of shock, Monami wasn't sure. She rather thought there was.

'Yes, she left a full confession when she committed her tragic act,' said Kumar.

'Vasudha killed my wife?' said Shekhar, wonderingly. 'Really? Why?'

'No, not your wife, sir, Mr Dhritiman Bhattacharya,' said DCP Kumar, a touch louder than before.

'Why did she do that?' said Samar, speaking for the first time. He was looking shaken. 'Why would Vasu want to kill DB?'

'*Because Anika Kapoor had asked her to*,' said the DCP. 'Anika was the only one with a motive to kill DB. We never considered it because of her own tragic death. But it's been well known that she was looking to take over DB's role at the *Delhi Daily*, that in fact this had been her ambition for many years. Finally, it was taken out of her hands for good by her family,' here he shot a sharp look at Shekhar, who looked blankly back at him, 'which caused her to take this extreme step. Perhaps she thought that only if he were removed permanently, as it were, would they have no choice but to fall back on her.'

Everyone looked stupefied at this. Monami looked around at all the faces, mouths curved into round Os, and thought back to when she had first heard about the crime. This was in fact her first theory. No one could have done it but Anika. She should have felt gratified, and wondered why she didn't.

Samar was the first to react. 'Wh-what is this you're saying, Deputy Commissioner? What is this?'

DCP Kumar looked at him. 'Ah, Mr Chishti. This comes as a surprise to you, does it? But I assure you, it comes directly from the source.'

'Vasu . . . and Anika? No, never. Something's wrong. First of all, they never got along. Second of all, Anika would *never*. She would never do this!'

'Ah, who knows with women? Some get along. Some don't. But what you always know is, you can never tell.'

'DCP Kumar,' said Shekhar, 'As fascinating as this insight is into the psychology of women, please watch what you say. You're talking about my wife.'

'Ms Kapoor? What about you? No objections?'

The whole group looked around at the new figure who was standing silently in the doorway. Anita Kapoor was dressed in a simple white linen shirt and jeans and looked thunderstruck. At this direct question, she jumped a little, and then said, quietly, 'I . . . I wouldn't have believed it of her.'

'No?' said the DCP, almost conversationally.

'No. Anika was . . . oh, I know, she was angry, aggressive. But this? No. I can't believe it.'

But her denial was quiet, and a far cry from Samar's white face, and Shekhar's indignant, loud voice. The whole group seemed to feel it.

'We leave that question for the time being, and move on to the second murder,' said the DCP, finally. 'The murder of Ms Anika herself. According to Ms Vasudha's account, after watching DB fall, she ran into the house, and up the stairs as she had previously agreed with Ms Kapoor, at which point she witnessed her murder.'

'There was a witness?' cried Anita. 'Why didn't she come forward before?'

'It was a man for whom she had a great deal of affection, a man that she had worked with closely.' He looked around at the whole group, who squirmed under his eye. 'A man who had the strongest motive of all to kill Anika Kapoor. A man who had been a close friend, until they had fallen out. A man who owed her money. A man who had exchanged heated words with her not more than a few hours previously, and then conveniently disappeared from the scene.'

There was a squeak from Jemin. DCP Kumar turned to face him.

'Her husband bought your label—that must have been very embarrassing for you.'

'Not at all,' said Shekhar, angrily.

'Not at all,' echoed Jemin, but with about half the conviction.

'You had the opportunity,' went on the DCP relentlessly. 'You were already upstairs, and once everyone's attention was elsewhere, you pounced. You killed her!'

'No!' cried Jemin. He blanched in terror. 'I didn't! I would never!'

'Jemin?' said Shekhar. 'It was you? Was it you, Jemin?' His handsome face dark with anger, Shekhar moved, jaw and fist clenched, towards the fashion designer, who started to back away.

'Shekhar! You can't believe this! You know me!'

Before Shekhar could get too close to the man, Samar stepped in between them and turned angrily to the DCP. 'Is this your idea of theatre? You're playing with a man's life!'

'I'm the scapegoat!' Jemin's voice rose so high it seemed the glass in the windows might shatter. 'Of course it's the gay fashion designer. That'll go down well with the media . . . I know most of them are saying it already . . .'

'Deputy Commissioner,' Kajal now also sprang out of her chair. 'This is ridiculous! You can't pin this on Jemin, not on such flimsy evidence! How will this stand up?'

'I have an eyewitness account madam,' said DCP Kumar with great finality. 'Constable!'

A young police officer stepped forward smartly.

'Please accompany Mr Sequeira down to the station.'

Jemin gave a howl of misery.

'We're not arresting you yet,' the Deputy Commissioner said, reassuringly. 'Just . . . ah . . . asking you to help us in our investigations. Just a little questioning.'

Jemin's howl rose even louder, but it was no use. Two burly policemen took a firm hold of his arms and, backed up by their colleagues, marched Jemin unceremoniously outside. His cries could be heard all the way down the stairs.

ii

The rest of the group looked at each other, shaken. DCP Kumar had followed his men out the door with a triumphant little bow to the group.

'I think Jem kept some brandy in his office,' said Shekhar, at last. 'Shall we?'

'I would be most grateful,' said Kajal, her voice tremulous.

They trooped into the office. Shekhar opened up a blue carved Jaipur cabinet, produced a bottle and several glasses. If anyone was reminded of the toast that had kicked off this whole horrible sequence of events, no one said so. They silently took their glasses and drank.

Mridula and Monami had stayed a little apart from the group, but now came in, too, and stood by the door.

'This is ridiculous,' said Kajal, suddenly. 'It's . . . it's not how justice is supposed to work.'

'The details will be kept out of the press,' said Anita, in a low voice. 'We have to keep it as quiet as possible. Lucky for Jemin, it'll protect him too. Not that he deserves it.'

'Anita, you can't possibly believe . . .'

'I can. I always thought it was Jemin. Always. Either Jemin, or *you*,' she said, suddenly turning on Samar. 'It was always one of you two.'

Samar knocked back his brandy, put his glass down and walked to the door. The whole group watched him, it seemed to Monami with bated breath. She couldn't imagine what was going through his mind. DB, Anika, Vasudha. Now Jemin.

Finally, he turned around at the door, and said, 'I don't know exactly what's going on here. But I agree with Kajal. This is not justice. I knew Anika, I know Jemin, and I knew poor Vasu. Not one of them would have done this. Vasu, kill a man she had no beef with? Anika, pay someone to kill? Jemin, kill someone with his bare hands? The whole thing is . . . it's laughable.' His voice was grim. No one laughed.

'You knew my sister better than me? Better than her husband?' said Anita, and there was a dangerous new tone in her voice. She stood next to Shekhar and they both looked at Samar, Shekhar still wearing the ugly expression he had had when advancing upon Jemin.

'If you think she was capable of all that,' said Samar, looking steadily at them both, 'then yes. Yes, I knew her better than both of you.'

'Be careful, Samar,' said Shekhar. 'Be careful now about what you say.'

Samar looked at him. And he looked at Anita. A new light came into his eyes, as though a realisation had dawned.

'So . . . she was right,' he said. 'She was right. I thought it was just paranoia, but it wasn't.'

He looked around, appealingly at the group, as though asking if anyone could understand him, if anyone had seen what he was seeing. Monami too looked around the group and saw faces that were still too shaken to read. All except one. As Samar caught Mridula's eye, she gave a very faint shake of her head, and nodded subtly towards the door.

Samar ran a hand through his hair in a familiar gesture, and, after pausing a moment, said again, 'She was right.' He turned and marched out of the room.

The rest of the group looked at each other, and then one by one, slowly put their glasses down as well, and followed Samar out. Kajal first, then Tina, Ishaan and Devika. Just as Shamik was about to leave too, Mridula put a hand on his elbow.

'Would you hold back a second?'

Shamik looked confused but stopped.

Mridula looked at Monami. 'Maybe you should step out, too.'

Monami knew the plan, but she was still reluctant to tear herself away. She asked, for about the eighteenth time that day, 'Are you sure?'

'Yes, yes,' said Mridula, crossly. 'Go on.'

Monami went.

30

Then the Spin

i

'Right, well, I'm glad that's over,' said Mridula, and poured herself some more brandy.

'Is this really the time for another drink?' Shekhar said, still scowling. Anita had sunk into Jemin's chair and was looking at Mridula with considerable scorn.

'We should also make a move soon,' she said. 'Nothing to be gained by hanging around here.'

'Oh, I was hoping to have a word with you and Shekhar here,' said Mridula. 'Can you hold on for five minutes?'

'Okay,' said Anita. 'What's up? We should probably talk about how to build the messaging around this in the paper. No time like the present.'

'First the story, then the spin,' said Shekhar. 'Isn't that what you said? You were right.' He perched on the chair, looking thoughtful.

'Yes,' said Mridula. 'The spin. That's the main concern here, isn't it? How we can spin it. I thought it might be helpful to listen to a last piece of evidence from Shamik here. Now, Shamik, perhaps you can tell us what you saw on the night of the 10th?'

Shamik had started to look more and more uncomfortable. He was sweating through his shirt and now wished he'd worn a t-shirt underneath so the patches wouldn't be so visible.

'Sure, Mridula. Er, if you're sure? Okay then. Okay. So on the night of the 10th. After the launch itself, you know I did some mingling, as it were, moving from group to group. But I'm not the most social, and so after a while I decided to head inside. Inside Kajal's house, that is.'

As no one responded, he continued, 'I went up to the balcony. And I was there when Anika came up the stairs. There were a few of us, we were all talking, and no one noticed her particularly. She looked as though she was in a temper, so we all avoided her. She started pacing up and down, talking furiously into her phone.'

'When Shamik told me this, he added a couple of details that I found very interesting,' said Mridula, softly. 'Can you repeat them, Shamik?'

'Er, what do you mean, Mridula?' said Shamik, looking nervously over at the glowering Shekhar.

'What was she doing, for instance?'

'She was talking furiously into her phone, as I said.'

'Whisper-shouting, I think you said, when we spoke.'

'Did I?'

'You did. And what about the marching?'

'Yes, she was marching up and down the balcony.'

'You said she was clomping around like a drill sergeant.'

'Er, maybe something like that.' Like the rest of the *Delhi Daily* office, Shamik wasn't overly sensitive when talking about Anika, and he was starting to feel that Mridula was rubbing it in unnecessarily now. There was a frown on Shekhar's face that was making him nervous.

'Such an interesting word, *clomping*. Very evocative, isn't it? I tried to imagine it.'

Mridula did a little stumpy walk across the room. Shamik looked on, appalled.

'I tried to put myself in Anika's shoes, you know. That's one of the first reasons we had to dig into this story—to use our imaginations. The one edge I felt we had over the police. So I tried to imagine that I was Anika, clomping around, whisper-shouting, or whatever it was you said.'

'Where are you going with this, Mridula?' said Anita tetchily. 'It's one thing to be eccentric . . .'

'Oh no, I'm being very practical,' said Mridula, putting up her hands. 'Because what I realised was that once I put myself in Anika's shoes, I found it very hard to scream-whisper. She never did that, you know. Most unlike her. It was either full on screaming, or nothing. And then, the clomp. Has any of us known Anika to clomp? What shoes did she wear that night, do you know?'

Shamik, deducing correctly that this question was meant for him, and still feeling that he was maybe the victim of some practical joke, said uncertainly, 'I don't know. I didn't notice.'

'Well, I can tell you without even having been there. She was wearing stilettos. Because she always wore stilettos. Samar even validated this for us without realising it. He said that when she walked off from their conversation, it was as if her shoes were stabbing holes into the grass—as heels would.'

Shamik said, slowly, trying to imagine it himself: 'You're right, actually. I don't think she was wearing her heels. Do you know, I think that's what was so peculiar about her. I thought something was off—that was it. Usually, she'd wear such towering high heels that she had a very distinctive walk. That night, she was just clomping around, er, like I said, like a drill sergeant.'

'Almost as though she were drawing attention to herself?' suggested Mridula.

'I don't know that she ever needed to draw attention to herself, but I certainly noticed.'

'So did everyone,' said Mridula. 'You don't know how many times she's been pointed out to us. Anika was on the balcony. Smoking. Ashing into a champa. Shouting into her phone. It was so distinctive, she even made it into Meena Bhattacharya's dreams.'

'What are you getting at, Mridula?' said Anita. 'How does it matter what shoes she was wearing?'

'How does it matter! You don't think it's interesting that your sister suddenly changed her usual high heels for . . . I don't know, combat boots, a few moments before she was killed?'

'Maybe her feet were hurting her?' suggested Shekhar.

'That's a very mannish suggestion,' said Mridula, smiling at him. 'Are you saying she just had a pair of boots around, ready to slip on? Perhaps they were in her clutch.'

'I'm not sure this is a very productive line of enquiry, Mridula,' said Anita, impatiently. 'I agree it's odd, but it could have been for any reason. If—Shamik, is it? If Shamik is even right about this.'

'I could be wrong,' Shamik said, quickly. 'Highly possible. Probable, even.'

'There, you see?' said Anita. 'Anyway, I'm fairly sure Anika didn't even own combat boots.'

'She might have borrowed yours. That's a very nice pair you have on, by the way.'

'Oh, thank you,' said Anita, uncertainly.

Shamik looked at the boots. And then he looked at Anita. His face was covered in confusion.

'All okay, Shamik?' said Mridula. 'You look like you've seen a ghost.'

'It was . . . it was you!' he said suddenly, pointing at Anita.

'What do you mean, Shamik? Spit it out,' said Mridula, encouragingly.

'That night on the balcony. It wasn't Anika. It was *you*.'

ii

'That's so interesting,' said Mridula, as if she were having a conversation at a cocktail party.

They all turned to look at her. Anita narrowed her eyes and her lips curled into a sneer. If Monami had been there, she would have attested to the fact that, with her veil of professionalism dropped, Anita now looked extraordinarily like her sister, despite her shorter hair and slightly smaller stature.

'I'm not sure what you think you're doing,' she said. 'Do you think you know what you're doing?'

'Now, Shamik,' Mridula said, ignoring Anita, 'would you say you're sure about this?'

'Yes,' said Shamik, surprising himself, staring at Anita. 'Yes. I'm absolutely certain. There was a lot about Anika that night that I couldn't quite place. It didn't even strike me consciously, but I think subconsciously I held on to those doubts.'

Mridula nodded. 'As had many people,' she said. 'Meena especially. She was quite intuitive, and she saw it at once, without realising what she was seeing.'

Anita was once again trying to radiate calm, albeit with less than her usual success. 'You are both insane,' she said.

'It was a good touch to dress the servers up in her usual outfit, by the way,' said Mridula, ignoring this. 'Long black robes, loose pants. Very clever. I suppose it was easy for you to slip away after your little act. But it's also where you slipped up. You don't seem to realise that they'll be able to corroborate our story. This way you have of not counting anyone who's not in your particular social sphere . . . ' she shook her head and made a tutting noise with her tongue. 'Tch tch. It's not done, you know. It's not the dark ages anymore.'

Shekhar now found his voice. 'Shamik, thank you for your contribution. I think Anita and I should talk to Mridula alone. This is a matter for the family. I'd ask that you don't discuss what you've said in here with anyone until one of us has been able to contact you.'

'But . . .' began Shamik.

'I agree with Shekhar,' said Mridula, firmly. 'Shamik, thank you for this. But now, I would go, if I were you.'

'Mridula, I can't leave you like this,' he said. 'The DCP . . .'

'Leave this to me, please, Shamik,' said Mridula, fixing him with a stare. 'I'm asking you to trust me. Go on.'

Shamik met her gaze for a few moments. He didn't like it, but he went. 'Call me if you need me,' he said, shuffling out with an agonised backward glance.

'So sweet. Who would have thought it? I must ask the people at the office to be nicer to him in the future. Everyone avoids him like the plague,' said Mridula, settling down comfortably on the Chesterfield sofa. 'Now. Cards are on the table. What do you intend to do about it?'

'Just to be clear,' said Anita, also taking a seat. 'You're accusing me of murdering my own sister? Is that what's happening here?'

'No, I think Shekhar did the actual murdering.'

'What?!' said Shekhar. 'Me? You think . . . you're crazy.'

'I'm not,' said Mridula, mildly. 'No, I'm not crazy. There have been lots of interesting things about this case. It's really been fascinating to work on. I was saying to Monami just the other day how much I was enjoying myself. Of course, the murders were not fun, particularly your last one. Vasudha, that poor girl, did not deserve to die. That one made me angry. More so than even the loss of my friend. DB was bad enough, but Vasudha? Particularly when she was in love with you.' Mridula shook her head at Shekhar. 'That was cold.'

Shekhar and Anita glanced at each other but didn't speak.

'I thought from the beginning,' Mridula continued, 'that the whole thing was a little too convoluted. Nothing was straightforward. Do you know what question I asked all of our interviewees first?'

Shekhar had by now sat down too and he answered, as if he still couldn't believe what was happening, 'No. What?'

'It was this: Why was this book launch held at all? Whose idea was it?'

'What do you mean, why was the book launch held? There was a book. We launched it.'

'As you know, most book launches happen in the backs of coffee shops nowadays. There is no budget. No one is spending on lavish launches. So . . . why a book launch for an unknown writer? Everyone said it had been someone else's idea. Kajal thought Jemin. Samar thought Vasu. Jemin was the only one who got it right. He said at once that he thought it came from you. Poor chap.'

'Poor chap? He killed my wife.'

'You know he didn't. You set him up. You're quite a dangerous man, you know.'

Shekhar's expression changed. A sneer came over his matinee idol face, an arrogance that would have been apparent all along if only anyone could have seen through the dazzle.

Mridula continued to speak, as though she hadn't noticed Shekhar's sudden ugliness: 'Of course, the answer to who could have come up with the idea for the launch, who could have organised the whole thing, should have been obvious from the start. It was you. It had to be you. Jemin couldn't have come forward to sponsor anything, even if he'd thought of it. He didn't have the money. Samar wouldn't have bothered. Vasudha—she was just the intern. There could have been only one person making all the decisions, pulling all the strings. You, Shekhar.

'You gave yourself away when we came to talk to you, and you said it hadn't been a business idea at all. But up until that point, that was all we heard—synergies, brand alignment, Venn diagrams. There was clearly some work done to sell it from a business angle, and there was only one person that kind of jargon could have come from. You.

'You see, the answer to the question about *why the book launch* is actually fairly simple. The idea was this: when someone gets murdered, who is the first person who is always suspected? If Monami were here, she would tell you. She doesn't deduce much, although she did provide a very valuable hint to me in this case. But when it comes to detective fiction, she's quite the expert. And this is a trope for the ages.'

'Anyone want to hazard a guess? Shekhar? Anita? It's the spouse, you know. And that's even more so in a high-profile murder like this. The husband, the sister, the family, the immediate focus would be on them! And in this case, that was what I found so astounding. No one was focusing on the family. Not the police, not the media. No one. In fact, the family was parading around demanding answers from everyone else. But if you use just the teensiest bit of imagination, it all becomes so clear. What's the motive to kill Anika Kapoor? All three main suspects had such thin ones—professional rivalry? Spite?

'But, *money*. Control of a vast business empire. That's the stuff murders are made of. *That's* why you both did it.'

Anita laughed then. 'You grotesque little woman. Money? Control? Power? You think we need more of these things? You think Anika was a threat to us?'

'Yes, I do. Your father told us, which you didn't expect, that he was trying to bring Anika back into the family business. It must have incensed you, Anita, that despite all your hard work, he was still thinking of bringing your sister back. Maybe he had started to have suspicions that you weren't quite . . . right?' She shook her head. 'I wondered about the seashell story you told. I rather think it was a story about *you*, not your sister. *I don't want to be sentimental*, that's what you said when we came to see you. I should think not! You hated her. She stood in the way of you controlling the family business and she stood in the way of you and Shekhar.

'And once I realised that you two were working as partners, it all became very clear. I think it started fairly early on, didn't it, this affair?

It explains so much about Anika, her frustration, her increasingly aggressive attitude. To have the ones closest to her turn on her, and not in a way that she could necessarily pinpoint. To have her husband and her sister profess love, companionship and loyalty to her, all the while plotting behind her back . . . she must have thought she was going slowly insane.

'And your father inviting her back to the firm was the last straw. I don't know if you were right the other day, if she would have come back or not, but it's not something you would have ever risked. And this way was so much neater—given your affair. It's the one thing the family would never, ever condone. They would have signed over the entire business to her if they had found out that you were having an affair with her husband. You and Shekhar would have been out, discarded without a second thought. This was such a neat solution—Anika dies, gets out of your way. Incidentally, the shock gets your father out of the way too. You get the business. And, after a suitable period of time, both of you can profess your love and live happily ever after. So many birds with one stone!'

The silence from Shekhar and Anita grew more ominous, but Mridula wasn't about to stop: 'You couldn't risk making a mess at home—no mysterious food poisoning, or getting pushed down the stairs. And even an external assassin, a bag snatching or something, with a knife in the back as a tragic by-product, would be tricky, firstly because she was never alone going down a street or anything like that, and even that could be traced back to you. No, the idea you came up with was fiendishly clever. To have her murdered in the open, and to deflect suspicion from yourselves. Organise a party, stack it full of people. So many people. At the end of the day, you didn't really care who got blamed; it could have been someone she had targeted through her columns. It could have been Jemin, with his silly, childish spat. It could have been Kajal, and Anika played into your hands there by insulting her at the launch. And it could have been Samar, her longest relationship, the one person who genuinely loved her. Honestly, it's surprising he hasn't incriminated himself more. It could have been anyone else, anyone else from the dozens of people you had Vasudha invite to this party. You literally didn't care, as long as the focus of the police was elsewhere. Why would it be on the husband, who was catching a flight to Hong Kong, and the sister, who wasn't even there?'

There was a short silence, and then Shekhar laughed. It was not a pleasant laugh.

'I thought you'd forgotten that I was halfway to Hong Kong when she died, so I couldn't have done it.'

'Ah, but that's what makes it all so brilliant. You killed her before you left, of course. Then your girlfriend here comes in and plays a rather ostentatious part for about half an hour, making sure everyone sees her. No one is likely to approach her too closely, because they've all heard the fight with Jemin, the shouting on the telephone, they know Anika's in a foul mood. All you needed was the long hair and the clothes. Oh, it was all very easy. You do look so much alike, you know,' she said in an aside to Anita.

'Something started to click when Kajal talked about finding the body and described it as cold. How could it have been cold if she had just been walking around on the balcony minutes before?

'Then, once the commotion started about DB's collapse, you moved Anita's body from the spare room to Kajal's room while everyone was distracted downstairs. You tweaked your costume to become one of the servers. What did it take, just removing the wig and the scarf? That's the thing about Anika's look, once the hair goes, there's really nothing there. Very easy to blend into the background and disappear. Ingenious idea.'

'This is ridiculous,' said Anita, jumping up. 'We don't have to listen to this.'

'Oh, but you do,' said Mridula, her expression finally growing stern, 'Because of DB, you do. You had Vasudha kill him merely as a distraction. You didn't care who got the poisoned glass, did you? It could have been anyone. The poison was already in one of the glasses when she pulled them out. What did you tell Vasudha? Did she know what the plan was? From her reaction afterwards, I think not. Poor girl. I think you told her that it was enough just to knock a person out, just to make them sick, to create a diversion. But it was enough to kill. It had to be a fatal dose, because it couldn't just be the murder of Anika. It had to be two people, to keep everyone guessing. And you very nearly succeeded, too! It was a daring plot. It was . . . audacious. It required only a complete disregard for human life. But, in the end, well, it failed. You failed.'

Shekhar and Anita looked at each other. Almost imperceptibly, Anita shook her head.

'And I think that was because you didn't plan it out as well as you thought, you know. Lots of holes. First of all, moving the body to Kajal's room—of course Kajal was going to discover it, and get rid of it! Did you think she would just leave it in her bed for the police to find?

'Secondly, the whole mess with having to silence Vasudha—first, transferring her over to Sea Lion with that ridiculous story about her wanting to work for a publisher. That girl who clearly just wanted to be an investment banker. Absurd. Anyone who would have spoken to her or her family would have seen through it in an instant.

'And that message you sent her through us, "I'm watching you." Did you think we were idiots? She burst into tears when we said it to her. Poor girl!

'And finally,' Mridula shook her head, 'killing her in that senseless way. Planting the suicide note. You were waiting and watching to see who best the suspicion could be fixed on. The way things had unfolded, it was Jemin.

'And the moment Kajal's staff came forward and you realised that the cat was out of the bag about when the crime had been committed, you had to do something quickly. Unfortunately for you, you didn't realise that *the body had already been discovered earlier*, before even DB's death. It was seen in the spare room. We have the evidence.'

In two bounds, Shekhar was across the room.

'You wretched woman!' he snarled. 'Do you think anyone will believe this nonsense? Where's your evidence? I believe you're just bluffing.'

His face was transformed with hate, the face of a murderer. With Herculean pluck, Mridula remained impassive as Shekhar advanced.

She looked calmly up at him. Her voice completely unchanged, she said, 'You overplayed your hand with Vasudha. She would never have given you away, no, not even after you betrayed her to marry your girlfriend here.

'Anyway, you know I'm not bluffing,' added Mridula. 'We have witnesses. And Meena, too. She guessed something was wrong with Anika. She couldn't quite pick up on what it was but no doubt with some careful prodding, she'll get there, like Shamik did. She's sensitive, you know. She's the noticing kind. I think she also noticed Anita as a waitress.'

Anita sneered again. 'An airtight case built on the word choices of a mediocre journalist and a bereaved, probably deranged wife?'

'And a couple of kids,' Mridula said, 'who can testify that Anika's body was cold even as DB died. These are the people who will put you both in prison.'

'No!' Shekhar cried. 'Let's end this now.'

He lunged at her, and this time, his hands tightened around Mridula's throat.

iii

Just when Mridula thought that it was too late for her, a cupboard door at the far end of the room opened and Constable Khurana popped out. He was holding a gun and it was pointed at Shekhar.

'H-hands up!' he said, self-consciously.

At the same time, as though a timer had been set, the office door burst open and DCP Kumar and his men were back. To Mridula they seemed like a pantomime band of merry men appearing magically out of a trapdoor just in time to perform the spectacular rescue. She wondered why the audience wasn't applauding; it was a fine entrance.

'Well, Ms Majumdar,' the DCP said, in a tone that perhaps should have been contrite but was actually triumphant. 'It appears that you were right! Constable, arrest them.'

31

The Story

'I didn't even get to blackmail them,' said Mridula, sadly.

They were back in Kajal's house, back on her balcony. It was a perfect Delhi evening, with a touch of night jasmine in the air, and a hint of winter to come. Samar, Kajal, Jemin, Monami and Mridula were drinking Irish whisky and discussing the case.

'That was the plan, you know,' Mridula continued. 'That I would blackmail them, and then they would confess under the strain. Sadly, they tried to kill me instead.'

'I did tell you,' said Monami. 'I said it was a crazy idea.'

'You did. You did,' said Mridula, raising a glass in acknowledgement.

'Now, you must tell us the story,' said Samar. He looked more tired, and older than he had just a week ago. 'Tell us everything.'

Everyone looked at Mridula, expectantly. She looked back, meeting everyone's eye in turn, very conscious that she had a role to play, a role that had been consecrated throughout the canon of crime fiction, but one that she nonetheless resisted.

She sighed. 'Must I?'

'Yes, you must,' said Monami. 'Spit it out! When did you first suspect, how, when, et cetera, et cetera. We're all dying to know.'

'I would certainly like the story,' said Jemin, still looking a bit pale after his ordeal. 'I really thought I was done for.'

'They just took you out the door, surely? It's not like you got frog-marched down to a prison cell,' said Kajal.

'You try being marched anywhere by the police, and I'll see how you like it. So tell us, Mridula—were we all played for fools?'

'Oh, I wouldn't say that,' said Mridula, managing to give them the impression that she thought that they had all in fact been played for fools. 'You were possibly a bit manipulated, yes. But it was a very clever plan, you know. No one would have been able to see through it.'

'I knew there was something off about my book launch,' said Kajal, triumphantly. 'I always said so.'

'You did. It made me suspect the worst of you, I'm sorry to say,' said Samar.

'Did you?'

'Only for about two seconds!'

'You did behave very suspiciously, Kajal,' said Mridula, severely. 'You probably muddled me up more than anyone.'

'Oh, sorry. Did my need to keep myself out of Tihar Jail get in your way? Sincere apologies.'

Monami laughed. 'Seriously, Mridula! Begin at the beginning! When did you first start to suspect them?'

Mridula sighed again. In a tone of long-suffering, she began, 'When I heard about DB, my first thought was what an unsatisfactory crime it was. If I wanted to kill someone, would that be the way to do it? First of all, it was too public; second of all, there was too much of a chance something would go wrong. In fact, I decided very early on that something *had* gone wrong. So many people, so many glasses. So many potential witnesses. And besides, no one stood to gain by his death, not even his wife. In fact, she stood to lose considerably since she was dependent on his income. There were only two real suspects,

Tina and Anika, and I couldn't see either of them carrying out a crime in this way.

'That's as far as I had got when we heard about the second murder. This of course provided a lot more fodder. My colleague Monami here stuck with her theory of Anika as the murderer,' and here Mridula allowed herself a tiny grin. 'A murderer who had been betrayed by her accomplice.'

'Very plausible, Mona,' said Kajal, with a snicker.

'Okay, pipe down. It was the theory that the police went with in the end, and everyone bought it. And hello, at least I wasn't a prime suspect,' said Monami.

'With the news of Anika's death,' continued Mridula, 'it somehow completed the picture of DB's murder, which hadn't made any sense by itself. But it also made the whole thing more complicated. There were many possibilities—first, that the crimes were connected, either because Anika was involved in DB's death, or because she had seen something. Second, that the crimes weren't connected, but someone had taken advantage of the chaos to commit a murder that they'd been thinking about but hadn't yet planned.

'The more I thought about both of these ideas, the more they didn't quite make sense. I couldn't see how the crimes could be connected; and I also couldn't see anyone risking everything to commit murder on the spur of the moment. And the more I mulled it over, I came to the conclusion that there must have been another option. Do you remember, Mona? *Option Three.*'

'All your options always confused me utterly,' said Monami. 'What was Option Three now?'

'Option Three was that there was *no motive for DB's death*. Someone needed to die, but *it could have been anyone*. They just needed the distraction, and equally, they wanted to muddy the waters, to somehow tie together the deaths, and have the police try to make futile connections instead of focusing solely on the murder of Anika.'

'A crazy idea,' murmured Samar. 'And Vasudha just went along with this?'

'I think she was quite in love with Shekhar,' said Mridula. 'He must have manipulated her, pretended it was a practical joke. Why else would she do something so out of character, so reckless? My guess is that he didn't tell her it was poison that she was putting in the champagne glass. Hence her look of horror as she rushed up the stairs.'

'And when she found out, she couldn't tell anyone without implicating herself,' said Monami. 'Why was she going up, by the way? To meet Anika?'

'Yes. Anika was Shekhar's wife, and my guess is that, since she knew Shekhar had already left, she was running up to ask what had gone wrong. And of course, once she got up there, Anika was gone. I can only imagine how she felt when the news of Anika's death broke too. She must have been scared out of her mind.'

'She was,' said Monami, sadly. 'When we went to see her that day. She looked . . . so sad, so alone and so scared.'

'Yes,' said Mridula. 'That was our biggest oversight, that we didn't guess when we went to speak to her. But by then, she must have been in full self-protect mode since she was actually guilty of one murder. No wonder she burst into tears when we gave her Shekhar's message.'

'When did you actually start suspecting Shekhar?' asked Kajal, curiously.

'He was always in the back of my mind as the husband, but he really did seem to have been well and truly out of the way. There's no way you can fake a flight to Hong Kong.

'I think I first really started to suspect him after that visit from Abhishek. He was clearly hinting *something* at us. But what? I couldn't put a finger on it. But the outcome of that meeting was very clear; he wanted us to keep digging, and he asked us to go talk to Shekhar. I found that interesting.

'And the moment we met Shekhar, I had a sense of something not being quite right. He firstly was a little thrown that Abhishek had sent us his way. He outright denied that he knew anything about Anika leaving the *Delhi Daily*. And there was clearly no love lost between him and his wife, although he tried to play it off as the usual marital blues. I couldn't see a kernel of affection, and also no real sense of mourning or loss. Very unlike when we went to visit you, Samar,' she said, nodding at him. 'Or Meena, for that matter.

'It was most stark when he talked about buying Jemin's business. He obviously hadn't cared about his wife's point of view at all. And, frankly, none of what he said there made sense. The business was losing money, but it was such a wonderful buy? Of course, he had actually bought it to bring Jemin closer to Anika and lay the groundwork for this type of suspicion to fall on him.'

Jemin shuddered. 'You think he planned it as far back as that?'

'I think so, Jemin. There was no other reason, really, for him to buy your business, you know.'

'I knew all that points of entry stuff was just nonsense,' said Jemin, darkly.

'Then we went to talk to Vasudha, and she told us a series of very transparent lies. Lies about how she had gone to work from Shekhar to Sea Lion because she wanted to be a writer and work in publishing! It made me think about the connection between her and Shekhar more carefully. Unfortunately, I didn't see through it in time.'

Everyone fell quiet. In the distance, an owl hooted softly. A fruit bat flapped its wings.

'When she burst into tears at the mention of Shekhar, I started to think about him more seriously. Could he have been involved? I went back to our notes. Could he have caught a later flight? I did some research and saw that there were two more flights that night. But that would be something the police would double check. So, if I couldn't change the time that he left, I asked myself, could I change the time that the murder was committed? But she had been seen right up until the death of DB.

'You unwittingly gave me a very key pointer, Mona. At one point, you said something about her being very *showily visible*, or something like that. That's what got me thinking about the motive of distraction.

'It suddenly dawned on me . . . what people were actually saying they saw when they said they saw Anika. They saw a figure in black on a balcony; they saw the long hair; they heard her talking into her phone; they heard her calling down to a waitress. But no one had spoken to her; Meena had even gone looking for her but couldn't find her. It finally struck me how odd this was. Anika wasn't the type of person to keep to herself at parties; she was almost always front and centre. And it seemed like someone putting on a very deliberate show.'

Monami made a movement. Mridula nodded at her.

'Yes, that aspect of the theatrical has always been a motif throughout this case. Your friend Tina mentioned it first—she said she was watching a play. Kajal didn't quite put it in the same words, but she had this sense of being strung along, directed. Jemin said that he thought Vasudha was just following instructions, which she was, of course. Meena said that in her dream, she would get mixed up between Anika and the waitstaff—because they were all dressed the same. When you get right down to it, it's very easy to create a persona, isn't it?'

'Is that why you asked her the question about the models, and the waitstaff?'

Mridula nodded. 'Yes, I figured that there was an accomplice there, and it was either one of the models, or one of the waiters. I wasn't sure which. But Vasudha didn't know about any of that. I really think that she was quite innocent. So when I spoke to Shamik, that's what I was looking for—confirmation that "Anika" was deliberately drawing attention to her persona.'

'All that clomping and stomping stuff? That was quite a stretch deduction,' said Monami, half-admiringly.

'Well, it wasn't so much a deduction as a sort of backwards construction. At that point I knew very definitely that Anika had been killed beforehand, so the person on the terrace couldn't possibly have been her. I pounced on the words Shamik used that sounded least like the Anika we all knew.'

'Lucky for Anita to be actually wearing combat boots when you accused her.'

'Yes, wasn't it? And Shamik played his part beautifully. They were so sure of having gotten away with it then. Both of them just showed up to watch you being carted off, Jemin.'

Jemin laughed bitterly. 'What a nasty shock when you sprung all of that on them afterwards, then.'

'Oh, that's just psychology,' said Mridula, modestly. 'We had to first give them the relief of seeing someone else arrested. And then, when they were least expecting it, pull the rug out. And you saw . . . it almost didn't work.'

'They were insane,' said Samar, softly. 'And so many lives lost in the meantime.'

'I still can't believe they killed DB just as a distraction,' said Kajal, and she shivered. 'Horrible.'

'On the plus side, both Anita and Shekhar are actually in jail and haven't got bail yet, a most unlikely outcome when you're as rich and connected as they are. Even her parents couldn't raise a peep. They've gone completely underground.'

'I heard the parents thought it was Shekhar all along,' said Samar. 'They really hated him, you know, especially the mother. When this happened, she knew instantly that he had concocted it in some way. He had always been in it for the money. But when they found that their daughter had been involved too . . . well, they went completely to pieces.'

'That reminds me, we found out how Anika and Shekhar met,' said Monami, looking at Jemin. 'Care to share?'

Jemin laughed loudly, the sound rupturing the still evening.

'There was never any secret. He used to model in my pop-up shows.

That's how they met, I introduced them. He was one of my big finds, a rangy hoodlum type. Anika was so taken by him. Her bit of rough. But when things got a bit more serious, when she thought she might want to leave her bedroom with him and go to a restaurant or a party, she paid for him to get elocution and etiquette classes. His name wasn't even Shekhar Malhotra; he was our project, a *desi* Eliza Doolittle. After they got married, Anika thought of it as a major skeleton in her closet, and she was terrified that I knew everything.'

'So that was the debt you guys were talking about?' said Kajal. 'I wondered.'

'Yes, she loaned me a lot of money, but I introduced her to her husband. I thought that went beyond money. But now that I come to think of it,' said Jemin, looking suddenly stricken, 'it doesn't seem to have been a very good exchange.'

'I think, you know,' said Mridula, softly, 'that she may have married him because she couldn't marry you, Samar. Did you ever wonder about that?'

Samar was silent for a while, and then slowly nodded. 'Yes—it was true what I told you when you came to see me. That the two of us were from two different worlds. But I think at the end of the day, this was more of an issue for me than it was for her. She would have wanted to make a go of it, in fact she did want to make a go of it. But I . . . I didn't.' He sighed. 'I didn't want the big business life. Her family were all so intense. I wanted to travel, to see the world. To live well but not the way billionaires do with their private jets and their hangers-on. I went abroad. And when I came back, she was already married.'

'Yes, that was when I introduced her to Shekhar,' said Jemin. 'You're right, Samar, that must have been it. And it explains so much. She never really loved him, I think. She was drawn to him, to his body and then to his ambition. With time, though, she grew to resent him, and by extension, she resented me.'

'And you *did* have a plan for the launch?' asked Monami.

'I did, I did. Mea culpa, although I don't really think it was as bad as all that. I just invited Suleiman. He was younger than Shekhar but they used to be great friends during their modelling days. I thought it would be terribly amusing if they bumped into each other and had a whole reunion. Anika would have been most embarrassed. Of course, in the end, she provoked me so thoroughly that I had to go and smoke a joint, and by the time I came back, Shekhar had already left.' Jemin looked abashed.

'Poor Anika,' said Monami.

'It's surprising to hear you say that,' said Kajal. 'Your attitude towards her really changed, didn't it?'

'Yes, it really did. As we heard more about her life, I just kept feeling more and more sorry for her. Her husband obviously didn't love her. She couldn't be with the person she did love. Her family didn't support her—her sister and husband were gaslighting her—and that was probably the last straw. I think her father, though, loved her and did have her best interests at heart. But he didn't really understand her. I just kept getting an impression of her as a lonely woman who, in the end, at best wasn't taken seriously by those who should have been in her corner, and at worst was manipulated and used by them. It was sad.'

Mridula nodded. 'She was a smart woman, too. As offensive as she was at the launch, she was perfectly right, you know. When she said she didn't understand why it was taking place, and all the business-speak around it was nonsense. She saw right through it. Unfortunately, she didn't guess why it had to happen—but who could have?'

There was another short, contemplative silence and then Samar raised his glass. 'To Anika,' he said. 'We're sorry that we couldn't save you. I'm sorry.' He let out a long breath, and Kajal patted him on the shoulder.

'Don't blame yourself too much,' she said. 'You were absolutely right not to want to get involved with her family. To do this in cold blood . . . monstrous.'

'I agree,' said Mridula. 'And I think they would have been happiest for you to take the fall, that is, if you hadn't been the one to drink from the poisoned glass. The affair would have been easy to prove. But unfortunately, Jemin disappeared during the toast and made himself look more suspicious than you did.'

'I still can't believe he bought House of Jems, even though he thought we were a failing business, just to keep me up his sleeve as some sort of trump card or scapegoat,' said Jemin. 'But now, I've been told, our sales numbers are *actually* through the roof. It seems there's no better marketing campaign than a murderous rampage.'

'What a terrible epitaph for us all,' said Kajal, gloomily.

'I think I blame the sister more than the husband,' said Monami. 'She was *family*.'

'I agree,' said Kajal. 'And all for a man.'

'And money,' pointed out Monami.

'Men and money,' said Kajal. 'The root of all evil.'

'Title of your next book?' enquired Jemin.

Kajal laughed. 'Maybe! But it'll be a while before I can write another. I don't want to put anything else out in the universe just yet. You never know the invisible strings you're pulling.' She turned to Mridula, 'And what's next for you? Are you joining the police force as a consulting detective? You and that Deputy Commissioner seemed to be having a gala time.'

Mridula gave Kajal her best impish grin. 'We did. It's been eye-opening to work with the police. I don't think I'll be underestimating them again. That was one of Anita and Shekhar's mistakes too.'

'They did miss a whole body,' pointed out Kajal.

'True. But you probably hid it very nicely.'

Kajal sighed. 'I can't joke about it yet, Mri.'

'Well, this all started with a toast, let's end with another one. To our very own amateur detectives, Mridula and Monami. To their continued success!'

Everyone raised a glass and clinked loudly. Monami looked out over the garden, which was now awash with moonlight. Nothing stirred, except for the fitful breeze which shook the leaves in the trees and carried the scent of the night flowers up to the balcony.

Acknowledgements

When I was eleven, sitting on the couch in my parents' living room, I read a book that blew my mind—*The Murder of Roger Ackroyd*. (If you haven't read it already, drop everything, including this book, and get yourself a copy.) Steeped in mysteries ever since, I've always wanted to try and write one of my own.

This novel, like Kajal's, has been many years in the making. But earning a living and having children (the two to whom this book is dedicated) got in the way. The pram in the hall is real. So, having found the time and taken the plunge, I have to thank Ambar Sahil Chatterjee, Hemali Sodhi and A Suitable Agency for championing both me and my book. They were key to getting it over the line.

I also have to send shout-outs to my earliest readers, Meenakshi Reddy Madhavan and Ashwati Parameshwar, my tribe, whose helpful comments and unstinting encouragement gave me the confidence to try and find both an agent and publisher. I owe you a lifetime supply of Aperol spritzes.

Chiki Sarkar and the team at Juggernaut—I am thrilled to have published this book with you. Thank you so much for believing in it.

My family, of course. My parents, for creating a Felu Da-shaped influence of mysteries around me since early childhood, and my sister, for always being my most ardent supporter.

And lastly, my long-suffering husband, aka my in-house editor. Your head was bloodied but unbowed.

And if you're still reading, I'd like to thank you! I want to write more Mridula and Monami mysteries, and I'd love it if you'd stick around.

A Note on the Author

Samyukta Bhowmick is a lifelong devotee of the Golden Age of crime fiction, written between the 1920s and 1940s, and its uniquely unsettling combination of outward respectability and inner turmoil. Born in Calcutta, raised in Kuwait and educated largely in the United States, she now lives in Delhi with her two children, her husband and her cat.